SINATRA SINGING

by
Richard Grudens

Books by Richard Grudens

The Best Damn Trumpet Player

The Song Stars

The Music Men

Jukebox Saturday Night

Snootie Little Cutie - The Connie Haines Story

Jerry Vale - A Singer's Life

The Spirit of Bob Hope

Magic Moments - The Sally Bennett Story

Bing Crosby - Crooner of the Century

**Chattanooga Choo-Choo - The Life and Times
of the World Famous Glenn Miller Orchestra**

The Italian Crooners Bedside Companion

When Jolson was King

Star*Dust - The Bible of the Big Bands

Mr. Rhythm - A Tribute to Frankie Laine

Published by

 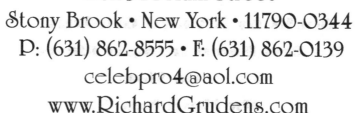

CELEBRITY
PROFILES PUBLISHING
Div. Edison & Kellogg
Box 344 Main Street
Stony Brook • New York • 11790-0344
P: (631) 862-8555 • F: (631) 862-0139
celebpro4@aol.com
www.RichardGrudens.com

Book Design and Editing by Madeline Grudens

Library of Congress Control Number in Progress

ISBN: 978-0-9763877-8-7
Printed in the United States of America
King Printing Company Inc.
Lowell, MA 01852

PRELUDE TO SINATRA SINGING

1923 - THE CAR RADIO WAS INTRODUCED

1933 - THERE WERE ABOUT TWENTY-FIVE THOUSAND JUKEBOXES IN OPERATION

1934 - CAR RADIOS WERE STANDARD IN ALMOST ALL CARS

1936 - RECORD SALES WERE ONLY 5.5 MILLION

1938 - HALF OF ALL RADIO BROADCASTS WERE RECORDINGS OF POPULAR MUSIC

1939 - THERE WERE 400,000 IN RECORD SALES

1940 - TOTAL RECORD SALES WERE 48 MILLION

1945 - RECORD SALES REACHED 109 MILLION THANKS IN PART TO FRANK SINATRA

FOREWORD

by Jerry Vale

My first performance at the Sands in Las Vegas was due to a generous recommendation by one of my early idols, Frank Sinatra. We maintained that cherished relationship for the rest of our lives. Earlier, I had heard so many negative stories about Frank that I was

Richard Grudens with Jerry Vale

somewhat apprehensive about approaching him. To my absolute surprise, he wound up being quite amiable and the most caring individual that I have ever known. During that period I had befriended a number of fellow entertainers. There was Jerry Lewis, Sammy Davis, Jr., Nat "King" Cole, but I was especially thrilled to work alongside

Glen Osser with Jerry Vale

Frank Sinatra.

I first met Frank at Lindy's Restaurant in New York City in the early fifties. Lindy's was one of the great show business restaurants whose walls were covered with caricatures of the great and near-great entertainers of our time. He was sitting at a table with friends, and when we were introduced, he stood up, which was an unusual custom for big stars. When he rose, he tried to ease the table away to make room for himself. I'll never forget what he said, "I'm trying to push this table back, but the damn thing is pushing me instead."

As time went by I would encounter Frank at various show business events and affairs. He was always the gentleman and made it a point to ask me if I needed anything, something he always earnestly inquired of his friends, either when seeing them face-to-face or over the telephone. One night he asked me when I was coming to Vegas to perform my act. "When somebody asks me," I responded.

Frank was a partner in the Sands Hotel and shot back without hesitation: "Come to Vegas next Friday and you'll start in the lounge." I almost choked up. I, of course, kept the date. That first performance lasted twenty-two weeks and was the first important start that has continued through my career. And it was all due to Frank's generosity and caring about people he liked. He didn't have to do that

Vic Damone, Sammy Davis, Jr., Jerry Vale, Jack Jones

When Buddy Hackett and I worked together in Florida, Frank would invite us up to his suite in the Eden Rock Hotel for sandwiches and pizza. Frank could stay up all night and perform a great show the next evening, without even napping. They were wonderful days spent with a great friend. I'll always treasure them.

Over the years Frank, his wife Barbara, and my wife Rita and I became kindred, especially when we lived in California and spent much time at Frank and Barbara's Rancho Mirage home. In 1996, I was honored to perform in a special tribute to Frank at the Frank Sinatra Celebrity Invitational Golf Tournament.

I was honored. The show also featured a powerhouse of great vocalists: Vic Damone, Andy Williams, Jack Jones, and Buddy Greco. We all belted out Frank's favorites as he sat at a front table and cheered us on. When it was my turn I announced:

"Frank, I'm going to sing some tunes that are associated with your great career. I only hope to do them justice, as God knows you already have," to a smile and a wave.

In the past Frank and I had performed together at a number of shows including some for the Italian American Organization.

And, I must tell you about the Sunday afternoon card games with Frank and our friends Gregory and Veronique Peck, "M*A*S*H" creator and writer Larry Gelbart, Angie Dickinson, Jack and Felicia Lemmon, at Frank's home. When Frank fell ill, we continued the games and talked about the old days, so to speak, trying to keep his spirits up. Frank would sometimes try to quit early, but I would say something like, "Hey, c'mon Frank, stay up with us. You're bringing me luck. Stay a while. Don't you remember singing 'Luck Be a Lady?' Then don't go to sleep. You can sleep tomorrow."

I was trying to keep Frank in the game and not allow him to give in so easily. We talked about many things he had enjoyed in the past like the Convair plane he bought in which he would take us for a spin when we were playing Vegas.

He would light up like a kid finding a set of trains under a Christmas tree when we touched on such antics and recall the fun we had back then.

When Frank reached his eighties and became too ill for the Sunday get-togethers, I would visit him as often as I could as I had done a hundred times before. Barbara would receive me warmly and excuse herself to bring her husband out to greet me. While waiting in the kitchen I would hear a familiar voice over my shoulder, "Hello, Jerry!"

When I turned around to see Frank standing there, I could not avoid the feeling of a deep emotional attachment. It was upsetting to see my teacher, my friend and idol Frank Sinatra, in such condition, his health deteriorated. It hurt, but wear and tear, illness and age had taken its toll on this marvelous man as it will someday on every one of us.

God Bless Frank Sinatra.

Jerry Vale

SINATRA SINGING

TABLE OF CONTENTS

THEN:

Al Jolson
Bessie Smith
Ethel Waters
Billie Holiday
Mildred Bailey
Russ Columbo
Rudy Vallee
Bing Crosby
Peggy Lee
Bobby Darin
Matt Monro
Mel Torme
Connie Haines

NOW:

Tony Bennett
Michael Feinstein

Patty Andrews
Tony B. (Babino)
Vic Damone
Johnny Mathis
Margaret Whiting
Kay Starr

Gia Prima
Carol Kidd
Bruce Springsteen
Pat Boone
Tom Postilio
Nick Hilscher
Julia Rich
Jerry Costanzo
Lou Lanza
Cristina Fontanelli
Roberto "Weatherman" Tirado
Daryl Sherman

Michael Bublé
Tony DeSare
Julia Keefe
Maude Maggert
Jane Monheit
Dana Marcine

The Main Event - Madison Square Garden 1974
The London Palladium - 1975
The Egytian Event 1979
The Rio Concert 1980
The Ultimate Madrid Event World Tour 1986

How it Works, How it's Different

Goal and Anthem

I Love to Sing-a

E.Y. Harburg and Harold Arlen
From the film, The Singing Kid with Al Jolson

I love to sing-a
About the moon-a and the June-a and the Spring-a,
I love to sing-a,
About a sky of blue-a, or a tea for two-a,
Anything-a with a swing-a to an "I love you-a,"
I love to, I love to sing!

Give me a song-a
About a son-of-a-gun that went and done her wrong-a.
But keep it clean-a,
With a cottage small-a by a waterfall-a,
Any sob-a that will throb-a to a bluebird's call-a,
I love, I love to sing!

I was born a singin' fool-a,
Lah-de-dah!
Ol' Major Bowes is gonna spot me,
Got through Yale with boula-boula,
Lah-de-dah!
Old microphone's got me!

I love to sing-a,
I love to wake up with the south-a in my mouth-a,
And wave a flag-a,
With a cheer for Uncle Sammy
and another for my mammy,
I love to sing!

The swingin'est,
Hot singin'est,
Bell-ringin'est,
Song singin'est
High tootin'est,
Sky tootin'est,
I love to sing!

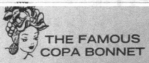

THE FAMOUS COPA BONNET

Only the really great are entitled to wear the Copa's symbol of success. It's the Night Club Academy Award... the Laurel Wreath of Stardom. Just look at the talented stars who have worn the Bonnet:

1	Jimmy Durante
2	Dean Martin
3	Dionne Warwick
4	Joe E. Lewis
5	Johnny Mathis
6	Richard Grudens
7	Danny Thomas
8	Tony Bennett
9	Peggy Lee
10	Steve Lawrence
11	Sammy Davis, Jr.
12	Joey Bishop
14	Diana Ross and The Supremes
15	Eydie Gorme
16	Bobby Darin
17	Jerry Lewis
18	Don Rickles
19	Jerry Vale
20	Connie Francis
21	Tom Jones
22	Paul Anka

THE CAPTIVATING, SCINTILLATING COPA! This is where it all happens . . . the glitter of sparkling entertainment . . . the fun and excitement of "anything goes". . . the electricity that makes the Copa "The Great American Night Club". The Copa —inventor of what's best in cafe entertainment, hands you the evening filled with the most dance-able music in town . . . the most star-strewn musical revues East of Broadway . . . and a night to remember!

THE GREAT COPA SHOW Where else but the world-famous Copa would such unbelievable talents perform for your entertainment pleasure? No where else—because the Copa is the showcase for the stars. The biggest stars can and do call the Copa home —stars like those illustrated above—like the one you'll see tonight . . . holders of the famed Copa bonnet . . . recipients of the world's acclaim. They're all here for your enjoyment. Watch and see for yourself!

...Frank Sinatra

CUISINE A LA COPA Just marvelous! This is because the Copa has a reputation to live up to . . . a reputation for the finest in everything. Master chefs whip up outstanding gourmet menus in kitchens any woman would adore. Service is a happy, courteous experience. Surprisingly enough, Copa Cuisine will cost you far less than most of our town's finest restaurants. You'll enjoy the sumptuous cuisine, the show, the dancing, and the excitement without a pinch to your wallet.

CHINESE FOOD SERVED HERE Oriental cooking is so important to the Copa's guests, we have separate kitchens, just to prepare it. Our native chefs keep everything authentic and serve up a tantalizing menu of savory Chinese specialties.
The Copa Cuisine and Kitchens are personally supervised by Jules Podell.

COPACABANA

MEMBER OF THE DINERS' CLUB—10 E. 60th STREET, PLaza 8-0900

The Andrews Sisters with Frank Sinatra

**Harry James with Frank at the
Hollywood Canteen**

INTRODUCTION
Richard Grudens

The first time I met Frank Sinatra, I was introduced to him by RCA's Vice President Manie Sachs in 30 Rockefeller Center's Room 253, the NBC Radio & Television Ticket Division office.

Manie was a regular visitor to the desk where, as Assistant Manager, I dispensed radio and television broadcast tickets to mostly out-of-town visitors, NBC personnel and studio executives, and, via mail, to the general public who wrote in for tickets. Legend had it that Sachs was a very nice guy in the very competitive business of A & R man in a major recording company. I found him to be a fine gentle-man and a down-to-earth executive and always respectful to one and all: musicians, singers, song pluggers and everyone else.

Frank Sinatra was working under the guidance of Manie Sachs at this somewhat dark time in his career, a time when his agency, MCA, had dropped him, as well as his movie studio, his network, and his record company. Frank and Manie were very close in those days of early 1952 and could be seen together frequently underlining the fact that Manie was working on strategies to help jump-start the upcoming, revised career of Sinatra, which was heading upward on a new course with massive changes leading to unparalleled success just a short distance down the road.

This could not yet be foreseen in early 1940 when Sinatra, after a successful almost full year with Harry James, had joined the Tommy Dorsey Orchestra. Harry James' band was faltering finan-cially and so James offered Sinatra an unconditional release with no strings attached. The same deal was offered to Sinatra's co-star Connie Haines, the band's regular girl singer. They both linked up with Dorsey. Regarding Sinatra, here was an entirely new breed of singer who was making the rounds of millions of jukeboxes in bars and restaurants throughout the country. Jazz influenced by Bessie Smith, Billie Holiday, Mildred Bailey, Ethel Waters, and even the great

Crosby himself, "Sinatra found a whole new audience. His natural phrasing, which even Bing Crosby couldn't match in sensitivity and interpretive imagination," as Gunther Schuller wrote in his book, The Swing Era, "subtle jazz inflections and a fine beat, even in those slow ballads, characterized his singing."

Like bandleader Tommy Dorsey, Sinatra possessed a natural way of offering original timing and phrasing. Unlike many weak-voiced singers and song interpreters of the time, Sinatra had remarkably quality and natural intonation which he learned on his own by closely and carefully listening to his predecessors and his own ear. The quality of his voice spoke for itself. "After many years of colorless, lightweight, expressionless male voices- mostly effeminate-sounding crooning tenors--Sinatra's virile earthy baritone, with a rich bottom voice, was a startling departure for the popular norm," Mr. Schuller added.

Sinatra's original phrasing could be heard on his first performance with Dorsey, and, of course, earlier with Harry James on recordings like Jack Lawrence's"All or Nothing At All."

On "Too Romantic," and "Shake Down the Stars" - his initial recordings with Dorsey, Sinatra is still not up to par and not as confident as he achieved in later years, but his basic talents shone through brilliantly, and most importantly, his innate ability to create and hold a musical line, thereby making a musical totality of a song rather than a series of vaguely connected phrases. Like Dorsey in his trombone solos, Sinatra would carry phrases across bar lines or phrase joining, balancing out weak points in songs or dramatizing their best structured musical elements.

Sinatra learned much from Dorsey's playing, especially in regard to breath control. On the other hand, it is undoubtedly those very talents in Sinatra - in immature form - to be sure - that Dorsey found interesting enough to hire him in the first place. Sinatra's instrument- like approach was the perfect compliment to Dorsey's highly vocal approach to the trombone.

In time Sinatra learned how to use dynamics and subtle timbral shadings, for instance on "Fools Rush In," (1940's) or to swing in that unique relaxed, lilting way of his, that he perfected later in his mid-1950s recordings.

Frank Sinatra sang beautiful, carefully chosen songs with charming melodies better than anyone else which made him an bona fide singing star due to that fact alone. His "singing" diction was flawless, assisted it's been said, by building up his vocabulary doing

Manie Sachs

crossword puzzles and reading books on diction, like Elements of Style, by Strunk & White, usually reserved for writers. Stardom can be a fickle phase in anyone's show business career. Some stars are really not stars, and there are some who are not stars but deserve stardom, but fate somehow overlooks them somehow. Some of the reasons may include management, not enough optimum use of their talent, breaks of one kind or another that can translate into an unexpected success brought about by of a single recording or movie role.

The truth is, if there is really talent present and it is brought to light, success usually follows. Some singers were one-hit stars, others, like Bing Crosby, who recorded with almost everyone in the business while under the direction of Jack Kapp of Decca Records, achieved immense success because of the unrelenting, prolific use of his voice and talent and who worked well with all his contemporaries whether they were a musician, vocalist, vocal group, entire orchestra, male or female, talented, or famous for different reasons, like the duets with songwriter Johnny Mercer or crossing swords and barbs with the great Bob Hope and dueting with "Satchmo" Armstrong.

Sinatra was beginning to replace a handful of familiar singers of the past namely Al Jolson, who sits at the top of the Sinatra Tree, Rudy Vallee, Russ Columbo, and even his personal hero, Bing Crosby, who still held on to his own.

Then, his career secede into an abyss for mostly unknown reasons: Sinatra in 1955: At that time I was my own worst enemy. My singing went downhill and I went downhill with it, or vice versa-

but nobody hit me in the throat or choked me, it happened because I paid no attention to how I was singing. Instead, I wanted to sit back and enjoy my success and sign autographs and bank the heavy cash. Well, let me tell you, nobody who's successful sits back and enjoys it. I found it out the hard way. You work all the

Manie Sachs

time, even harder than when you were a nobody."

Sinatra rolled up his sleeves and went back to work. He changed record companies, changed attorney's, accountants, motion picture companies, and even his style of dressing.

Sinatra's voice was still very much his instrument that controlled phrasing, production, dramatic acting within the lyrics, unmatched interpretations on many songs, including some songs that were written expressly for him by a number of song-writing teams, and his careful selection of arrangers who understood his music and delivery of a notable list of songs that will be heard for many years to come. Dozens of singers at the beginning of their career have tried to emulate his singing including Bobby Darin, Steve Lawrence, Tony Bennett, Billy Eckstine, Johnnie Ray, Perry Como, Jerry Vale, Julius La Rosa, Jack Jones, Andy Williams, Eddie Fisher, Dean Martin, Vic Damone, Al Martino, Dick Haymes, James Darren, Mel Torme, Harry Connick, Jr., Tony B (Babino) who actually wrote a song he calls "I Wish I Could Sing Like Sinatra," and a few new, young entries Michael Buble, Tony DeSare, who blatantly emulate him and sings the songs Sinatra made famous over his career. Sinatra was an original as was Jolson, Crosby, Frankie Laine---meaning that no one before them did exactly what they subsequently accomplished in sound, production, style, and performance. And among the ladies it was Mildred Bailey (the first Big Band singer), Billie Holiday, Ella Fitzgerald, Peggy Lee, Doris Day, and the Andrews Sisters. This book will present this material in detail.

Sinatra's early, pleasant, landmark recordings with Dorsey were just that. He graduated, after a two-year hiatus, redefining style and delivery, that led to greater things beginning in the mid-fifties and continuing beyond his second, final retirement. Sinatra was a great singer. No question exists to challenge that claim. Nobody could surpass him.

Frank was always able to "get it" whether the lyric contained a hint of philosophical depth, or a administration of wit, and he always had a taste and an intuition for jazz nuances, as well as the ability to add little touches of, and neat pieces of, jazz phrases that does his talents justice which are beyond the call of what the song may require. And Frank was aware of the fact that there were songs that are called standards, and above that they are named classics. Classics and standards become exactly that when Frank does his justice to them one at a time. Otherwise a number of songs remain below such designations and are lost until someone lifts them from their doldrums in music's overfilled garage sale for singers. Songwriters have to be grateful for what Frank does with their lyrics, always faithful and carefully making sense of every verb, adjective, and pronoun or adverb, as if he were talking to someone instead of singing to them.

Singing "Ol' Man River" from "Till' The Clouds Roll By"

Schuller: "He also learned to stretch slow tempos almost beyond the point of emotional endurance. Songs like those early recordings with Dorsey 'I'll Never Smile Again' and 'This Love of Mine' were not only big million sellers but were remarkable musical breakthroughs, instantly initiated by hordes of other singers and vocal groups- mostly with disastrous results. For an abnormally slow tempo can be carried off only by a singer with perfect breath control and an exceptional sense of musical line; and these were talents only a handful of singers commanded. In time, of course, singers worthy and capable of imitating Sinatra did come along, but even such were rare, and then they would always find their own voice."

And, Sinatra made about twenty-five recordings as the borrowed voice in the group called the Pied Pipers. Many were wonderful achievements, beautifully romantic performances with great commercial successes that included Hoagy Carmichael's "Stardust," "I Guess I'll Have to Dream the Rest,"and perhaps the most compelling, "The Night We Called it a Day" written by Matt Dennis, and thanks, too, to the masterful arrangers Axel Stordahl, Paul Weston, and the great Sy Oliver, of the Dorsey stable of accomplished and most suitable arrangers.

And, we will not overlook commentary and support for what may have been Frank Sinatra's greatest singing, live concert achievement at Madison Square Garden in New York on October 12th 1974 when he sang " The House I Live In," and other significant Sinatra gold at a time when he was, perhaps, at his very best voice. This book will omit, except when necessary, mentions of the Sinatra antics, public brawls, the Rat Pack, the effects of his marriages, the alleged mafia connection, in-depth film material or the early hysteria that at times developed and showcased and highlighted his rise to everlasting fame. This is a book about the music and all those associated with the music. There will be no room for the psychological and the sociological Sinatra history. This book is Sinatra Singing, and that's all.

And, we pay full respect to Sinatra's entire family in this endeavor.

Frank

Connie Haines

John Huddleston

Chuck Lowry

Billy Wilson

Tommy Dorsey

Jo Stafford

The Tommy Dorsey Band

AT THE NEW YORK PARAMOUNT

"Not since the days of Rudolph Valentino has American womanhood made such unabashed public love to an entertainer." - *Time*, 1943.

On December 30,1942, Sinatra played his first solo concert at the Paramount Theater in New York, the fans, known as Bobbysoxers, came out in droves. It was famed comedian Jack Benny who

first appeared, then introduced Frank Sinatra. When Sinatra came on stage he was greeted to endless feminine shrieks and screams that seemed to never end.

"That amazing greeting," Frank recalled, "was deafening. I couldn't believe it, It was a tremendous roar. Five thousand fans, stamping, yelling, screaming, applauding. I was scared stiff. I couldn't move a muscle. Benny Goodman couldn't speak. He was so scared he turned around, looked at the audience and said, 'What the hell is that?' I burst out laughing."

The female gender screamed in delight; some even fainted. They also crowded back stage after the show shrieking for his autograph, and spilled over into Times Square, messing up traffic. Sinatra by then had become a recording sensation. He was so popular at the Paramount that his engagement was extended to February 1943, lasting four solid weeks, first with Benny Goodman and his Orchestra and then with Johnny Long's Orchestra.

Sinatra's drawing power and talent was terrific and never waned. By early 1943 Frank had twenty-three top ten singles on the Billboard music chart, while through those years, at Paramount and places where he performed, the girls continued screaming and swooning for their singing hero, Frank Sinatra.

"In various manifestations, this sort of thing has been going on all over America lately," wrote Time magazine.

Fans had not swooned or screamed as much over other singers, such as Bing Crosby. So what was it with Sinatra? Something else was going on, the critics surmised. Although his singing was certainly a factor, some charged it was also Sinatra's blue-eyed charm,

his youthful innocence, and his vulnerability that evoked these passions.

Newsweek magazine then viewed the Bobbysoxer phenomenon as a kind of madness; a mass sexual delirium. Some even called the girls immoral or even juvenile delinquents. But most of us simply saw very young girls spending their emotions. By now Sinatra fan clubs were growing in numbers all over America, and not just among teenagers, because forty- year-old women were joining up, too!

In October 1944, after Frank had appeared in two films, "Step Lively" and "Higher and Higher," he returned to New York's Paramount Theater once again, where some 30,000 to 35,000 fans, mostly female teens, caused a another great commotion outside. Coined "The Columbus Day Riot," the police were called in to calm the situation. The problem had to do with fans who refused to leave the theater after having seen one complete show. Repeat performances were being scheduled in close rotation, running nearly all day and into the night. In theaters with a capacity for 3,000 to 3,500 fans, sometimes as few as 250 would leave at the show's end. Some would sit through many performances. Some reached the point of fainting, but nevertheless remaining in their seats for six or eight hours without food and refusing to leave until gently removed by attendants.

In January 1945, the New York correspondent for the London-based Guardian newspaper filed this report on Sinatra for readers back home:

'"The United States is now in the midst of one of those remarkable phenomena of mass hysteria which occur from time to time on this side of the Atlantic. Mr. Frank Sinatra, an amiable young singer of popular songs, is inspiring extraordinary personal devotion on the part of many thousands of young people, and particularly young girls between the ages of, say, twelve and eighteen." The adulation bestowed upon him is similar to that lavished upon Colonel Lindbergh fifteen years ago, Rudolph Valentino a few years earlier, or Admiral Dewey, the hero of Manila Bay, at the turn of the century. Mr. Sinatra has to be guarded by police whenever he appears in public. Indeed, during the late political campaign he broke up a demonstration for Governor Dewey, the Republican candidate, merely by presenting himself on the sidelines as a spectator.

"It is reasonable to suppose that his popularity with young people was at first a fiction invented by his press agent; it is not uncommon for myths of this sort to be set going by those enterprising gentlemen, and young people have even been hired to riot on a small scale in a music-hall or cinema to demonstrate the popularity of a performer. There is no doubt, however, that the matter has now become a genuine phenomenon. . ."

By 1946 Frank Sinatra's recording company, Columbia, estimated that he was selling 10 million records per year. Yet these were still the early years for Frank Sinatra. He had another 40-plus years of performing and music-making ahead.

Sinatra: "I'm twenty-five. I look maybe nineteen. Most of the kids feel like I am one of them - the pal next door. So maybe they feel they know me. And that's the way I want it to be. What the hell, they're nice kids."

Jo Stafford, lead singer of The Pied Pipers: "Once you heard him, you knew he couldn't do a number badly."

He started big at the Paramount, where, as Connie Haines, his co-singer with both Harry James and Tommy Dorsey said: "Call it talent, Richard, it was magical, and we all knew it...and he knew it. Why we couldn't even cross the street to get a hamburger without a Police escort."

He was the Voice that thrilled millions. And that would continue for the next 50 years.

The House I Live In (That's America to Me), words by Lewis Allan, music by Earl Robinson. As featured by Frank Sinatra.

THE HOUSE I LIVE IN

Frank Sinatra sang "The House I Live In" in 1974 so beautifully during his concert at Madison Square Garden. However, years earlier, in 1945, he performed it in a ten minute film short The House I Live In.

In 1945 Frank Sinatra received an Honorary Academy Award and a special Golden Globe Award in 1946 for that effort. The recording was a sensation. The film was produced to oppose anti-semitism and racial prejudice at the end of World War II.

Frank Sinatra liked and believed in the song so it became a part of his repertoire. He also sang it before President Nixon in the White House and later at President Reagan's inaugural.

In 2007, the film, with Sinatra, was selected for preservation in the United States National Film Registry by the Library of Congress. Indeed, a historic piece of film with Frank Sinatra, who treasured it himself.

Directed by Mervyn LeRoy, composed by Lewis Allen and Earl Robinson, and produced by Frank Ross and Mervyn LeRoy.

THE HOUSE I LIVE IN

What is America to me?
A name, a map, a flag I see?
A certain word, "Democracy"?
What is America to me?

The house I live in, a plot of earth, a street
The grocer and the butcher, and the people that I meet
The children in the playground, the faces that I see
All races and religions, that's America to me

The place I work in, the worker by my side
The little town or city
where my people lived and died

The "howdy" and the handshake,
the air of feeling free

And the right to speak my mind out,
that's America to me

The things I see about me,
the big things and the small

The little corner newsstand,
and the house a mile tall

The wedding in the churchyard,
the laughter and the tears

The dream that's been a-growin' for
a hundred-and-fifty years

The town I live in, the street,
the house, the room

The pavement of the city,
or a garden all in bloom

The church, the school, the clubhouse,
the million lights I see
But especially the people - That's America to me

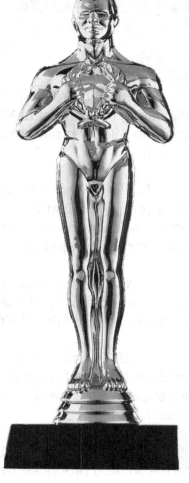

Frank Sinatra in the Wedgwood Room

THE WALDORF-ASTORIA

STRICTLY SINATRA
By Ron Della Chiesa

    Swing Easy, Songs for Swingin' Lovers, In The Wee Small Hours, No One Cares, Come Fly With Me, those are just a few of the remarkable recordings made by Francis Albert Sinatra. Doing a weekly Sinatra radio show is one of the great joys in my almost forty years as a broadcaster. People ask me, 'Do you have a favorite Sinatra recording?' That is a difficult question to answer. It is like asking, 'Do you have a favorite sunset, do you have a favorite Michelangelo painting, do you have a favorite Mozart Symphony or do you have a favorite Puccini Opera?' I think my good friend Tony Bennett summed

it up best when he said, 'Sinatra's music is art, and a work of art is a joy forever. Just as the great artists going back hundreds of years in history left their mark, Sinatra left his in this century.' What makes this man's music so unique is his emotional honesty in everything he sang. He combined superb musicianship and open enthusiasm for

Ron Della Chiesa and His Wife Joyce

the fine musicians and arrangers that he worked with. He had the greatest respect for the music and lyrics. Every time I had the pleasure of hearing him sing, he always credited the composer, lyricist and arranger.

     "Looking back at Sinatra's career as a recording artist one is amazed. I think much of what Sinatra brought to his music was part of his Italian -American roots. Not only just for his star quality and the beauty of the voice, but because he was a true Italian "bel canto" singer. Growing up in Hoboken, New Jersey, he was exposed to Italian music and song at a very young age. He once mentioned that one of his favorite composers was Puccini, an obvious choice for him to make. For Puccini's music touches our heart, as Sinatra's voice touches our soul. He also listened to recordings played on the old family Victrola by the great tenor Enrico Caruso. I am sure this had an impact on his future development as a singer and recording artist. Peggy Lee said that Sinatra is irreplaceable because of his emotional honesty. I think that is one of the most valid comments about his recordings. His career spans over sixty years in the technology of the recording industry, from the 78 RPM'S, to the 45'5, to the LP, and finally the compact disc.

"A couple of years ago I had the pleasure of attending the first world conference on Frank Sinatra, that took place at Hofstra University, Long Island. Hundreds of Sinatraphiles gathered together for four days to discuss and define his accomplishments in the world of music. One of the participants at the conference was author Pete Hamill. He sums it up best in his marvelous book titled Why Sinatra Matters. At the very end of the final chapter, Hamill says, and I quote, 'Frank Sinatra was a genuine artist and all his work will endure as long as men and women can hear, ponder and feel. In the end that is all that truly matters.'

"Now Frank has his own All Star Big Band in the sky. Satchmo is wailing on trumpet, Count Basie is swinging on the piano, with special guest appearances by Sammy and Dino. I can hear the introduction now by my dear friend, the late disc jockey Bill Marlowe......... ."Ladies and gentlemen join me in welcoming Francis Albert Sinatra" ....Is there another? I hope you will join me each Saturday night from 7 midnight, and every Sunday evening from 7 to midnight on WPLM 99.1 FM, as we celebrate the career of this remarkable man who dedicated his life to the Great American Songbook of beautifully written clasic songs and left a legacy of unrivaled recordings that have become true monuments of art. Old Blue Eves lives!

MUSICALLY SPEAKING, ITS SINATRA "ALL THE WAY"

The View from Massachusetts
By Frank E. Dee

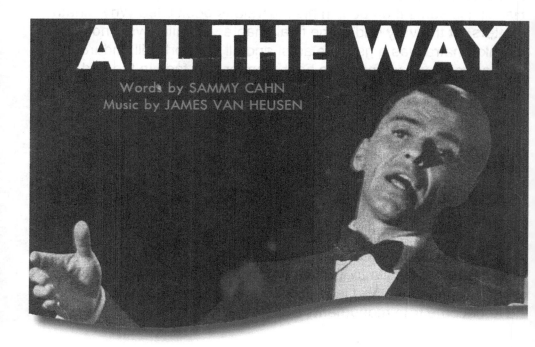

If I don't begin this article about Frank Sinatra in the usual, chronological manner, its because I have to choose different Frank Sinatra era's from the 40s, 50s and up into the 1990s. As I recall, Frank Sinatra was the biggest hit singer of the World War II years and into the 1950s. He had a captivating voice and style that delighted millions with his recordings. I was one among his millions of fans.

At the age of ten I recall hearing Frank Sinatra for the first time on our family wind-up Victrola. The song, "Dream," was the door that opened my heart to becoming a Sinatra fan. I need no reminder that Frank Sinatra was the most popular singer of our time. We all knew the man was an iconoclast legend of song, from his recordings, radio, television, concerts, and films. From the 1940s up into the 1990s his successful, professional career lasted 60 years. I think the key to Sinatra's vocal fame and popularity was due to him being a 'Doer,' meaning a very hard worker, because he stayed on top up to the 1990s.

Sinatra was the Star of our 1950s Record Hops

In the 1950s one of the hottest swinging Sinatra albums *Songs For Swinging Lovers* captivated the teenagers in my home state of Massachusetts. Every teenager with whom I associated and who attended Record Hops, owned a copy of *Songs For Swinging Lovers*.

The record hops in the early 50s flourished every Friday and Saturday night with the great Frank Sinatra hit songs. He had the musical power of taking all of us on a sentimental musical journey with the songs being played over and over by radio disc jockeys. One particular radio personality of the great 1950s was Boston's radio personality Bill Marlowe, who introduced a thousands of us teens to the voice of Frank Sinatra. At these record hops, and on his radio show Bill Marlowe used to introduce Mr. Sinatra as; King Farouk, or Mr. Ring-a-Ding- Ding, or "Welcome To Sinatra-

ville," and every time he mentioned these sobriquets, the over-packed record hop rooms filled with Sinatra fans would scream and applaud. Although Rock music was coming in, Sinatra still attracted a large turnout of teens at the record hops.

As record hops dwindled, Sinatra became an iconoclast feature on Bill Marlowe's four-hour *Sinatra Saturday* show, that lasted for more years than I can remember. This same Frank Sinatra show was passed on to one of New England's leading radio personalities, Ron Della Chiesa. Now called Strictly Sinatra and featured every Saturday night on radio station WPLM-FM Boston, it still broadcasts today in the year of 2010 featuring the voice of Frank Sinatra.

In the early 1970s, not ever thinking I would one day be a disc jockey on the same radio station, WHET-AM, in Waltham, Mass, under the guidance of Bill Marlowe, who also became my radio mentor and best friend, took me under his musical wing and taught me the music library of Frank Sinatra.

If there was anything one wanted to know about Sinatra's singing, Bill had the right answer. In the early 1990s I was honored to be a special surprise guest on Bill's Frank Sinatra Show, with a special Frank Sinatra presentation tribute to Bill Marlowe's 50th year in radio featuring songs of Frank Sinatra. Mr. Sinatra was very gracious to send me a dedicated letter and photo for presentation to Mr. Marlowe on his Sinatra show. What a wonderful memory and a Sinatra treat, one I shall never forget. Thank you Bill for educating all of the teens, from the 50s through the 90s keeping "Sinatra Singing" on radio show.

Sinatra Remains a Hit in Mobile Senior Parks.

If you were to tour any Senior Mobile Park or Senior Center in your local area across America, and mentioned the name of Frank Sinatra, it would be as if you mentioned a Saint. Some of the overwhelming reactions I receive, "Are you kidding?" Then the stories began: "I saw him perform at the Copa in New York City" or "I was one of those teens screaming when he sang "Night and Day" at the Paramount." How could anyone of us in this park ever forget the songs Sinatra sang for us?" One lady said; "Frank Sinatra was our musical hero. His songs are still featured at our weekly dances."

If there is any place on earth one is seeking information about the songs Frank Sinatra sang from whatever era, these seniors will share a wealth of musical information on how they remember Frank Sinatra. Indeed, it is a joy to be able to hear how Sinatra's songs influenced even their marriages. Most of the seniors commented on how they recalled how Sinatra's songs dominated the jukeboxes of their time. Several pointed out; "Who could forget those juke boxes of the 1950s greeting you with the smooth sounding Sinatra voice. And just think? You could get six plays of your favorite Sinatra songs for twenty-five cents, 2 plays for ten cents, one play for just five cents. Try finding a juke box today."

Remembering Sinatra's 78 and 45
Recordings Of The Rare 1950s Jukeboxes

Talk about hearing some wonderful memories from various seniors. One tune, in 1959, was a real tearjerker titled "Just Friends," The LP made its debut that March. In my 1970s Radio years at station WHET in Waltham, Mass., this song was one of the most requested songs played on my show. I recall introducing the song title and adding; 'We loved, we laughed, and we cried, then suddenly love died, the story ends, and we're just friends." I may add Sinatra influenced the New England radio audiences with his magical songs.

On GMMY Radio, Sinatra's songs are aired daily, and, again, in the evening. One of our streamlined shows *Strictly Sinatra* hosted by New England's favorite radio host, Ron Della Chiesa, are   aired weekdays by Ron who hosts the same shows on WPLM-FM in Boston. Ron also hosts annual Sinatra Dances and Sinatra Cruises. He is keeping Frank Sinatra's songs alive on his shows and on Gmmy Radio. In due respect Frank Sinatra is a must to be aired on any radio station, for he has maintained an unwavering popularity over a long period of time, over years that witnessed the rise and decline of many artists and musical trends. In today's society of upcoming popular singers, there are many, many singers who imperson- ate this vocal genius in nightclubs. However, I found most of them unable to come close to the quality Sinatra Bel-Canto style of singing. There was and only will be one Frank Sinatra.

Frank E. Dee
Golden Radio

Jumping back to the time of the old radio years when Frank Sinatra was a mainstream feature on the *Your Hit Parade* radio show of the 40s, folks gathered around a floor model radio to hear 'Sinatra singing', and in those years, folks would stare at the radio as though it was a television. I often wondered what they were staring at. What I did understand was they were mesmerized listening to Frank Sinatra singing their favorite songs.

Gene Lees On Sinatra Singing

"When it comes to American popular song in the English speaking language the ones who can deliver a song like none other are Peggy Lee and Frank Sinatra. He was the best. No one came close to his artistry. Even Placido Domingo agrees to this. Technically he was superb. His sound; he had a great natural instrument which he constantly trained by swimming underwater to expand his lungs. His voice production; the way he made the sound with his diaphragm, ribcage, and throat. He had a range of two octaves and he was terribly in tune with the musical surroundings and the instruments.

"Sinatra sang in relationship to the chord and the sound of the orchestra and whichever scale they were in. There was a dramatic inwardness like some of the very best actors. Sinatra was an actor of the song. An actor cannot control the muscles of his face by conscious effort. If you want sadness to register you have to feel it and then it will show on your face. Sinatra felt the music like none other. Nobody could surpass, nobody could get into the emotion of it like Sinatra. He does difficult songs and tosses them off like there's nothing to it. I love a lot of singers, actually, but Sinatra is like Shakespeare; there's him and then there's everybody else."

**Frank sings and records "Somethin' Stupid,"
with daughter Nancy**
Words and Music by C. Carson Parks

VAN ALEXANDER

I first met Frank Sinatra when he was singing with Harry James and I watched his rise and fall and his rise again as did the rest of the music world.

Frank was so truly musical. He was always cognizant of the work of arrangers and orchestrators, so much so that he never neglected to give name credit to the arranger of the song he had just performed.

As a past president of ASMAC (American Society of Music Arrangers and Composers) I feel that all arrangers and orchestrators owe him a sincere debt of gratitude.

This treatise on Frank Sinatra has been told many times, but just in case you're not familiar with it. Frank was fascinated with Tommy Dorsey's' playing, and tried to emulate his breathing and phrasing, which he studied and practiced. This was a part of his success. He also had a great feel for 'swinging' and had a natural good beat. Singers like Gordon MacRae (who really studied voice control) would go through vocal gymnastics before going before an audience. I remember distinctly how he would steam up the bathroom and do 10 or 15 minutes of just vocalizing musical scales. He had a glorious voice but had no beat, and couldn't swing so there was no competition between he and Frank. Eddie Fisher had a nice voice, and also would do some vocalizing before going on stage, but he had trouble keeping in time with the orchestra.

A good, attractive arrangement of a song has much to do with its success or failure. An arrangement with attractive, colorful musical sounds will enhance the performance of the singer, whereas a dull arrangement adds nothing and actually detracts from the singer's performance. Frank always worked with great arrangers and never neglected to give them credit for their work, especially at live concerts. The singer, pianist, Michael Feinstein is a natural. He never vocalizes, always seem to be in top shape, and coupled with his marvelous musical inventions at the piano, he's never at a loss for pleasing an audience. Last week (last week of October 09) he presided over a tribute to prolific songwriter Johnny Mercer at the Motion Picture Academy, and beautifully interpreted Mercer's lyrics. So, Richard, being of the old school, I'm not familiar with the new singers of today, so I have no comment to pass on any of them. It's someone else's turn for evaluating the new crop.

BEN GRISAFI

Frank Sinatra was unique more so in his interpretations of each song and not necessarily the timbre or resonance of his voice. His voice had the distinct quality like no other singer before him. There were nuances in Russ Colombo's voice and Bing Crosby, to name a few, but Sinatra milked his nuances to the hilt. His ballads always contained a certain amount of passion and emotion. In essence he was reciting the lyrics accompanied by a beautiful voice. My saxophone playing has been described by my fellow bandsmen as sensuous, passionate and soulful. Sinatra had all if these attributes and more. I be-

Richard Grudens, Connie Haines and Ben Grisafi

lieve that he first concentrated more on the interpretation of the lyrics and then absorbed the essence of what the composer had in mind, added the icing on the cake by showcasing his unique style to convey the composer's thoughts to his listening public.

Sinatra was wise enough to align himself with some of the world's finest arrangers: Nelson Riddle, Alex Stordahl, Gordon Jenkins, and many, many more.

A voice, like a musical instrument, can convey many emotions providing the recipient is astute enough to recognize the case in point. In Sinatra's case he appealed, right from the start of his career, to the young, female bobby soxers who first saw him perform at the New York Paramount Theater. As a youngster, I can recall seeing photos of those teenagers going wild in the aisles, and together with my fellow young musicians concluded that that fad would soon blow over.

It didn't, however, for it wasn't until many years later that those musicians finally recognized that this skinny youngster had a story to tell and he told it well.

Frank Sinatra's career had many ups and downs and he "paid his dues" through the years and earned the respect of professionals as well as laymen throughout the world.

When I play a ballad I utilize the warmest sounds that can be emitted from a tenor saxophone. I produce what is called a sub-tone sound which sounds like I am breathing into my instrument in a most intimate way. Sub-tone playing was very prevalent in the 30's & 40's with legendary stars like Coleman Hawkins ("Body & Soul") Ben Webster, Charlie Ventura, and many more. However it is almost a lost art and I have had many young players approach me and asked how they too, can produce that warm, hard to achieve sound. They wonder if it's the instrument, mouthpiece, or reed. I respond: "No" the sound is fixed in your brain and in your heart."

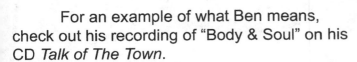

For an example of what Ben means, check out his recording of "Body & Soul" on his CD *Talk of The Town*.

Ben Grisafi
Big Band Hall of Fame Orchestra
Palm Beach, Florida

THE SINATRA BASICS AND ESSENTIALS IN A NUTSHELL

Born on December 12, 1915 to Anthony Martin Sinatra and Natalie Garavante in Hoboken, New Jersey.

Graduated from David E. Rue Junior High School in 1931.

Attended just a few months of High School.

Worked on a delivery truck for the Jersey Observer newspaper.

Between 1932 and 1939 he worked on and off manually at local shipyards, but dreamed of becoming an engineer.

In 1935 he saw Bing Crosby perform in Jersey City and changed the direction of his life hoping to become Crosby's successor.

Major Bowes Sounds the Gong on the Amateur Hour Radio Show

Sang, often unpaid, on WAAT radio in Jersey City under the name The Romancer.

Organized a group of singers coined the Hoboken Four to appear on the Major Bowes Original Amateur Hour and won singing the Crosby-Mills Brothers-styled tune "Shine."

Sinatra traveled briefly with Bowes then returned to New Jersey singing in roadhouses including the Rustic Cabin in Englewood Cliffs.

Hearing Sinatra over his car radio on WNEW's hookup to the Rustic Cabin, Harry James hired Sinatra to join his band along with vocalist Connie Haines. He joined up at the Hippodrome Theater in June 1939. Remained with the band for 6 months.

Joined Tommy Dorsey in January, 1940, along with Connie Haines, and just a bit earlier, the Pied Pipers with Jo Stafford came on board, too.

His first hit was "I'll Never Smile Again," with the Pied Pipers. Frank remained with the band for three years.

On his own he appeared at the New York Paramount with the Benny Goodman Orchestra to mass hysteria success by his fans.

From 1943 to 1945, known as the "Voice" became the main singer on the radio show *Your Hit Parade*, followed by his show *Songs by Sinatra*.

Recorded with Columbia Records between 1943 and 1952.

Moved to Capitol Records in 1953 and recorded with arrangers Nelson Riddle and Billy May where he produced the albums *Songs for Young Lovers*, *A Swingin' Affair*, *Come Fly with Me*, *Only the Lonely*, *In the Wee Small Hours* and *Songs for Swingin' Lovers*.

During the 1960s he recorded with his own company Reprise Records with hit albums *Ring-a-Ding-Ding*, *September of My Years*, *My Way*, and *Strangers in the Night*.

Began his motion picture career in 1941 and appeared in over 50 films. Won an Oscar in *From Here to Eternity* in 1953 and a special Oscar for "The House I Live In."

Retired in 1971 and returned in 1973 with a television special and the album *Ol Blue Eyes is Back*.

In the 1990s he released two albums recorded with many popular artists, *Duets* in 1993 and *Duets II* in 1994.

Sinatra donated more than one billion dollars to charities private and public and was bestowed with the Jean Hersholt Humanitarian Award in 1971, the Kennedy Center Life Achievement Award in 1983, the Presidential Medal of Freedom in 1985, the NAACP Lifetime Achievement Award in 1987, and in 1997 the coveted Congressional Gold Medal, America's highest award.

Frank Sinatra was one of the most successful entertainers of the 20th century, a career that spanned seventy years of recordings, films, radio, television and countless live performances in nightclubs, stadiums, and concert halls.

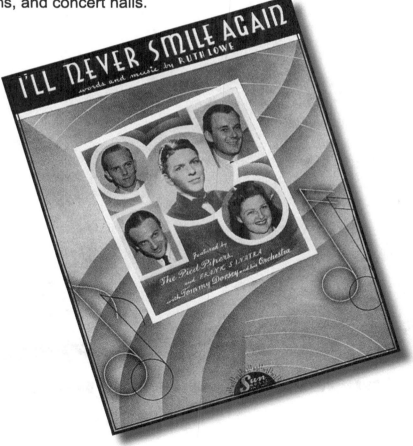

Dine and Dance at the

RUSTIC CABIN

A TYPICAL MOUNTAIN -LODGE-

We Cater to Balls, Banquets, Parties, Weddings, Etc.

Two Miles North of George Washington Bridge
Sylvan Boulevard, Route 9-W, Englewood Cliffs,
New Jersey.
Telephone: Englewood 3-1245

MENU

MINIMUM CHARGE

AFTER NINE P.M.

Weekdays 75c per person
Sundays & Holidays $1.00 per person
Saturdays $1.50 per person

RESERVATIONS
Englewood 3-7709
Englewood 3-7931
1939

Where Frank Sinatra First Started

SINATRA SINGER RELATED STATISTICS

1. For the Grammy-winning album Frank Sinatra Sings for *Only the Lonely* he painted the cover art for the album.

2. Four Number one singles with Tommy Dorsey: "I'll Never Smile Again," "Dolores," "There Are Such Things," "In the Blue of Evening."

3. Frank Sinatra was mentor to Harry Connick, Jr. whom he referred to as "The Kid."

4. For the album *Frank Sinatra Conducts Tone Poems of Color,* the orchestra was conducted by Sinatra himself and was the first album to be recorded at Capitol Records' Tower in Hollywood.

5. Frank won a special Oscar for singing "The House I Live In" in a short feature directed by Mervyn Le Roy directed against racial prejudice.

6. Frank's first starring role in movies was in Higher and Higher.

7. Frank's favorite albums are *Only the Lonely* and *Wee Small Hours*.

8. At his retirement concert in June 1971, Sinatra closed his last show with the song "Angel Eyes," and in a cloud of cigarette smoke, he sang the final line of the song: "...excuse me, while I disappear." The lights went completely out, and when they came back up, Sinatra was gone. Life Magazine's Tom Thompson wrote, "The single most stunning moment I have ever witnessed on a stage." (From the book Sinatra 101).

9. Arrangers Billy May, Gordon Jenkins, and Ernie Freeman each won a Grammy for the best arrangement of a Sinatra chart. Nelson Riddle--Sinatra's greatest arranger, was never accorded the same honor.

10. Sinatra's singles of note were "Strangers in the Night," "That's Life," "My Way," and "Something Stupid" with his daughter Nancy, which hit number one, all in the 1960s. "'Something Stupid" was Sinatra's first Gold single.

11. Sinatra performed on more than 1,800- recordings.

12. He was awarded 31 Gold records, nine platinum, three double platinum, and one triple platinum by the Recording Industry Association of America.

13. He won ten Grammys, while his albums won a total of 21.

14. Sinatra performed in Rio de Janiero before an audience of over 175,000, setting a world record in the Guinness Book for highest attendance at a concert by a solo artist.

15. Sinatra appeared in 58 films and produced 8 films; won three Oscars.

16. Sinatra has three stars on the Hollywood Walk of Fame: Recording at 1637 Vine Street, Motion Pictures at 1600 Vine Street, and Television at 6538 Hollywood Blvd.

17. On Sinatra's eightieth birthday the Empire State Building glowed for Ole Blue Eyes and repeats the ritual on his birthday lighting up the building with blue lights to commemorate his sobriquet "Ol' Blue Eyes."

18. Sinatra's last public appearance concert on February 25, 1995 in Palm Desert, California, was opened by none

other than iconic country singer Willie Nelson. Willie closed with his old favorite,"You Were Always on My Mind" and Sinatra's last song was a stirring version of "The Best is Yet to Come," a phrase which also appears on his gravestone.

Willie Nelson

Harry James Band 1939 - Atlantic City Steel Pier
Harry James Front and Center With Connie Haines on His Right
and Frank Sinatra on his Left.

THE FOUR SINATRA WIVES

NANCY BARBATO was seventeen when she met Frank Sinatra. He was nineteen. They married, five years later in 1939. They had three children: Nancy, Frank, Jr., and Tina. The couple divorced and remained friends after a few years passed.

AVA GARDNER- The bombshell movie star and Frank married in 1951. She had been married to Mickey Rooney of Mickey Rooney and Judy Garland fame, from all those MGM movies and also to famed bandleader Artie Shaw. At this point Frank's career was at an all-time low and Ava was an up-and-coming star. They divorced in 1957, after two years.

MIA FARROW'S marriage to Frank Sinatra was a surprise to everyone. Totally unexpected. She was nineteen and he was thirty years older. She was tomboyish and a little childlike bride. Frank was the first love of her life, but the marriage was short-lived and the divorce followed. They remained friends for the rest of his life.

Jerry Vale with Barbara Sinatra

BARBARA MARX had been married to one of the famous comic Marx Brothers, Zeppo, although he was not much of a factor in the group. Barbara and Frank knew one another for several years. They married and remained happily married from 1976 until Frank's passing. Barbara and Frank's two daughters did not get along from the beginning and there were issues over Frank's fortune and legacy. Barbara protected Frank in those late years when he became ill. Barbara and Frank spent over 20 happy years together. Today, Barbara and the girls get along as one family.

Frank and Barbara Sinatra (Courtesy B. Sinatra)

THE CONFERENCE

FRANK SINATRA

The Man, The Music, The Legend

November 12, 13, 14, 1998

Joining with the world in recognizing
Frank Sinatra's 82nd birthday,
Hofstra University invites
scholars and professionals
to participate in a major
scholarly conference on the
life, career, and worldwide
societal influence of this
legendary personality.

HOFSTRA UNIVERSITY
Hempstead, New York 11550-1090

With the cooperation of **The New York Friars Club**

Natalie Datlof
Director for Liaison and Cultural Development
Hofstra Cultural Center
Coordinator, *The Frank Sinatra Conference*

Tel: (516) 463-5669
Fax: (516 463-4793
e-mail: HOFCULCTR@hofstra.edu
www: hofstra.edu/sinatra

Works Consulted

Academy of Motion Pictures Arts & Sciences, Los Angeles, CA, Clipping files on Dick Haymes.
Dick Haymes Society Newsletter, Numbers 32-42.
Friedwald, Will. Jazz Singing. New York: DaCapo Press, 1996.
Giddens, Gary. Visions of Jazz. New York: Oxford U Press, 1998.
Grudens, Richard. The Music Men. Stony Brook, NY: Celebrity Profiles Publishing, 1998.
Leaming, Barbara. If This Was Happiness: A Biography of Rita Hayworth. New York: Ballantine, 1989.
Lees, Gene. Singers and the Song. New York: Oxford U Press, 1987.
_____ Singers and the Song II. New York: Oxford U Press, 1998.

Sinatra Speaks
"WHEN I SING, I BELIEVE, I'M HONEST."

"I can still close my eyes and visualize its blue and purple label. It was a Bessie Smith recording, "Bleeding Hearted Blues" with "Midnight Blues" on the "B" side. I laid that phonograph needle on the turntable and I began to have goose bumps and felt excited because it was my first exposure to jazz and blues, although I was not able to identify the genre, but I knew I needed to hear a lot more of it. It was my kind of music. I knew I could handle it with my own voice."

At Hoboken College in May, 1985, when he received an Honorary Degree in Engineering, he stated: "May you live forever and I hope the last voice you'll hear is mine."

"I tried to vary the arrangers so that there's a different quality to the songs."

"Most singers did not understand the microphone, and still don't, that a microphone is their instrument. You don't crowd it, you must never jar an audience with it. You must know when to move away from the mike and when to move back into it. It's like a geisha girl uses her fan."

"I'm sixty-one and full of activity. I'm singing well. I feel marvelous. I vocalize a least 45 minutes a day. Barbara chases me around the tennis court. When I'm home alone, I punch a sandbag. That's great for the breathing. Then I tap my chest that produces the tones. Gotta keep the bellows nice and big." To Neil Hickey, TV Guide April 1977. Life Magazine "Me and My Music 1965."

"When I started singing in the mid-30's everybody was trying to copy Crosby-the casual kind of raspy sound in the throat. Bing was on top, and a bunch of us-Dick Todd, Bob Eberly, Perry Como and Dean Martin-were tying to break in. It occurred to me that maybe the

world didn't need another Crosby . I decided to experiment a little and come up with something different. What I finally hit on was more the bel canto Italian school of singing, without making a point of it. That meant I had to stay in better shape because I had to sing more. It was more difficult than Crosby's style, much more difficult."

"The great man Crosby brought to music what has grown into an American institution."

"I'm a performer. I'm better on the first take."

"I hate the song "My Way"- you sing it for eight years and

you would hate it too." (Said at Caesars Palace, 1978)

'"Fred Astaire was a great singer, supremely musical, but not a great voice....short notes."

"My favorite albums were *Only the Lonely* and *Wee Small Hours*."

"Mel Torme told me that my old pal, drummer Buddy Rich hid his tears when I sang 'Stardust,' and he was a tough guy. I never knew that."

"Dinah Shore is a fine vocalist who puts a tremendous amount of feeling, understanding and expression into every note she sings."

"I"ll never forget the night when a fan grabbed my copy of the lyrics out of my pocket as I came through the studio door--and for a half hour the Hit Parade's audience was treated to an unending series of boo-boo-boo-doops."

"Singing one night with Tommy Dorsey and we broke the all-time record at an Ohio Dance Palace. We broke the attendance record and the promoter broke the record for the 100-yard dash--with all the money. Boy, Tommy was mad."

"Besides Bing, Bob Eberly is my favorite singer. As for the girls, I think Jo Stafford is the future star to be discovered." (Bob Eberly sang with Jimmy Dorsey: "Green Eyes," "Amapola," "Maria Elena.") Some with Helen O'Connell.

"I can't stand hearing my own records. If I'm out visiting someone, I say to them, 'If you play my records, I'm going home.' Because often I was a little impatient in making a record, and I said, That's it, press it, print it. And there was one little note in it that isn't right, and every time I hear that record, it comes back to me. If I'm in my car listening to the radio, I cringe before the note comes and I think to myself, 'Why didn't we do it one more time? Just one more time.'" (To Bill Boggs, 1975).

WILLIAM B. WILLIAMS

MAKE-BELIEVE BALLROOM

WILLIAM B. WILLIAMS

My very fine friend, once the best-known and best-loved disc jockey, William B. Williams, long time host of the Make Believe Ballroom radio show on New York's WNEW, was also a great friend to Frank Sinatra. It was William B. (as he was affectionately known) who coined the Sinatra sobriquet Chairman of the Board, which Frank, himself, admitted he always tried to live up to. In 1984, Williams, who consistently said, "I don't care how a record sells, just how it sounds," held a rare interview with Frank on the air and sent me a copy of the tape which began:

"Hello World! This is William B. and I'd like to introduce you to Francis Albert Sinatra , a practically unknown singer. Say something, Francis, don't be shy!" (He chuckles.)

"Hello World! This is Francis Albert Sinatra. You know, Willy B., about forty years ago I started at WNEW, and do you know what I got paid - zilch - but --they gave me thirty-five cents in carfare to get back to New Jersey. Well, I'm back again for those of you who ever wondered what happened to me. I know they're still paying the same kind of bread which may explain why Willy B. has been able to keep his job here."

Some time before that interview a guy named Major Bowes fronted a talent show on the radio called The Amateur Hour, a mini-version of today 's American Idol television show, where performers got their start. One night in 1935 the Major introduced a new group: "Good evening friends. We start the dizzy spin of the wheel of fortune...around and round she goes and where she stops nobody knows," the Major said in gravely eloquence. "Now, first four youngsters in kinda nice suits - The Hoboken Four. They seem so happy, I guess, and they seem to make everybody else happy (gentle laughter from the audience). Tell me, where do you fellers work in Hoboken?"

"I'm Frank, Major. We're looking for jobs. How about it! (more appreciative laughter to Frank's good-natured boldness). Everyone that's ever heard us - liked us. We think we're pretty good."

"All right, what do you want to sing - or dance - or whatever it is you do?"

"We're gonna sing 'Shine' and then we're gonna dance." "All right! Let's have it!" Then the Major announced: "Here's the Hoboken Four" The boys closely and nicely emulated a Bing Crosby/ Mills Brothers version of the then very popular song. They got the job. The Hoboken Four toured with the Major Bowes Amateur Hour Show earning seventy-five dollars a week. "We were getting paid, so we were no longer amateurs," declared Frank, triumphantly.

It was a very slim looking Frank Sinatra in his first public appearance on the world's stages that would last over 62 musically eventful years. For most of those years he sang his heart out while the world listened.

Let 's leap ahead some 10 years to 1945... things have changed. Frank was now singing to thousands of screaming bobby soxers at New York's Paramount Theater with the popular band of Harry James, and later, Tommy Dorsey. Were you one of those screaming youngsters who helped catapult Frank to everlasting fame?

In 1981, while interviewing Dorsey clarinetist Johnny Mince, he told me about meeting Sinatra for the first time:

"We were ready to go on a one-nighter, and Tommy says, 'C'mere, John.' He took me across the street and they had on a juke-box - playing that thing he did with Harry James - 'All or Nothing at All.' I said to Dorsey, 'Boy that guy is good!' But my impression when meeting Frank was something else. He was such a skinny, beat-up looking guy compared to Jack Leonard, our singer who just left the band, who had lots of class and was good-looking. Of course, Frank sure turned out to be the great one."

During my interview with Harry James in 1981, he said exactly this: "At that time Frank considered himself the greatest vocalist in the business. Get that! No one ever heard of him. He never had a hit record. He looked like a wet rag. But he tells me he's the greatest. He believed. And, you know what, he was right."

By this time Frank was now out on his own as a single and the screams and carrying-on continued wherever he appeared. "Kiss me once and kiss me twice and kiss me once again....it's been a long, long time..." Frank's way of embracing a microphone with a new approach to putting over a song completely won over a fast growing female audience. He admittedly copied Bing Crosby and he absorbed Billie Holiday's way of bending a tune and bringing it back.

When he was with Harry James and Tommy Dorsey, Frank was the boy singer and Connie Haines, my best friend in this business, was the girl singer: "I was just eighteen and I remember the police escorting Frank and me across the street from the Paramount over to the Astor Hotel, through the lobby into the drugstore just to get a hamburger," Connie and I have frequent conversations about the history of popular music of the time: "We could not get away from the screaming kids even to eat."

Tommy Dorsey Plays His Trombone

Connie recalled some early enthusiasm three years before when they both sang with James. "Richard, it was something about the way he'd hang on to that microphone. Something in his singing that reached out to the audience - like he was saying...'I'm giving this to you with everything I've got....so, what have you got to give me?' I guess they came backstage afterwards to tell him.

"Frank and I didn't always get along in those days, but, Frank showed his true colors one night - even though we were feuding while we sang the songs 'Let's Get Away from It All,' 'Oh, Look at Me Now,' and 'Snootie Little Cutie.' -- when my dress caught fire when someone tossed a lit cigarette down from the balcony and it got snared in my dress netting. Tommy was still vamping, unaware of what was happening. Frank reacted quickly, throwing his suit jacket over me and flinging me to the ground, snuffing out the flames - probably saving my life."

When Sinatra joined Tommy Dorsey, Jo Stafford was the lead and only female singer of the four member Pied Pipers singing group: "Frank made a special effort to get a good blend with the Pipers. Most solo singers usually don't fit too well into a group, but Frank never stopped working at it and, of course, as you now know, he blended beautifully with us. He was meticulous about his phrasing and dynamics. He worked very hard so that his vibrato would match ours. And he was always conscientious about learning his parts. The first song I ever heard him sing was 'Stardust'. I thought, wow, this guy is destined for great success."

BING CROSBY: "FRANK IS A SINGER WHO COMES ALONG ONCE IN A LIFETIME, BUT WHY DID HE HAVE TO COME IN MY LIFETIME?"

FRANK SINATRA TALKS ABOUT LEARNING PHRASING FROM TOMMY DORSEY'S TROMBONE PLAYING

"I used to sit behind him on the bandstand and watch, trying to see him sneak a breath. But I never saw the bellows move in his back. His jacket didn't even move. So I edged my chair around to the side a little and peeked around to watch him. Finally, I discovered he had a 'sneak pinhole' in the corner of his mouth---not an actual hole but a tiny place he left open where he was breathing. In the middle of a phrase, while the tone was still being carried through the trombone, he'd go 'shhh' and take a quick breath and play another four bars. So I began to 'play' my voice like he did with his trombone."

Sinatra's first recordings with Columbia Records exposed the public to a former band singer who no longer sang songs to which you could only dance. Axel Stordahl was his arranger helped by arranger George Siravo. Frank was just twenty-six and Stordahl about the same. Both Dorsey alumni, they produced some classic sides together with music that had some imagination and gutty arrangements. Remember, "Dream," "The Girl That I Marry," "Put Your Dreams Away,"and "Day by Day?"

At the end of the 1940s, Frank Sinatra's career changed. He rebelled against Columbia's chief Mitch Miller, who was producing his own kind of music that bothered Sinatra and which he thought demeaned his skills as a singer. He would not sing silly ditties Miller had set for him to record.

Talking with Rosemary Clooney in 1986, she loved Frank. Manie Sachs, A & R man at Columbia and later one of my own associates at NBC, answered Sinatra's request for a girl singer by suggesting Rosemary. Frank said, "O.K."

Rosemary: "We did two sides of that first date together, but later on we did some other things. That first session was the thrill of my life because I was such a fan. I adored him when I was in high school, and it was great working with him. He kept up the quality in every recording date."

By 1952 Frank Sinatra was without a movie or recording contract, or even management. Because of those late 1940s forty-five to fifty shows a week, which meant 100 songs a day, the great voice tired, his personal life tumbling into a shambles. But, Frank Sinatra promptly restarted on the road to an even greater success than he had known before, propelled by his acting-only role in the film From Here to Eternity, his move from Columbia to Capitol Records, and his magnificent union with master arranger Nelson Riddle.

"I first met Frank Sinatra when we were with Tommy Dorsey," said Duke Ellington in 1973,"They all came down one night at the College Inn at the Sherman Hotel in Chicago where we were playing, about the time he was ready to split the Dorsey gig. I could tell that by the way Tommy said good -night to him. He was young, crispy-crunch fresh, and the girls were squealing then. He was easy to get along with, and there were no hassles about his music. Every song he sings is understandable and, most of all, believable, which is the ultimate in theater. And I must repeat and emphasize my admiration for him as a nonconformist. When he played the Paramount the chicks were screaming. He was an individualist , nobody tells him what to do."

"In 1961 my father asked Morris "Mo" Ostin, who was with Verve Records, to head up his own label, Reprise," said daughter, Nancy," It was very important for dad to have his own recording company."

According to Frank himself, "I always like to choose my own songs for an album...to keep all the songs in the same genre' - swing, love songs, et cetera. Once I decide what type of music I want, I make up a list of song titles, and my associates - arrangers - suggest songs. When we actually get down to where arrangements have to be done, I go through the list again and pick out eight to ten songs and go with them." The first Reprise selections were "A Foggy Day," "A Fine Romance," and "Be Careful, It's My Heart."

When I talked with legendary jazz vibraphonist Red Norvo in 1998, he championed Frank as a great singer: "We worked together in Vegas and then at the Fountainbleu in Florida and also in Atlantic City. We also went on tour in Australia. I was used to handling singers in my various bands (Red Norvo was married to the first regular Big Band singer Mildred Bailey and is a recognized Jazz Master,) so Frank was never a problem to me. When we first worked together I had a trio, which was too small, so I told him we needed a drummer and sax, and he said OK. We made a couple of movies - *Kings Go Forth*, where I wrote some of the music, and *Oceans Eleven*, a kinda funny movie where Frank plays a bank robber in Vegas. Our Capitol recordings of the late sixties are just being issued now. Heard they are number four on the charts. Isn't that somethin'?"

Frank Sinatra continued his singing activities, although he really did not do many Italian numbers as some of his counterparts were singing. He announced his retirement in 1971, after pouring out albums like *Cycles* and *A Man Alone* in the late sixties. He returned gradually doing some concerts into 1973 and produced an album, *Old Blue Eyes Is Back*, arranged by Gordon Jenkins and Don Costa.

The songs: "Send in the Clowns," and "You Will Be My Music."

Frank toured triumphantly with Woody Herman in 1974 and spawned the album The Main Event. which included "The Lady is a Tramp," "I Get a Kick Out of You," "Autumn in New York," "My Kind of Town," and "My Way. "

Richard Grudens with William B. Williams, Westbury, Long Island, NY

1975 produced a series of appearances at the Uris Theater in New York and then London with the driving band of Count Basie which included the presence of the divine Sarah Vaughan.
In the eighties, Quincy Jones' talents became linked to Sinatra's musical career, beginning with the album L.A. Is My Lady.

"Frank is remarkable. When we recorded at A & M studios in New York, I called the orchestra for three hours before. We rehearsed and set the balance. Frank came in at seven o'clock and, so help me God, at eight-twenty he went home. We had done three songs, he said. The songs: "Stormy Weather," "How Do You Keep the Music Playing?" and "After You've Gone."

Again, appearing with William B. at WNEW on the *Make*

Believe Ballroom, Frank had a speaking part: "Hi there, my name is Francis Albert Sinatra and I've got news for you. Here is your host William B. Williams."

"Name dropper!" William B. answered tongue-in-cheek, "A question, Francis, that is somewhat philosophic. I know how keenly you feel about your family and your two granddaughters. The legacy that you leave them, is there any particular way you want to be remembered as a man...as a performer...as an American...as a human being?"

"Well, Willy, I realize it's a broad question, but I can narrow it by saying that I'd like to be remembered as a man who was as honest as he knew how to be in his life and as honest as he knew how to be in his work...and a man who gave as much energy in what he did every day as anybody else ever did. I'd like to be remembered as a decent father, as a fair husband, and as a great granddad...wonderful grandpop. And, I'd like to be remembered as a good friend to my friends."

William B.: "I think the only addendum he would have added is ...'as a man who enjoyed.'"

Frank Sinatra has always worked for the benefit of those in need . Helen O'Connell told me that Frank secretly paid all the medical bills for fellow singer Bob Eberly and many other actors and people, some of whom he never actually met. Frank always contributed his time and talent for the Italian American Organization through personal appearances to raise needed funds.

William B. also once told me about Frank's great work that gathered in millions for Sloan-Kettering Memorial Cancer Hospital in New York. At the 67th Street outpatient entrance between York and Ist Avenue of that hospital there is a plaque on the wall that states" "This Wing of Sloan-Kettering is Through the Efforts of Frank Sinatra"

During his final years Frank and Barbara Sinatra worked hard for the Barbara Sinatra Children's Center at Eisenhower Center, Rancho Mirage, California. And, profits from their book The Sinatra Celebrity Cookbook by Barbara, Frank & Friends, have supported that worthy project.

Read on, the best is yet to come.

William B. once told me he ran a no-prize contest on his show, the *Make Believe Ballroom*, pitting the Mammy singer, Al Jolson, the Voice, Frank Sinatra, and Der Bingle, Bing Crosby in a fifteen minute segment. Close to 2000 letters and cards were received from nine states. The final count: Jolson came in first, Sinatra second, and Bing in third place. That was in the late forties when the very popular film *The Jolson Story* was still showing in theaters.

FRANK SINATRA

August 6, 1993

RE: WILLIAM B. WILLIAMS

WILLIAM B. WILLIAMS WAS AN IRREPLACEABLE
TALENT. I AM AMONG THE LUCKY ONES WHO HAD
THE GREAT FORTUNE TO HAVE KNOWN THIS
TALENTED GENTLEMAN. I AM FOREVER PROUD
THAT I WAS HIS FRIEND. WILLIE, HERE'S
TO YOU AND ALL THE MEMORABLE TIMES WE
SHARED TOGETHER.

Frank Sinatra

Mr.Al Monroe
287 Country Club Drive
Oradell, N.J. 07649

Al Monroe is a Radio DJ in New Jersey

Sinatra Interviews With Only His Voice

In 1975 Bill Boggs interviewed Frank Sinatra on New York's television station WNEW. Frank had just come off an engagement at the Uris Theater in New York. However, the interview took place in Philadelphia. Here are some revealing highlights:

Sinatra: More than anything else I felt that this new show was a love-in with the people. It was like coming home. The effect of performing in a cavernous coliseum or a large theater like those in New York, Chicago, and Philadelphia where the people seem so far away- and up so high, the exchange of feelings is tough to measure because its so overwhelming, and when I look up all that affection comes forward like a wave.

I have always trained myself since the beginning to capture a song with real emotion. I think that after I've chosen a piece of material that I feel I must be doing-something in a somewhat serious vein or something slightly dramatic like "Send in the Clowns," --- I think it has to do with something in my background that comes forward and it presents itself rather than just reading a piece like poetry - I, as a singer, have to do it in that sense. So I try to transpose my thoughts about the song into a person at that moment saying those words to somebody else - like his making the case for himself. I don't know where it started but I've always worked in that vein all the way back with Tommy and even before Tommy - - when I was a kid working from one small joint to another.

When I wasn't working and had decided not to go to college my father threw me out of the house. To him education was every-thing. He wanted me to go to college. That was his big point. I had planned to go to Stevens Institute in Hoboken - a very fine engineer-ing school - to become a civil engineer, which at one time was my great desire, until I got mixed up in vocalizing. So he got fed up with me because I was singing for pennies to get experience singing with a megaphone like Rudy Vallee. So Dad ordered me out of the house, so I packed up a suitcase and went to New York leaving my mother in tears. I was shocked…I remember the moment.

My honest plan was to get to sing with Tommy Dorsey. He had the best orchestra and a good singer in Jack Leonard. And Jimmy Dorsey had Bob Eberly and Glenn Miller had Ray Eberle, his brother. I wondered at my chances.

I would go to see Tommy at Roseland in New York and stand in front of the bandstand and watch how he handled his singers. He would showcase his singers with much respect and set them up to feature them. Tommy has a simpatico about vocalizing, something I didn't know at the time.

The trombone had the same qualities as the human voice in the way of execution- much like a flute. There's something quite soft about the trombone when it's played well like a cello. I kept trying to find out how Tommy was able to breathe enough to get past ten mea-sures. He kept it a secret until after a year or so with me watching his back to see when he breathed in and out. One day Tommy said to me, "Haven't you seen it yet?"

Well the secret was that he had maintained a pinhole in the corner of his mouth so he could catch a cat's breath, which allowed him to breathe those extra two measures that no one else could do. All I had to do was to copy that secret. Soon people would ask me, "When do you breathe?"

That led me to begin exercises by swimming underwater to keep the bellows as strong as I could. I had to stay in good physical condition. For the Uris show I had to really work out because I had retired so I had a tough time bringing back my breathing strength, but with time I was able to work it all out. The greatest training that any youngster can have today, if he really wants to become a pop singer, is that you have to sing all the time and every day.

Today, there is no opportunity for young, up-and-coming singers to train with a band -with no one nighter's night after night for you to learn. With me, who had that opportunity, I used the lyrics of the song as a script. I didn't know I was doing that at the time but I was doing it anyway.

Hard work and nothing different than hard work, concentration, choosing the best material and trying to find out what the audience wanted to hear. You have to think like a baseball pitcher. I'd say to Bill (Miller, piano accompanist), skip the next two tunes and go the a third because there is something about the audience not getting the vibes - so you go to something different that might grab them a bit more-like throwing a knuckler, or a slider, or a fast ball, which will amuse them and even mystify them.

I believe when you are in a saloon you get a response, and you know they have been there too, experiencing some kind of sadness in the song and it brings it back to them.

I always love working with Ella Fitzgerald. She is a good musician and vocalist. We both have been blessed with good fortune in our lifetime. She is so wrapped up in her singing like Benny Goodman is in his playing the clarinet. Once I asked Benny why he sits in corners playing after he just finished playing a concert, or even during a party, and he said that he must practice every day: "If I'm not great - I'm just good. You have to work just as hard during the slow periods to keep it good and never below the standard." I listened to that advice carefully and remembered it.

People ask whom I followed to learn my craft and I can mention Bing Crosby, Bessie Smith, Mabel Mercer, Bob Eberly, Jack Leonard did some fine things with Dorsey and the great Robert Merrill, who, by the way, when I come to New York we would meet and we'd have a clinic and he always straightens me out.

When listening to other singers who sound a lot like me when I'm listening to the radio in my car, I say to myself, "when did I record that song, I don't remember it?" Then there's the other side, for instance, when I'm visiting someone and they have my records playing-I can't stand that! I ask them to turn it off and if they don't I'll leave and I tell them so.

Many songs that I have recorded have flaws, even that one little note that's way off I cringe even before the note comes. When I am in my car and hear it I think to myself, "why didn't we do it just once more time?"

I want everyone to know that when the year 2000 arrives, I will throw the biggest party anyone has ever seen. Now, about the privacy issue, like when you are walking on the avenue and folks say hello and even some will ask for an autograph. I always oblige- it's great flattery. In fact, it's a delight. But there is that rare bird that will ask you to come over to their table while you are in the middle of actually eating. That's the bad guy who insists, but most people have better sense that that, they really do.

If I wanted to go to Coney Island in the daytime or even the evening there would be bedlam, or at any popular place where a lot of people congregate. So I go out at night, to the park, or window-shopping in New York, when there is nobody around. Sometimes I'd be strolling along and you'd hear someone say, 'Is that really him?' You can get a few quiet moments now and then. And, you know, I swear I have never, never been heckled in all my lifetime-my entire career or at any performance. That amazes me. I know some performers who will never sign an autograph and I don't understand why.

A particular annoying item is when flash bulbs hit your eyes alighting from a car. That is not good. It can hurt our eyes-and I've got to take care of my baby blues. Sometimes they are red from time to time.

During a performance, someone will run down the aisle to take a picture, and what I do is stop and let him take it because I want him to go back to his seat, otherwise people begin to shout at him - or her- disrupting the performance. It's best to let them take the photo and sit back down.

Bill Boggs Today

My obligation to the audience is high. How well you do depends on your physical condition. With ten minutes to go on I will vocalize in the dressing room. I'd sing an "F" for 4 to 5 minutes, it being the best exercise before a performance. Sometimes I will get Bill Miller and do scales. And you never sing AH…you only sing UH, which is the right sound to help you warm up. These short exercises give me an extra-added sense of security. Then I am ready to pitch. I usually sing for about one-and-a-half hours a day. I'd break it up, but you must keep the singing because it keeps those singing muscles going.

During my retirement I wouldn't even hum for anyone and I did not miss singing. It lasted just under two years and I had the time of my life, the most wonderful period of my life. I wanted to stop singing and working for a while. Then, when I was ready, I came back and, thank God, the public allowed me back.

When I was first starting, all those little places fitted into my scheme at the time. I would sing anywhere, and wait tables and act as emcee too. Now they are gone by the wayside (1975). Those who work the rooms in Vegas may go to Miami for Easter or Christmas. That's all there is because New York has closed. When the Copa closed that was the end of the so-called cabaret era. The Copa and similar places were where all the name acts performed. Now there are no rooms in New York like that anymore to work.

When I was singing at the Rustic Cabin, it wasn't far from a place called the Riviera near the George Washington Bridge in New Jersey. After work we would stand at the door and listen to the Dorsey Brothers play. The place had a roof that opened up and it was a beautiful place that did most of its business during the summer. There should be a few places like that today. Maybe someday it all will return and give new singers a chance at achieving a singing career.

Editor's note: Today, many of the Big Bands are active and on tour as Ghost, or Tribute, Bands. Many movie theaters have been converted into Performing Arts Centers and have attracted singers and others acts. Such places are the new Copacabana's. But without the drinks and food service.

JACK ELLSWORTH INTERVIEWS FRANK SINATRA

Interview. July 11, 1949.

(Questions omitted)

Jack, thanks for inviting me for this interview, something I don't do too often. I love to sing only good songs. An artist is as good as his material. We've done a few things lately like "Let Her Go, Let Her Go," in a new studio with Sy Oliver arranging, and Jule Styne's "It All Depends on You," a very nice George Siravo (arrangement) thing.

For the past couple of years the songs these days are very poor. I guess the songwriters are all tied up doing Broadway shows or working on films and don't have much time to do pop songs any-

Richard Grudens with Jack Ellsworth at the WALK studios on Long Island more. Amateur songs are being written, but they don't belong in the music business. They hurt the artist and the orchestra.

We did things with Dorsey like "This Love of Mine," "Fools Rush In," which are great tunes done with Dorsey's fine orchestra. I don't think there were many bad songs written then, but now it's an uphill battle to find something good---something that has some thought behind it.

Speaking about my leaving the *Hit Parade*, it was amicable, and now I'll have a five night a week show where I can sing songs I like to sing and songs the audience wants to hear. I got fed up with songs like "The Woody Woodpecker Song," but I had to sing it because the policy was that the star had to sing the number one song each week. But songs like "I Beg Your Pardon" was terrible, and songs like "Lavender Blue" and "Near You" and a couple of other broken-down tunes like that I had to sing.

The show will be sponsored by Lucky Strike and then we may be doing a daytime radio disc jockey-type talk show where sometimes I will sing live with a piano along with playing records. I think television will be taking over from radio from 7:30 p.m. and daytime radio will take over in the daytime.

As for today's singers that I like, one would be Kay Starr who has made some fine records as she is a tremendous singer. Everything she does is wonderful. She will be on the top before long as the top female bracket. And, Doris Day on Columbia. Well I was fortunate to be on the record with her. We did a song from Irving Berlin's *Miss Liberty* called "Let's Take an Old Fashioned Walk." Doris is so cute. She has something special about her. She is bubbly and I love her style. I mean that sincerely. I like working with her. And Crosby is turning out some nice tunes lately. I guess the singing business is here to stay.

Thanks Jack for all you do for fellows like me.

On March 10, 2010, I spoke to Jack Ellsworth who has been playing Sinatra recordings on WALK, Long Island for all these years and continues in Jack's 86th year.

FRANK SINATRA

April 15, 1997

Dear Jack,

We've traveled many musical miles
together, my friend. I am delighted
to send cheers and bravos to you
on 50 marvelous years of championing
our kind of music.

As I raise a glass of bubbly, I thank
you for your generous support of my
career -- you're a good man!

Frank Sinatra

Mr. Jack Ellsworth
WLIM Radio
Woodside Avenue
Patchogue, N.Y. 11772

ARLENE FRANCIS

1980 Interview with Frank Sinatra

"Talking about preserving your vocal cords, Arlene. You have a second set of vocal cords above the first set that protects the main vocal cords. They vibrate and make the sounds that we achieve singing. The throat is the most antiseptic part of your body because nothing stays there, maybe except bacteria. The throat is easy to get to for a doctor to check and treat. Getting rest and not speaking for six to seven hours a day is important to protecting the vocal cords. Not even whispering. Whispering strains the vocal cords even more.

"A few years ago when I was doing five radio shows a week and singing nights at the Copacabana, I took a gig singing at the Capitol Theater each night and going from there to the Copa. One night I opened my mouth to sing and not a sound came out. I left and called my doctor, Irving Goldman, who directed me not to say a word until I saw him a few hours later. It was a sub-mucosal hemorrhage of the throat. Fortunately, Billy Eckstine was able to fill in for me. I did not speak not even one word for forty days. My songwriting friend Jimmy Van Heusen and I went to Florida to help me and speak for me. When I went back to the doctor after the forty days voice vacation, he looked at my throat and told me my throat and vocals were pink like a baby. He asked me to say something and in a squeaky voice I said," "What do you want me to say?"

JONATHAN SCHWARTZ INTERVIEWS NELSON RIDDLE

They are speaking mainly about the recording "I've Got You Under My Skin" and the trombone solo improvisation by Milt Bernhart in the Nelson Riddle arrangement of Frank Sinatra which is legendary. According to Jonathan, "What a great man Nelson was: modest and funny. Direct. Wonderful with language."

The Interview Verbatim:

Jon: But, Nelson, as it happens, you were there that night. Was it at night ?

Nelson: Well, Frank always liked to record at night.

Jon: Do you remember about that recording of that date, the arrangement, how long did it take you, the writing, where you did it, and the conditions?

Nelson: Well I was living in Malibu Canyon in Malibu - but it was a work of pressure because I had to stay up quite late one night and finish it. That was 1956.

Jon: As you wrote the arrangement could you clearly hear an orchestra playing it in your head?

Nelson: One always does. I work from a piano which is a form of a crutch. In truth, I can really hear the instruments then when I try to find harmonies or a line on the piano I just have to look at the keys from a nearby table to get the feel of it. But, yes, you can hear the orchestra.

Jon: This arrangement , you were obviously the first to hear it, you probably said to yourself, WOW, this is awfully good.

Nelson: No! I probably said, wow- isn't it nice that I would be able finish it in time. I think that most of my wows are reserved for that particular purpose in those days. And I was so naive that I thought my major problem was getting my work done, and isn't that stupid, because there were many potential problems around me which I ignored in favor of getting it done because I wasn't dealing with them.

Jon: So, in arranging this song in this eleventh-hour city, you had sixteen arrangements to write. So let's take a step backwards: The songs- "I've got You Under My Skin," "You Make Me Feel So Young," "Our Love is Here to Stay," "How About You," "Anything Goes!" Did Sinatra, and Sinatra only, select those songs, or did he do it in collaboration with you and the producer?

Nelson: No, that wasn't possible. Voyle Gilmore (President of Capitol Records) presided as a benign presence over the proceedings. He was a very pleasant man, very easy going. Sinatra picked his own things, he has always to my knowledge, although he may once in a while listen to a suggestion. Don Costa told me some time ago that it was a problem with Frank, and Don is a fine arranger, but basically he prefers producing an album, that's the big thing with Don, he does it by the package and not by the arrangement.

Jon: What was the problem?

Nelson: The problem was that, Don, the producer usually picks what goes into the album, but when he came up against Frank, he found he was dealing with a man who was used to producing and selecting his own albums for years before Don arrived on the scene. Don finally dealt with it in the most practical way possible by taking one short step backwards and let the status-quo continue.

Jon: Are you suggesting, Nelson, that by describing Voyle Gilmore as a rather benign presence and a very affable man, it seems to me then that Sinatra had basically produced all his own albums at Capitol though the years.

Nelson: I believe so, I really believe so. When he gets an idea that he feels works, he won't tolerate any interference. When you hear a Frank Sinatra album it's a product of Frank Sinatra's head. Jon: Well, this album Songs for Swingin' Lovers--- does that mean you received a list in the mail saying 'these are the songs we are going to do?'

Nelson: No, not by any means. Frank, or someone, would call me and then I would have a meeting with Frank. When I first worked for him, some of his instructions went on ad infinitum, and he'd say, I want this kind of sound here, and that kind of sound there, he's fairly versant with classical music and he would give me many examples from classical music.

Jon: For example?

Nelson: There's a song "To Love and Be Loved," and there's another where he wanted a Puccini sound behind him. Well, anybody with half a thorough musical knowledge would immediately know what that was, but I had to go to the library and open a Puccini score because I had studiously avoided operatic music, which I didn't enjoy as much back then.

What he meant by a Puccini sound was that the melody is doubled in octaves in the orchestra. And that was what he wanted.

Jon: That's well reflected in your arrangement of that song. Nelson: That's right. And when he heard it he came right over to the bandstand and said,"That's a beautiful arrangement." Frank was always appreciative and enthusiastic in his praise regarding my efforts, just as I was enthusiastic about his, but I must say we didn't interchange too many compliments because we both expected that of each other. Getting back to "I've Got You Under My Skin" he mapped out a lot of these things and was specific in coloration's at times, but at least he was very coherent about what he wanted...where the crescendos took place and where the diminuendos and tempo belonged, and naturally, the key, and sometimes it was painful discussing an album of twelve to fourteen songs.

You look at your watch but he wasn't looking at your watch. How much longer is this going to go on? Because it was a very tight and intense atmosphere and I was taking copious notes so that I could reconstruct this meeting later on. Sometimes I wanted to blow my stack, but he never knew it, because we would take an hour on each piece, but then human nature would set in. After five, six, or seven of those he would get tired and he'd finally say, "Do what you want with the rest of it." And that would be the end of the thing and we both would be relieved.

Jon: Do you remember any specific song that was subjected to careful scrutiny?

Nelson: "Last Night When We Were Young"...(for the Wee Small album) we did thirty takes. As a result I learned a lot from Frank about conducting for a vocalist. The importance of tempos, which are just as important as the coloration's of the orchestra, and so are the dynamics. And I learned to have an orchestra breathe with him phrase by phrase. But I was still in the learning process and he was extremely patient with me. Not all my fault, but at least half. In those days he had voice to burn, obviously.

Jon: On the arrangement of "I've Got You Under My Skin" do you recall any prearrangement or conversation with Frank Sinatra about it?

Nelson: There must have been one but I think he wanted a crescendo. I don't think he was aware of the way I was going to achieve that crescendo. He certainly wanted an instrumental interlude which would be exciting and carry the orchestra up into the instrumental part and then come down and he would finish the arrangement vocally. I know the night we did it he experienced enthusiasm for the arrangement, and I guess later on when he took the tape home and played it he was even more enthusiastic. As it turned out, it was a cornerstone recording for both of us.

Jon: It changed American popular music. That's not overstating the case, Nelson, that is a fact. Nothing was the same after that. Nelson: Frank stood for quality. I think the brought out the best in me, and I like to think that at times I brought out the best in him.

Jonathan Schwartz began at New York's WNEW in 1976 alongside DJs William B. Williams, Jim Lowe, and Bob Jones.

He is the best DJ playing America's Best Music, the Great American Songbook. He knows more about Frank Sinatra's career than anyone else and plays his music on Sirius Sinatra on XM radio every day from 12 noon to 3 pm, 7 days a week. If he has to go somewhere personal, Jonathan tapes the show for airing in its regular spot. He plays everyone, including up and coming girl and boy singers. He calls his program High Standards and Siriusly Sinatra. His favorites are Frank Sinatra, Peggy Lee, Tony Bennett, Ella Fitzgerald, and Bing Crosby, as well as all the other singers we all know so well. Jonathan is the son of Arthur Schwartz, who wrote, among others, my favorite song to play on the piano, "Dancing in the Dark," and all the songs from the movie The Bandwagon that starred Fred Astaire and Cyd Charisse.

There's a story that once on a Superbowl Sunday, he played recordings with only baseball themes, being a staunch Boston Red-Sox fan. Jonathan frequently talks about the music and hs been known to present the premiere of an album before anybody else. There is little Jonathan doesn't know about or care about when it come to Frank Sinatra. Rumor has it that he will be joining with the Sinatra family on Sirius radio in presenting Sinatra material and talk about it too.

"I think it's criminal to go on the air without an intimate knowledge of every record by each of the artists. No only one album but every album. Every song on the albums. Every note."

THE BODY OF WORK OF FRANK SINATRA AND NELSON RIDDLE WAS COMPOSED OF 318 RECORDS-WHICH INCLUDED SIXTEEN ALBUMS, SEVEN MOVIES, TWENTY-FIVE TELEVISION SHOWS.

Their friendship closed with Sinatra snubbing Riddle at a testimonial dinner in 1978 causing them to no longer working with one another, but Sinatra always praised Riddle.

"Of all the orchestrators I've ever worked with, Nelson is the finest musician of them all" Frank Sinatra to Frank Sinatra, Jr.

Author Robin Douglas-Home.

"Nelson is the greatest arranger in the world--a very clever musician--and I have the greatest respect for him.. He's like a tranquilizer--calm, slightly aloof....There's a great depth somehow to the music he creates....Nelson's quality of aloofness and way of detachment give him a particular kind of disciplined air at sessions and the band respects him for it."

In 1971 the Congressional Record praises Sinatra. Sinatra sent a copy of it to Nelson Riddle with a note that read: "Dear Nelson: You are as much a part of what was said about me by these great men in the Senate, and at the risk of my doing something hokey,The rift had been healed. I wanted you to have a copy of the enclosed. All the best always, Love. Frank."

Nelson Riddle compilation of Capitol Albums

- Songs for Young Lovers and Swing Easy (CDP-748470-2)
- In the Wee Small Hours (CDP-746571-2)
- Close to You (CDP-746572-2)
- Songs for Swingin' Lovers (CDP-746570-2)
- Swingin'Affair (CDP-794518-2)
- Only the Lonely (CDP-7 96827-2)
- Sinatra's Swingin'Session (CDP-746573-2)

Capitol Singles and soundtracks

- All the Way CDP-791150-2
- Capitol Collector's Series CDP-792160-2
- Frank Sinatra at the Movies CDP-99374-2
- Can-Can CDP791248-2
- Pal Joey CDP791249-2

The Reprise Albums:

- The Concert Sinatra (FS 1009-2)
- Sinatra's Sinatra (FS 1010-2)
- The Days of Wine and Roses (FS 1011-2)
- Moonlight Sinatra (FS 1018-2)

In 1984 Nelson Riddle was asked to name his favorite Capitol Records project works with Frank Sinatra.

"I would have to say the album *Swing Easy* was the most inventive and most exciting work we did together."

Other sources name the album *The Concert Sinatra*, a Reprise undertaking, as his best, and in 1984, in an interview.

Anatomy of a Song - My Way

"My Way" is an English version of a French song. English lyrics were added by Paul Anka and popularized by Frank Sinatra on his 1969 album My Way. arranged and orchestrated by Don Costa. The melody is "Comme d'habitude" composed in 1967 by Claude François and Jacques Revaux. Paul Anka's English lyrics are unrelated to the original French lyrics.

The lyrics of "My Way" tell the story of a man who is nearing death. As he reflects on his life, he has few regrets for how he lived it, saying that, as he reviews the challenges he's faced, he is comfortable with and takes responsibility for how he dealt with all the ups and downs of his life while maintaining a respectable degree of integrity.

Paul Anka heard the original 1967 French pop song, "Comme d'habitude" performed by Claude Francois with music by Jacques Revaux and lyrics by Gilles Thibault, while on vacation in the south of France. He flew to Paris to negotiate the rights to the song. In a 2007 interview, he said: "I thought it was a bad record, but there was something in it.

"I was lucky, said Anka," I acquired publishing rights at no cost, and two years later I had dinner in Florida with Frank Sinatra and he said he was quitting the business, "I'm sick of it, I'm getting the hell out."

Anka rewrote the original French song for Sinatra when he got back to New York, and carefully altered the melodic structure and changed the lyrics: "At one o'clock in the morning, I sat down at an old IBM electric typewriter and said to myself, 'If Frank were writing this, what would he say?' And I started, metaphorically, 'And now the end is near.' I read a lot of periodicals, and I noticed everything was 'my this' and 'my that'. We were in the 'me generation' and Frank became the guy for me. I used words I would never use: 'I ate it up and spit it out.' But that's the way he talked. I used to be around steam rooms with the Rat Pack guys - they liked to talk like wise guys."

Paul Anka finished the song at five a.m., so "I called Frank up in Nevada - he was at Caesar's Palace - and told him, 'I've got something really special for you.'" When Paul's record company caught wind of it, they thought he should've kept it for himself. "I said, 'Hey, I can write it, but I'm not the guy to sing it.' It was for Frank that I did it, and no one else."

Frank Sinatra recorded his version of the song on December 30, 1968 and it was rush-released in early 1969. It reached the U.S. charts, but in the UK the single achieved a still unmatched record, becoming the recording with most weeks inside the Top 40. It spent 75 weeks between April 1969 and September 1971. It has spent a further 49 weeks in the Top 75 but never bettered the numer 5 slot achieved upon its first chart run.

Interesting note: The two takes that made the song went well, but there was a split in the recording where Sinatra reaches "I've loved, I've laughed, I've cried," but it goes unnoticed except for the vocal quality. He goes from a big voice to a moderate voice in a split second or two. The song is not a strong song in itself, but with Sinatra it becomes a grandiose theme of great proportions that mesmorize Sinatra fans worldwide and almost without exception.

Just about everybody had a shot at "My Way," including Elvis Presley who began performing the song in concert during the mid-1970s, in spite of suggestions by Paul Anka, who told him it was not a song that would suit him. Nevertheless, on January 12th and 14th of 1973 Presley sang the song during his satellite show Aloha from Hawaii, beamed live to 43 countries via Intelsat, the only time that a single entertainer faced such a worldwide audience. In the continental U.S., the show was carried by NBC, and shown in prime-time on April 14th thus achieving very high ratings and eventually helping the show reach a worldwide viewership of over 1 billion.

On October 3, 1977, several weeks after his death, Elvis Presley live recording of "My Way" (recorded for the "Elvis In Concert" CBS-TV special on June 21, 1977) was released as a single. In the U.S., it reached number 22 on the Billboard Hot 100 pop singles chart, number six on the Billboard Adult Contemporary chart, and the following year reached number 2 on the Billboard Country singles chart but went all the way to number one on the rival Cash Box Country Singles chart. In the UK, it reached number 9 on the UK Singles Chart.

In 1972, the Spanish singer Raphael recorded a close translation to Spanish "A Mi Manera" from the lyrics of Paul Anka that got to number one in sales in Spain and Latin America. Vicente Fernandez followed suit in 1983 when he recorded a cover of it in his album *15 Grandes*. Beatrice Arthur sang a version of the song in an episode of Maude, Paul Potts recorded "A Mi Manera" for his album *One Chance*.

Anka also duetted with Julio Iglesias in a unique Spanglish version of "My Way" on Anka's duets album *Amigos*. The song "A Mi Manera", on the Gipsy Kings' eponymous 1988 album *Gipsy Kings*, is a loose translation of Anka's lyrics into Spanish.

Robin Williams, voicing the penguin character Ramón, sings A Mi Manera in the CGI animated movie Happy Feet. The song was featured on the soundtrack album Happy Feet: Music from the Motion Picture.

In a segment for Sesame Street, Oscar the Grouch sang an antilittering song called "Just Throw It My Way", a parody of the song. In 2007 Paul Anka released the album Classic Songs, "My Way" which included the song in a duet with Jon Bon Jovi. In 2007, in the second of their specials covering the 2007 Australian Federal Election, Andrew Hansen of The Chaser performed a version summarizing the events of the local government elections.

The identification of the song with Sinatra became so strong, and the song so iconic, that the Soviet government of Mikhail Gorbachev jokingly referred to its policy of non-intervention in the internal affairs of other Warsaw Pact countries as the Sinatra Doctrine.

It was briefly sung in Russian in Superman IV: The Quest for Peace by an astronaut. His crew are irritated by the song and shout "Sing at home!", while the singer replies, with a giggle, "At home, they tell me to sing in space."

"My Way" is one of the most popular songs sung in karaoke bars around the world, to the point that it has been reported to cause numerous incidents of violence and homicides among drunkards in bars in the Philippines.

"My Way" was in the Buffy season 3 episode "Lover's Walk" twice, first sung by the character Spike in a drunken moment of self-pity, then again at the very end Gary Oldman's version from the film 'Sid and Nancy' was played (as the producers were unable to get permission from the Sex Pistols to use Sid's version).

"My Way" was played at the 880th victory of Bobby Knight. He passed Dean Smith as the coach with the most wins in NCAA Division I basketball with this win.

When former Australian Prime Minister, John Gorton stood down as the leader of the Liberal Party and consequently, as Prime Minister, a video montage was put together with photos of his career, with "My Way" as the backing song.

However, the song belongs to Frank Sinatra as surely as "Over the Rainbow" belongs to Judy Garland, "I Left My Heart in San Francisco" belongs to Tony Bennett, " White Christmas" belongs to Bing Crosby, and "God Bless America" belongs to Kate Smith. Questions anyone?

Paul Anka

THE FRANK SINATRA SCHOOL OF THE ARTS

From Tony Bennett:
To Whom It May Concern:

For a number of years the idea of creating a school of the Arts has been important to me. My interest was sparked by an experience I had with a public school in Chicago, some time ago, where I saw the following things: an abandoned vest-pocket park was taken over by a school: the park was cleared, murals were painted and the kids put on performances for the community. This showed me how powerfully the arts could be used for a community's well-being.

The school I envision would stress community service, just like Chicago, where the kids could practice their craft. I would like students to know at the onset that fame and celebrity are not the true goals of the arts. The true artist is at the service of a rigorous arts and academic program... and his craft.

I also see a school where artists and entertainers themselves are intimately involved with the school. Toward this end, I have asked a number

Susan and Tony Bennett with Quincy Jones

of prominent businessmen and performers to support and work with the school (i.e. Harry Belafonte, Wynton Marsalis, and Eli Wallach, to name a few). These performers could be involved in a number of ways, including mentoring, giving master classes and if need be, co-teaching a class.

Through the years, beginning with his Academy Award winning performance in "The House I Live In," it was always Frank Sinatra's desire to help children receive a quality education involving the arts. I can think of no better way to remember, celebrate and honor my best friend and colleague, the great performer and entertainer, Frank Sinatra, than to create a wonderful, vibrant school in his name.

Sincerely,
Tony Bennett

Frank Sinatra School of the Arts, Tony Bennett Founder
30-20 Thomson Avenue, Queens, New York 11101

THE ARRANGERS

Nelson Riddle with Frank

AXEL STORDAHL

Axel Stordahl for the soft, beautiful and nostalgic, Billy May for upswinging and Gordon Jenkins for enriched downers, Johnny Mandel for the touch of modern jazz, Neal Hefti for earthy swings, Robert Farnon for love songs. George Siravo was more like a musical designer, Don Costa for special all-around, but more contemporary material. And then there is the true musical genius of Nelson Riddle. Frank would assign an arranger to a song he thought would fit the style of arranging required for that particular song.

Sinatra would always credit the tempo and outline of a number when he performed publicly. He made demands on all his arrangers, which mostly at first would upset them. He had excellent musical taste and authority over arrangements and all musical events. At a recording session, when important parts of a take break down at the last minute, Sinatra would not hesitate to abort and start over again - even, at times, up to over twenty-five or more takes, that is, until satisfaction is achieved.

VAN ALEXANDER - "AN ARRANGER IS A SONGWRITER'S BEST FRIEND"

Arrangements either make a song either like a million bucks or ten cents. Sinatra tried to vary the arrangers so that there was a different quality to the songs.

Frank: "Singing with Harry James was an important part of my career. I learned a lot about pacing and programming and fine musicianship from Harry, because you are bound to learn when you work closely with someone. I performed with him and made some fine records for over eight months. Then I received an offer from Tommy Dorsey, who was the number one band in the country, and Harry was a relatively unknown band by comparison. After three years with

Tommy, and singing shoulder to shoulder with Connie Haines and the Pied Pipers I decided to strike out on my own, and because orchestration and arranging is over sixty percent of a recording, I asked Axel Stordahl, a Staten Island, New York born native from across the river from where I was born, who was one of the best band's arrangers, if he wanted to take pot luck with me, and he did, and we grew together five years. Axel worked on untold inspirational arrangements and great orchestrations. Being essentially a composer, he was able to do everything a singer required for recording.

Axel Rehearses Frank

"When Axel arranged for me it was like a separate composition. When I went to Capitol, Nelson Riddle, who I did not know at first,was the house arranger so I had to work with him, but Axel remained with me too because you need up to five or six arrangers when you are putting an album together. Nelson couldn't do it all alone." Stordahl's first Capitol recording with Sinatra was "I'm Walking Behind You" before he got started with Riddle.

Frank had a commitment to Stordahl, which was his largest expense. He had offered Stordahl more money than Dorsey was paying to lure him away. Axel was a definite romantic who developed Sinatra's role as a singer of intricate love songs and delicious slow ballads and helped him up the ladder before the Sinatra-Riddle association existed. Sinatra was searching for a unique and special sound and he thought Axel Stordahl could continue the success they both had with Dorsey with his early recordings that shared in the introduction of new Sinatra singing ideas, a new manner of singing in what became the beginning of the era of the vocalists, sans the big bands, who were beginning to break up in favor of this new revolution in singing styles. The war had broken up most of the bands and with the war being over and automobiles became available, people exchanged the big band pavilions and venues for traveling to new places to spend their weekends.

Sinatra and Stordahl had just about perfected Sinatra's style on the Sinatra V-discs with "I Only Have Eyes for You," "She's Funny That Way," "The Way You Look Tonight" and a few other beautiful ballads that were never recorded commercially because it was during the war and the musicians strike was in full swing in 1942-43 when the only recordings allowed to be waxed by the strike were exclusively for servicemen serving overseas and were designated "V" discs. Stordahl never received the early recognition he deserved but was held in awe by up-and-coming arrangers including Don Costa. Stordahl was way ahead of his time and was clearly the best arranger of Sinatra's musical product until later on by the circle of arrangers comprised of Billy May, Gordon Jenkins and Nelson Riddle that came upon the scene at Capitol.

Columbia Records producer Mitch Miller considered Axel Stordahl the "consummate craftsman, a man with no negative temperament or divisive attitude among his fellow musicians," or even Sinatra himself.

Axel Stordahl was at first a moderate trumpet player and an occasional arranger, preferring the later and became a regular arranger for Jack Leonard, the Dorsey pre-Sinatra boy vocalist, and the number-two arranger beneath Paul Weston, who soon left the band leaving Stordahl as lead arranger for the Dorsey band and his fair-haired vocalist, Frank Sinatra.

Stordahl actually arranged more charts for Sinatra than any

other arranger, including Nelson Riddle, although they match on the number of recordings, Stordahl arranged almost every chart on a variety of Sinatra radio shows, which were endless and were never added up.

Stordahl shared the arrangement of early Sinatra's super-gem "I'll Never Smile Again" with Fred Stalk. Here was the beginning of an arranger arranging specifically for the vocalist, the new specialist of song and not just a fill-in the one-two-three formula employed by most bands of the period: First the band, then the vocal, then the band as a closer.

According to Paul Weston, who later married lead singer Jo Stafford, Tommy Dorsey's only female member of his singing group par-excellent, the Pied Pipers: "Axel was a very good writer for strings and was originally oriented in the classical style. He and I would always listen to classical material in our off time, Debussy being a favorite. It is recognized that the classical composers influenced Axel Stordahl that ultimately produced the lovely Sinatra countermelodies and codas and repeated intros that relied heavily on his favorite instruments, the violins."

I love the Stordahl arrangements of the dreamlike "Laura," and "Stella by Starlight."

When Sinatra emigrated to the west coast, taking Axel with him, he was able to convince the sponsors to relocate The Hit Parade radio show to California. Mark Warnow had led the Hit Parade Orchestra when it was in New York and the arrangements for Frank were Axel Stordahl's. When the show shifted to Hollywood it allowed Axel Stordahl to conduct, as well as arrange.

However, Sinatra often battled with the sponsor to allow him to develop songs that he felt his fans wanted to hear, and not the songs that the sponsor selected for his own satisfaction.

The *Hit Parade* radio show, although it held a high rating, did nothing for its vocalists. Sinatra insisted on better arrangements for his part of the program that would show off his style, but the sponsor did not want to pay for the extra arranger salaries. So, when it came to Sinatra's portion, the arrangements of Stordahl took over the otherwise mundane, standard tempo arrangements that dominated all the other singers spots.

Axel Stordahl and Frank Sinatra appreciated deeply that most of the songs they recorded were already perfectly balanced ballads and did not require alteration, but just a smooth and perfectly suited arrangement for Sinatra's voice and style. No substitutions of harmonies or paraphrasing would improve the song. The collaboration between arranger, musician and vocalist, excellently presented was the obvious requirement to fashion a musical gem. Every arrangement has its own considerations and Stordahl worked out the musical devices the song and the vocalist deserved, with this vocalist always interjecting his proverbial "two cents."

Axel experimented with guitar openings and interludes and other odd, but suitable to the song intros which Sinatra relished, although he sometimes rejected them if he wasn't comfortable. And he was always his own master.

Great Sinatra/Stordahl songs are, among others: "These Foolish Things," J.Fred Coots (my old friend at NBC) masterpiece "You Go to My Head," Gershwin's "Someone to Watch Over Me," "That Old Feeling," and "Try a Little Tenderness," demonstrating the richness and tenderness of songs that stand up even today over and above much of his future Capitol days. The album *The Voice* was the one Stordahl arranged group of tunes that became an important influence on future Sinatra peers and imitators who were sitting down listening over and over to these great 78's dreaming of their own future prospects as a pop vocalist- like the Voice himself.

But now, much of that was over with Capitol Records Alan Livingston, deciding to sign Frank Sinatra at the request of William Morris agent Sam Weisbord. Alan said,"Sure, send him in." Alan said that Sinatra said he was glad to be there. Reportedly, the deal was that if it didn't work out in one year, the company would fail to pick up his option. He would receive $ 145.00 per recording session. Sinatra signed the contract in Lucey's Restaurant in Hollywood with his manager, Hank Sanicola, present and a couple of witnesses. Some, at Capitol, were disappointed, but Livingston reminded them, "Look, I only know one way to deal and that's with talent, and Frank Sinatra is the most talented singer I know!"

And, that was that! Livingston knew that Sinatra would work out well. "Riddle," said Sinatra, "but I've been with Axel for so long now."

So Livingston allowed Axel to make the first Capitol recording with Axel and it was "I'm Walking Behind You." The song was done beautifully, but Eddie Fisher's version outdid Sinatra's. A few more were recorded with Axel arranging but they were not very successful, so Livingston paired Sinatra with Riddle, and you know the rest of the story. The first Capitol/Sinatra/May/Riddle recording was "South of the Border" with Billy May's slurping saxes. It was followed by "I've Got the World on a String." And Frank asked, who was the arranger on the recording.

"This guy--someone pointed- Nelson Riddle." "Beautiful," said Frank.

Frank with Skitch Henderson

Noted in Metronome Magazine in later years:
Frank Sinatra once more changed his musical director when he announced that beginning with his current New York appearances, on radio and at the Copacabana, Skitch Henderson would permanently take over the post. Skitch broke up his big band to work with the Voice again, replacing Jeff Alexander on the air and indicating a rather definite split between Frank and Axel Stordahl, an association that began when both were with Tommy Dorsey but which seems to have been on the edge of a breakup for some months.

Nelson Riddle

Nelson Riddle was one of the most respected arrangers in popular music and will be musically connected forever to some equally respected vocalists, mainly Frank Sinatra. Then you may add Ella Fitzgerald, Peggy Lee, Steve Lawrence, Dean Martin, Nat "King "Cole, Judy Garland, Johnny Mathis, Rosemary Clooney, all among the vocal artists of our time.

More importantly, the classic concept albums *Only the Lonely*, and *In the Wee Small Hours* have become probably the best of all the classic albums of the Great American Songbook.

The arrangment of Cole Porter's "I've Got You Under My Skin" with the Milt Bernhart's sensational trombone solo, recorded on Janauary 12, 1956, is linked with Sinatra more than any other arrangement of Riddle's career. The opening with George Roberts nineteen bar trombone chorus that sounded like continuously spaced "burping." Milt Bernhart told me that it took about fifteen takes, every-one different, until he was satified and "got it right," meaning about his trombone solo.

It is said that Frank Sinatra took home the acetate of the song and played it over and over and realized the quality and arrangement of the recording would be counted among his best.

Cole Porter, the composer and lyricist said: "It's the best, the crest, the works, the top." It was Riddle's shining hour, according to Frank himself.

Johnny Mandel: "Frank was into it. They tore the world apart. It's one of the outstanding vocal arrangements---'My Way' and 'New York, New York,'if that's your bag, fine. But forget it, this one wipes 'em all out."

Nelson riddle was described by most as a generally unhappy personality and gloomy charactor despite his genius writing great music. Another small-town New Jersey born artist associated with Frank Sinatra (Axel Stordahl was one), Nelson Riddle was a product of Oradell, across the Hudson River from the big town of New York City.

His father loved popular music and played trombone and jazz piano. His mother enjoyed the classical music that she heard in her birthplace, Mulhouse, France, and raised in a convent.

Nelson took piano lessons when he was eight, which helped him later on with his composing and arranging career. The trombone lessons began at age fourteen, but didn't last very long because his parents was never able to pay the teacher. Neverthless, Nelson continued playing in small bands and developed a reasonalbly reliable playing ability.

A friend, arranger Bill Finegan, who arranged later for the Glenn Miller Orchestra, showed his protége Nelson how to write music for dance orchestras. Nelson's first assignment was to write a chorus of "Swanee River" for five saxophones, that included two altos. two tenors, and one baritone), and how to mix clarinets with muted trumpets, and other varied ways of combining instruments for color and nuance.

Of course, Finegan went on to write hundreds of pieces for

Nelson with Rosemary Clooney

Glenn Miller including the famous Miller recording of "Little Brown Jug," and later, with fellow arranger Eddie Sauter, formed the Sauter-Finegan Orchestra and signed with RCA records when Jack Kapp, who later formed Decca Records with his brother Dave, was the A & R man.

Sinatra: "When you talk about arrangers that can swing, you talk about Nelson Riddle and then you list the other arrangers. His arrangements can

A young Nelson on Trombone

never be called corny because they don't age. They are like fine wines. They get better, they don't get old. No matter what we write, we took from him. He's as important as oxygen. I don't know a bigger compliment to pay him.

Nelson Riddle was a very smart kid and grew to be even smarter. If he never wrote a musical chart, he would have turned to anything and made it a success. His friends collectively agreed that Nelson could have been a CEO if he turned to any kind of business because he was honest and forthright, as well as very, very smart.

In his non-Sinatra works, Nelson Riddle was involved heavily in television in the early seventies. He wrote the score for *Emergency* in 1972, which was a drama that starred Bobby Troup and the vivacious Julie London of "Cry Me a River" fame.

André' Previn, orchestra leader and great pianist, recommended Nelson for Julie Andrews' first adventure into television. He became Julie's musical director.

Nelson won an Emmy for actor William Holden's *The Blue Knight* miniseries. At the same time Nelson was musical director for *This is Your Life*, Ralph Edwards popular TV show which surprised a famous and popular show-business subject showcasing their career and inviting the subjects friends, coworkers, associates and family. It was tear-jerker kind of show that Nelson enjoyed working.

However, the producers of some of these shows felt that Nelson had taken on too many projects at one time and Jack Webb, the

Nelson receives his 1975 Academy Award for his score for
The Great Gatsby

producer of the *Blue Knight* shows, replaced him with Billy May.

On Julie's show Nelson wrote for the show as if it were a great

Nelson on Trombone with Julie Andrews and Henry Mancini on Piccolo

concert, with lush chordal changes, medleys, key changes and employed additional arrangers to assist him so he could concentrate on Julie's numbers only.

And...Nelson worked the Steve Lawrence, Eydie Gorme' Las Vegas shows. Because the couple was impressed with what Nelson accomplished for Sinatra, and they had hoped his orchestrations and arrangements would help lift their own career to greater heights than they had achieved with other arrangers.

Nelson with Sammy Davis Jr. while Dean Martin
and Bing Crosby listen

Nelson with arranger Billy May, 1980

GORDON JENKINS

If you have ever listened to Gordon Jenkins' "Manhattan Tower Suite," you will discover it is a forerunner of his work that would engulf the music and distinctive voice of Frank Sinatra.

As a songwriter, musical director and, most importantly, an arranger, Gordon Jenkins had an absolute influence with his arranging the many remarkable recordings of Frank Sinatra, employing those minor chords and lush strings.

Jenkins always worked with the cream of musicians. He has arranged for Paul Whiteman's King of Jazz Orchestra, Benny Goodman, Andre Kostelanetz, Judy Garland, Bing Crosby, Lennie Hayton, Sinatra rival Dick Haymes, (who took Frank Sinatra's spot in the Tommy Dorsey Orchestra after Sinatra left), Ella Fitzgerald, my wonderful friend Patty Andrews on her exquisite recording "I Can Dream, Can't I," and even Louis Armstrong's pivitol recording of "When It's Sleepy Time Down South."

Jenkins wrote his signature composition "Goodbye," a song

Benny Goodman always used as his closing theme. Add in "P.S. I Love You," "Blue Prelude," "This is All I Ask," "San Fernando Valley," a major hit for Bing Crosby, and "When a Woman Loves a Man," and you have a neat pile of excellence in songwriting. There were others,

(Trademark Registered U. S. Patent Office)

VOL. 19—No. 20 **CHICAGO, OCTOBER 8, 1952**

(Copyright, 1952, Down Beat, Inc.)

ARMSTRONG AND JENKINS, that unlikely pair who turned out to be a perfect team for best-selling records, are seen here at a party thrown jointly for Satchmo and Gordie during their joint engagement at the Paramount theatre. Decca records and the *Pittsburgh Courier* combined to throw the shindig. —

too.

So, Jenkins early experiences were well grounded with a lot of great singers, including his stellar work with Nat "King" Cole, notably on his hit "When I Fall In Love," and his complete album *Love is the Thing*. And, of course, his little-known work with folk artist Pete Seeger and the Weavers on the hit recordings "Tzena, Tzena, Tzena," "On Top of Old Smoky," and "Goodnight Irene," all mega hits back in the early 50s.

Gordon Jenkins association with the greatest female pop vocalist Peggy Lee occurred on two of her most exceptional pieces "Lover," and "I Hear the Music Now."

Jenkins' association with Frank Sinatra began at Capitol Records in the late 50s. He arranged songs on the album *Where Are You?*, *No One Cares*, and later *September of My Years* in 1965, and the comeback album *Ol' Blue Eyes is Back*, and later on *She Shot Me Down*, his last album in 1981.

After Gordon Jenkins passing, his son Bruce, a sports writer for the San Francisco Chronicle, began writing a book about his father's career. After three years of waiting to interview Frank Sinatra, finally, in 1990, Sinatra called Bruce Jenkins and agreed to an in-person interview.

"I could feel the strength of my father's music as I pulled in the driveway of Sinatra's home on Foothill Drive."

Sinatra rarely gave interviews at this time of his life and Bruce believed it was allowed as a tribute to his father.

Sinatra: "I never saw a man step up in front of an orchestra and get as much attention without saying a word. You'd go into a date, and the guys are unpacking and yakking and everybody's laughing and having fun. But when you heard this [taps the table loudly, four times], there was silence. Absolute silence. Anybody who can do that has got some kind of authority. And I loved Gordy for it, because I needed that from time to time. You can't just run around wildly all the time, or you'll wind up in the can."

To Sinatra, Gordon Jenkins was the most solid and best-equipped musician he ever worked with because he regarded the music, all the music to be serious as is reflected in his entire career as songwriter, arranger and conductor. Sinatra knew that as a conductor, Gordon was a great assistant to a singer because he knew a lot about vocalizing and was able to dissect problems as they came up before a singer got into trouble. And he would hear a "clinker" and correct it on the spot.

Some interesting things about their relationship:

"There were times when Gordy had me sit behind the orchestra. First guy who ever did that. He wanted a balance, and in the back, there was never a mixup or a bad time mixing the vocal and the

orchestra. Nobody ever thought about that before. I sat against the wall with a microphone, so the orchestra could play as freely as they wanted and he had better control of them. And I think we discovered something quite marvelous. I had guys tell me later on that it worked for them, too."

Sinatra remembered when he asked Gordon about the song "Laura" that he really liked and wanted to have it recorded with him as the arranger. He told Gordon that it was his favorite song of all time. When they began to record it Sinatra had a lump in his throat, much like he did when he recorded "Lonely Town."

For Sinatra, the song lifted his spirit and always gave credit for the recording to the authors, (W) Johnny Mercer and (M) David Raskin, and especially the perfectly crafted Gordon Jenkins arrangement, that literally drove him to tears.

"Nobody else had heard anything like Gordy's arrangement before," Sinatra said to Gordon Jenkins son, "That's when I realized what he was doing for me. He was sensitive, he got angry, he was warm...well, cheers, here's to him. I can't say any more."

The Best of Sinatra/Jenkins collaborations - author's opinion:

From the Capitol album WHERE ARE YOU, 1957:

- Laura
- Maybe You'll Be There
- Lonely Town
- I'm a Fool to Want You
- Where Are You?

From the Capitol album *A JOLLY CHRISTMAS* FROM FRANK SINATRA, 1957:

- I'll Be Home for Christmas
- Jingle Bells
- Silent Night

From the Capital album *NO ONE CARES,* 1959

- A Cottage for Sale
- Here's That Rainy Day
- Just Friends

From the Reprise album *ALL ALONE,* 1962

- What'll I Do
- All Alone

- Remember

From the Reprise album *SEPTEMBER OF MY YEARS*, 1965

- Last Night When We Were Young
- This is All I Ask
- It Was a Very Good Year
- Hello, Young Lovers
- September Song

From the Reprise album *OL'BLUE EYES IS BACK,* 1973

- There Used to Be a Ballpark
- Send in the Clowns (Gordon considered this his best collaboration with Sinatra)

BILLY MAY

Frank with Billy May

My introduction to Billy May coincided with the research of my book Chattanooga Choo Choo, the history of the Glenn Miller Orchestra. Glenn needed an intro to the song "Serenade in Blue" and asked all three of his arrangers to work on it. Well, Billy May told me he wrote the beautiful introduction to the song, featured Glenn's famous recording of the song, in fifteen minutes. A classic, but true story. The intro is a gem. Actually Bill Finegan wrote the arrangement, and May the intro, but, Oh! What an intro!

Besides writing arrangements over the years for many of America's best singers: Sarah Vaughan, Anita O'Day, Ella Fitzgerald, Keely Smith, Nat "King" Cole, Frankie Laine, Bobby Darin and Mel Torme, among others. Early-on, Billy May was an arranger and composer for a handful of mythical cartoon characters background music that included the Green Hornet and Batman as well as Daffy Duck and Tweety and Sylvester. That went on for years. When Al Hirt played his trumpet on The Green Hornet theme, which was an adaptation of Rimsky-Korsakov's "Flight of the Bumble Bee," it was May who adapted it for Hirt's trumpet.

May's arrangement of Charlie Barnet's theme "Cherokee," written by bandleader Ray Noble, is legendary. It set the band's future style. "I worked with Charlie Barnet for two years. That was 1939 in New York. On the day Roosevelt was elected president, I joined Glenn Miller. I had met with Glenn and Helen in Hurley's bar, that little bar set at the corner of 49th street and struck a deal. I joined the trumpet section and also played solos that Glenn asked me to do. I did lots of arrangements for Glenn along with Miller regulars Jerry Gray and Bill Finegan."

After a stint with Les Brown, and two years on the road with his own band, Billy May settled down in the vicinity of that big, round building in Hollywood called Capitol Records. When Frank Sinatra joined Capitol, Billy May was already writing arrangements there for Nat "King" Cole, Peggy Lee and Vic Damone. Being an upswinging stylist Billy was commissioned to write for Sinatra's albums *Come Fly with Me*, *Come Dance with Me*, and *Come Swing with Me* (the later which arranger Heinie Beau wrote seven of the twelve tunes with Billy May conducting).

Notably, Billy May was a prolific arranger and especially known for his playing style of slurping saxes and muted trumpets in a unique way that became his signature style notably represented on many of Frank Sinatra's recording sessions. It was Frank who requested that Billy arrange the tracks on *Come Fly with Me*.

"They invited me to Frank's house in Palm Springs and Jimmy Van Huesen and Jule Styne was there. We talked over the track choices and they gave me a few tunes to work on, so I went home and wrote up the charts."

In discussing the subject of arranging with Billy May, he identifies his craft as "when someone like Irving Berlin writes a song, they usually write just the piano part. If a vocalist is added, they can simply work it out. But, an arranger takes that song and does the background of, say, an instrumental version, keeping in mind perhaps the addition of a vocalist---figures the key and the vocalists range, and, depending on the mix of instruments you employ, arranges it for orchestra charts.

"I was born with a good ear and harmonies worked for me when I tried to couple them. Some sounds worked well together other sounds were not working, that's how I learned.

May: "Now take a guy like Sinatra, who besides being a great singer, is really a better musician (with fine musical taste) than people give him credit for. He will sit with you for hours and work out what he wants. Does he want to do a ballad with strings, or does he want to work with a dance band sound? With all those singers and bands, it's always a meeting of the minds. You work together to produce the sounds you both want to achieve.

"For me, it was always a pleasure to work with Frank Sinatra, with the jokes and good times with all the musicians--- we had fun together. Frank would only work with better tunes with better chances of succeeding, rather than working with songs that you can't do much with-- musically."

Ironically, setting Sinatra aside for a moment, Billy May, a gregarious and pleasant fellow to talk with, actually wrote the silly song "I Tawt I Taw a Puddy Tat," which master voice impressionist Mel Blanc recorded with May's orchestra and it became May's greatest claim to fame. This clearly attests to the variety and contrasts of Billy May's musical taste. On serious material he will go a few bars with violins, revert to heavy brass, and then back to strings, to maintain his penchant for instrumental musical variety.

Sinatra will instinctively pick up on the energy and tempo Billy May may present in a given piece. While backing Axel Stordahl when he was writing for Sinatra on the radio show, May worked indirectly for Sinatra- a secondhand music relationship for certain. `Frank enjoyed the backing of May's slurping saxophones. Although the slurping sax sound was really common to many individual musicians, that included Johnny Hodges when he was with the Lunceford band, and Willie '"the Lion" Smith' with the Ellington band, it introduced the idea of writing it for an entire section of saxes, thereby creating an ensemble sound of a entire chorus of slurping saxes:

"Well, it didn't last long because everyone and his brother decided to copy the style and it lost its distinctive quality and got lost and drowned out over time," said Billy. Ironically, one of the most recognizable May arrangements employing the slurping sax sound is on the recording "South of the Border," (which was really arranged by Nelson Riddle in May's copycat style because May was on the road at the time, but gave his permission), Bill's theme "Lean Baby," "Isle of Capri" and "Road to Mandalay," the later which Billy said was banned in England, being an offshoot of a poem by revered author Rudyard Kipling, so they removed it from the *Come Fly with Me* album and replaced it with "Chicago."

When Billy arranged for Sinatra, he used many of the musicians Sinatra was used to working with when Riddle was conducting, so Frank knew them and that made May's job easier.

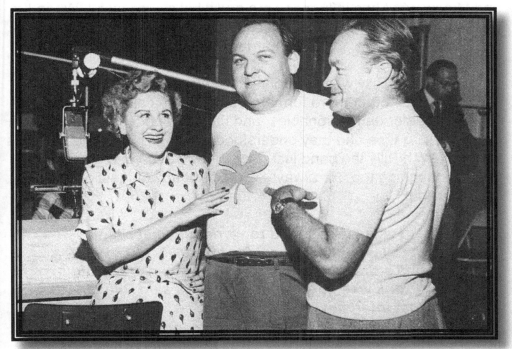

Margaret Whiting, Billy May and Bob Hope - at rehearsals for Bob's Radio Show

In 1979 May was called in to arrange the Sinatra *Trilogy* album, which was produced by Sonny Burke. Sinatra and Nelson Riddle were not talking to one another at this time over some disagreement. Billy May said "That's how I got to do the *Trilogy* album. It was sad that any one of them could have called the other and made up, but both were stubborn." They made up shortly before Nelson's death.

Everyone concerned with *Trilogy* met at Sinatra's house to plan the album. That included producer Sonny Burke, arranger Don Costa, and Billy May.

A diversified musical genius whose arrangements were, in Sinatra's words: "Always great!, Billy May was a well-loved resident of the Big Band Era and a friend to almost everyone else who was a part of it, and that included America's greatest voice, Frank Sinatra.

Billy May was never impressed with the likes of Frank Sinatra and considered him just another singer, but when it came time to get together for an album. "I know what I like , I know what I like to write, and I know what has influenced me and what's successful. When I'm gonna arrange an album with Frank Sinatra singing, it's gonna be a major project, so I'm gonna try harder."

Sinatra: "Billy was a roughneck in his old pants and a sweat-shirt, unlike my other more formal arrangers. He called his musicians "cats" and other unmentionables, and they responded. Billy had been around a long time and they understood him, which kept the sessions informal. With Billy the band just goes on and everyone has fun. He kept me laughing,too. He always worked out my suggestions and I appreciated it."

I was always glad to work out what Frank needed. I would change it for him. Why not? What the hell's the difference. And it always worked out and Frank was happy and so was I," said Billy on our last interview.

Frank Sinatra on Billy May: "Recording with Billy May is like having a bucket of cold water thrown into your face. Nelson Riddle will come to a session with all the arrangements carefully and neatly worked out beforehand. With Billy you sometimes don't get copies of the next number until you've finished the one before. Billy and Nelson work best under pressure. Billy May is always driving while Nelson has more depth, and with Gordon Jenkins, it's just plain beautiful and simple.

DON COSTA

Don Costa was another of Frank Sinatra's stellar arrangers. His early session with his and Bucky Pizzerelli's guitars backing Vaughn Monroe's very popular recording of "Ghost Riders in the Sky" validated his membership as one of the better musicians of the era.

Costa's early success with the singers Steve Lawrence and (his wife) Eydie Gorme further certified Don's ability for arranging songs for contemporary pop singers. This led to his becoming top A & R (Artists and Repertoire) executive for the ABC-Paramount label. His works included efforts for Paul Anka, Lloyd Price and George

Hamilton IV. Costa also cut some instrumentals that enjoyed success, namely the hits "Never on Sunday," and the Theme from "The Unforgiven," establishing his reputation for quality arrangements.

Don Costa's connection to Frank Sinatra began just as Frank

was forming his own record company, Reprise. As usual, Sinatra chose his arrangers or any musical associate because he heard something he liked that that person wrote or performed. Sinatra called upon Costa to be the arranger for his album Sinatra and Strings in 1962, that included established ballads "All or Nothing at All," an early Sinatra-Stordahl hit "Night and Day," in ballad form, Harold Arlen's "Come Rain or Come Shine," and an unusual version of Hoagy Carmichael's "Stardust" but only the verse after an introduction, with Costa's orchestra' completes the song without voice. Costa enjoyed great success with Sinatra. So, at this point, Costa replaced Riddle and Jenkins because of his ability to keep up with current trends. A few years later it was Costa again, but this time it was "My Way," with full orchestration that chills your body as the crescendo raises the song to great heights that is absolutely thrilling. "My Way is Sinatra's anthem personified and a Sinatra classic, no matter how many times you hear it played.

Costa also arranged the albums *Cycles*, *A Man Alone*, as well as *Sinatra & Company*. He was also involved in the *Trilogy Album* along with Billy May and Gordon Jenkins, a 2-CD event. *Trilogy* was an immediate hit and found early gold.

Don Costa also worked with Sinatra in Las Vegas. During that period, however, Costa suffered a heart attack, recovered, then did some arranging for Sammy Davis, Jr. ("Candy Man"), and some Osmond Brothers recordings, as well as Petula Clark's "My Guy."

Don Costa was known in the trade as the "Puccini of Pop" because he wrote extremely well for strings reminiscent of the great operatic composer Giacomo Puccini, a favorite of Frank Sinatra, as well, who admired Puccini's brilliant music so much that he wove it into some of Nelson Riddle's works in his past albums. The albums *Ol' Blue Eyes is Back* and *Some Nice Things I Missed* were arranged jointly by both Gordon Jenkins and Don Costa. Jenkins had come out of retirement in 73 & 74. The tunes "You Will Be My Music" and "Noah" had beautiful openings but were not commercially successful. The mix of music was not Sinatra material and therefore the poor arrangements did no favors for Sinatra's career.

According to songwriter Sammy Cahn, Don Costa was the missing link who was a Stordahl but with deeper strings. Costa filled

Stordahl's shoes in many ways for Sinatra. Those repeated Dorsey/Sinatra gems in the 1940s restored Sinatra, and many have opined that Costa's rendition of Hoagy Carmichael's "Stardust" was "Sinatra's best of all his other 'Stardust' recordings," said Sinatra's elite guitarist Tony Mottola. "He made it a classical performance above all his other works. And Don Costa opens and closes it to insure everything. It's simply beautiful--- both verse and refrain. He does just as good with the other songs of the album." Harold Arlen's "Come Rain or Come Shine," "Georgia on My Mind," and Jerome Kern's classic ballad "Yesterdays," (Not Paul McCartney's "Yesterday.")

Costa was a good arranger but preferred not to conduct. He selected others to perform that service. He liked to sit in the control booth and listen for errors or flaws. Costa rehearsed the musicians, which was an easy chore since most of them didn't require rehearsing. Then he passed on the baton to others. Sinatra really liked Costa since he brought music up-to-date from the 40s and 50s into the 70s. Costa was the addition Sinatra needed in an arranger. He was not the ultra-serious Jenkins that May, and Riddle were. They were specific and identifiable unlike Don Costa, who never settled into a niche and always reached for new ideas, and was also responsible for producing and setting up arrangements. He was new and fresh, exactly what Sinatra needed to complete his musical life's cycle.

Costa worked in and out of Sinatra's singing career both alone and with others. On the Trilogy album the arranging was split up with Billy May on the Past, Costa on the Present, and Jenkins on the Future, the later with very special, unique sounds that proves Sinatra was very innovative and always took chances. Trilogy's music was mostly comprised of standards already done in the past and included other popular works of the day: Presley's "Love Me Tender," Billy Joel's "Just the Way You Are," and Neil Diamond's "Song Sung Blue." Frank's rendition of a tune by the Beatles' George Harrison, "Something" a song Frank once called, the greatest love song ever written, and he does it justice, although differently, backed by Nelson Riddle's arrangement and soulfully performed by Frank. This collection of songs was the right material for a great album, although it's not above his Capitol efforts, but nevertheless excellent with the four Sinatra strengths in his singing: mental, emotional, physical and spiritual.

Don Costa passed at an early age, fifty-seven in 1983. A very stressed and tense individual, he also was involved in a marital dispute. He would have lived longer had he chosen a more amiable life's work, according to those who worked with him.

GEORGE SIRAVO

A practically unknown and underrated Frank Sinatra arranger was George Siravo. Siravo is the arranger who was the orchestrator of the albums *Sing and Dance* with Frank Sinatra and Songs for Young Lovers, two very important and significant albums bringing Frank Sinatra into performing more swinging tunes rather than the earlier ballads only with Dorsey, with then, and later with arranger Axel Stordahl.

George Siravo was first a musician having played alto sax in many big bands of the 1930s and 1940s that included the famous Cliquot Club Eskimo's led by bandleader Harry Reser who favored dixieland music, and the bands of Glenn Miller and Gene Krupa.

It is said that Axel Stordahl called in Siravo to assist with Frank Sinatra's recording of "Saturday Night" (Is the Loneliest Night of the Week), one of Sinatra's most popular recordings.

After some freelance arranging with a handful of big bands, George Siravo was hired by Columbia Records when Mitch Miller was the A & R man and Sinatra was a staff singer. Siravo had already had experience with Sinatra on *The Hit Parade* radio show.

Siravo told me during a 1985 telephone interview from his home in Oregon: "Frank would hang out with real hip swing musicians. That's where Sinatra learned to swing. He was easy to work with when we were recording, a real professional. But, as expected, he dropped me suddenly in the early sixties because he wanted me to do things I didn't want to do with some songs. After that we didn't get along and when he asked me to join him in some social events, I turned him down. Didn't like the attitude he flung at me. After all, I worked with him quite a bit, even tough on those radio shows which were never recorded. A lot was lost. No one realized it." George Siravo was a great friend to vocalist Kay Starr when she sang with Charlie Barnet.

Frank Sinatra actually admired George Siravo, especially for his orchestration for the music on Sinatra's Australia tour in 1959 which also involved Nelson Riddle's arrangements.

On a further note, George Siravo arranged and orchestrated Doris Day's single in 1950, "It's Magic" from her first movie *Romance on the High Seas*, Doris' best single in this writer's opinion. His album *Swingin' in Studio A* is one of George Siravo's best-known albums.

Doris Day

Neal Hefti

Not much of Neal Hefti's career was spent with Frank Sinatra's music. In 1961 Hefti, an accomplished trumpeter, was closely involved with Frank Sinatra's album *Sinatra and Swingin' Brass* where he was fully credited as both arranger and conductor of the album's twelve cuts.

Most of Hefti's career was spent with his own band of the 1950s and created a strong association with both the Woody Herman organization and the Count Basie Band.

His musical life was vast, stretching from the big bands and into television and motion pictures on a dozen tv shows including *Batman* and *The Odd Couple* and a handful of motion pictures.

Count Bill Basie: " I loved the charts Neal wrote for us. So we went out to California and did ten tunes in two, four-hour sessions with Frank (Sinatra). All of those tunes were standards which I am pretty sure he had recorded before (and had hits on). But this time they were arranged by Neal Hefti with our instrumentation and voicing in mind.

"Neal did a lot of marvelous things for us, because, even though what he did was a different thing and not quite the style, but sort of a different sound, I think it was quite musical."

"Many of the original instrumental charts Hefti wrote for Herman and Basie had become widely accepted as big-band classics, and several eventually attained acceptable lyrics," according to Will Friedwald. Some were "Li'l Darlin,' "Softly, with Feeling," "Oh, What a Night for Love," and "Girl Talk."

Count Basie, during my personal interview with him back in 1982, told me he loved working with Sinatra, whom he felt had a lot of respect for his hard-driving band of the time, and he had a special affection for the piano-playing icon from Red Bank, New Jersey.

Neil Hefti received two Grammy's for Basie, aka *Atomic Basie*, and three nominations (and one award) for the Batman TV score, and two nominations for the Harlow movie score "Girl Talk".

ROBERT FARNON, JOHNNY MANDEL & QUINCY JONES

I'll tell you who they are! Collectively, they have arranged innumerable, quality songs for Frank Sinatra. Like Stordahl, May, Riddle, Jenkins & Hefti, they are among the top arrangers in Frank Sinatra's life's work.

JOHNNY MANDEL

Johnny Mandel's fame was earned from composing the theme from the *M*A*S*H* television show, originated and devised by Bob Hope writer Larry Gelbart, and also composed the songs/themes for *The Russian Are Coming*, the *Russians are Coming*, *The Sandpiper,* and *The Last Detail*. And the beautiful song "Emily."

Johnny is as much a songwriter as he is a musician (trumpet) and played with jazz violinist Joe Venuti, trombone with Jimmy Dorsey, Buddy Rich, and accompanied June Christy, the Stan Kenton big band singer. He arranged for Count Basie and went on to write jazz material for bandleader Woody Herman, musicians Stan Getz, and musician/vocalist Chet Baker.

With Frank Sinatra Johnny arranged the Reprise album *Ring-a-Ding-Ding* in 1960. He arranged albums for Shirley Horn, Tony Bennett, Barbra Streisand, Diana Krall and worked with Quincy Jones on some selected material. Mandel won a Grammy for the 1991 Natalie Cole and her late father's duet single "Unforgettable."

QUINCY JONES

Quincy Jones became an important wheel in the cycle of work for Frank Sinatra when he was invited by Princess Grace in Monaco for a benefit. There he met Frank. A few years later Quincy was sought out by Sinatra to arrange and conduct Frank's second album with Basie, *It Might as Well Be Swing* in 1964. After that success Jones conducted and arranged the 1966 live album with Count Basie, Sinatra At the Sands.

In 1965 he was both arranger and conductor with Sinatra, Sammy Davis, Jr., Dean Martin, and Johnny Carson, performed with Basie in a St. Louis benefit. The CD was released on DVD. Jones also worked on The Hollywood Palace TV show in 1965, again with Sinatra and The Count. A full nineteen years later, Frank and Quincy produced the project *L.A. Is My Lady*. Of course, Quincy Jones was deeply involved with working on Michael Jackson life's work including the mega hit Thriller which has sold over 100 million copies, as well as the album Bad. He worked with Dinah Washington, Dean Martin, Stevie Wonder, Will Smith, and Marvin Gaye.

Quincy Jones, a musician, conductor, producer, composer, is one of the most revered people in the music business. He won a Jean Hersholt Humanitarian Academy Award in 1995.

ROBERT FARNON

Robert Farnon: "Frank is an inspiration. You know when you're writing for him or in anything you do for him, you have to do your very best, very best. "

With Sinatra, Farnon was the architect of the more tranquil love songs that Sinatra loved to sing in those early days. In 1962 Farnon arranged the album Great Songs from Great Britain, containing songs written only in England. The album was manufactured and sold only in Great Britain and the earnings from the album were directed to the Duke of Edinburgh's favorite charities.

This was on Reprise where Sinatra wanted a more diversified representation from different arrangers as he launched his own record company. Farnon had met Sinatra back in the early Dorsey days when he was a musician in the Percy Faith orchestra. "I was a Crosby fan back then, but when I heard Sinatra I changed and became a really big Sinatra fan."

It would be some twenty years later when Sinatra and Farnon would work together. When Sinatra performed in Vegas, arranger Don Costa recommended Farnon for a British album Sinatra was planning.

Farnon was a great orchestrator whom many others emulated, especially when working with strings and for large contingencies and it comes out smooth as glass whether it's for 100 musicians or even more.

When Frank got together on an album with Robert Farnon, he allowed full-range to the arranger because of his pristine reputation. They accomplished the song "If I Had You" after some hard work, and completed the remaining ten songs with the great orchestra and it had been said that Sinatra's voice was too "thin" to compete with the overwhelming orchestration. Some said he was tired and not in full

Sinatra voice. The album contained a nice version of "A Nightingale Sang in Berkeley Square."

Robert Farnon

Nevertheless, the album *Great Songs from Great Britain* remains an important album of quality Sinatra song performances with the equally great arrangements by Robert Farnon.

The Eleven Songs from the Album.

1. **The Very Thought Of You** - w.m. Ray Noble 1934
2. **We'll Gather Lilacs In The Spring** - w.m. Ivor Novello 1945
3. **If I Had You** - w.m.Ted Shapiro, Jimmy Campbell 1928
4. **Now Is The Hour** - w. m. Dorothy Stewart, Maewa Clement Scott 1948
5. **The Gypsy** - w.m. Billy Reid 1946
6. **Roses Of Picardy** - w. Frederick Edward Weatherly, m. Haydn Wood 1916
7. **A Nightingale Sang In Berkeley Square** - w.m. Eric Maschwitz, Manning Sherwin, Jack Strachey 1940
8. **A Garden In The Rain** - w. James Dyrenforth, m. Caroll Gibbons 1928
9. **London By Night** - w.m. Carroll Coates 1950
10. **We'll Meet Again** - w.m. Ernie Burnett, Gerald Griffin 1939
11. **I'll Follow My Secret Heart** - w.m. Noel Coward 1934

Of course, by now the album has been released for sale everywhere through Amazon.com and here and by another name through Frank Sinatra Enterprises, released on January 27, 2009.

VINCENT FALCONE

"I first met Sinatra when he was fifty-nine years old, and at that time he was starting to suffer some vocal deterioration, but it didn't matter because he worked so hard at keeping his voice in shape. He got exited about what we were doing and began to do vocal exercises. I'd meet him every afternoon and we would spend a couple of hours going over scales and arpeggios, and so forth. And then, later, for at least an hour immediately prior to every performance, he would do still more exercises."

Frank would frequently meet with the great classical singers

Steve Lawrence, Buddy Greco and Vincent Falcone

whenever he could arrange it. Especially the greats Robert Merrill and Pavarotti and he would ask their advice. He went so far as to quit smoking and drinking, knowing alcohol was bad for the throat, so he settled for drinking hot tea.

During the period Vinnie Falcone was conducting for Sinatra he brought up the quality level of the concerts. Vinnie was very respectful and serious, always addressing Mr. Sinatra as *Mr. Sinatra*, never *Frank*.

Vinnie Falcone's first encounter conducting for Sinatra was to be at Caesars in Las Vegas. It was a time when Bill Miller was on piano, Al Viola on guitar, Irv Cottler on the drums, Gene Cherico was the bassist, and Charlie Turner played lead trumpet, all regulars and favorite musicians of Sinatra.

The first event, with the songs, "I've Got the World on a String," "The Lady is a Tramp," "What's New?" and "Witchcraft" was nerve-racking for Vinnie Falcone. Sinatra came on stage without an introduction and the applause was deafening. Vinnie began his baptism of fire conducting for Frank Sinatra.

Vinnie had always paid attention in the past when Sinatra was dishing out advise to his main pianist, Bill Miller and carefully retained that information. "I tried to pickup on any nuances and dynamics that Mr. S. was searching for during rehearsals and in performances." Upon meeting Gordon Jenkins, Vinnie was invited to his home, which he arranged shortly thereafter. "Gordon gave me lessons in conducting, tips on writing, and showed me examples of how to arrange for large orchestras."

Jenkins also told Vinnie never to take his eyes off Sinatra when he was conducting.

"The orchestra needs to see your hands, but they don't need to see your face," Jenkins explained.

"Apparently if you watch the singer, you can tell what's going to happen next," said Vinnie, "When I look at the person for whom I am conducting, I can see the vibrato, I can see when it is going to end, I can see the breath that's going to continue, I can see when the voice is up to par or not, and then I conduct the orchestra and make them meld with what he's doing, rather than force the singer to do what the orchestra is doing." Other conductors over the years never looked at Sinatra wen he was singing and that got them into trouble now and then.

For Vinnie, it was great advise he used over his entire career, "Fortunately, I understood what Gordon Jenkins was trying to tell me." According to Vinnie, Sinatra liked the big ballads with the fat, lush strings, and loved the bass notes and the bass trombone, the celli and the more deeper sounds."

The first time Sinatra asked Vinnie to double the bottom of the orchestra with the piano. Sinatra was pleased that Vinnie remembered to provide the same when they next met and performed at

Caesars, where Vinnie was now the house pianist.

Vinnie got the chance to work with Don Costa on a Nelson Riddle arrangement of two songs that were to be a medley. The songs "The Gal That Got Away" and "It Never Entered My Mind" were arranged individually, but they were now to be worked out together as a medley. It was Frank Sinatra's idea.

Vincent Falcone with Tony Bennett

'"We rehearsed the medley with the orchestra and then he pointed to me to accompany him alone on the piano. That night I practiced it as if I was going to play it alone. I now knew it backward and forward until I was satisfied." When the show was ready, Sinatra let him know that he would be accompanying him on the piano alone, without the orchestra.

Vinnie Falcone's first road trip gig with Sinatra was at Lake Tahoe where he gradually became the pianist of choice and became one of Sinatra's favorite musicians.

Soon Vinnie became Sinatra's vocal exercise routine accompanist which took place at the Sinatra home that eventually led to him becoming Sinatra's conductor at Radio City Music Hall in New York. "Let's go Vinnie," Sinatra said to Vinnie just before going out on stage.

Frank Sinatra and Vincent Falcone became good friends and shared stories of Frank Sinatra's personal life, and reflected on Sinatra's early days with Dorsey and about his family life in Hoboken. Vincent Falcone always kept up the personal respect in this professional/personal association with Frank Sinatra, which was more like father and son. Frank Sinatra always called him "Vinnie," or "kid," and Vinnie always called Frank Sinatra, "Mr.S." or just plain "Boss." Vinnie Falcone continued to conduct and play piano for Frank Sinatra including on the album *Trilogy and She Shot Me Down*. Gordon Jenkins was there to help and encourage Vinnie.

"It was really an era to be remembered. I am glad I was included in that moment in time. There doesn't seem to be very many Gordon's, Don's, and Billy's around these days," Vinnie wrote in his recent book (with Bob Popyk), *Frankly Just Between Us-My Life Conducting Frank Sinatra's Music*.

A COMPLETE LIST OF SINATRA'S ARRANGERS

FROM 1939 THROUGH 1980

Of course, most of the names listed here were very limited in their association with Sinatra as a regular arranger. Where an asterick is shown, it designates the more well-known arrangers.

1. Andy Gibson
2. Axel Stordahl*
3. Paul Weston*
4. Sy Oliver*
5. Heine Beau *
6. Alec Wilder *
7. Xavier Cugat
8. Mitch Miller
9. Page Cavanaugh
10. Alvy West
11. George Siravo *
12. Tony Mottola
13. Jeff Alexander
14. Mitchell Ayres
15. Phil Moore
16. Hugo Winterhalter
17. Morris Stoloff
18. Percy Faith
19. Ray Conniff
20. Joseph Gershenson
21. Nelson Riddle *
22. Dick Reynolds
23. Conrad Salinger
24. Gordon Jenkins *
25. Billy May *
26. Felix Slatkin *
27. Skip Martin
28. Johnny Mandel *
29. Don Costa *
30. Neal Hefti *
31. Robert Farnon *
32. Gil Grau
33. Jack Halloran
34. Quincy Jones *
35. Dick Reynolds
36. Ernie Freeman
37. Torrie Zito
38. Freddie Stultz
39. Claus Ogerman
40. Billy Strange
41. Eumir Deodato
42. Joseph Scott
43. Bob Gaudio
44. Charles Calello
45. Al Capps
46. Joe Beck

Paul Weston

Sy Oliver

Percy Faith

Count Basie and Joe Williams

FRANK SINATRA'S FAVORITE MUSICIANS

William Count Basie

THE BAND WAS LIKE SOME GREAT LOCOMOTIVE

On a bitter cold evening in February of 1982, I set out to meet Count William James Basie, the enduring piano player from Red Bank, New Jersey, who led the longest-running jazz institution at the even older Northstage Theater in Glen Cove, New York where he was appearing with his band for a one-nighter.

The Northstage stage entrance was dark, the stage door decrepit, and the backstage facilities bleak, cold, and bare. It was

hard to believe the great Count Basie was to use these facilities this night. We waited around, talking to band member Freddie Green, the veteran Basie guitarist who has been with him since 1937, the acknowledged true pulse of the band.

When Basie and his party arrived, cold winds blew in behind them further chilling the backstage corridor the old steam radiators could not adequately heat. We slipped into the warmest dressing room. Catherine, Basie's wife of over 40 years, was literally holding him steady. He held a cane for added support. He look a bit wasted, physically diminished, but cheerful and even enthusiastic, Basie, his valet and myself sipped some Chablis and talked about the Count's great career. At one point we had to excuse the women, while we helped Bill change from street clothes to stage clothes. Basie placed his hands across my shoulders as he attempted to stand up receiving added assistance from his valet until we finally got him dressed for the performance. Friends and acquaintances showed up, popped in their heads for a handshake or a glass of Chablis that the theater manager furnished. The manager also handed Basie a fistful of cash which Basie waved over his head like a winner in a crap game, then pocketed it with a grin.

We began the taped interview talking about myriad Basie personnel, a who's who of jazz artists who played or vocalized with him over many years: Lester "Prez" Young, Illinois Jacquet, Harry "Sweets" Edison, Clark Terry, Jo Jones, Roy Eldridge, Benny Carter, Buddy Tate, Stan Getz, Buddy De Franco, Lucky Thompson, and singers Billie Holiday, Jimmy Rushing, Helen Humes, Dinah Washington, and Joe Williams. I chided him about his three-note signature, the beguiling, "Plink, Plank, Plink" piano ending and he simply smiled and explained that it was, "a trademark, you know, just like Bing's bub-bub-boo-in', but our band is like some great locomotive- then it ends quiet-like, you know."

Basie spoke endearingly about his one time, magical vocalist, Billie Holiday, who spent one year or so with the band early-on (he was 34 and she was 25) and concluded with: "She and I kinda almost started up together--you know," lowering his voice to escape his wife Catherine's listening range, but didn't quite make it. Catherine delivered an understanding and knowing smile and the wry comment:

"Well, I don't know about that!" as Bill Basie turned quickly away. The only recordings Billie made with Basie were those rare radio broadcast air checks performed at the Savoy Hotel just before she went over to Artie Shaw.

Bill Basie and Frank Sinatra got together several, notable times and "Swing' was definitely the thing.The albums were *Sinatra-Basie: An Historic Musical First*, arranged by Neil Hefti and *It Might As Well Be Swing* with Quincy Jones' arrangements, his first with Sinatra.

"I have waited a long twenty years for this moment. To me the Basie Band is the greatest orchestra at any time in the history of the world," Sinatra said anticipating the album's taping. Sinatra loved Basie and was always happy in his presence even to placing an affectionate arm around him. Sinatra also had an affection and respect for the great tenor sax genius Lester Young: "I took what he did and he took from what I did," Young said: "Sinatra is my main man."

Sinatra worked well with Basie's band. Basie's swing charts carried him along easily on almost all the tracks, and was always interpolated by Basie's familiar piano magic pouring it on along with his undisciplined veterans who knew how to produce the old man's unmistakable sound like they did on their famous recording of "April in Paris."

Ella with Count Basie and Sinatra

The musicians liked Sinatra, who, to them, never became bothered by recording glitches. They were musical bumps in the road and Sinatra never carried on when they occurred. "Let's try something else," guitarist Freddie Green heard Sinatra say at such a point.

The ten charts on the second Basie album *It Might As Well Be Swing*, were spun together by Quincy Jones, even adding unlikely strings to the regular powerhouse brass section. A few tracks on the album have become Sinatra standards: "Fly Me to the Moon," "The Best is Yet to Come," and "I Can't Stop Loving You" are the most played.

In the mid-sixties Bill "Count" Basie backed Frank Sinatra in Las Vegas for a good month, and recorded the final week and turned it into the Basie-Sinatra album, the first live show Sinatra released, and named it appropriately Sinatra at the Sands, on Reprise, of course.

If there was a Pulitzer for hard-driving big band music, Basie deserves it more than anyone. He employed more worthy musicians, he changed the direction of the sounds of jazz by allowing his players to use the devices they employed best with their instruments in a slightly undisciplined manner, unlike Ellington who worked his stricter arrangements around his players. Those offbeat accents and jarring dissonance's blew away many recording sessions and concerts than you could count (no pun intended). Call it swing or call it great influential jazz music: it is more magnificent than you could describe. America should be grateful for its music royalty in Count Basie.

Count William Basie told me he wants to be remembered: "Just as I am right now...sittin' in front of a piano." I was a very humble human in the presence of William "Count" Basie, the kid from RedBank.

L-R: Buddy Rich, Woody Herman, Willard Alexander, Benny Goodman, Count Basie, Stan Kenton, Mel Torme

Skitch Henderson

Skitch Henderson and I go way back to the early fifties when he was the Summer guest conductor on the Sunday NBC Symphony's radio program under the baton of the great Arturo Toscanini. As a member of Guest Relations for NBC and involved in reserving seats for guests, I recall Skitch Henderson cavorting around the studio with his open love for Faye Emerson, all of us having a grand time in those grand times.

It was Bing Crosby who coined the sobriquet "Skitch" because of Henderson's uncanny ability to almost instantly sketch out a lead sheet in any key for a singer who needed the change or a chart for a change in orchestration for any instrument. Much of his musical training occurred under the guidance and teachings of conductors Fritz Reiner, the conductor for the Metropolitan Opera, and Albert Coates,famed Russia- English conductor In the 1930s.

Skitch Henderson at Five Towns Music College with President Stanley Cohen

Skitch worked with Judy Garland rehearsing the magical song for the Wizard of Oz, Harold Arlen and "Yip" Harburg's classic "Over the Rainbow."

Skitch toured with Mickey Rooney and Judy Garland on an extended MGM promotional tour for the Andy Hardy motion picture series as pianist, musical arranger and conductor.

Then: "When I became part of the Axel Stordahl-Tommy Dorsey group, and because pianist Joe Bushkin had an altercation with management and was fired, I was selected to do a solo session with Sinatra. Sinatra was always confident of his skills so it went easier than I thought possible." Although he was not immediately accepted by the other musicians, Skitch was a natural for the upcoming date and a natural substitute for Bushkin." The recording was "The Song is You," which became a Sinatra classic.

When Frank Sinatra left Dorsey while the band was on the road performing in Indianapolis, Sinatra called Jimmy Van Heusen at the hotel, and Skitch was there: "The old man goosed me for the last time," said Sinatra, "so I'm leaving the band," Connie Haines told me during me during one of our day-long interviews.

After the war Skitch Henderson became the musical director for the radio show *Songs by Sinatra*, Frank Sinatra's NBC *Lucky Strike Show*, and later on the famed Bing Crosby *Philco Hour*. Skitch had played piano for Frank on some earlier Bluebird sessions and also accompanied Frank on his Waldorf Astoria appearances in 1945. Henderson: "The Lucky Strike show was a lot of work. It was only for fifteen minutes, but complicated, having to perform a medley of three songs in just a few minutes with more commercials than there was music. There were only two solo spots, usually Frank alone and a duet with a guest. Constrictions like this helped fuel the angst that added to Frank's slowly, upcoming problems."

Frank Sinatra, who first avoided singing dates at the Copacabana, finally gave in and performed two dates with Skitch at the piano both times. Sinatra was worried about inflicting damage to his voice trying to perform the three shows nightly required by the Copa. For Henderson it was a memorable, wonderful experience. For Sinatra, a bad turn of his life's fortunes - for the moment, that is.

Henderson also became the original *Tonight Show* musical director with Steve Allen. He continued with the *Tonight Show* right into

Johnny Carson's realm. But the two were oil and water and Henderson eventually left the show.

In 1983 Skitch Henderson founded the New York Pops Orchestra and settled his musicians into New York's Carnegie Hall, and guest-conducted with numerous orchestras all over the world. Skitch Henderson remained as director and conductor of the New York Pops until his passing on November 1, 2005.

Skitch with Richard Grudens

In early 2005 I was reunited with Skitch Henderson at Five Towns College on Long Island where I presented him with a copy of my book Bing Crosby-Crooner of the Century with a Foreword by Bing's wife, Kathryn, and talked over old times at NBC over lunch, which also included the presence of songwriter Ervin ("It Was a Very Good Year") Drake, his wife Edith, and school President Dr. Stanley Cohen, who presented Henderson with a very deserving Lifetime Achievement Award.

Skitch Henderson sat at the piano and played some enjoyable music from Lerner and Loewe's *My Fair Lady* while relating his association of how the songs were developed. A few tears were shed by host and honoree, and myself. Musical tender moments.

Bill Miller

Frank Sinatra's long time piano accompanist from 1952-1995. Bill Miller, actually started in 1952 during Sinatra's last period with Columbia. Bill Miller provided the harmony, rhythm and general support, but also knew Sinatra's performance choices well and where he was going and what road he was traveling musically.

When I asked piano player Bill Miller how he started with Sinatra, he said, at that time he was performing in Las Vegas in September of 1951 with his own trio:

"I was doing pretty well and was in good shape, and I had understood he was going to make a change in the piano chair, and, well I happened to be in the right place at the right time. His manager asked me to do a TV show they were about to film and I said, 'Sure, I'd love it.' And that's how it happened. Real simple and easy.

"When we were recording "One for my Baby and One More for the Road" on the *Only the Lonely* album, we ran it down once, rehearsed it, then recorded it in one take, believe it or not." It is a pensive introduction that glorifies that opening to one of Sinatra's best recordings. The intro that Miller invented contained the tinny sound of a saloon piano and was kept musically in a tipsy frame-of-mind-playing form. The piano works its way throughout the recording and is the final, failing wipe-out that takes Sinatra out of the saloon and moves him out of sight. There is a fading echo prevailing that the piano performs as a final bevy of goodbye notes.

"Frank usually would let me do what I wanted on the up-tempo pieces, but on the ballads you had to kinda underperform to keep him happy. I would work in some nice changes which I managed to creep in gradually. He would usually like them, so we worked together well because I knew him and how he needed to be satisfied musically. I knew him and he knew my piano."

Miller was born in Brooklyn, New York, just across the river from Frank's birthplace, Hoboken, New Jersey. He learned the piano himself - no lessons - I am told. He played with all the giants: Tommy Dorsey, Benny Goodman and Charlie Barnet, and others of note. Bill Miller was the wind beneath Frank Sinatra's wings for over 40 years. His light touch on those Sinatra ballads are memorable and will remain so as long as records are played. If Sinatra's voice is the last voice you hear before you leave this earth, as was his constant wish for all of us, its probably accompanied by Bill Miller's piano. Bill Miller was one of the privileged insiders within the Sinatra circle. "Once I figured out what I was going to do on any particular tune, we kept it that way. When I played, it's only with minor variations, because Frank is used to it a certain way, and it works. So why not leave it alone, I always said."

Millers' contribution helped shaped the rhythmic background for many Sinatra hits including "Fly Me to the Moon," "The Lady is a Tramp," Ervin Drake's "It was a Very Good Year," and "My Way." Frank Sinatra, Jr. claims Bill Miller was the greatest singer's pianist ever.

Bill Miller passed away in Montreal, Canada, while traveling with Frank Sinatra, Jr. He was 91 years old and still playing for the Sinatras.

When his first boss, Frank, Sr. passed in 1998, Bill Miller played "One for My Baby" at his funeral.

Milt Bernhart - Trombonist. Originally a staunch Stan

Kenton musician, Milt scored with his exciting trombone solo in 1956 being featured on Frank Sinatra's original recording of Cole Porter's "I've Got You Under my Skin," which has never been equaled on any other version.

Harry James - The best damn trumpet player with the most emotion, Frank enjoyed the six months he spent with the Harry James band and co-singer Connie Haines. They recorded songs on

Brunswick, then with Columbia. The recording of "My Buddy," "Who Told You I Cared," "Every Day of My Life," "Ciribiribin," are rare collector's items.

Herbie Haymer - Saxophonist, a favorite of Frank who also played with all the great bands, but who was killed in a car accident on the way home from a Sinatra recording session in 1949.

Irv Cottler - Drummer. Frank hailed Irv as the "best in the

business, "He was considered as having the most reliable sense of rhythm of all the studio drummers and extolled by both Billy May and Nelson Riddle. He always spoke his mind at recording sessions to the chagrin of many observers.

Ruben "Zeke" Zarchy - Trumpet - An alumnus of the Glenn Miller Orchestra who has played with Artie Shaw, Tommy

Zeke Zarchy and Peanuts Hucko in Paris WWII

Dorsey, Red Norvo and others including being featured lead trumpet player on Bing Crosby's very popular Kraft Music Hall radio show. It was Frank who first urged "Zeke" to California to became a first-call studio musician.

Lee Castle - Trumpeter. Lee fronted the Jimmy Dorsey band through the 1980's. He is a favorite of Frank Sinatra and Kay Starr, as well.

Tony Mottola - Guitar. Stellar guitarist who worked with Perry Como and was a regular guitarist with Doc Severinson in the *Tonight Show* band.

Al Viola - Guitarist. Worked regularly with Frank Sinatra between 1956-1980 on recording dates and in concerts. He was a flawless player, self-learned from an early age and played for hundreds of recordings, movies, television shows and was the mandolin player on the *Godfather* film soundtrack. Sinatra called him "one of the world's greatest guitarists." Viola was featured on Frank's original recordings of "New York, New York," and "My Way."

Harry "Sweets" Edison - Harry "Sweets" Edison served with Frank Sinatra for many years, participating on his albums *Complete Capitol Singles* in 1953, *It Might As Well Be Swing* in 1964, and *Capitol Years* in 1998. Edison has played his sweet trumpet within the Basie organization, as Basie's best trumpet player for many years, and has backed the creme-de-la-creme of singers that includes Ella Fitzgerald, Anita O'Day, Bing Crosby, and almost every singer of note over the last fifty years. He was a favorite of Nelson Riddle at Capitol, and his fame was established with Frank Sinatra at

Capitol and earlier with Billie Holiday. His reputation of excellence kept him in demand on thousands of recordings and concerts throughout his lifetime until he passed in 1999.

Harry Edison was happiest, according to his own word, when he worked with Sinatra and the great jazz artist, the one-and-only Billie Holiday. Later Harry taught music seminars at Yale University and was honored as a Master Musician in 1991 with a National Endowment for the Arts Award at the Kennedy Center.

The fabled story of Edison, racing to be on time for a Sinatra session, when he was stopped by Police. He told the Police he was going to the session, but they didn't believe him, so he invited them up to the session to prove his story. When the Policemen were introduced to the musicians and Sinatra himself, they felt chagrined and smiled as they released Edison to the music.

Frank Sinatra, Jr. - The son of Frank Sinatra, Frank Sinatra, Jr. became his dad's last conductor which lasted eight years. Frank Jr., obviously knew his fathers repertoire better than anyone and they worked well together.

Beginning in 1988, at the request of his dad, Frank stepped

---

away from his own growing career to became his dad's musical director. Sinatra Sr. had just about exhausted all his former arrangers, musical directors and conductors. Most of them had either passed on or were retired. Sr. trusted Jr. who was forty-four at the time and successfully performing in Las Vegas and other venues.

"Yes, my father's name has opened many doors for me, but, on the other hand a famous father means that in order to prove yourself, you had to work three times harder than the guy off the street." Frank Jr. knew it had to be him to keep his father going at this time of his life and career, and he did it well. The love was there. Frank Sinatra, Jr. knew the Sinatra book of music and has a background of the American Songbook under his arms and in his heart and has the experience to back it all up. He's not a bad singer, either. I like him!

THE SINGERS

AND

Frank Sinatra

Harold Arlen, Peggy Lee and Vic Damone

WHEN JOLSON WAS KING

You may ask what's the relevance of Jolson today? Well, it's like asking what's the relevance of the Wright Brothers or Thomas Edison? Like them he started it all---everything that we take for granted today.

I had long ago decided to set out a on an Al Jolson search, he being someone who has haunted me before, and ever since my first writings and interviews of many of his successors, both singers and musicians, and in all cases, entertainers. His name cropped up regularly and from every direction. It followed me everywhere in my quest to learn about Crosby, Sinatra, Como, Laine, and others who claim him as mentor. He is the rock they built their careers upon. The first superstar. The first crooner, and for certain, the first popular singer. And he didn't need a microphone.

Like many lifetime Jolson followers, my personal introduction to Al Jolson's repertoire of songs occurred in 1946, long after his great success, when Columbia Pictures produced an autobiographical movie entitled *The Jolson Story*. In this terrific and entertaining film, filled with Jolson's greatest songs sung with a more mature voice, Larry Parks, a young, tall and handsome actor with shocks of wavy hair, lip-synced Jolson's timeless evergreens while Jolson actually sang them off-camera. The vitality of the Jolson mature voice matched well with Parks' bearing and physical simulation. It was so convincing that, when I later saw photos of the then actual Jolson, I couldn't believe that, although short and diminutive in stature like many performers of his day, he was a perfect show-business specimen and suited to his bearing, and Larry Parks was the best match that could be found to represent him.

Parks' brilliant portrayal of Jolson paved the way for an unexpected Columbia Pictures blockbuster and a renewal of Jolson's tumultuous career as the greatest entertainer America has ever known.

Al Jolson became a totally reincarnated super entertainer upon the big screen mirrored through Larry Parks. His recordings once again sold in the millions. An entirely new generation had discovered old Jolson classics previously communicated live to his audience 30 years before from elevated proscenium stages of the world's majestic theaters, music halls and palaces where he had to shout out his songs over the heads of orchestra pit musicians to an anticipating crowd until he discovered the use of a runway.

Al Jolson and Sybil Jason Sing "You're The Cure For What Ails Me"
From the *Singing Kid Movie*

Jolson's countenance was eternally eager, his need for an audience's admiration of him almost desperate. He broke the barrier, developing personal intimacy between audience and performer for the first time as he vigorously strode those runways that extended deep through the center of the theater. Bent down on one knee, crooning his classics to a mesmerized crowd, all he ever wanted was to see into their faces to certify that they idolized him.

The Jolson Story sharply elevated my interest in all singers and their songs that has translated into a career of writing about singers and musicians from that day through today.

Playing earlier Jolson recordings led me to realize that Jolson's mature voice as recorded for *The Jolson Story* was clearly superior to earlier recordings that were tinny, although I must admit that I enjoy them just as well. Due to improved recording technical equipment and some other reasons, Jolson was at his best voice in 1946.

Meanwhile, a very good singer waited in the wings to take his place among great singers like Jolson and Crosby, then, as Bing wisely noted, along came Frank Sinatra.

THE SINGERS - THEN AND NOW

BESSIE SMITH

Henry Pleasants: "Sinatra was neither pioneer or radical. He was simply a musical genius who arrived at a moment predestined for that genius. The ground as been prepared for him as a singer by Al Jolson, Bessie Smith, Ethel Waters, Louis Armstrong, Billie Holiday and Bing Crosby."

In the beginning God made Heaven and Earth and then, in a wild, extraordinary moment, added the powerful vocal influences of Bessie Smith. In 1923 Ma "Gertrude" Rainey, another original and undisputed top blues singer, she was known in those pioneer days as the *Mother of the Blues* who shouted and moaned the laments of her life's condition.

One day she came to the town of Chattanooga, Tennessee, heard Bessie Smith sing, and took her in tow as a member of her famous traveling blues troupe. Legend has it that Ma Rainey literally

kidnapped Bessie at the age of twelve, forcing the girl to go with her show, teaching her how to sing the blues, Ma Rainey style.
But those who really knew later denied that. Actually, they got along just fine, but Bessie never learned much about singing from Rainey's troupe. She was in herself a natural singer and her own person who learned all aspects of her craft. She could Charleston and does funny turns then send an audience into a trance with her shy, but earthy blues. Rainey was more like a mother than a teacher to Bessie Smith. Remember, too, history will bear out that there was just no blues predecessor to Ma Rainey.

Historically, for unknown reasons, female blues singers followed male blues singers. According as told, by Lionel Hampton, during my interview with him: "Bessie Smith, had she lived a full life, would have been right up there on top with the rest of us in the Swing Era." Bessie became known as the Empress of the Blues. With a raucous and loud voice, a complete command of a lyric and the ability to bring first-hand emotion to a song, there was misery in what she did, but some say she just had to bring it all out in her music.

The post World War I period propelled the blues north. By the early, 1920s Bessie Smith was a recording and performing giant, two hundred pounds of human emotion packed behind her vibrant, powerful voice. She made over 150 recordings and was so successful that her record sales literally saved Columbia Records from bankruptcy, even though they had Eddie Cantor and Al Jolson under contract. Her record sales surpassed a stupendous ten million in a time when there were relatively few phonographs and little available money for the average person to purchase them. Bessie earned a great deal of money, but, just as easily, lost it all. She gave it away or spent it on liquor, or lost it to men predators.

There was magic in her voice, a magic that attracted the fledgling singers Frank Sinatra and Tony Bennett. Frank Sinatra felt her songs represented man in his sorrow and sometimes-terrible condition. "Bessie Smith's main themes were love, sex, and misery." The recordings "Sorrowful Blues" and "Rocking Chair Blues" were promoted heavily by Columbia. Magazine and newspaper ads in 1924 read: "Having a phonograph without these records is like having ham without eggs."

Louis Armstrong recorded with Bessie when he was only twenty-four years old and fresh from King Oliver's Creole Jazz Band in Chicago. He joined Fletcher Henderson's orchestra and, with Bessie, he had met his match. He later said: "She thrilled me always. She had music in her soul." That recording date, January 14, 1925, although not important at the time, would, for critics and scholars, stand as a memorable date in jazz history. The session started with W.C. Handy's endlessly recorded "St. Louis Blues," and became the definitive recording. The selections on the rest of the session, "Reckless Blues," "Cold in Hand Blues," and "Sobbin' Hearted Blues," all became classics, attesting to her greatness.

By the 1930s, when Frank Sinatra was starting his climb to his own greatness, good blues singers' popularity began diminishing, falling behind the proliferating jazz singers who were out working the scene. Bessie saw the day when Ethel Waters' more sophisticated torch singing pushed her off the boards. Bessie went down - still trouping. Here untimely death, at the age of forty-one in a September, 1937 automobile accident, virtually coincided with the renaissance of traditional jazz that began in the late thirties. By 1938, Columbia released he first Bessie Smith reissues, recordings that began to fill the mind and heart of a young singer named Frank Sinatra.

ETHEL WATERS

Ethel Waters lived several musical lives. She started out in black vaudeville as a long-legged dancer known as Sweet Mamma Stringbean. One of the first black singers to be accepted on the same level as white singers, Ethel Waters was the first to demonstrate the many possibilities for jazz singing in good commercial tunes. As an example, she made the first recording of the immensely popular "Dinah," later

Ethel Waters

performed by many other notables including Bing Crosby. Although her style was different from Bessie Smith's.

Ethel had an enormous personality and talent, but it was difficult for her to compete with Bessie Smith - the star. In 1932 and '33, Ethel Waters recorded with Duke Ellington, along with a group of other well-established singers like the Mills Brothers, performing selections from all-black revues, including the *Blackbirds of 1933*. Her rendition of "I can't Give You Anything But Love," recorded with Ellington in 1932, is the definitive version, eclipsing that of Aida Ward's in 1928. Ethel also recorded with Benny carter and Teddy Wilson earning respectability even as a Bessie Smith-type blues singer. When beginning her stage appearances, she devised a cute opening where someone off stage would ask, Are you Ethel Waters?" and she'd answer, "Well I ain't Bessie Smith." It would excite the audience and then she would break out with a heartbreaking blues number.

Ethel Waters was also a remarkable lady of the theater. From early childhood she envisioned herself a great actress. Her later celebrity as an actress eclipsed her importance as an accomplished singer of the blues. Along with Bessie and Louis, she shone as a distinctive singer of her time. She considered Ma Rainey and Bessie Smith and other blues singers as shouters. Her acceptance by the public was due to advised change in her repertoire. Stepping away from Smith-like songs, she adopted songs other than blues. Although she never could read music she would say, "My music is all queer little things that come into my head. All queer that I hum." This led to engagements at the Cotton Club in Harlem and the Plantation Club on Broadway to recording sessions with Jimmy and Tommy Dorsey, Benny Goodman and many more, and finally to the movies notably *As Thousands Cheer* in 1933 and *Cabin In The Sky* in 1940, where she sang her unexpected success "Taking A Chance On Love", thereby achieving success as both singer and actress.

Her rendition of "I Can't Give You Anything But Love" with the Duke Ellington Orchestra in 1932 is the most enduring version on record. On the second chorus of this recording, she almost sounds like a man, the voice lowdown and bluesy. Find a copy if you love early jazz/blues prizes. Ethel Waters, a blues singer, jazz singer, actress, and thriving personality, could swing in the jazz idiom of the times. In the book *The Real Jazz*, author Hughes Panassie wraps it up accordingly: "Her voice, although a miracle of smoothness, is nonetheless firm and penetrating, clear and supple, swinging, caressing, cynical, with myriads of little touches and inflections... since 1930 she had been influenced to some degree by Louis Armstrong." Later, Ethel Waters became a star of the religious world when she traveled and preached with the Reverend Billy Graham's troupe.

MILDRED BAILEY

Mildred Bailey was an immensely successful singer of the newly established Swing Era with her particular mastery of phrasing. Part Couer d'Alene Indian, she was xylophonist (not vibes) Red Norvo's wife and later sang with her husband. She credited her Indian heritage for the unusual quality of her high-pitched tone, which balanced her warm lower range. After running away from home because her father re-married after her Mother died, Mildred originally got in the

Mildred Bailey with Guitarist, Remo Palmieri

music business in Seattle Washington. "She has a job demonstrating sheet music in a ten cents-a-copy music store. She played piano and sang each song for customers." The eighty-nine year old Red said in a conversation I once had with him. "She had an excellent memory. Before a recording date she would go over a song once or twice with me at home and simply memorized it. She always recorded it in one take."

I

In the 1930's Mildred Bailey and Red Norvo were known as Mr. and Mrs. Swing, a sobriquet levied on them by George Simon in his column for Metronome magazine. With Norvo and pianist-bandleader Teddy Wilson of Benny Goodman Quartet fame, Mildred waxed some great recordings. Her recordings of "Melancholy Baby," "A Lull In My Life," and "Russian Lullaby" (a little known tune but a favorite with jazz performers) are the best examples of her superiority in the genre.

Red Norvo's Band in Atlantic City w/ Mildred Bailey

"Rockin' Chair," Hoagy Carmichael's evergreen classic, became a hit that was always identified as Mildred's own. "She used it as a theme song," Red said. It was a variation of the blues, although somewhat closer to the new swing patterns. Hoagy used to hang around on the movie set of King of Jazz (Paul Whiteman and Bing Crosby's landmark film). He wanted Mildred to introduce the song because he thought she could sing it better than anyone else: "Her recording of 'Lazy Bones'- you know, Johnny Mercer's tune- he was her friend and she always did his tunes- and 'More Than You Know' were her best recordings as far as I'm concerned."

Mildred Bailey remains one of the finest jazz vocalists of the era. "She possessed a clear voice and excellent diction (a 'la Frank Sinatra) and vocalized with conviction and warmth. Her diction was so exceptional," Red reiterated. Again, like the later Sinatra, she consciously surrounded herself with the best musicians available. Red Norvo and others, too, have said that with her recording of "Rockin Chair," Mildred Bailey became the very first girl singer of the Big Bands. Credit for this goes to the uncanny ability and foresight of Brunswick Records A & R Man Jack Kapp (who later formed Decca and worked with Bing Crosby and was responsible for the success of the Andrews Sisters, Rosemary Clooney, Tony Bennett, among others). Mildred was Al Rinker's sister. Al was one third of the Bing Crosby group The Rhythm Boys along with Harry Barris. It was Mildred who encouraged the three friends to go to Hollywood. The rest, as they say, is history. Many years later Mildred appeared with Bing Crosby on his landmark radio show in L.A. in 1950 and together they sang Harold Arlen's "I've Got the World on a String," just like they did in those early Paul Whiteman big band days.

Mildred passed in 1951 in a Poughkeepsie, New York, hospital, not far from her upstate farm. She had retired in 1949, and although mostly unknown to the modern world, she was the catalyst for many singers including Frank Sinatra, as he readily admitted. Tony Bennett told me in no uncertain terms that it was Mildred Bailey who influenced his singing career the most, as did Frankie Laine. "Bing told me many times he learned to sing from Mildred," Red Norvo proudly declared. In his autobiography Call Me Lucky, Bing said, "I was lucky in knowing the great jazz and blues singer Mildred Bailey so early in my life. She taught me so much about singing and about interpreting popular songs."

And, there is this little-known story: "She was actually responsible for discovering Billie Holiday along with help from John Hammond," Red recalled. "They were up on the second floor of the Apollo Theater in New York where the white people sat, when Billie appeared on stage in an amateur show, and Mildred excitedly said, 'That girl can sing!' and ran downstairs to find out her name. "Take a moment one quiet day and put some Mildred Bailey records on the turntable and simply listen.

BILLIE HOLIDAY

Frank Sinatra learned very early that when it comes to improvisation, it's a rule that the singer must keep the song recognizable.

Billie Holiday

The lyrics can stray off the melody line but must arrive back on track by the end of the phrase. For Frank Sinatra, Billie Holiday was the master of this kind of singing. If Bessie Smith's example enabled a tradition, Billie was the singer whose life spelled out that tradition. "It's not a matter of what you do, but how you do it," Fats Waller once declared. Billie Holiday's recording of "What a Little Moonlight Can Do" with Teddy Wilson clearly demonstrates this musical necessity. Here a plain song takes on jazz expressions of major proportions. Billie's best recordings, I believe, were made with pianist and bandleader Teddy Wilson.

"She made the most beautiful records with her friend Lester Young, when she recorded with me back in the thirties," Teddy Wilson personally told me back in 1982.

Lester Young's tenor sax suited Holiday perfectly. Her voice was also her instrument, as Sinatra's became his own. Like both Crosby and Sinatra, Billie skillfully took advantage of the advent of the microphone, using her supple, sensitive voice to embrace it, delivering a song in a totally different way than when not using the microphone. Remember that Billie was not a blues singer, as 95% of her recordings were not blues by any account.

In later years Billie's voice became a mere shadow of her earlier, greater days. The voice and spirit was worn and sounded old. Her stressed life of drugs and abuse, heaped on her mostly by others, ended an early death at forty-four. There was no doubt as to Billie Holiday's credentials as a major, influential jazz voice of the 20th century. Almost every vocalist who followed, as acknowledged by Sinatra and others like Tony Bennett, followed her career and learned from her.

When Tony was 70, he recorded an album entitled Tony Bennett: On Holiday, a tribute recording where the magic of modern electronics permits Tony to sing a duet with Billie with the song "God Bless the Child." Frank Sinatra followed releasing his own duet album with other deserving singers he admired.

ELLA FITZGERALD

Frank Sinatra learned from listening to the singing of Ella Fitzgerald, among others. Ella was Sinatra's favorite female singer.

Before Billie Holiday there were a host of female singers performing on the swing circuit. You can never say too much about the success that was Ella Jane Fitzgerald. So much has been written about Ella who rates as one of the best voices of the Jazz Age and the Big Band Era. Growing up, she absorbed the sounds of Connee Boswell and her Sisters, Bing Crosby, and Louis Armstrong. Her big hit with the Chick Webb band that led her to the big time was "A - Tisket, A-Tasket," which she co-wrote with my long-time friend, band-leader Van Alexander. It was a late 1930's swinging, pouty version of an otherwise dull song and an auspicious beginning for the talented teenager. Shortly after her mother died, Chick Webb actually rescued Ella from a fate in an orphanage by adopting her as his own. Ella was a somewhat gawky, rather unruly - scarcely chic- bandstand singer.

Ella Fitzgerald

But it was her voice that appealed to Webb.

In the forties, Ella scored with "How High The Moon" and George Gershwin's "Lady Be Good," both durable Big Band Era favorites and a prelude to her scat vocals, leading jazz straight into bebop by the late 1940's. She was the prototypical swing singer. "She uses the blues structure when she improvises: she can hum a blues languidly or drive it joyously through fast tempo and melody changes," said Stuart Nicholson in his biography of Ella. Her story is strikingly opposite Billie's. Although both were initially handicapped by poverty and race, the difference was temperament and personal strength.

There was no alcohol, addiction, or degradation. Ella Fitzgerald was constantly amazed at her fame. A somewhat nervous performer, she was never at home with interviews or publicity even up to the end. I know about that very well. I once had an opportunity to interview Ella, although I had met her several times, but, as luck would have it, a terrible snow storm prevented me from traveling the twenty-five miles to the theater that appointed evening. I never got a second chance.

The *Songbook* albums produced by her manager and producer since the 1950s. Norman Granz, were definitive interpretations of songwriters George Gershwin (within it the best version of "Of Thee I Sing" ever done), Jerome Kern, Cole Porter, Harold Arlen, and Irving Berlin. They are considered lasting treasures of American music. They are all so exceptional. William B. Williams, then legendary host of New York's WNEW's, *Make Believe Ballroom* for many years, named Ella the *First Lady of Song*, or sometimes just plain *Ella*. As Leonard Feather astutely observed in his 1972 book, *From Satchmo to Miles*: "Ella Fitzgerald is one of the most flexible, beautiful, and widely appreciated voices of this century."

Her thirteen *Grammy Awards* started with the 1958 Best Vocal Performance, Ella Fitzgerald Sings *The Irving Berlin Songbook*, to the 1990 Best Jazz Vocal Performance for *All That Jazz*. She has been honored with honorary doctorates at both Yale and Dartmouth Universities. Accepting the Yale award, she said with characteristic modesty, "Not bad for someone who only studied music to get that half-credit in high school." In 1979 she received a *Kennedy Center Honors Award.*

During her final days, her old friend Bea Wain, a wonderful Song Star herself with those treasured recordings "Deep Purple" and "My Reverie" recorded with Larry Clinton's orchestra, went driving around town together with Ella and her chauffeur.

"It was April 25th, Ella's 78th birthday. Our mutual friend Joyce Garro and I were at her home celebrating her special day. We were

Frank Sinatra with Ella

laughing , singing and eating birthday cake. We reminisced about our past, beginning in the latter part of 1937 when I was singing with Larry Clinton and she was with Chick Webb. Although she was ill, Ella usually went for a ride in her big beautiful car every day. On this day she invited me to come along. She sat in the front with her driver and I was in the rear with her nurse. The radio was tuned to one of the jazz stations and, of course, we were listening to Ella coming over the air. She sang along with herself and clapped her hands in time. She called out the names of some of the musicians and remembered them really well. I have to say that the ride with Ella on her last birthday was a tremendous thrill. I loved her so much and I miss her so...."

A tribute was held at Carnegie Hall on Tuesday, July 9, 1996 to celebrate the life and career of Ella Fitzgerald. Margaret Whiting, Bobby Short, John Pizzarelli, Harry "Sweets" Edison, Lionel Hampton, Ruth Brown, Herb Ellis, Jack Jones, Diana Krall, and Chris Conner were there contributing through song. It was voiced by Jonathan Schwartz, the excellent disc jockey of New York's (at the time) radio station WQEW, the most listened to radio station playing standards in the United States. It was intended to be a testimonial to a living legend, but wound up as a fitting eulogy to the excellence of Ella Fitzgerald.

Frank Sinatra loved and admired Ella and appeared with her on a few occasions, particularly on television show *A Man and His Music* in 1967. It is unfortunate they never recorded together, due to personality problems among the various participants of the business side of recording.

When *Duets* came into being, Ella had already been retired a while, so they opportunity was lost forever for the two best singers of all time to get together in song.

Connie Haines with Ella

Russ Columbo - A Career Cut Short

Bing Crosby spoke kindly of his only rival of his time, Russ Columbo, the Camden, New Jersey born "Prisoner of Love" recording star of the 1930s: "I worked with Russ in 1930 at the Cocoanut Grove in Los Angeles. We were both working in the Gus Arnheim band. He played violin and accordion and sang. I just sang. I am sure if Russ had lived longer he would have been a big, big star."

Russ Columbo's baritone crooning style is sometimes mistaken for Bing's, as Bing was more widely known and people tend to forget the talents or even existence of Russ Columbo. Appearances at the famous Cocoanut Grove night club catapulted both Crosby and Columbo's aspiring careers higher. When Bing was late or didn't show up for his appearance, Arnheim would cue in Columbo to take his place for the bands vocals.

Within a short time, both he and Bing had their own competing radio programs. Russ on NBC and Bing on CBS. Coincidentally, both shows were scheduled on the same night and at the same time, inviting radio and newspaper columnists to inquire whether or not they were actually different people.

Newspaper reporters dreamed up a feud, calling it The Battle of the Baritones, but none existed. The singers actually admired and praised one another, and Russ was a guest of Bing's at his first son Gary's christening. Bing, although usually one to avoid such events, became a pallbearer at Russ Columbo's funeral.

There was much resemblance in their voices, delivery, and choices of material. Bing, however, generally performed brighter, lighter, richer, and more livelier - and at times, outright jazzy songs. Columbo's approach was more morose, serious, and sadder sounding. He sometimes blatantly imitated Bing and learned from watching him manage tricks on the microphone, using what he witnessed to his advantage. To most observers there was no mistake as to who was superior. It was clearly Bing. Both recorded "Prisoner of Love," "Out of Nowhere," "Sweet and Lovely," "Paradise," "Goodnight Sweetheart," and "Where the Blue of the Night, " (which became Bing's theme) all being among the most popular songs of the moment. It was Russ who composed the sullen torch song "Prisoner of Love."

Russ was a child prodigy, an accomplished violin player by age five. He first played professionally at a theater in San Francisco at the age of thirteen and played violin in his high school orchestra in Los Angeles. In 1928 he joined the Gus Arnheim Orchestra after some playing experience at other ballrooms and dance pavilions in the Los Angeles area. In other work, his voice was substituted for actors who could not satisfactorily sing in films with Metro Goldwyn Mayer, a common problem in films at that time.

In 1931 Russ formed his own band and became a sensation with a more silky, ballad style of singing. One of the songs that heralded him was his own composition written with his manager and promoter, Con Conrad, "You Call It Madness (But I call It Love)." Russ toured the country and Europe singing "Prisoner of Love," "Paradise," "Auf Wiedersehn," and "Too Beautiful for Words."

Russ appeared in a dozen films in his short career and also recorded with Jimmie Grier's fine orchestra. Early in 1934, Russ performed on his new NBC radio show from the Hollywood Roosevelt Hotel. His exciting, promising career, including his quest to become an operatic singer, came to a sudden end in a bizarre accident. On September 2, 1934, a close friend, photographer Lansing Brown, Jr., was showing him a pair of old dueling pistols at Lansing's home and struck a match to one of them that, unbeknownst to anyone, turned out to be loaded.

The gun discharged and Russ Columbo was struck in the eye by a ricocheting bullet. He was rushed to the hospital but did not survive. His death was officially listed as an accident by an official Court of Inquiry. Lansing Brown was crushed by his friend's death. Russ Columbo was twenty-six.

Frank Sinatra hadn't started his career as yet, but had his eye and heart on the sound of Bing Crosby. As Frank said later: "He was the father of my career."

RUDY VALLEE

Rudy Vallee was first a musician, having had earlier experience with the clarinet and saxophone, forming a band and became a reluctant vocalist, and despite doubts from fellow band members. Vallee, however, became a special kind of singer, known as the first "crooner." His rather thin voice required uplifting so Vallee employed the use of a megaphone. His wavering tenor and sweet vocals combined with his boyish looks attracted the admiration of young women. He predated Bing Crosby by a couple of years. Armed with a recording contract he began performing his vocals on the radio. He was indeed the Sinatra of the twenties. His tag line was "Heigh-Ho Everybody," adopted when he played at the Heigh-Ho Club in New York where he first began singing. His opening & closing theme was the song "My Time is Your Time."

His singing, although weak, was augmented by his use of the new invention, the microphone, that

Rudy Vallee "Disk of the Week" (Plastic record - 78 RPM One-Sided)

inspired Crosby, Sinatra, Perry Como, and others who began to copy his phrasing. Vallee's long-time radio career with his group "The Connecticut Yankees," recorded throughout the '30s and 40s. According to most critics, his vocal quality was really bad, but charming. He nevertheless succeeded with songs like "Life is Just a Bowl of Cherries," "The Stein Song," and his swan song, "As Time Goes By," years before it captured success in the film Casablanca.

When he recorded an unusual series "Hit of the Week" in the early thirties, which was pressed on laminated cardboard, his photo appeared on the record face along with the weekly song. I had a copy of one that I recently donated to singer, pianist Michael Feinstein, who is working hard collecting old sheet music and special related products that he is turning over to the Smithsonian Institution archives permanent collection.

When Crosby took over the crooning business, Vallee turned to making movies and appeared in a number of musical and other type films and later appeared on Broadway in How to Succeed in Business Without Really Trying, projecting his now mellower baritone.

Rudy Vallee was a songwriter too, with "Deep Night" and "Oh! Ma-Ma." (the Butcher Boy), his two best-known compositions, as well as "I'm Just a Vagabond Lover" which he recorded himself.

It is said that Rudy Vallee's eye for talent discovered singers Frances Langford, Alice Faye, and comedian Edgar Bergen and his wooden friend Charlie McCarthy. In his time Rudy Vallee was a big singing star for many years.

BING CROSBY

BING CROSBY

"Some people insist that Sinatra was a reader of books, a devotee of classical music, which was the basis for his own music, an admirer of great art, a man graceful before women, a generous, although anonymous contributor to people he didn't even know or ever met. "

SINATRA

"Bing made you think you could sing as well as he could, especially in the shower. He was relaxed and casual and if he forgot some words, he slipped in a buh-bub-boo here and there and they loved it. He was the first popular singer just as Mildred Bailey was the first big band girl singer. But behind it all was the hard work you didn't see. Same thing with Fred Astaire. After you came out of a movie you thought you could sing and dance like him. When Bing sang, I sang along with him and it became a duet. Bing was the father of my whole career. Blame him if you didn't buy my records.

You can't imagine how big Bing was back when I started. Everybody listened and watched this great man. Records and movies and even radio. Everybody copied him, including me."

BING CROSBY:

"Dear Frank, I want to tell you what a laugh it was to me when some people in Hollywood tried to steam up a feud between us. One reason it worked out is because I've known from away back what a right guy you are.

Unlike some of the young performers who hit the Hollywood gold coast for the first time, you didn't try to make a big flash, throw-

Bing Crosby, Grace Kelly and Frank Sinatra From the Film *High Society*

ing big parties and spending all your spare time in movietown's fancy bistros in the hope that some big studio man would spot you.

My advice is for you to keep on being yourself. I think it's swell - the classy, down-to-earth way you've taken your amazing flood of high-publicity in your stride, without losing your head. You'll not have too hard a time keeping that up if you listen more to your critical friends than to the back-slappers. It's the easiest thing in the world for your friends to say, "You were terrific tonight, Frankie boy. Greater than ever."

Yep, those are the lads to listen to. Those are the fellows

who will still be all out for Sinatra when you and I aren't top singers any more. The others will be too busy throwing posies at the newest sensation in songland to bother with you. And don't let knocks in the press upset you! You'll catch such blasts every once in a while. I know I have. The funny part of that sort of brick-throwing is that it brings your fans out fighting mad, does you more good than harm.

Another tip, Frankie boy. Don't be guided in your selection of songs by those most plugged on the air. I guess it's no secret to you that those plugs can be bought. What shows true popularity are sheet music and record sales.

Another sure-fire barometer you'll find in our fan mail. I take consensus of fan mail opinion. When a man or woman admires you enough to take the trouble of writing you "Please sing this, Frank!" he or she is worth pleasing.

Keep riding that skyrocket you're on, Frankie! I'm all for you. Yes, when I heard the whispers about you and me being bitter rivals, I just smiled. What did those would-be troublemakers think, anyway? That we were running for Governor, or something?

All that gossip reminded me of a story I heard about George M. Cohan, the greatest of all American performers. I'll never be a George M. Cohan, but I like to think that in all actors there is something of his spirit. Here's the story: Once, George was here to make a picture in which he was supported by Jimmy Durante. The movie front office kept calling in Jimmy and giving him the fat lines that had originally been written for the star.

Kathryn Crosby with Richard Grudens - 2003
(M. Grudens Photo)

Jimmy, who like all actors held the great song-and-dance man in reverence, became embarrassed after a while. Meeting George on the lot one day, he told him what was going on.

"I can't let them give me a chance to steal your show, Mr. Cohan. You're too big a man for a punk like me to do that to."

Cohan laughed, "Grab all they throw you, kid. When anyone steals the show from me, it means that I'm not good enough any more. I've been up there with my name in lights for a long time now. Any added time I get as a headliner is velvet. I like velvet but I can live without it. You're just coming up. Yep, grab everything they throw you, boy. It's okay by George M. Cohan."

Well, what's good enough for George M. Cohan is good enough for Bing Crosby now or any time, Frankie. And I hope you keep a riding that skyrocket as long and happily as I've been riding mine.

Your true friend, with every good wish.

Bing Crosby"

A LETTER FROM KATHRYN CROSBY
Something Special about Bing.

Dear Richard.

I have nothing of moment to add about my dear Bing with respect to Mr.Sinatra. As usual, you've hit the nail on the head, and I'm just an observer, without your research or expertise.

But now that I think of it, I might mention one small thing of which only a member of Bing's immediate family might be aware: He sang all day long----snatches of opera, foreign favorites, the latest rock numbers, even medleys of radio commercials.

At our home in Las Cruces, Baja California, Bing woke his friend Dr. Sullivan one morning with a fortissimo of YOU CAN TRUST YOUR CAR TO THE MAN WHO WEARS THE STAR.

"If you want to appoint me your agent," Sullivan mused, "I'll bet

I can get you some bread for that sort of work."

"Oh, I dunno, Bill, "the assassin of sleep replied, "I hear they got their own fella, that guy Sinatra."

And off he strode into the dawn, roaring out TOREADOR EN GARDE.....

NANCY FOR FRANK

Recently, listening to Sirius XM Satellite Radio, Nancy Sinatra hosts a wonderful thrice-weekly tribute to her dad and plays endearing recordings and entertains guests who share her love for her dad's recordings. When she invited Mary Crosby, Bing and Kathryn's daughter (famous for her role as the girl who shot J.R. on television) on the program, Nancy dedicated two four-hour shows about their

famous singing dads.

Mary often sang with her father on his television specials with mother Kathryn and her two brothers, Nathaniel and Harry, and, of course Nancy shared on her dad's biggest single, "Something Stupid."

Mary Crosby

The girls played Nancy's favorite Bing recording, Irving Berlin's "You Keep Coming Back Like a Song," and Mary talked about Bing welcoming Frank to his radio shows when Frank was just starting to become an important singer in his own right. All in all they played dozens of songs in each segment. Each show ended with Bing's Irish recordings and a warm goodnight to Bing and Frank from two dedicated daughters who have now, after all the years, become friends.

L-R: Frank Sinatra, Rosemary Clooney, Dean Martin, Kathryn and Bing Crosby

PEGGY LEE

"Well, I've never been able to define a jazz singer," Peggy Lee said, "but I can tell when I hear one." Then she leaned back and added : "I believe it's a composite thing of good taste and understanding harmonic structures. It doesn't necessarily mean that they have to "scat" sing at all. Frank Sinatra doesn't skat much and is not considered a jazz singer, although he sings jazzy compositions frequently.

Peg thinks that it's good phrasing and good material that qualifies a capable or almost any singer including a jazz singer. That means the voice has to maybe jump a couple of measures- if needed- to reestablish where you started out - always knowing where 'one' is."

Sultry singer Peggy Lee, formerly Norma Deloris Ekstrom, instituted the important part of her career when, after slipping into Helen Forrest's shoes with the Benny Goodman band in 1941, she recorded her sulky, jazzy rendition of "Why Don't You Do Right?" in 1942. That recording made her an international star.

Peg really started her professional career quite modestly at the age of fourteen. It was an unheralded debut on local radio station WDAY in Jamestown, North Dakota. It was there that program director Ken Kennedy christened her Peggy Lee. She eventually landed a job with the popular novelty band of Will Osborne, the slide-trombonist, vocalist, and drummer leader who composed the swing era hit "Pompton Turnpike."

In a cocktail lounge at Chicago's Ambassador Hotel shortly before Helen Forrest quit, Benny heard Peggy sing and promptly hired her. After twenty months with Goodman, that molded her into one of the most famous female vocalists of the time, Peg and her guitarist husband, former Goodman sideman Dave Barbour, quit the band in 1943 and went on to record a batch of great hits they wrote on their own in the years following, while Peg impersonated a retired, professionally inactive, simple housewife. "Dave would come home," she said, "the dinner wasn't ready - but the song I worked on all day was."

These are the numbers I most identify with when it comes to Peggy Lee's hits: "It's a Good Day," "I Don't Know Enough About You," and a deft little ditty they composed in 1948 while vacationing in Mexico, "Manana."

Aside from teaming with her husband, Peggy has written over 500 songs with various collaborators including Broadway's Cy

Coleman who penned "Witchcraft" and many other Broadway tunes; producer and leader Quincy Jones; orchestra leader and composer Victor Young, and "Emily" and "The Shadow of Your Smile" composer and arranger Johnny Mandel. She was careful not to mark them with slang or things that might date the piece so they would not be overtaken by time. "I guess that's an instinct. It's not just good luck to keep a song's standard quality," she noted.

When singing, Peg's voice sort of whispers confidential resonant passion even on the most fragile numbers. Hard songs become dreamy; harsh songs translate into soft songs. Novelty songs become ballads. Some have called her the "Actress of Song." It was Duke Ellington, however, who christened her the "Queen of Song."

F E V E R !
The Peggy Lee Fan Club Newsletter
Issue 29 · Volume 8

In those days, Peggy had always entertained her fellow celebrities and just anyone she knew who wasn't in the business at her lavish home on Kim Ridge Road in Beverly Hills. It was through these parties that Duke Ellington and Peggy got to know one another and became very warm friends. They had always admired one another. Peg had written the lyric for Duke's theme melody for the film *Anatomy of a Murder*, 'Gone Fishin'. Peg threw a special dinner party for the occasion in the Duke's honor. Charlie Barnet and Frank Sinatra were invited, as was Cary Grant. That party deepened their friendship and established her relationship with Frank Sinatra. At a later gala tribute held at Madison Square Garden and sponsored by the NAACP, so the story goes, Peggy showed up with Quincy Jones to support the Duke. While Peggy was on stage performing, Duke, who was backstage talking with Louis Armstrong, turned to him and said, "Louis, now we really have royalty on that stage. She's the 'Queen.'"

Some critics have suggested Peg emulated the styling of Billie Holiday, but that was impossible. "We had no radio where we lived in North Dakota," she said, "we didn't even have electricity. When I finally heard Count Basie coming out of Kansas City, I didn't think of it as swing or jazz or anything. It just sounded like good music to me. I can't say I emulated any special singer, until I first heard Maxine Sullivan. She communicated so well - I liked her simplicity." Nat King Cole, however, said that when Peg sang "Sometimes I Feel Like a Motherless Child," she sounded just like Billie Holiday, but Peg just shrugged it off.

Peg always got very involved in her music, favoring best the theme song she wrote for the 1950 movie *Johnny Guitar*. Her favorite album was *The Man I Love*, recorded in 1957 and orchestrated by musical genius Nelson Riddle, and actually conducted by Frank Sinatra himself . One selection, "The Folks Who Live On The Hill," a quiet, prayer-like piece recorded earlier by Bing Crosby, is a typical reverie style Lee rendition.

When Peggy recorded her swirling, stampeding Decca version of Richard Rodgers' evergreen waltz "Lover," he was quoted as lamenting, "Oh, my poor little waltz, my little waltz. What happened to my little waltz?" Later, being the very kind and amiable figure he was known to be, he approached Peg: "You can always sing anything of mine." Peg felt that comment from the great composer was quite a compliment.

In a change of pace, Peg's "Is That All There Is?" is a life-weary mystical selection written by rock writers Jerry Leiber & Fred Stoller that sticks in your mind and may even keep you awake at night. "Though the song wasn't written for me, it just happened that the lyric paraphrases my life, "Peg said. "I've been through everything including the death experience, but I believe the song is positive. Of course, we all know there is more." Few know that Peggy Lee's very early life was that of an abused child at the hand of a cruel step-mother. The abuse that lasted until she was seventeen had an odd effect in that Peggy became a mild, nonviolent person, which countermands the expected future life of an abused person. She came to hate violence of every kind.

As a Bing Crosby specialist, I recall a Bing Crosby movie in which Peg appeared. It was a so-so film, the 1950 *Mr. Music*, but, in a peppy party scene, Peg and Bing warble several bubbly choruses of the song "Life Is So Peculiar." Although her role was a short cameo, the two entertainers became good friends and singing partners. Peg sang regularly on Bing's radio show.

"Before I met Bing, I had always secretly loved the Rodgers and Hart song 'Down By The River,'" Peg explained, "that he sang years before in (the 1935 film) *Mississippi*, and I told him how I felt about it. One night, when I went to dinner with him to a little place in San Francisco, he actually sang it for me. He somehow convinced the piano player to play it and then sang it for me personally. Can you imagine that? It was a memorable evening. There was always a certain security for me in just thinking about Bing."

Although she wasn't much a movie star, Peggy had, of course, appeared on countless television shows including the one in which a young Frank Sinatra made his debut performance on Bob Hope's second ever TV show.

Peggy Lee was really in a class with counterpart Frank Sinatra. Although she too began her career with the Big Bands, Peg continued her lifelong career as an individual artist choosing her own songs, backup musicians, tailored format, and a very classy wardrobe. Peg has emerged an accomplished and respected, world-class entertainer.

"I learned more about music from the men I worked with in the bands, "she says, " than I've learned anywhere else. They taught me discipline and the value of rehearsing and how to train. Even if the interpretation of a particular song wasn't exactly what we wanted, we had to make the best of it."

P.S. I almost forgot to mention Peg's stellar version of "Golden Earrings" from the Ray Milland, Marlene Dietrich film of the same name. It's on my personal all-time top ten list. Another note: It was Peggy Lee who changed the name of the song, "In Other Words," to "Fly Me to the Moon, after recording it. Thought it sounded better with a new title.

Bobby Darin

Bobby Darin has been described as a singer graced with a Sinatra framework and with basic Tony Bennett overtones. Add a little bit of Crosby and a healthy portion of rock and roll to his roots. When I hear a Bobby Darin record in the earliest bars I hear a bit of Sinatra until it clears up to become Darin. Bobby Darin originally wanted to become an actor.

Gene Lees qualifies Darin as a Sinatra with firecrackers. Sure, I agree with Lees in this assessment, although I cannot place Darin in a league with Sinatra. Darin unfortunately did not live long enough for a final judgment. Sinatra was almost 20 years Darin's senior, and comparisons were drawn in the heart of his career. Biographer and my personal friend, David Evanier, designated Darin as a fascinating singer who had a promising career but was cut down by illness and died very early in life. Bobby was born in 1936 and passed on in 1973. Who knows what kind of future he would've had had he lived a full life.

Influenced by Frank Sinatra, in his short life Bobby tried everything. He performed at the Copacabana in New York, recorded an album with the great composer/lyricist Johnny Mercer, backed by legendary Billy May, and performed mightily on television and in films. From his album *That's All*, Bobby won two Grammy's at the age of twenty-three. One of the tracks "Mack the Knife," was named Best New Artist, and one for Record of the Year. A prolific actor, composer, and vocalist, Bobby Darin did it all. He appeared in no less than thirteen films, had his own television show in 1972-1973 and composed a startling number of songs, some for motion pictures.

Bobby Darin was posthumously inducted into the Rock and Roll Hall of Fame and into the Songwriters Hall of Fame in 1999, and in the same year his prolific and exciting life and career were documented on Public Television.

His best were "Mack the Knife," "Beyond the Sea," "Clementine," "Artificial Flowers," "Dream Lover," and "Mame."

MATT MONRO

with daughter Michelle

Sinatra observed upon Matt Monro's passing in 1984: "His pitch was right on the nose: his word enunciation's letter perfect; his understanding of a song thorough. He will be missed very much not only by myself, but by his fans all over the world."

Matt Monro, whose given name was Terence Edward Parsons and his alias' were Terry Parsons, Al Jordan, Fred Flange, used in his early appearances.

His first recording was with Decca, where the name Matt Monro was christened by Decca. The LP was called *Blue and Sentimental*. It was followed by a radio series where he was signed for the *Show Band Home* series, and then embarked on a long list of recording over 40 commercials for well-known sponsors.

It was a demonstration recording that made it for Monro.

Producer George Martin wanted Matt to record a takeoff of Sinatra for one of the tracks on the second Peter Sellers album he was working on. It seemed that Sellers could not emulate Sinatra so he engaged Matt for the opening track "You Keep Me Swingin" for the album *Songs for Swingin'Sellers*. On the track the credit was to Fred Flange, a mysterious singer, indeed, and remained so, stirring up a lot of interest, and eventually it leaked out and Matt became in demand internationally.

Eventually Matt Monro recorded some stellar sides that included Jimmy Van Heusen's "Polka Dots and Moonbeams," "Gonna Build a Mountain," the unforgettable Monro gem "Portrait of My Love," "Softly As I Leave You," which closely rivaled Frank Sinatra's version, and "My Kind of Girl," to become England's Number one male vocalist.

Monro set his sights on America where he was solidly billed, performing in all the great venues all over the 48 states and Hawaii: Resorts International in Atlantic City, The Persian Room in New York City, The Roosevelt Hotel in New Orleans, Harold's Club in Reno, Nevada, The Sands in Las Vegas, sharing the television stage with Jack Benny, Johnny Carson, Liberace, Pat Boone, and on Ed Sullivan's *Toast of the Town* television show no less than four times.

Matt Monro's following was phenomenal, his rise to fame coincided with the Beatles era, but Monro held his own and even recorded a version of "Yesterday," and the recording reached a respectable number eight.

Matt Monro was happiest working with musicians Quincy Jones, Nelson Riddle, Billy May, England's great Ted Heath Band, Robert Farnon, Henry Mancini and the London Philharmonic Orchestra.

Matt Monro was a respectable, natural rival of Frank Sinatra almost more than any other singer in their time. Unfortunately, Matt Monro passed away too early in any case. He was a fine singer and will be remembered.

In February, the 25th anniversary of Monro's passing, a new book will be released named The Singer's Singer. Two other projects *The Complete Singles Collection* and *The Greatest*, a collection of twenty-five tracks chosen for their popularity, will be released. Matt Monro's daughter, Michele, is behind this highly expected moment for her dad and issued a warm statement of good wishes for all his fans and hopes 2010 will be Matt Monro's year.

MEL TORME

Once, under a massive tent at Planting Fields Arboretum, Oyster Bay, New York, Mel Torme and I talked about his ability as a singer. The date was a hot August 5, 1994. He had just finished a fine singing performance. In his book It Wasn't All Velvet, Mel described that phenomena like this:

"I have lost track, in the past few years, of the number of times reviewers have commented on my increased strength in the vocal department. I recall the numerous TV, radio, and newsprint interviewers who have asked me why, when middle-aged-and beyond-normally ushers in diminishing strength, wobbly vibrato, and increasing hoarseness in certain singers, I seem to have reversed the process."

Mel Torme never smoked cigarettes. He never drank hard liquor. He always made certain he got enough sleep before performances. He credits those items as a reason for his successful singing career and the ability to keep longevity and production in his voice.

Like many other singers, including Frank Sinatra, you have to keep the vocal cords rested with ample sleep. When singers perform night after night after night during long engagements, there must be a consistency. That means you have to sound good on every performance. Not good on Monday and lukewarm on Friday. You have to be effective in strength and freshness at the same time.

"As Frank Sinatra once told me, the key is concentration, and when it works and you 'touch' the audience, there's no feeling in the world like it."

Mel Torme was always known as "The Velvet Fog" because of his soft, romantic style of almost whispering through some of his material. In the film *Good News*, in which he costarred with Peter Lawford and June Allyson, he sang "Be a Ladies Man" and "The Best Things in Life Are Free," both songs were my introduction to the Velvet Fog. It was also Mel's first film singing performance after the film *Higher and Higher*.

Mel Torme had gained fame for his versatility: actor, songwriter, arranger, drummer, author, singer, dancer, and musical director. He first started as a child of four singing solo with the then world-famous Coon-Sanders Orchestra on a coast-to-coast radio show originating from the Blackhawk Restaurant in Chicago.

"It was 1929. I loved radio. My first hit was 'You're Drivin' Me Crazy,' with the orchestra. It became a hit for me in 1947." In 1949 with Crosby's big hit "Dear Hearts and Gentle People," and Frankie Laine with his big winner "Mule Train," Mel kept pace with "Careless Hands," although it didn't reach nearly the fame. His recording of "Blue Moon" certified the Velvet Fog sobriquet until Mel changed his style and began singing jazz pieces a little later on. The creamy singing turned to jazz singing.

Here's the wrap-up on Torme from his own voice: "I was a drum-and-bugle corps kid in grammar school. I loved Chick Webb and, obviously, Gene Krupa, and finally Buddy Rich. Those are the people who motivated me as a young man." Then, an actor: I was a child radio actor, probably one of the five busiest child actors in America, from 1933 to 1941. I did the soap operas *Mary Noble, Backstage Wife, Captain Midnight; Little Orphan Annie*, and even *Jack Armstrong*."

Add songwriter, vocal group (Mel Tones) director, and very influenced by Frank Sinatra's break with Tommy Dorsey, and since Mel was a singer, too, he followed the handwriting on the wall that Sinatra had written and became a soloist singer.

So, for Mel Torme, it wasn't all velvet. But, the fog had finally lifted.

Connie Haines

Connie Haines, actually Yvonne Marie Ja Mais, sang shoulder to shoulder with Frank Sinatra in the bands of both Harry James and Tommy Dorsey, along with the Pied Pipers singing group that featured Jo Stafford, whose husband Paul Weston was Dorsey's arranger.

Like many of her singing contemporaries, she followed the styles of Mildred Bailey, Billie Holiday, and Kate Smith as her heroes. Connie was with Harry James when they took a trip to New Jersey to see Frank Sinatra perform at the Rustic Cabin where he was waiting on tables and singing for his supper. James liked him and suggested Frank call himself Frankie Satin, to which Frank responded, "You like the voice, you take the name."

Connie Haines and I spent some great times together. I was able to write her biography which I called "Snootie Little Cutie," the name of one of the duets she and Frank performed while with Tommy Dorsey.

"After the eight New York Paramount engagements, we prepared our first cross-country tour of one-nighters.," Connie said. Earlier, with Harry James, Connie and Frank toured together in appearances from the Atlantic City Steel Pier, Roseland Ballroom, and the Hotel Sherman in Chicago.

"Life on the road was fun. Frank was the soft crooner and I was belting out my tunes, like 'What is This Thing Called Love,' 'You're Nobody's Baby.' the first tunes I recorded with Tommy.

The story of the little girl with the magnificent voice who sang out to America with the Big Bands

Frank was a lot of fun on the bus trips. He was always in good spirits. He got along with everybody and really pitched in, always doing his share and more. Once, the band's drummer was late, so Harry asked Frank to get behind the drums. The opening theme was no problem for Frank, but, the next number was a jump tune called 'Night Train.' It featured an opening sixteen-bar drum solo. Frank grabbed the sticks and pounded away. Harry was so convulsed with laughter that he had to keep his back to the audience.

Harry soon disbanded because he couldn't keep up the payroll payments. Frank went with Tommy, and I followed. Soon after, Tommy heard me sing 'Honeysuckle Rose" at the Frank Dailey's Meadowbrook in New Jersey."

One night while Connie and Frank were at the Paramount, Connie literally saved Frank's life. As the huge stage was descending into the pit, a group of teenage girls were screaming and groping at Frank. One reached over and grabbed Frank's tie while we he singing the finale 'I'll Never Smile Again' with the Pipers.

"I could not believe what they were doing," said Frank, "and I began to choke." The girls were actually trying to pull Frank over the railing as the stage was being lowered.

Connie: "I screamed for help over the mike and reached over to Frank, trying to beat the girls off him and release his tie. By then the ushers were racing over and the musicians were helping as the stage hit the bottom. Those were the days Frank and I began to have Police escorts even when just crossing the street for a hamburger or cup of coffee."

"Boy, did we ever sing up a storm in those days, especially at the Palladium. 'Let's Get Away from it All,' 'I'll Never Smile Again,' 'Snootie Little Cutie,' 'Comes Love, Nothing Can Be Done,' 'Marie,' 'All or Nothing At All,' 'Song of India,' 'Oh, Look At Me Now,' 'What is This Thing Called Love?' all those wonderful chestnuts with Tommy and Frank, Jo Stafford and the Pipers, the crisp sound of Johnny Mince's clarinet and the exciting drums of Buddy Rich, and the great piano of Joe Bushkin. And don't forget Ziggy El-

man's trumpet.

Life with Frank Sinatra and the entire Dorsey group was a magnificent run for the petite Connie Haines. She left Tommy and got a show of her own with Skitch Henderson as musical director and made her first recording for Capitol Records with Gordon Jenkins called "He Wears a Pair of Silver Wings."

In 1990 Connie was called to appear on her old singing partner Frank Sinatra's 75th Birthday television special.

"How exciting it was to be on the show. Frank was so pleased: after all, we had been friends for over 60 years. Oh, my God! Sixty years. Well, I sang with the Manhattan Transfer vocal group, and, just like the old days, I stared at Frank while I sang to him like I used to do singing with him. His offstage wink told me he remembered. It was a memorable evening."

Significantly, Will Friedwald in his book Sinatra! The Song is You, reminds us that "The best remembered of the Sinatra-Haines duets 'Oh Look At Me Now,' also represents Sinatra's first really up-tempo performance."

More about Connie Haines and her great career in the book I wrote for her, Snootie Little Cutie - The Connie Haines Story.

Larry O'Brien, Musical Director, Glenn Miller Orchestra, Connie Haines and Richard Grudens

Frank Sinatra and Connie Haines Debut with Dorsey on Opening Night

Frank Sinatra and Connies Haines Debut with Tommy Dorsey on Opening Night

ANTHONY DOMINICK BENEDETTO

Tony Bennett -The Other Saloon Singer, Who Still Sings Today in 2010

The first time I met Tony Bennett, I was being detained by theater security when Tony came forward and called out to me, "Hey! Richard," and he waved me through," C'mon over, I've been waiting for you."

I hope that will not happen this upcoming November when I am scheduled to meet up with Tony once again at the same, but renamed, Capitol One Theater.

Well it was an extremely cold evening and Tony was waiting to go on. We had made a date for an interview, but his people never left my name at the door. Tony, however, true to everyone else's image of him, rescued me and we had our long conversation and even took some photos. That was in 1986.

Since then, instead of a diminishing career, Tony Bennett's star spiraled upward, thanks in part to his son Danny, who took on his management: "My career was never at a standstill. It just may have seemed that way, because I was performing just like always, and everywhere. It just made the back page because all the rock stars took center stage over those few years. But my fans are civilized and my following is now stronger than ever."

In 1988, a chapter covering his career appeared in American Singers by Whitney Balliett. In 1997 Tony was a subject in my book The Best Damn Trumpet Player, and in 1998, in a book dedicated to his mom, entitled The Good Life, written with his good friend Will Friedwald, Tony has been well covered in print over the years, including help from Mark Fox of the UK, who maintains an almost daily log.

"I feel Sinatra exemplifes the best music that ever came out of the United States. No only was he a great interpreter, but he had a magic voice. I've mentioined that Bing Crosby had really invented intimate singing, but Sinatra took it a step further, in a way that one one could have imagined. He comunicated precisely what he was feeling at the moment. He knocked down the wall between performer and audience, inviting listeners inside his mind. Before Sinatra, no one had ever told such vivid and beautiful stories through song," Tony said in The Good Life.

Tony Bennett with Composer Harold Arlen

Tony Bennett credits all the American Songbook songwriters for his success. "It's not whether a song is new or old that makes it great...it's whether it's bad or good that makes a song live or die." He never gets tired of singing the worthy strains of Irving Berlin, Cole Porter, Harold Arlen, George Gershwin, or Harry Warren. He has sort of an instinct for selecting the songs that suit him. In the case of his immensely popular gem "I Left My Heart in San Francisco," he recalls that while rehearsing it with his piano accompanist Ralph Sharon in a Hot Springs hotel bar before he first introduced it at the Fairmont Hotel in San Francisco, "a bartender was listening and, after we finished rehearsal, he told me he would enthusiastically buy a copy if we ever recorded it. That was the first tip-off that we had a hit in the making. Right up to today, it's still my biggest request - it gets the best reaction, and San Francisco is really a beautiful city - it's a musical city - and I love to sing about it." The recording won a Grammy.

Some argue the song is too sentimental and weak, but it brings in the faithful and will probably be the song with which he will always be identified. No one else sings it as well.

While we talked backstage, Sarah Vaughan was on stage singing and he was slated to follow her. We could hear her over the speakers loud and clear. "What a magnificent background for our interview, listening to Sarah." Tony said. Tony makes an art out of feelings: "I conjure up emotion much like the impressionist artists who work with light. Feelings are the opposite of coldness...I try to sing in a natural key...choosing strong lyrics with meaning...then I inject my own feelings into it."

It's more than feelings that drives Tony Bennett. Ever since he won an *Arthur Godfrey Talent Scouts* Contest, coming in second to Rosemary Clooney, Tony's career has always expanded, helped by a battery of million sellers, namely "Because of You," "Rags to Riches," "Blue Velvet," "Cold, Cold Heart" and "Boulevard of Broken Dreams." It was Bob Hope who told me that it was he who changed Tony's early stage name of Joe Bari back to Tony Bennett because he thought Bari sounded phony. Hope had invited Tony to join his show at the New York Paramount after hearing him sing at the Village Barn in Greenwich Village, in lower Manhattan, where he was appearing with Pearl Bailey. "Right there and then at the Paramount Bob announced what would be my new name and told me I was going on tour with him all over the U.S. - it was great. Who could argue with Bob Hope?"

Tony was brought up in a non-affluent Manhattan suburb known as Astoria. His father passed on when he was ten, and his mom had to support the family. Uncles and Aunts helped feed that family of four in those hard times. "It was a warm feeling among all of us, and I would sing for the family on Sundays."

Tony loves to be associated with Sinatra as the other saloon singer, as he has been often identified by Frank himself. With Tony Bennett, he believes every show is his last show. When he had to record what record executives wanted back in the 1950s, he did it and luckily succeeded. But since then he chooses his own tunes to record.

"I would get record execs angry at me when I would not record some of the garbage, so they labeled me a fanatic and troublemaker. I considered that a compliment. They were forcing artists to take a dive. Remember, they are accountants and marketing guys and don't know or care about the product." Over the years Tony has matured into a more disciplined performer who communicates with his audience and never really ever sings a song the same way twice, one of the things I love about his performances.

At the outset, Tony was warned by Columbia A & R man Mitch Miller, who signed him after hearing his rendition of "Boulevard of Broken Dreams," not to try to sound like Frank Sinatra, which many others singers made the classic mistake of trying to sound like the leading singer of the time, much like Russ Columbo and Frankie Laine

Richard and Tony, Westbury Music Fair - Back Stage (C. Smith Photo)

tried to sound like Crosby early in their career, among others. Sinatra had just left Columbia at that moment. With an orchestral arrangement by Percy Faith, Tny went on to record his first hit "Because of You."

Whitney Balliett: "Bennett is an elusive singer. He can be a belter. He drives a ballad as intensely and intimately as Sinatra. He can be a lilting jazz singer. He can be a low key, searching supper-club performer. But Bennett's voice binds all his vocal selves together. His voice has a joyous quality, a pleased, shouting-within quality."

Sarah Vaughan: "Richard, Tony is frisky and fresh. You've just got to look at the movements in his face when he sings. He's not Sinatra, but Sinatra isn't him, either.

As a young man, Tony was trained to be a commercial artist at Manhattan's School of Industrial Arts. "But, I always had to sing.

It was something in my genes..my Italian heritage. I have spent my whole life studying and thinking about my singing. My whole family sang, too."

Tony was influenced early by the school's choral director. He joined the chorus to learn his craft, and, after singing with military bands while serving in the armed forces in Europe, he came home and entered the American Theater Wing professional school under its director, Miriam Spier. While studying, he rounded out a livelihood by playing club dates around Manhattan and even served as an elevator operator at the Park Sheraton Hotel to make ends meet.

Tony Bennett also credits Art Tatum's ingenious piano playing and Mildred Bailey's jazz voice as mentor's. In 1986, shortly after the time of my first interview with him, his *The Art of Excellence* album was doing pretty well on the charts: "Listen to this," Tony declared over the telephone from Atlantic City when I called to congratulate him, "It's number one...and it's wonderful...and to think it's in front of the Rolling Stones and the great Bruce Springsteen. It's full circle for me." The album, still available, contained an amazing duet with the late, great Ray Charles on James Taylor's "Everybody's Got the Blues" and a number called "City of Angels," which was written by Fred Astaire, plus my favorite of the album, an almost forgotten song from Irving Berlin's *Annie Get Your Gun,* "I Got Lost in His Arms." In 1993, his album entitled *Perfectly Frank*, a tribute to Frank Sinatra, but in the Bennett mold, won a Grammy.

Speaking of Grammy's, Tony's 1994 Album *Tony Bennett: MTV Unplugged* won another Grammy. It was the biggest selling album of Tony's long career. It was actually nominated for three Grammy's, including Album of the Year. Tony was sixty-eight. "And, I did it without compromising my music," he said. In 1995, paying tribute to all the lady singers, Tony's album *Here's to the Ladies*, won another Grammy for Best Traditional Pop Album.

Up to 1999, Tony Bennett had won eight Grammy's. In 2003, another Grammy for *Playin' With My Friends*, composed of duets with B.B. King and Sheryl Crow. According to B.B. King, "To work with this man is a great highlight of my life. I've met two presidents and the Pope, Pavorotti - and now Tony Bennett."

Tony Bennett is another kind of artist, for you readers who do not know this. Tony is a portrait and landscape artist. He signs his works Benedetto and sells them all over the world, which is where he paints his subjects on canvas between shows and while on tour. I saw a handful of them at Westbury Music Fair where they were on display during a show he performed with Rosemary Clooney. They were mostly cityscapes and landscapes. From my interview with Tony one evening a few years later, I was able to write a piece for an art magazine about his art alone.

Bob Hope used to tell Tony some good advice: "Come out smiling, show the people you like them."

"To this day,, I still follow that rule. Some performers say they don't care if the audience likes them or not. With that philosophy, they should stay home."

Tony's kids, Danny, who brought his dad into the current scene via MTV, Daegal, a recording engineer and producer, Joanna, an actor and art designer, and Antonia, a graduate of the Berklee School in Boston, who is breaking into a singing career of her own, remain the true loves of his life. They have furnished him with some beautiful grandchildren. There exists a world famous Hirschfield cartoon depicting A Group of America's Great Artists. "There's Ella, Bing, Nat Cole, Fred Astaire, Judy Garland, and I'm in that group. I can't believe it, but it's true."

"When you first start painting, or doing anything, and it doesn't work out, you're devastated. But you keep painting. Then you're not bothered by your mistakes. You just say, 'The next time will be better.' That's what happens in life. That's why I wouldn't change anything, because I made mistakes, but those mistakes taught me how to live, and boy, am I living." Tony still tours and records today, 2010.

Tony had won his twelfth Grammy for Best Traditional Pop Album *A Wonderful World* performing duets with his long time singing partner and friend, k.d.Lang, that contain the many favorite standards he loves to sing. The album is dedicated to his cherished friend, the late Rosemary Clooney, featuring her own "Tenderly." Tony has long past the 50 million record sales mark, been honored by the Kennedy Center along with Robert Redford, Tina Turner, Julie Harris in 2005 by President and Mrs Bush.

Tony Bennett and his wife, Susan Crow, have founded the Frank Sinatra School of the Arts in Queens, New York, a public high school dedicated to the performing arts. It opened in 2001. This was Tony's way of honoring his friend Frank Sinatra, who once said of Tony:

"For my money, Tony Bennett is the best singer in the business. He excites me when I watch him. He moves me. He's the singer who gets across what the composer has in mind, and probably a little more."

Tony Bennett is 83 today and still singing. His 2010 UK tour will be a big year for the veteran, singing twenty-one of his favorites all over England. With 50 million records sold and fifteen Grammy awards and two Emmy's, Tony Bennett seems as though he may just be beginning instead of winding down.

MICHAEL FEINSTEIN

A Personal Reflection by Michael Feinstein

"I do research into the songs I perform because I like to know where the lyric came from and what led to the creation of the song. That may give me a little insight or a clue as to how to interpret it. Knowing the plot situation for which the song was created is sometimes helpful, although it can get in the way if it's a ridiculous plot. Frank Sinatra has had an instinct for being able to interpret lyrics as they were envisioned by each respective song writer. One of my favorite memories is of the night I first met him at Chasen's Restaurant in Los Angeles over 20 years ago. I'd been hired to play the piano for his wife Barbara's birthday party and accompany several of the guests in carefully prepared special material, and I was well aware of the importance of playing all the right songs and proper chords for the Chairman of the Board.

I prepared my selections exactingly and was gratified when he would cast glances at me as I struck up a particular song. Sometimes, to the delight of the other guests, he'd spontaneously sing a phrase or two.

When Barbara introduced me to her husband, the first thing out of his mouth was "Jesus, how do you know all of those songs? How old are you, 12?" I was, of course, delighted. Frank invited me to sit and talk, and we immediately began discussing songs and song-writers, and, eventually, his films.

The film *High Society* stands out for me as a personal favorite, due to the combined talents of Sinatra, Bing Crosby, and Louis Armstrong, as well as the pairing of Nelson Riddle with the resident M-G-M musical genius Conrad Salinger.

Cole Porter was delighted with the song interpretations, even commenting on Armstrong's diction. The crooner and the groaner seemed to bring out the best in each other.

I am left with a feeling of gratitude for Frank Sinatra's high

Sheldon Harnick, Michael Feinstein and Richard Grudens

standards, his passion for the lyrics he sings, and his natural talent. In other words, the short version of this tribute is...You're sensational, Mr. Sinatra. And that's all.

Author's comment: Michael Feinstein is a singer, songwriter, author, and a friend. Michael has recorded over 20 albums and appears at his Feinstein's at the Regency Night Club in New York where he frequently appears and sings the songs of the American Songbook.

The Johnny Green anecdotal Sinatra Story by Michael Feinstein: "Johnny Green and I were talking about Frank's work one day,and he launched into this terrible diatribe, explaining to me all the things that were wrong with Frank's singing; the vocal swoops, his penchant for interpolating words, and some other points. Sensing that there might have been a bit of tension between them, I asked,'You mean you don't like him?' Johnny just looked at me incredulously. "'No!' he exclaimed. 'I love him!'

Receiving Doctor of Music Award from Stanley Cohen, President of Five Towns Music College

Johnny Green was musical director at MGM during Frank Sinatra's heyday.

Sinatra And The Andrews Sisters

The Andrews girls, Patty, Maxine and LaVerne, worked with Frank Sinatra on their very first radio show called the Andrews Sisters Show sponsored by Nash autos and Kelvinator home appliances.

It debuted on New Year's Eve, 1944 and featured Frank Sinatra as the first guest. Frank also appeared on the March 4th show of that year. The story revolved around Frank rounding up some ruthless cattle rustlers. It also starred the curmudgeon character actor Gabby Hayes. After some comedic exchanges with the girls and Hayes Frank sang "Empty Saddles" with the singing group, Riders of the Purple Sage, and the girls.

The girls blended well with Sinatra, who was used to blending voices with singing groups like The Pied Pipers, so it all went off well. Somehow, the girls and Sinatra never made recordings together, which would have worked well. They sang together on radio and television, but never did get to

Maxine, Patty and LaVerne

making records together.

With a host of great performers that included Frank Sinatra and the girls, they appeared and sang together on February 15, 1945 for a Command Performance show entitled Dick Tracy in B-Flat, spoofing the famous comic strip character. Bing Crosby and Judy Garland were also on the show.

The Andrews Sisters would always swap appearances on their guests show, if they had one, of course. On Songs by Sinatra, Patty sang a duet with Frank on November 14, 1945. The song was "A Kiss Goodnight," then the girls followed with a swinging rendition of "Begin the Beguine."

I have been personal friends with Patty Andrews since 1980 when, after an interview, I wrote a few articles about her and wrote promotional material for her one-woman acts with the Tex Beneke orchestra and other venues. On her 91st birthday, my wife Madeline and I sent Patty a gift of flowers to help her celebrate the day with her devoted husband of over 60 years, Wally Weschler.

TONY BABINO

As a kid growing up in Brooklyn, it was the Bobby Darin recording of "Mack The Knife" that initially drew me to music. Like the lyric of the famous Sinatra tune, "All Or Nothing At All," I was "caught in the undertow." Soon I was mesmerized yet again by the unique legendary voice of the great Al Jolson. Back in the early 1960s, WOR television in New York played films several times a day on *The Million Dollar Movie*. As a kid, I watched *The Jolson Story* several times a day for a week straight. Larry Parks' portrayal of Jolson, along with his unmatched lip-synch performance to Jolson's voice made me an

Tony at the "Italia Mia" Luncheon, 2004 (M. Grudens Photo)

instant fan. I then began my quest to find Jolson records. Although he had passed away many years before, Jolson's recordings were still being sold in stores under the MCA label. After acquiring a few re-

cords, I began to learn the songs and spent countless hours singing along with the great Jolson.

Jolson was a "song-belter" most of his career, primarily because he was a Broadway stage performer at a time when microphones did not exist. Without the benefit of a mic, performers like Jolson had to rely solely on their vocal power to reach the back row of a theater. I and my wife Elayne have always believed that singing along to Jolson records and constantly belting out song after song, increased my lung capacity, and gave me the ability to become a "song belter" able to sing long phrases, and hold notes longer than other singers, much like Sinatra. Perhaps a bit unorthodox vocal training, but it was how I learned to sing.

Next, it was The Beatles. Amazingly, except for Sinatra, I pretty much discovered all of my musical influences during the same time period. The Beatles were, and remain, an amazing phenomenon…. writing, singing, and playing many of their own songs. I and the rest of the world were completely captivated. As with Jolson & Darin, I also sang along to all of their tunes. Since Paul McCartney sang in a higher range than I, it forced me to sing the high notes in my falsetto range. Having had no formal musical training, this actually became a vocal-stretching exercise for me, and eventually increased my range, strength and production ability.

By 1979 I really became a student of everything Sinatra. However, I was caught up with all my other musical tastes to really give Sinatra full attention. In 1979, the release of Sinatra's recording of "New York, New York" compelled me to buy the *Trilogy* album that featured songs from a different era…the past, present, and future. Songs from the past were arranged by Billy May; the *present* by Don Costa; and *future* by Gordon Jenkins. I can vividly recall my anticipation as I placed the needle on the grooves of the first track. What followed was a life changing experience. My ears were treated to an incredible Sinatra performance of "The Song Is You," accompanied by a driving Billy May arrangement. I was totally blown away, and have been a huge fan ever since.

By then I had to hear every recording I could possibly get my hands on. Capitol, Columbia, Reprise…I went down the line listening intently to every nuance, every breath, and every phrase. It was intense…and it was strikingly different than all of the other vocalists. After listening to recordings, reading books, watching movies, and having the opportunity to perform many times with Connie Haines (she was the girl singer with Frank in both the Tommy Dorsey and Harry James bands for over three years) I finally understood why Sinatra stood out from the rest of the pack.

Unlike anyone before him, Frank Sinatra had an ability to read the lyrics and clearly understand exactly what the songwriter was trying to convey. He tied those words together in long phrases that were unmatched, often imitated by his contemporaries, as well as those who followed. His unrivaled phrasing and diction were sheer perfection. Listen to his recordings of "Moonlight In Vermont" and "I Have Dreamed"...it simply doesn't get better than that. Mel Torme once said that Sinatra held the patent, the blueprint on singing the popular song, and I agree.

How did he do it? Marveling at how Tommy Dorsey was able to play long phrases on his

Top L-R: Richard Grudens, Remo Capra
Bottom L-R: Tony B., John Primerano - (M. Grudens Photo)

trombone, he decided that he wanted to use his voice similarly....like an instrument in the orchestra. In order to do that, he had to be able to hold those notes and stretch those long phrases. Sinatra always said that he accomplished this by swimming underwater while humming a song, that helped to increase his lung capacity. Whether he was swingin', singing a ballad, or a gut wrenching, emotional saloon song, no one could touch him.....he stood alone.

Frank Sinatra understood that the only way he could grow and create different sounds was to use different arrangers. Like a vocalist, every arranger has their own unique writing style, giving their charts a unique sound. Sinatra recognized this, and used it to his advantage. He recorded with Billy May, Nelson Riddle, Don Costa, Gordon Jenkins, and many more...the crème de la crème. He also created the concept album, and recorded one with Antonio Carlos Jobim. Sinatra was never afraid to record current songs, translating several rock and pop songs to fit his own style. In my own career, I have tried to emulate this to a degree. I have several wonderful arrangers with whom I work, and I always try to infuse my repertoire with modern day gems as well as classic songs from the Great American Songbook.

Choosing songs for repertoire is a trying process. Should you do a familiar song that's been done thousands of times? If it's a crowd pleaser, I say why not! However, you have to bring something new to it. Whether it's the musical or vocal arrangement, it's got to be fresh and do justice to the original. I love having new arrangements written, especially by musicians like Richie Iacona or Dave Gross, because they always write a chart for me that breathes new life into the song, and makes it my own. Their arrangements aren't busy…. and they breathe. In other words, the orchestra (especially trumpets, saxes, and trombones) aren't constantly playing lines, and never step on the vocalist and vice versa. I'm not really big on having transcriptions of other peoples charts written for me when I'm doing a song in my own show. Generally, I try to choose songs that the audience will enjoy. I also enjoy searching for obscure tunes that I think should be dusted off and given new life. We did that with "I Gotta Get Back to New York," which was a terrific Rodgers and Hart song that Jolson introduced in the film *Hallelujah I'm A Bum*, and then it kind of fell through the cracks. It remains one of my favorite tracks on my first album.

Putting a solid show together involves song selection, great arrangements, and the writing of interesting patter that allows for smooth transitions from song to song….thereby creating a seamless flow. When I'm preparing for a show, I go through a few rituals beforehand. Like most entertainers, I have my little superstitions and traditions that I follow before I go on stage, which is prefaced by warming up with various vocal exercises. I never walk on to the stage without saying a little prayer and thanking the Good Lord for allowing me the opportunity and good fortune to be able to do what I so very much love doing….singing for people.

One thing I've learned from Sinatra is that some songs, more than others, have the ability to touch people. Recently, I've had the wonderful good fortune to experience that with my original song "Fifty

Years." It's a beautiful song that I wrote for my grandparents when they celebrated their 50th wedding anniversary. Disc jockey Paul Richards, of WHLI radio on Long Island began playing the song on his show, and soon it became the most requested song on the station. I know that my grandparents, God rest their souls, would've been extremely touched and proud to know that the song I wrote for them was being enjoyed by so many others.

Another tune that is near and dear to my heart is one I wrote in tribute to Frank several years before he passed away. The tune, "I Wish I Could Sing Like Sinatra" was my homage to Mr. Sinatra, a true thank you note from me as a fan, a performer, for all that he meant to me. I was glad he was able to hear it a few times, and honored that

"I Wish I Could Sing Like Sinatra"

When I sing a love song
When the band strikes each chord
There is only one singer
I wish I could sing like.....
He's the chairman of the board

I wish I could sing like Sinatra
Make each word seem to,
Jump right off the page
I'd tell a story about two lovers
Caught in a tender trap
Aah they better watch out,
They never know when Mack-ie is
back ....in town

Wrap my arms 'round each lyric
And caress it, I'd finesse it
With each new phrase, you can hear it
It's such bliss
I'd be flyin' to the moon
On a warm summer wind in June
If I could sing like Francis Albert S.

Don't wanna sing like Connick,
Not Martin or Davis or Vale
I don't wanna sing like Crosby,
That kind of style is stale
But if swing is the thing,

Sinatra's the king
I gotta swing like that man, that man

I wish I could sing like Sinatra
With a song in my heart,
From the start it would be such a thrill
Singin' songs his way or mine,
I'd keep singin' through rain or shine
I wish that I could sing like Frank

(Orchestra Interlude)

Don't wanna sing like Connick,
Not Martin or Davis or Vale
I don't wanna sing like Crosby,
That kind of style is stale
But if swing is the thing,
Sinatra's the king
I gotta swing like that man, that man

I wish I could sing like Sinatra
With a song in my heart,
from the start I'd be king of the hill
If Chicago lets me down
Old New York's my kind of town
I wish that I could sing like
Nobody else can swing like
I wish that I could sing..... like Frank

he enjoyed it. Over the past few years, the song has been used by numerous Sinatra tribute radio shows, and was also the centerpiece of a hit show in Atlantic City.

I Wish I Could Sing Like Sinatra

Words and Music by: Tony Babino
Arranged by: Richie Iacona

The most important thing I've learned about being on stage came from my dear friend Connie Haines. One night after our show, I asked her if she could give me some advice. In her best Georgia accent, she said "Honey….when you walk out on that stage, you just be a real person….'cause the audience knows when you're fakin' it". And…that's all I've tried to do ever since.

If I've learned anything from Sinatra besides the obvious, it's that you've got to appreciate all that you have, and never take anything for granted. Every once in a while, stop, take a good look around, and enjoy. A good song is like a good friend…so treat it that way. Give it the respect that it deserves. Treat it with passion….caress and finesse the lyrics…and always acknowledge the songwriter and arranger. Finally….like Sinatra, and Jolson before him, make love to the audience. It's reciprocal.

VIC DAMONE

Steve Lawrence and Vic Damone at Frank Sinatra's 75th Birthday Party

Vito Rocco Farinola, known to all as Vic Damone - the guy who Frank Sinatra claimed, "...has the best set of pipes in the business," is celebrating 63 years in the singing business in 2010, twelve years after he performed at a sold-out, one-man Carnegie Hall concert on January 24, 1998. Afterwards, his publicist Rob Wilcox told me the show was a terrific success.

Vic worked as an usher at the New York Paramount Theater when he was a kid and became influenced by Frank Sinatra. Vic's voice, although clear as a bell, was similar to Sinatra's style and voice tone in his early period, especially on his 1946 radio air-checks "You Go to My Head" and "All Through the Day," Sinatra style songs Vic performed on New York's WHN station."

"Most songs have been recorded by Frank Sinatra," Vic said, "but you have to try to give them a new interpretation." Vic cheerfully admits the emulation was deliberate at the time, "I tried to mimic him. My training, my learning process was watching performers onstage. I decided that if I could sound like Frank, maybe I did have a chance." At sixteen,while working at the New York Paramount as an usher, with a hopeful heart to one day become a singer like those, like Sinatra, who occupied the great stage and sang to thousands of fans. At one point during a concert, Tommy Dorsey fired one of his singers, and Vic thought he had a chance. He approached Dorsey's road manager Nick Savano and asked to have Dorsey allow him an audition to replace the freshly- fired vocalist.

"Listen, kid, Dorsey only holds auditions by listening to a recording. There was a nearby studio called Nola Studios where many of the bands rehearsed and recorded. "But it cost five dollars and I didn't have five dollars, so that was out for me."

Years later, when I stopped in a Dorsey rehearsal, I saw Nick Savano and asked him if he remembered me and the day I wanted Dorsey to hear me. He said he didn't. But he told Dorsey about it at that moment, but I had already reached success, and after Dorsey found out who I was, said to his manager, 'Why didn't you let him sing for me?'"

When Vic got to know Sinatra, who became his mentor, although Sinatra didn't know it, Vic listened and learned from some very important points from him.

"'Enunciate clearly, make every word of the song distinct, emphatic and unmistakably perfect.' He told me to use my emotional memory and provide a good story, using the emotionally experienced moments of my life. 'Use that approach, revert back and live that special moment,' he said.' Take the songs "Sometimes I'm Happy," and those great tunes from the Broadway show Kismet, for example."

For me, Vic Damone's most appealing recording was "You're Breaking My Heart," which will always be his song as Tony Bennett's is "I Left My Heart in San Francisco." Vic, of course, did not come up with the Big Bands, but he appeared in a movie, The Strip, with the great Louis Armstrong, trombonist Jack Teagarden, and genius pianist Earl Hines. In the 1955 film *Hit the Deck* , Vic sang Vincent Youmans' wonderful song "Sometimes I'm Happy," and arranger/conductor Percy Faith directed Vic singing "An Affair To Remember," the title song from the 1957 hit movie. The recording enjoyed a tremendous success.

Vic sometimes avoids those old tunes in his current work, but always does Lerner and Loewe's classic "On The Street Where You Live," from *My Fair Lady*, for my money the definitive recording of that song. Vic also toured with Bob Hope's USO troupe at Chu Lai, Vietnam in 1966.

Vic was responsible for discovering the prolific songwriter, arranger, composer and musical director John Williams of *Star Wars* fame. He was the third piano player tryout for Damone after firing Burt Bacharach, who would not provide Vic with an audible intro chord he could hear, and accordingly would not accommodate Vic during concerts and appearances. The first two were inadequate, but the third guy played well, and was able to arrange and conduct, so Vic hired *John Williams* who remained with Vic for four years. John, of course, did well in Hollywood and later as conductor for the sensational Boston Pops.

"Back in the early days I always told John to 'keep it simple' and when we met many years later at a concert, he said, 'Vic, I still keep it simple, and it has always worked well for me.' Thanks!'" Vic kinda retired for a while then appeared back on the scene in the early eighties, mostly because of a renaissance he enjoyed in England. It seems a DJ, BBC's David Jacobs, gave Vic a lot of play, especially on his 1961 album *The Pleasure of Her Company*. Vic toured the British Isles to standing room audiences during the eighties.

"When he walked on stage, before he sang a note, he received a standing ovation every time, everywhere," wrote Denis Brown of The Dick Haymes Society in a society newsletter. In 1996, twenty-five of Vic's Mercury Recordings were reissued under the title, *The Mercury Years*.

Vic Damone appeared on stage as Sky Masterson at Westbury Music Fair in a revival of the 1940's Broadway musical Guys and Dolls. Over the years he has performed regularly at Michael's Pub and Rainbow and Stars in New York, and in important venues in Las Vegas and Atlantic City.

Peggy lee, Vic Damone and Lena Horne

Some one once said Vic Damone hates show business, "But, I'm never tired of singing," he says emphatically. Luckily, Reader's Digest had issued The Legendary Vic Damone quality CD with 30 new and 30 old recordings.

Vic sings with snapping fingers, bobbing his head and tilting his shoulders, savoring each syllable, singing in a rich, conversational baritone that's still robust and romantic. A true Italian troubadour.

He is never full of anxiety when he is about to perform, which he owes to his keeping in top physical condition and being always prepared. He never smoked which keeps his breathing strong to meet those high and lengthy notes. He once took Kung Fu lessons from non-other than Bruce Lee himself to help strengthen his vocal cords and his breathing ability. Vic also keeps his spirituality in tune following Bahai, emphasizing the spiritual unity of all humankind.

Vic's "Farewell Performance" on February 10, 2001 at the Kravis Center for the Performing Arts in West Palm Beach, Florida, backed by a 60 piece orchestra, was a night to remember. As Yogi Berra is fond of saying, "it's deja vu all over again."

Vic plans a concert on January 22nd, 2011 at the famed Kravis Center once again with a full orchestra, "Be the Good Lord willing," Vic said this day, April 23, 2010, when we last talked. He is counting the days and getting ready.

Vic with his wife Rena Rowan

Vic Damone lives in Florida now with his caring wife Rena Rowan-Damone, a former designer at Jones, New York, and who heads philanthropic foundations to help various charities.

JOHNNY MATHIS
The Voice of Romance

Like Frankie Laine, Perry Como, Tony Bennett, Jerry Vale, and Guy Mitchell, Johnny Mathis never sang with the big bands. Take his interpretation of just these four songs alone: "Chances Are," "A Certain Smile," "Wonderful, Wonderful," and "It's Not for Me to Say," and you have a singing career solidly constructed through Johnny's incomparable phrasing and articulation, not to mention a brilliant microphone technique reminiscent of the early singing innovators Bing Crosby and Frank Sinatra.

On a warm January day Johnny Mathis and I sat around his great indoor pool in the Hollywood Hills in Los Angeles, California, in a clearly Southwestern garnished room filled with exotic palms, totems, and cactuses growing in large baskets, among rattan chairs and soft, wide couches, under a high, box-framed glass ceiling. It has been his home for over 30 years.

"Welcome to my home, Richard, I hope you love it here as much as I do!" Johnny had just returned from a three-day engagement in Clearwater, Florida. We had been trying to get together for a few months.

No secret, Billboard charts have established Johnny as a world-class romantic singer who has prevailed over 40 years. By some accounts, Johnny Mathis is second only to Frank Sinatra as the most consistently charted albums artist. His Greatest Hits spent 490 weeks - count them: nine-and-a-half consistent years on the charts. Johnny Royce Mathis owes a lot to his dad, Clem Mathis, who fostered his son's career from the time he was a small boy living with his large family in a San Francisco basement apartment. "I learned an appreciation of music from my father who taught me my first songs. He had worked in vaudeville back in the 1920s, and always encouraged me and my sisters and brothers to sing."

When Johnny was only 13, his father, realizing his son's exceptional singing ability, took him to see a Bay area voice teacher, Connie Fox, who taught him vocal scales and exercises, voice production, and some operatic skills. "I paid for these lessons by working around Miss Fox's home doing odd jobs, and what little time we had together was very precious and very special. We concentrated mainly on voice production. I tried to take more theory, harmony, and piano, but I had so much going on with my athletics. Connie told me that if I learned to produce my tones properly (precise use of diaphragm and vocal chords, and accurate breathing techniques) that I'd probably sing as long as I wanted to. If I ever had an advantage, it was that I learned to sing correctly right from the start so I didn't get sick all the time. Over the years, I probably canceled only two or three performances.

Unlike his hero, Nat King Cole, the whole singing experience did not come natural to Mathis. "The sound that I have did come naturally, I mean God gives us these little gifts, but Nat, Sarah, Frank, and Ella --people like that -- they never studied voice in their lives. Johnny admits he never tried to be different; "I actually tried to copy all the other singers. Nat Cole was my big hero and I think the best singer of all of them. I listened to his music over and over again. Then I listened to Frank Sinatra, Billy Eckstine and Sammy Davis, and then I took all the girl singers like Ella, Peggy Lee, and Lena, of course, and I tried to emulate the high, soft singing that they did. The women have a very flexible sound. I have the advantage of having a big register so I could sing a lot of high and middle range and low notes." "You mean --like in Maria - the closing notes of that song?" I said. "Exactly -- that's amazing that you picked that up...that night after night, year after year, I can still sing that delicate, little high note. One Sunday afternoon, while singing weekends at the BlackHawk night club, Johnny was spotted by the club's co-owner Helen Noga, who promptly took charge of Johnny's career and who asked Columbia Jazz A & R man George Avakian, who was in the area on vacation, to come to hear Johnny sing at Ann Dee's 440 Club, where she had just booked him.

After listening, Avakian quickly sent this now famous telegram to his record company: "Have found phenomenal 19-year old boy who could go all the way. Send blank contracts."

I guess you would have to say Johnny Mathis is mostly a romantic ballad singer, although he manages to make Christmas carols sound magical, the way they should be interpreted. Nevertheless, he was booked into jazz oriented New York's Blue Angel, Basin Street, and the Village Vanguard. Then, fortunately, Johnny was placed under the management of Columbia's Mitch Miller, who told him to avoid jazz and record pop records. Miller's magic was at work once again. He found "Wonderful, Wonderful" and It's "Not for Me to Say" for the young balladeer.

"The first time I heard my recording of "Wonderful, Wonderful" on the radio, I knew I would become a singer for the rest of my life. I had made the recording about a year before and they took a long time to release it. I had played it myself on my own phonograph, but it wasn't magical until I heard it played on the radio."

"Were you surprised by the phenomenal success of that re-cording?" "I was flabbergasted. To this day I am still in awe. I cannot believe that I've had this career, because I did not plan anything." Although Mitch Miller, Artists and Repertoire man at Columbia Re-cords was often trashed by music critics, I have maintained over and over that he constructed a stable foundation for many of the after Big Band Era non-jazz singers like Frankie Laine, Tony Bennett, Rose-mary Clooney, Guy Mitchell, Jerry Vale, as the antidote to the rock and roll music of the time. He helped them establish their careers. "When Johnny chooses a song for a recording, he sets priorities: "The first thing I hear, which is probably what most people hear, is a melody. If it has a pretty melody, I love it. And then, of course, I have to have some literate lyrics."

Those two songs were followed by "Chances Are," a monu-mental hit of its own, and the most requested song at his concerts right up to today. It was Johnny's first # 1 hit. Another great tune, "The Twelfth of Never," made it big in 1957.

Johnny's rapid vibrato imparted a sentimental, bittersweet quality to that type of love song. He mesmerized his generation. In 1978, Deniece Williams and Johnny recorded a duet album that included the single "Too Much, Too Little, Too Late," that reached number one in 1978, in a time made difficult for balladeers to infiltrate the singles charts, and with his friend Dionne Warwick, he recorded "Friends In Love" that made the Top 40.

When you add it all up, it must be realized that Johnny Mathis' incredible commercial recording success ranked third, just behind Frank Sinatra and Elvis Presley. "I've always been proud of my two Grammy nominations, for "Misty" in 1960 and my album *Salute to the great Duke Ellington* in 1992."

When Johnny prepares for a concert: "I make sure that I can sing everything that I have to sing on stage. That gives me the con-fidence I need. There's no one in the world who had less confidence than I did- - I didn't like the way I looked or acted or sang, I was shy and wasn't in command."

Johnny Mathis keeps going strong. What's his secret? I believe it's his consistency to purpose, uncompromising professionalism, great organization, and lots and lots of hard work. "And I really take good care of myself these days. I watch my diet and quit drinking alcohol some time ago. I work out five times a week, and the whole process has actually strengthened my voice. At this point in my life I am really excited to see just how long I can sing at a level that I'm comfortable with. I think I'll be the first one to know when I no longer sound good. Then I'll quit. I'm very careful. I stretch out my performances, and do no more than three days in a row and then I come home for two to three weeks and rest up, play golf, and visit with my friends."

On April 19, of this year 2010, Johnny appeared in Clearwater, Florida, at Ruth Eckard Hall, and it was one of the best concerts ever, according to some observers. The house was sold out and Johnny sang practically his entire repertoire from "Chances Are," to "Misty." They say his voice was smooth and strong. It has been since he started. It looks like he and Tony Bennett are keeping the songs coming at you like always.

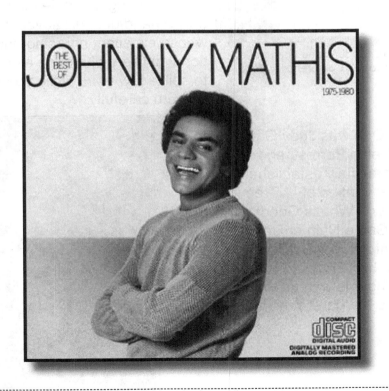

MARGARET WHITING
KAY STARR AND GIA PRIMA

During our lifetime, there have been dozens of songwriters who have written many wonderful songs but there have been very few singers who have been able to interpret those musical masterpieces to perfection.

Richard Grudens and Margaret at the Al Jolson Conference in 2005

Among the boys, of course there was our own powerful performer in Al Jolson, followed closely by an easy-going feller named Bing Crosby. And then came the perfect song interpretations of Frank Sinatra.

Among the ladies there were only a handful of great vocalists whose excellent phrasing and emotional delivery of a song allowed you to spill a few tears while you listened to them carefully.

One was Judy Garland, another Helen Forrest, and my favorite, who beautifully established standards with her version of "A Tree in the Meadow," "What's Good About Goodbye," "Come Rain or Come Shine," "It Might As Well Be Spring," and her first big hit, "That Old Black Magic," That singer is with us today and her name is Margaret Whiting.

Louis and Gia Prima with Frank Sinatra

GIA PRIMA

The wife of the great Louis Prima speaks about Sinatra.

"This is short, but very to the point. "In my opinion only two performers were possessed of, or by, Magic. "An aura of fiery dust exuded from them and directly into the audience and transported that audience to a magic kingdom usually experienced only in the minds of children.

"A blissful state of euphoria for certain. "The first being my husband Louis Prima, and the second being Frank Sinatra. "These two men stand alone among all others."

KAY STARR
"YOU CAN FEEL THE MEMORIES STARTING"

When she recorded those very sweet Glenn Miller evergreens, "Love with a Capital You." and "Baby Me," Kay Starr emitted a light and fluffy female delivery. She was just a mere fifteen then and had recorded these two sides for the Miller band because their regular girl singer, Marion Hutton, was ill. It wasn't the "Wheel Of Fortune" Kay

Starr you would easily recognize, it was the pre-Charlie Barnet- who-would-change-her voice-forever-era Kay Starr, but it was definitely the best female vocalizing ever heard on a Miller recording, although there were only a few recognizable traces of the legendary vocalist we all know so well.

"Yes, then much later when I was fourteen, I went with Joe Venuti and was with him every summer ' til I was sixteen...then briefly with Glenn Miller where I made those two recordings.

"My voice was so different."

Richard Grudens: I learned somewhere that you had (voice) trouble when you were with Charlie Barnet."

"I did, after singing for three years with Charlie, and you're singing over George Siravo's arrangements, you can bet that it affected my throat. It actually ruined my voice temporarily.......a lot of people said that it made me sound different....the keys didn't change, so....I don't know."

It took her a year to recover and: "I started with piano and they let me add bass after many weeks then drums with no sticks, just brushes, for more weeks and it took me all that time before I was able to sing with a full-blown band again. I had to learn everything all over again like having to walk from a crawl.

"Charlie would say, 'So your throat's bad. So what...sing anyway." ...and I listened to him like an idiot."

"She sang over, around and under colds the whole time she was with Barnet: "But then I finally developed a sort of pneumonia and was on the verge of (throat) polyps, and I'm sort of a frontier woman, I don't get sick easily or stay sick very long and it was not my nature to faint, but I did for the first and only time in my life. Even on those Miller recordings you just mentioned, I wanted to make those records so badly that I sang above my key.

"Some say that after all that throat trouble I developed a huskier, throaty voice, which is really my trade mark, the sound that unmistakably identifies me.

"Well, maybe...." She gives in a little..... "maybe I just grew up." Of all the familiar, successful songs she recorded with Capitol during her career, including "Side-By-Side," "Bonaparte's Retreat," "Angry," and her golden "Wheel Of Fortune," she names the latter as her favorite and claims never to get tired of singing it. "When I think I'm wearied of it, and I wonder, Oh, maybe people are tired of it. But what happens is, every time I start to sing it, somebody reaches over and touches somebody next to them, or they just smile, and you can just feel the memories starting, you know, and you can't deny that's what it's all about."

"It was like the marriage between Tony Bennett and 'I Left My Heart In San Francisco' and Frankie Laine with 'I Believe.'

"Well, actually a singer is no more than an actor or actress set to music, because you are only as good as the story you tell and people like to hear things they can identify with, and that's the story."

About Frank Sinatra: "His long breath technique was the single most essential element of his artistry. Tell a story, as I have always said, "The most expressive way possible get listeners to believe. A singer must also be a dramatic actor. Someone like Sinatra has lived much of what he sings about so he has experienced the emotions and sad transfers the emotions to the band to swing or any other inspiration needed to promote the song Sinatra style."

CAROL KIDD

FRANK SINATRA AT IBROX STADIUM IN GLASGOW: "Carol Kidd is the best kept secret of British Jazz," after she opened for him before the concert. Almost immediately she was invited to appear at the acclaimed Ronnie Scott's Club in London and has been an icon herself ever since.

"I have hero-worshiped Frank Sinatra all my life, his voice, his diction, vocal integrity - his "honesty" in delivering the story of song. the mischief in his gorgeous blue eyes and the way he made you believe every word of the song.

"You can imagine how I felt when I was asked, personally, through his people to my people, if I would open his stadium concert at Ibrox Football Stadium in Glasgow, Scotland, my home town in 1991. I truly thought someone was playing a joke on me.

"Frank Sinatra was performing in London at the time and had requested my albums to be sent to him. It seems he said after listening to the recordings "Book her!"

"I arrived at Ibrox just in time for Frank's rehearsal. He was dressed in a black satin bomber jacket with the word "GUV" on the back ---the rehearsal for him was a chat with the band and a sound check of about 3 minutes.

"I was delighted but filled with trepidation when I was taken to meet him. Frank's dresser was straightening his bow tie and I mumbled something, but don't remember what was. I was in awe of this Icon, so I beat a hasty retreat and as I left he gave me the most beautiful wink and thumbs up.

"I was taken to start the show into a room adjacent to the stage and there on a little table was a pack of Camels cigarettes with one cigarette placed sitting out of the pack with a gold lighter beside it and a bottle of Jack Daniel's - for Mr. Sinatra, of course!

"I sang my heart out, full of pride and dignity, to 25,000 in my home city and loved every minute of it. There I was on the same stage as the man himself. When I finished my 45 minute set of mostly Frank Sinatra related songs - who, by the way had asked for my set list and did not ask for any changes to be made, I walked into the marguee as Frank was passing me to go on stage and the words from him were exactly this: "Carol Kidd is the best kept secret in British jazz!!"

"There are singers out there who try to imitate Frank Sinatra but like all the greats there will only be one, and as far as I'm concerned he was the best. He was the one. I can't say I ever "Learned" to sing it was something which came naturally.

"I've been singing since my early childhood, my mother told me I sang all the time, nursery rhymes and as I got older songs from the radio but my mother was an avid American musicals fan and she took me to see all the films so much so that I could hear the orchestration in my head every time I sang-----singing in tune is a given thing that I seem to have inbuilt and diction has always been very important to me----the story in the song just brings out the emotion needed to relate to an audience.

"I usually rehearse with my guitarist then take it to my piano player and we then work out the routine, keys,beginnings and endings.

"Making my albums really works in the same way ---I choose the songs I want to do and the rest is rehearsing them to find the right groove or tempo. I love performing live, I am a talker and love the interaction with a live audience. I try to make my concerts both funny and reflective."

BRUCE SPRINGSTEEN

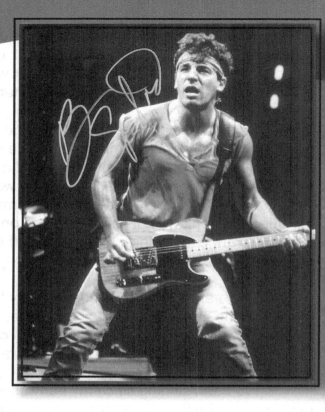

From one New Jersey born performer to another, Bruce Springsteen recalls:

"My first recollection of Frank's voice was coming out of a jukebox in a dark bar on a Sunday afternoon, when my mother and I went searching for my father. He was singing 'Angel Eyes.' And I remember my mother saying, 'Bruce, listen to that, that's Frank Sinatra. He's from New Jersey, too!'

"It was a voice filled with bad attitude, life itself, beauty excitement, a nasty sense of freedom, sex, and a sad knowledge of the ways of the world. Every song seemed to have as its postscript --- 'And if you don't like it, here's a punch in the kisser.'

"But, again, it was the deep blueness of Frank's voice that affected me the most, and, while his music became synonymous with black tie, good life, the best booze, women, sophistication, his blues voice was always the sound of hard luck and men late at night with the last ten dollars in their pockets trying to figure a way out. On behalf of all New Jersey I am happy to state to the memory of Frank Sinatra: Hail, brother, you sang out your soul."

Springsteen had met Sinatra at Sinatra's house in Beverly

Hills in early 1995. According to John Lahr of the New Yorker Magazine written in 1997, the guests performed for the Sinatra's including musical expressions from the talents of Steve and Eydie, Bob Dylan, Springsteen's wife, Patti Scialfa, and others. They gathered around the piano and collectively began to sing "Guess I'll Hang My Tears Out to Dry."

"Hold it!" Sinatra held up his hands, "You know I sing solo!" He finished the song alone.

PAT BOONE

As my career was just getting underway, and I had had several rock and roll hits, the word filtered back to me that Frank Sinatra had announced, "Pat Boone is the new Great White Hope." Later, some national magazines quoted both Bing and Frank with the same opinion.

This is not racist in any way, of course. It was part of their mutual concern that rock and roll, and loud, noisy music sung by non singers, was going to take over the industry. Frank explained that he heard in me a singer who could do rock and roll, but also sing meaningful lyrics and nice ballads. You can imagine what those words of commendation meant to a young kid from Nashville who was just starting to feel his way into the music scene.

Later, when I got to know both Frank and Bing on a first name basis, Frank and I laughed about our early days on the *Ted Mack Amateur Hour* as contestants. Actually, Frank was on the earlier incarnation of the original "American Idol" show, which was then called the *Major Bowes Amateur Hour*. Eventually, Ted Mack took it over and it bore his name. Still, we had both been anxious, starry-eyed young kids looking for a break, an entree' into the music business, and national amateur shows opened the door for us.

I always felt that Frank had a paternal feeling towards me,

and I welcomed it warmly. And his matchless singing certainly had an influence on my efforts, especially when I stood in front of a big orchestra and sang a great ballad or an exciting swing tune. Nobody ever generated more genuine excitement as a pop singer, no matter what he sang.

Well-perhaps I shouldn't mention his one effort into rock and roll, "Mama Will Bark" with Dagmar. I'm told Frank actually tried to buy up every record in the country and destroy them. He never got the hang of rock and roll.

TOM POSTILIO

History repeats itself. There is nothing new under the sun. What goes around-comes around, and lots of other clichés you have heard many time before.

However, this is a story of dyed-in-the-wool winner (another cliché) by the name of Tom Postilio-who, like Frank Sinatra, lives and works in the limelight under his own name. Tom Postilio was twenty-five when we first met and had already appeared at the fabled Village Gate and the 88's and the Rainbow Room in Rockefeller Center, and had a run in 1995 at the prestigious Tavern-on-the- Green, all in New York.

During the the following year Tom toured with Larry O'Brien and the World Famous Glenn Miller Orchestra for nine months. His first album *What Matters Most* featured shades of Frank Sinatra, Tom's first musical hero. Tom first fell in love with his dad's archived Frank Sinatra albums when he was but thirteen. Frank Sinatra inadvertently became his teacher and mentor. At the time some had told him not to emulate Old Blue Eyes too much, that it may be a dangerous career road, but rather to find his own niche in both voice and delivery. The only direct Sinatra song in the album is "Let's Get Away from it All."

Tom was completely committed to the music of the big bands and dedicated to the standards of Berlin, Porter, Rodgers and Hammerstein and Jerome Kern, to name a few. Meeting Tom, at the time, was like meeting the young Sinatra. Tom is charismatic like Sinatra and better looking at his age.

Tony Bennett and Tom Postilio (T. Postilio Photo

"It was hard to find song selections that Sinatra didn't record. I really tried hard not to choose selections for which he was famous. I didn't want to be another Sinatra.

Larry O'Brien told me that Tom couldn't help sounding Sinatra on certain tunes, especially on Billy Joel's "Just the Way You Are," when he was on tour with the Glenn Miller band. Tom had taken three years of voice to learn the right way to vocalize. When he finds the time, tom will opt for musical checkups.

Tom with Jerry Vale

Tom Postilio is one of the new generation of singers, an antidote to the mostly incoherent Top 40 products. He's in a class with Michael Feinstein and Harry Connick, Jr., as well as Lou Lanza of Philadelphia and the emerging Michael Bublé, who also sings Sinatra -style.

REVISITED -2009

Now, Tom Postilio goes on more relaxed in his regular gigs

Tom with Richard Grudens

like Vegas and Atlantic City. "One of the natural hazards of the business is getting a little nervous before performances. They say it happens to everyone. You do pick up extra energy - I go through jumping jacks to get the blood flowing."

Tom once met Frank Sinatra his distinct idol and inspiration. "I really didn't meet him. It was that I shook his hand for two seconds. But it was kind of a weird, incredible feeling...like touching God! It was at Carnegie Hall in 1987. I couldn't believe his hand was so small...I don't know, it seemed unusual.

"I love the word *crooner*. It's so evocative of that era with its great music and all the people who are my heroes. Sometimes I even think I don't belong in this age; that I should have been around 40-50 years ago when pop music was music and not just noise as it is today."

Tom, with his fourteen piece orchestra and his Sinatra-like voice, can be found performing and singing at the Rainbow Room on the 65th floor of Rockefeller Center above the NBC studios.

with Rosemary Clooney

NICK HILSCHER

Though Frank Sinatra was known and respected in the world of entertainment, the most important influence he had on my singing was his great musicianship. Sinatra would approach a lyric as if he were talking to his listener. His enunciation was impeccable. Every word understandable. His breathing and phrasing sounded natural, although his phrases could be extremely long and his taking a breath was never heard, and there was that beautiful tone and pitch that never missed.

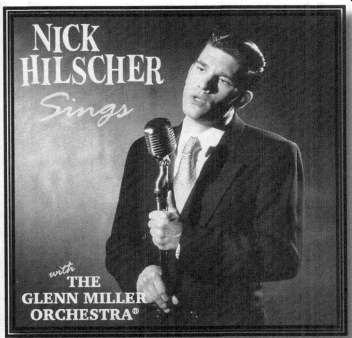

The development of Frank Sinatra's singing style throughout his career was fascinating. If one has only been exposed to the Sinatra of the 1960s and 70s, and then hears one of Frank's earlier recordings with Tommy Dorsey, the listener will not easily identify the singer. Sinatra's voice sounded so pure and innocent at that time. Yet, that's the voice that most fits the style of a that era's big band singer. During my days singing with the Glenn Miller Orchestra, I would approach ballad singing in the same way, due to the influence of the *Voice*. Recently, when I have toured with the Tommy Dorsey Orchestra, I have been able to use this same technique when approaching the songs "I'll Never Smile Again" and "Daybreak," among others.

As Sinatra's recording career took a turn in the early 1950s, his singing style developed into the rich, dark, mature sound that most of us identify as being his. This is the era, the '50s and 60s that had the most influence on my singing. I would sit for hours listening to the concept albums that were recorded in that period. The maturity of Sinatra's voice and overall approach to the music surfaces beautifully in such albums as *Where Are You*?, *Only the Lonely*, *Nice N' Easy* and *Point of No Return*. These albums are filled with lovely ballads and torch songs that any serious singer desiring to sing the American Songbook needs to study and master. Then there are the albums where Frank shows his other side: the up-tempo singer, supported by the best big bands and arrangers of that period; Billy May's *Come Fly with Me*, Nelson Riddle's *Songs for Swingin' Lovers*, and Sy Oliver's *I Remember Tommy* are a few examples, and I could list a dozen more. It cannot be stressed too much as to how these recordings have influenced my own approach to this style of music.

Kevin Sheehan, Julia Rich and Nick Hilscher

It's a good idea as an artist not to mimic or try to become a complete recreation of another artist. But it is a good idea to study and learn from the great singers of the past. Frank Sinatra tops that list. I am appreciative that someone introduced his music to me and his artistry at an early age. I have learned so much from him, and still learning even today.

JULIA RICH

Frank Sinatra became a voice for me in the 1960s via "Strangers in the Night," "Somethin' Stupid," and "It Was a Very Good Year." I heard those songs on the radio alongside what I really sought: Beatles music. I recall Dean Martin on his variety show, incredulous over Frank's "doo-be-doo-be-doo" ending on "Strangers."

In the '70s, college mentor Margaret Wright answered my "What do you think of Frank Sinatra?" with "he's a pretty good pop singer." Her husband Neil, also a band singer, and later, head of the music department at Middle Tennessee State University, was at the Vanderbilt with Dinah shore. In the early '80s, I watched Joe Piscopo mock "the old man" on *Saturday Night Live*. Then I joined the Miller band and discovered Frank Sinatra as trinity: party of one.

When I became the girl singer with the world famous Glenn Miller Orchestra in 1985, Joe Francis was the boy singer (which spoiled me for life). A dashing chap with a golden voice, Joe has a little Sinatra and a bit of Crosby; but he is mostly Joe. Likewise, GMO singers Nick Hilscher and Bryan Anthony can "do" Sinatra with the best of them, but they've drawn from many wells to cultivate their own styles. However, certain of the myriad number--I stopped counting at twenty-one--who've filled the boy singer chair during my tenure with the GMO introduced me to the "Sinatra clone" phenomenon.

For them, tackling the Great American Songbook starts and stops with Frank. These devotees never consult a lead sheet for the actual melody and lyrics to songs such as "Come Fly With Me," "I've Got You Under My Skin," or "The Lady is a Tramp." They sing the Gospel according to Frank: his licks, his alternate lyrics, his endings. Pass the Fedora!

To give the boys a break, I will allow that audiences love a guy who can bring forth Frank. Sinatra draws the applause. I once lamented the fact that no matter how I try, I will never look and sound like a young Frank Sinatra. I'm not sure who the girl singer is supposed to represent; but I do not see many filling the pumps of Ella (Fitzgerald), Sarah (Vaughan), June (Christy), or Helen (Forrest).

The carbon copy approach not only halts the ripening of today's male vocalists into unique artists but also distorts the brilliance of the man who studied Tommy Dorsey for his phrasing. We forget that Frank Sinatra had a beautiful voice. Larry O'Brien, my bandleader and comrade for twenty years, made sure I heard *Sinatra and Strings* and the *Wee Small Hours* albums. Sinatra, by the way, is quoted as calling Larry the guy who could play Tommy Dorsey's solos after Tommy died. But the trend is pervasive, and one finds current artists including Frank's version of Frank's arrangement of a Sinatra tune on their recordings, without credit to the source. With Elvis impersonators, at least you get the jumpsuit.

Here's how I feel about Frank's singing during the period that made him Sinatra and gave good reason for imitation: When Sinatra sings, he opens the door to his home and invites you in. He hands you a drink, calls for the hot hors d'oeuvre tray, and walks you toward the fireplace. Everything is there! No one tells so true a story, effortlessly and yet with such authority. When he swings, you want to throw up your hands and testify. When he croons, you see the players like in a movie.

Some artists cannot be trumped. We will never see the Beatles again, and there will never be another Frank Sinatra. Thanks to multimedia, we still have both. And, as far as I'm concerned, there ain't nothin' like the real thing!

Julia Rich- February 2010

JERRY COSTANZO

I learned to sing by listening. The great American standards were always playing at my house. It was the background music of my youth. As a matter of fact, when traveling in the car with my parents, we were not allowed to listen to rock and roll. My father would say "turn that crap off" and would immediately push a preset button on the dashboard AM radio, and out of the speaker would come Sinatra, Tony Bennett, Jerry Vale, Glenn Miller, Count Basie, and all the music of their generation, music that was still commonplace all over the radio dial during the 1960s and 70s. My Brothers and I knew the lyrics to songs like "Stardust," "I've Got You Under My Skin," "I Left My Heart In San Francisco," and many others as well as the popular rock bands of the time: the Beatles, Rolling Stones, and the Beach Boys. At this time I never dreamed that twenty-five years later I would be standing in front of a crowd belting out "I've Got The World On A String." I can't say I hated rock and roll, but I can't remember too many pop and rock tunes that brought out the feelings, emotions, and tears, that the American popular songbook did for me. I just fell in love with the music.

There's a very simple reason why I started singing signature Sinatra tunes. The arrangements were great, and readily available. The audiences always expected to hear some of his music such as "Summer Wind," "Lady Is a Tramp," "My Way," and other Sinatra mainstays. It wasn't that Sinatra was my biggest influence, or that I was trying to be a Sinatra impersonator, and I was a huge Nat King Cole fan as well as Joe Williams, Billy Eckstine, Tony Bennett, and Mel Torme to name a few. This is how I learned to sing; I stole bits and pieces from all my vocal heroes and incorporated them into a unique style that helped create my own. When I sing a tune, I want people to know its Jerry Costanzo singing, not anyone else. My goal has always been to avoid impersonations, but rather to pay tribute to these legends with my own voice.

I was very fortunate to have a father who was also a founding member of a local New York Big Band called the "Memories of Swing." There is where I learned to sing, or I should say, this is the place where I learned I had a lot to learn. My biggest problem was stage -fright and lack of self-confidence. I realized that if I wanted to be a serious singer, I would have to get over these problems. I sought out experienced vocal coaches who could not only teach me proper singing techniques, but who were working singers themselves with years of experience, working musicians that could help me overcome my fears and boost my self-confidence. They always said, the more you work and the more you put yourself out there, the easier it will become to perform without such fear, and they were right. One singing coach explained that the audience wants very much to like you, so you had to connect with them and enable them to like you.

People ask me if I continue to practice. The answer is, yes! I don't practice vocal exercises anymore, instead I spend much time learning new tunes to stay fresh and continue to work on my ever-expanding song repertoire. I will usually warm up in the car on the way to a gig by singing along to a CD which helps stretch my vocal chords. I work often enough these days that I consider the gigs where I perform to be my best practice studio. I also exercise to stay physically fit. As a singer, it is important to maintain good breathing and lung capacity. I accomplish this by mountain bike riding and when I can't ride due to inclement weather, I'll walk for miles.

A lot has happened since I first stepped in front of a microphone staring out at the crowd with shaking knees. I can even recall the song. It was Sinatra's "How Little We Know," a Nelson Riddle arrangement. This was one of the first charts I had acquired, and a song I knew I could perform easily. It was also the beginning of my addiction to collecting big band charts and orchestrations. I can now boast of a collection of both vocal and instrumentals that currently consists of over one thousand big band and combo arrangements, and still growing. I have also been fortunate enough to meet some of the best composers and arrangers in the business. When I hear a tune that really moves me, I can easily have a custom arrangement written, and, oddly enough, it helps that I'm a jack-of-all-trades. Many of my musician friends can't screw in a light bulb, so bartering becomes my first choice: "I'll help you fix your car if you will write an arrangement or two for me." This method has worked out pretty well so far.

I said earlier that Sinatra wasn't my most important singing influence, but you've got to give him much credit. His music and style has transcended generations to become timeless, and a valid and important part of music history. There were a lot of great crooners out there, and some may have been better then Frank Sinatra, but it was Frank who had the "World on a String." If I'm going to survive as a singer and entertainer into my senior years, it's definitely the ever cool and classy Frank Sinatra who will be my music mentor for constant direction well into the future.

Dedicated to the preservation of this true American art form, Jerry Costanzo is considered one of the best and busiest singer/bandleaders on the scene today. Jerry has gained popularity among connoisseurs of this great music. He appeals to audiences young and old. His interpretations of timeless "American Standards" from the song writing greats will set the stage and carry listeners back to an era when this sultry and swinging music was the "Pop" of the day.

LOU LANZA

Sometimes I feel like a case study of musical talent being the result of heredity or environment. My father's side of the family was populated almost entirely of professional classical musicians, most notably string players in The Philadelphia Orchestra. As I was growing up I felt as though I had grown up in Philadelphia's famed Academy of Music. My mother's side of the family was populated by professional jazz and commercial musicians as well as talented folk who played for "fun" at extremely high levels. My uncle would give jazz saxophone lessons to such notables as Michael Brecker while I danced around with a toy sax. The only way they could get me to quiet down was to play the theme music from the animated Spider-man series from the 1960's, "Bad, Bad Leroy Brown," or the "Theme from The Monkees." Was I influenced by constantly being surrounded by music or was it in the genes? Probably a combination of both, but to this day I still hear songs that I "know," even though I know I never consciously learned them.

Family lore says I sang the Schubert "Ave Maria" prior to speaking. Because of that I would have to conclude that I learned to sing from hearing my mother around the house and in church. I remember going around singing the Ave and "The Lord's Prayer" by Malotte the way other kids would sing "Old MacDonald." She was one of the most wonderful singers I have ever heard. Her vocal quality was reminiscent of a cross between Barbara Cook and Julie Andrews, and her beautiful phrasing and musicianship came from extensive classical training on the flute and piano. She made it sound so easy when she sang even as she often accompanied herself on piano or organ. When I sing in church or for wedding ceremonies, I find myself approaching many of these very same songs in the manner she would...and never quite doing them as well.

I would be remiss if I didn't include my father in this conversation. To this day he is a proud member of The Philadelphia Orchestra violin section. He makes such a beautiful sound on arguably the most difficult instrument to play. When he was teaching me the violin, legato phrasing, dynamics, and beauty of tone were constantly at the forefront of each lesson. The way a violinist bows is very similar in approach to the way a vocalist uses his breath control. For that reason, I am very much a stickler with my own diaphragmatic support. Also, I don't know whether this is a good thing, but I have never received an unqualified compliment from my father. In many ways, it has rubbed off on how I look at my own work. I'm rarely satisfied and am constantly trying to do better.

Early vocal influences included the Capitol era Frank Sinatra and Verve era Ella Fitzgerald. Their distinctive styles and the way the arrangements and orchestrations were constructed around the way they approached the songs were very attractive to my young ears. Even now I hear subtle things in their performances as well as in the charts. I suppose that you could make a case for Sinatra being the greatest pop singer of all time and Ella being the greatest jazz singer of all time, but I didn't know anything like that, I just liked to listen and sing along. Eventually I became enamored with Sinatra's early work with Dorsey and on the Columbia label. I absolutely tried to imitate the sound, the phrasing, as well as the intimate way he would "read" the lyric. He made it sound effortless in such a way that many people feel it's easy to sing that way. I can tell you from personal experience that it's not. Ella's influence came in the way I tried to improvise, first with the lyric and subsequently with scatting. Her voice was so pure and flexible...a perfect instrument for jazz vocalizing. I could go on and list many other influences such as Miles Davis, Mark Murphy, Billy Joel, The Doors, Tony Bennett, Stephen Sondheim, and Vivaldi, but these two made the most indelible marks on my musical psyche beside my family.

When I select songs, I am drawn to them for many different reasons. Sometimes it's a melody or a set of chord changes, but more often than not it's the lyrics that grab me. They are the reason why I fall in love with a tune, and often why I will take a tune out of my repertoire. They reveal something that I want to let go from within or a feeling that I want to share. The lyrics can be cathartic, joyous, painful, or funny (sometimes all of the above), but they are all expressing something that happened in my life or imagination.

I really love to discover tunes in all kinds of songbooks, scores, anthologies, and fake books. That way if I find something I don't know, I can try it out at the piano without any preconceived notion of how it should be performed. Once I find how I want to approach the song, I start "debugging" the changes or putting them the way I want them to go or "hear" them. Then I select a key and write out a lead sheet or skeleton chart. Instrumentation for a jazz musician is most often out of necessity due to budget. On most gigs, whether to sing with a piano, Fender Rhodes, Hammond B-3, guitar, or vibraphone based rhythm section is something that is also based a great deal on client or club preferences. However on my recordings, I choose instrumentation based on the vibe or feel of the song or album. For example, on my CD *Opening Doors: A Jazz Tribute To The Doors*, I wanted a real earthy funkiness on a good number of tracks, so I went with B-1 organ, guitar, electric bass, drums, and a horn section. When I wanted vulnerability and absolute emotional nudity, I did an album entitled *An Intimate Portrait In Blue* with only piano to accompany my voice. Sometimes the concept extends only to individual tracks, but more often than not I find it makes its way throughout a project.

When I prepare a set list, a concert, or an album's order, I try to tell a story, sustain, mood/vibe, or keep a musical forward motion.

I don't generally start a set or concert with a ballad, and only end on a ballad as an encore. I don't do two "ballady" pieces consecutively, and also try to build in mini musical climaxes. If I am doing a live set, I also feel at least one song that is funny and another that is lesser known are good things to throw in. I try to keep the audience a little off balance by not only switching tempo, but also feel, time signature, and key. Some of these things go unnoticed but can have a great affect on how the performance is received by an audience. Most of all, I go by what I am feeling that day as well as what I am getting from an audience. Even in concerts I will switch things up or drop a tune if I feel it won't work on a particular crowd. On most of the albums I have done it seems as if I have fallen more into the "concept album" format popularized by Sinatra. It seems a shame that very few people by full CD albums anymore. They miss out on that feeling of hearing an artist's conception carried out to fruition like missing the end of a good movie.

Since I teach voice at two institutions of higher learning a couple days a week, I am always warming up and doing exercises along with my students. At Moravian College I teach jazz vocal lessons and direct the jazz vocal ensemble while at DeSales University I teach musical theatre styled vocals. It is a good way to constantly review everything from the basics to more advanced concepts and keeps me on my toes. It also keeps me around young talent with creative ideas that are fresh and new. They are constant sources of inspiration.

While I know of some very fine singers that don't vocalize daily, I can't say that I'm one of them. If I don't sing for a day or two, I can really feel and hear a difference in my voice. I also have never smoked. My dad did and I found it to be a disgusting habit, so for that reason I never took it up. I don't drink any alcohol within a few days of having to sing in public. It's not that I'm a prude, but I don't like how my voice feels afterward. As far as illegal drugs, I've never done them either, but primarily because I have so many allergies to medicines that I felt discretion was the better part of valor. I find it very important not to push or strain my voice. Sometimes my wife thinks I am having a bad time at a party with loud music since I may not talk to many people if at all. Part of it is a natural shyness, but I am saving my voice from having to shout (without even realizing it) to be heard.

This ties in with the way I was taught to sing by Carlo Menotti. He taught, among others, Tony Bennett and Bobby Darin. He very much instructed me in the bel canto style of singing. I find that it is a very flexible, pliable, and durable way to sing a long time and stay vocally healthy.

How do I keep it together? I just try to do at least one positive thing for my career every single day. It makes me feel better and it adds up to positive emotion over time. I also am blessed with a very supportive wife and family. That makes it so much easier to fight the fight to make a living when you have a safe haven at home. For these reasons and many more I consider myself blessed and most fortunate. As Sinatra said on a live album, and I may be paraphrasing, "I get to sing for my supper and get paid for it."

I've learned so much from Sinatra's innate musicianship and phrasing that it would be hard to go into much detail without Rich telling me to "zip it!" If you want to know that, listen to me sing and you'll be able to hear where he is within my style. That being said, I do feel I have been able to get a great deal of comfort from knowing that even the best go through difficult personal and career troubles. He was a survivor and that is the most important lesson for anyone in the arts to learn: to keep moving forward and never stop learning.

CRISTINA FONTANELLI

My story - I originally wanted to be an actress and graduated from the American Academy of Dramatic Arts. Some famous alumni include Edward G. Robinson, Robert Redford, and Danny DeVito. As a child I used to perform on neighborhood shows, both singing and dancing. I studied singing in high school. I was told I had a great voice with operatic potential, but I couldn't relate to a musical language in a foreign tongue, so I had no idea at that time that I would become well-known as a singer. When I graduated from the Academy, I read the libretto to Tosca and realized that it required very dramatic acting as well as singing and that is when I decided to study opera.

My singing technical "road" had been very "rocky". I did not receive the proper vocal training in the beginning, so I had to search for my hard-earned vocal technique. Along the way, my jaw went into spasm from improper breath support. I couldn't open my mouth. My pitch was off because of it. I couldn't reach the high notes with the ease that is necessary for singing opera. I worked long and hard to achieve the rock-solid vocal technique I now own. I can roll out of bed and be able to sing throughout my vocal range with very little warmup......square on the money and without vocal fatigue. However, the fact that I had an incomplete technique, but yet, such a desire to perform, led me into becoming an entertainer and concert/show singer. I must say that my vocal road is unusual because I have legitimate reviews from well-respected news sources such as the New York Times bestowing upon me a number of very fine reviews of my operatic performances.

Forbes Magazine: "Cristina Fontanelli performing at Fein-stein's at the Regency is like seeing a cross between Maria Callas and Ethel Merman. She has no equal."

With respect to Sinatra....well, our roots are the same. My Mom is from Hoboken, New Jersey, too, and as a very young girl, she recalls often seeing Frank walking down the street.

Almost every year I sang at the St. Ann's Festival in Hoboken at the same festival where Frank performed!

One of my early singing teachers, a well-respected woman named Carolina Segrera, noted that she and some of her colleagues, studied Sinatra's phrasing and breathing techniques. He was, and is known among classical singers as someone to emulate with respect to his diction, phrasing, and breath support. As I noted in the Frankie Laine book, Mr. Rhythm, Frankie Laine told me he was studying op-era at one time, but didn't have enough money to continue. But, what he learned about breath support allowed him to continue to sing even into his 80s.

To keep my voice in "fighting shape," I have developed a series of vocalizes that I know work for me. These are based on the Bel Canto (which means beautiful singing) method of singing which encourages legato (the seamless connection of notes, clear diction, singing on the breath, phrasing, diminuendo and crescendo, the art of getting louder and softer on one note). People think that singing popular music requires less preparation, and in some cases, this is true. But in my voice, I have to warm-up almost as much for pop music singing as opera and classical. Because, if the vocal chords are not toned and vocalized to within an inch of their lives, I cannot achieve any colors and therefore will only sound, so to speak, heavy-toned, and don't have nuances because I won't have full-control over my voice and what tones I am producing.

However, I make sure, as much as possible, to rest, and not to talk above loud music or in loud, public places. I drink lots of water. I am not the kind of singer that relies on medication. I believe in naturally taking care of excess phlegm. There are singers that have taken something called humibid, for example, that thin our your mucous secretions. That medication has been known to block the body's ability to produce natural mucous, and your vocal chords become dried out. I do not believe in such crutches.

Since I sincerely believe I should give back some of the hard-earned knowledge that I have acquired that has set me upon solid vocal ground, I am now teaching voice and have limited openings for a few who wish to learn.

Check out Cristina Fontanelli's web site.

Roberto Tirado

"It should be conveyed with a great deal of phrasing, timing, clarity and diction."

No, that's not how a drill instructor speaks to a Marine recruit. That's how how you Sing a Song.

Irving Berlin's favorite singer was Fred Astaire, who was able to capture the essence of lyric and melody in a manner that escaped the ordinary singer. Again, Astaire's voice, secure and comfortable, did not possess the liquid warmth and sensuality of our next singer who once stated, "May you live to be a hundred and may the last voice you hear be mine."

Francis Albert Sinatra soared above all other singers of the golden age of American music, not because he had the greatest set of pipes, but because he connected his heart to his voice. He conveyed the clarity of a lyric in a manner even better then HD television; he was the Laurence Olivier of crooners. And anyone attempting to sing the American Songbook had better pay close attention to his total musicality.

Sinatra called himself a "saloon singer" and herein lies the crucial pathos that he alone was blessed with. The saddest stories in the world are told to bartenders and Sinatra's bartender was the microphone.

While others sang in stentorian tones with gimmicky emotions, Sinatra broke your heart with a sincere and revelatory image. Never mind the incredible breath control accompanied by a baritone voice that you could warm your hands to but long after the song is gone Sinatra lingers. No wonder Luciano Pavarotti called him the American Mozart. Like Mozart, he too walked in the waters of an innocent truth that could not be reproduced.

Roberto Tirado

JULIA KEEFE

Following jazz singer Mildred Bailey is no easy pickings. Julia Keefe, a very young jazz vocalist, is heading up a Mildred Bailey revival. Mildred Bailey, the very first big band singer, and a Coeur d'Alene American Indian, is being emulated beautifully by Julia Keefe, a Nez Perce tribe member.

Julia was influenced by Frank Sinatra, following his regimen by swimming underwater to strengthen her vocal cords, and by Billie Holiday, who spurred her original interest in singing in the jazz idiom. Julia sang regularly at the popular night club, Ella's Supper Club in Spokane, Washington, up on the third floor, ever since she was seventeen. The club has since closed, but it was there Julia launched her career. She is now in her very early twenties and attending Frost School of Music in Coral Gables, Florida.

"I sound like a saxophone when I improvise. When people scat like a trumpet there are a lot of B's, but sax sound has more V's and S's, softer, soothing kind of sounds," Julia told me. Fortunately, Keefe started serious training under the wing of Kristina Ploeger when she was in the seventh grade.

"I dabbled in classical to keep my voice healthy, but it's so structured. You have to do what the composer intended, so I stuck with jazz."

Julia Keefe is a name which will always be associated with the Rocking Chair Lady, the also young singer who encouraged a young Bing Crosby, who was friends with his partner Al Rinker, who was Mildred Bailey's brother. She advised them to go to Los Angeles where they made their way to the top. Now it's Julia's turn.

JULIA: "I can't really remember when I first heard Frank Sinatra sing, but I do remember hearing that when he was a kid growing up in New Jersey, he would practice developing his lung capacity by swimming under water as far as he could, holding his breath. That sounded good to me, so when I would swim in the Clearwater River down on my tribe's reservation in Kamiah, Idaho, I would do the same thing. Later, when I began singing in my school and church choir, I learned of some conventional techniques, and tried them.

"Before practicing my set list and even before getting up to sing at a gig, I warm up my voice. This includes lip trills, humming scales and melodies, and loosening up my neck and shoulders. The lip trills are helpful for waking up the muscles in the face but also a safe way to move any materials that may be coating the vocal folds. Humming scales and melodies is helpful for placing the voice where it's comfortable and capable of healthy vocal production. In my speaking voice, I tend to rest on my vocal cords and resonate in my throat and/or chest. This is what not to do. Because of my placement, I put a lot of strain on my voice that will lead to less than exemplary vocal performance. So it is even more important for me to use correct techniques while singing. Strain is put on the voice when the muscles around the vocal cords are tense, thus placing the voice in an unnatural point of resonance. If my placement is right, I will be able to sing stronger for a longer period of time. Finally, relaxing the muscles of the neck and shoulders encourages good vocal technique and allows for a more comfortable look and feel to the performance.

"Another important step in the pre-gig preparation is staying hydrated. While a person, especially a singer, should be staying hydrated all the time, this is not always easy given our hectic schedules. However, when it comes to a performance, hydration is no-negotiable. One of my voice teachers, when I was first gigging, told me that water doesn't begin to affect the vocal cords for about 45 minutes after drinking. So about an hour before the gig, I start sipping water so that my voice is loose and ready for performance.

"I usually get nervous before and after the gig. When it is performance time, I am a nervous wreck! I have done many gigs for many people, and yet I still get horribly nervous. I cannot eat before the show and talking to people is never easy, either. What could I possibly say? "So, I really hope I don't choke up there and start crying." No, that will not fly with me. But I do have to calm the nerves. I do a series of breathing exercises and stretches. I try to find my center and let all my tension go. I relax my body, which then relaxes my mind. I feel completely ready. Then, the split second before I go on stage, I get nervous again. I feel like I'm going to faint. But once

I'm on stage, the nerves are gone and I feel at home. After the gig is over, the nerves come back and I have to do more breathing exercises and stretches to calm down.

"Instrumentalists are given a set of chords and a melody and can interpret the song in whatever way they choose. But as a vocalist, I am given a set of lyrics to also take into consideration when I am performing. My job is to communicate to the audience the emotions behind those lyrics. When preparing a song, I analyze and recite the lyrics as a monologue. I try to determine who or what is the focus of the speaker and what message the speaker is trying to convey. This gives me a deeper understanding and connection to the tune. My phrasing should be reflective of the meaning. Sinatra was famous for his conversational phrasing. He was able to express such depth in his music because of his amazing ability to connect and communicate the songs he made famous.

"My own personal role model as a jazz vocalist is Mildred Bailey, a Native American woman who also grew up in Spokane, and became the first female big band singer in America. Mildred influenced a lot of singers, including her brother Al and his band-mate, Bing Crosby. And Frank Sinatra also appreciated Mildred's breakthrough role as a vocalist. When Mildred was down on her luck, near the end of her life, Mr. Sinatra heard about her problems, and helped pay her hospital bills. For that one act alone, I'll always have a warm spot in my heart for him, and for his music."

DARYL SHERMAN

"According to Sherman family lore I was singing as a toddler before I could even speak. "On Top Of Old 'Mokey" was the first 'tour de farce' followed by "Goodnight Irene" which I must have heard on the radio at the time. My dad, Sammy Sherman, had played trombone with New York big bands like Buddy Morrow, Sonny Dunham and gigs in the Catskills. After he married and moved to Rhode Island he regularly played weekends leading his own combos. I grew up with a steady diet of standards and jazz tunes under his influence -either hearing them live at his gigs or on radio and records. We got one of those clunky old uprights and I'd plunk out tunes by ear, then started taking piano lessons around age 7. My dad also would sit with me and show me how to form chords from the symbols on song sheets he'd written out and sing along. Also he subscribed to Tune -Dex, which were melodies and chord symbols printed on small card stock by the publishers. (This was pre fake books era, which were illegal then). By about 13 or so I was starting to sit in singing with his group. These musicians were like an extended family and also helped mentor me. My dad was exacting about my knowing the keys and terms used in communicating to the musicians like "go back to the bridge" or "take it out" He'd point his finger and chide "don't come

on like an amateur" or "I must talk to you about your vibrato!"

"Around the house there were lots of brass recordings -trombonists like JJ Johnson, but also lots of Kenton, and of course, Tommy Dorsey. So naturally I had Sinatra's singing in my ears at an early age. Ella was a favorite in our household and I was encouraged to listen and scat like her. I always had a natural bent towards improvisation and swing but in retrospect I wish I'd paid more attention to lyrics and diction.

"It wasn't until much later when I'd moved to Manhattan in the 70s that I began to see the light. I began listening more to Billie Holiday and Mildred Bailey, but it was my relationship with Sylvia Syms which had the greatest impact on me. I went to hear her every chance I could and got to know her quite well personally. Her knowledge and aesthetics about songs was invaluable and she wasn't shy about expressing her opinions.

"Stop listening to your voice so much and just tell the story!" she'd say. Sinatra was certainly a central figure in her life referring to him as 'the old man'. She never introduced me to him but I do remember seeing him and Barbara in her audience a couple of times. When he was in town Sylvia would be summoned to meet them at Rocky Lee's or the Waldorf Towers and she'd speak with him on the phone a lot --oftentimes discussing songs.

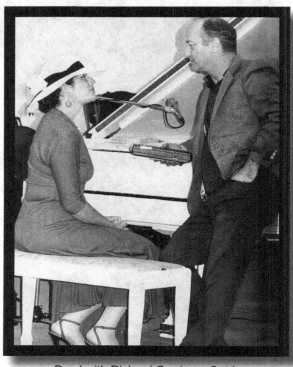

Daryl with Richard Grudens, Outdoor Concert, Port. Jefferson, NY

"My one actual encounter with Frank Sinatra came earlier, thanks to one of my very first gigs in NYC -- at Jilly's. It was a trio gig and the shift was 10pm to 4am. Even if no one was around that last hour, you'd get the vibe that you'd better stay put. Ironically, it was my night off when my folks were visiting and I wanted them to see Jilly's. We approached but noticed a sign on the door saying "closed for private event'. I was crest -fallen but luckily the door opened and Joey (Jilly's son) invited us in. Wouldn't you know, it was a party for Sinatra, who walked by just at that moment. Joey piped up "Daryl's our new singer/pianist" to which Frank replied as he pat his hand on my head "Yeah, kid!" then he dashed off. That was my 5 second brush with greatness.

"If there is a theme to the show, naturally I think about what's appropriate. If it's a particular songwriter, I'll spend time listening and researching a cross section of their material with different collaborators. Then I try to combine a program of well-known, slightly lesser known and perhaps some oddball piece that works into the scheme somewhere. The lyrics must tell a story expressed in a way that sounds and feels believable coming from me. Most of all, my objective is to connect with the listener and hope something especially resonates. Even if there's no particular theme, I work from a structure where songs and their placement have certain functions -balancing moods, tempos, even key relationships. I like to vary the colors and sonority. If I'm playing piano for myself with a rhythm section, I'll usually prefer guitar to drums because that will give me another chordal support if I want to stand up and sing.

"I also like the lighter texture of the guitar --which blends with my vocal timbre. I also like using a reed player who doubles on clarinet or flute to provide even more contrast. and the exercises, physical and voice, and how you keep it all together as a Singer, Sinatra paid great attention to details of his sound, phrasing and diction that I wish I'd done more of. When you're not performing on stages, in concert halls or recording sessions and instead spending long hours on a gig where people don't necessarily pay close attention to you, it's easy to get into some bad habits. Some hotel gigs could be five or six hours, five days weekly, where one would practice right in the hot seat. However, when the stakes are higher, slow focused practice and lots of repetition is the rule. I phrase in many different ways just to get a song into my head --searching for some special pattern that clicks and sticks. Every singer I know who swims has especially good breath control and I try various techniques to relax and concentrate on breathing from down deep. Blowing slowly through a straw while gently pulling in the diaphram seems to help.

"Frank Sinatra remarked once about Johnny Mercer's lyrics that they were 'all the wit you wished you ever had and all the love you ever lost.' Sinatra got inside each song he chose to sing and made you also feel that lost love or make you chuckle at some cleverness. His famous swagger in addition to his masterful understatement are incomparable. No matter how many times you've listened to one of his recordings, especially of a blockbuster standard, there's always some new facet to discover in oftentimes, the most simple and direct of deliveries."

Daryl was a 2010 winner of the MAC Award in the MAJOR RECORDING category for "Johnny Mercer: A Centennial Tribute."

Dick Haymes

Dick Haymes followed Frank Sinatra into the Tommy Dorsey band when Frank decided to leave to go on his own. Dick had previously followed Frank into the Harry James band when Frank switched

L-R: Connie Haines, Dick Haymes and Helen Forrest

to Dorsey. They spent time together on the Dorsey bandstand before Sinatra actually left, as Frank wanted to make it comfortable for the new boy singer in the Dorsey organization. Sometime later, Dick, with the wonderful Helen Forrest, performed together on the Autolite Radio Show with musical director and arranger Gordon Jenkins. The show lasted four years and showcased many fine guests, and had special material written for Dick and Helen by Matt Dennis and Tom Adair, each week a different theme for the thirty-minute, weekly show.

"Dick Haymes had discovered his own method of breath control," Margaret Whiting said during one of our interviews, "it produced a distinctive, masculine sound, with his deep baritone voice." Unlike Sinatra, Dick always felt the stress of singing directly to audiences. One day Frankie Laine and I talked about the comparison during a long conversation we had about Frank Sinatra vs. Dick Haymes. We think Frank Sinatra's life would have been different had Haymes lived longer. We always sensed a promise of great things to come when we heard Haymes sing. His voice was, no doubt, rich and warm, a great baritone with great intonation and projections of warmth.

A comparison of Dick's and Gordon's recording of "Little White

Lies," to Frank Sinatra's recording of "I'll Never Smile Again," confirmed the chance of an equalization of the two great singers.

Jack Jones

Jack Jones started, like so many others, imitating the then preferred sound of Frank Sinatra. He passed that point in his life employing his own engaging style that led him to success with such winners as "Lollipops and Roses" and "Call Me Irresponsible," both Sinatra classics, but Jack made them his own.

Steve Lawrence

Sometimes when Steve Lawrence's recordings are played on the Siriusly Sinatra daily show on Satellite radio, you would swear it's Sinatra himself, but then Steve's own recognizable voice comes through later in the recording. Steve's rendition of "Portrait of My Love" and "Go Away Little Girl" are distinctly his own.

Jimmy Roselli

Jimmy Roselli has his own faithful following as a true Italian troubadour. His rivalry with Sinatra is legendary, even to winning first prize on a *Major Bowes Amateur Hour* program where Sinatra first won his singing wings. Jimmy is retired now and living in Florida. His great song "When Your Old Wedding Ring was New," keeps the tears running at every performance and has endeared him to millions.

Al Martino

Al Martino was a soft-singing, Sinatra style vocalist, who created his own style of singing early in his career. "Spanish Eyes" was his best single. He was influenced by other singers on the radio, Tony

Martin, Perry Como, and Frank Sinatra. "I bought their records and sang along with them." Al actually got to sing in *The Godfather* film portraying the Frank Sinatra character, Johnny Fontane. The song "I Have But One Heart," and also recorded the theme song"Speak Softy, Love."

Eddie Fisher

By his own admission Eddie Fisher admired both Frank Sinatra and Bing Crosby. He became the protégé of the great vaudeville star, Eddie Cantor, who heard him sing in the Catskill Mountains of New York at a place called Grossinger's and invited him to sing on his radio show and then actually toured with the famous star who introduced him to Jack Benny, Bob Hope, Bing Crosby, and comedian Danny Thomas, whose act he opened for at Bill Miller's Riviera in Fort Lee, New Jersey, his first big break.

Sammy Davis, Jr.

Sammy Davis, Jr. started out imitating every singer, including Frank Sinatra, and made lifelong friends with Sinatra, toured with him in the late eighties, and appeared in some of Sinatra's films. He was a terrific dancer, a versatile singer, and an all-around performer. His best was "Candy Man," "Old Black Magic," "Hey, There," and his very best was "Mr. Bojangles." He was a member of Frank Sinatra's elite Rat Pack.

Nat "King" Cole

When I talked with Maria Cole, regarding her husband Nat "King" Cole and his association or emulation of Sinatra, she could not recall anything startling. "Nat's love of the music, playing piano in his trio, and singing such excellent renditions of songs like "Stardust,' rendered him a star of his own." William B. Williams of New York's *Make Believe Ballroom* fame, played a Nat Cole record every day he was on the air, after Nat passed away.

"No particular singer influenced his career," said Maria. Nat never had a problem with breath control and wound up teaching Metropolitan Opera artists breathing techniques at the request of Met impresario Rudolph Bing. With compact, syncopated backup chords

Gordon Jenkins with Nat "King" Cole at Capitol Records

and clean, spare, melodic phrases, Nat emphasized the piano as a solo, rather than a rhythm-style instrument in his arrangements. His playing complimented his singing. Highlights were "Nature Boy," "It's Only a Paper Moon," and "Route 66" with the trio. And, with Nelson Riddle, "Mona Lisa."

It looks as though Nat "King" Cole's only connection to Frank Sinatra was his use and appreciation of the same, selective arrangers in their body of work: Nelson Riddle and Gordon Jenkins. George Gershwin would've inquired: "Who could ask for anything more?"

Dean Martin

Dean Martin, of course, was allied with Frank Sinatra through their personal association and performing at mostly Las Vegas rooms, in some films, and performing their Rat Pack routines. They worked the shows together, however it was not considered serious performing. It was usually fun and games accompaning the singing. Dean Martin had his own show on TV for nine years. Frank Sinatra was a now-and-then guest.

Buddy Greco

To many, Buddy Greco is acknowledged as a Frank Sinatra-Style vocalist performing all the classic tunes of the great composers in the "bel canto" style, adding his own endings and vocal charm to his performances. He is loved the world over for his fine interpretations of these songs. His recordings "The Lady is a Tramp," styled after Bobby Darin. "Call Me Irresponsible," "Around the World in Eighty Days," and "Don't Worry About Me," keeps the whole Sinatra school of music fresh and new for all those who may have missed the Chairman's own live performances of the past.

THERE are many worthy singers who, with no influence whatsoever from Frank Sinatra, managed great careers singing for bands or on their own, and I make respectful mention of them here in Sinatra's own book: Julius La Rosa, Perry Como, Don Cornell, Billy Eckstine, Bob Eberly, Ray Eberle, Herb Jeffries, Buddy Clark , Tony Martin, Joe Williams, Tex Beneke, Andy Williams, Guy Mitchell, Johnny Hartman, Buddy Clark, Vaughn Monroe and Fred Astaire...yes! It was Fred Astaire who introduced more standards through his films, than any other singer in the business.

Fred Astaire

Sammy Davis, Jr.

THE NEW CITIZENS OF THE JAZZ COMMUNITY

Michael Buble' - Songs by Sinatra

Michael Bublé is not really new, but his Sinatra sound is very impressive, although a bit softer and without the deep range and production. Buble started out

Sinatra and remains essentially a soft Sinatra. Sometimes his deeper tones remind one more of Dick Haymes than Frank Sinatra. He possesses good phrasing and excellent romantic-styling diction. Hailing from Canada, he was first noticed by producer David Foster of Warner Records who signed him with Reprise Records. His rendition of "Moondance," "Come Fly with Me," "The Way You Look Tonight," and "How Can You Mend a Broken Heart," is proof enough of his Sinatra-like star capabilities. Lately, he recorded a duet with Jane Monheit and it is simply ter-

rific. Michael is "here to stay," to paraphrase Ira Gershwin.

Maude Maggert

Maude Maggert is a fine singer and a rising star who follows tradition and with excellent phrasing sings with piano and violin, almost *a capella*. The voice is sooth-ing and compelling and each note is car-ried to the final phrase, no short-cutting at the end, she stretches her music without cutting it off at the end that so many older singers seem to do. Are they tired? Why do they clip off at the coda?

Anyway, she has recorded Ellington, Richard Rodgers, George & Ira Gershwin, Johnny Mercer and Hoagy Carmichael (Stardust, of course). Her sister is Fiona Apple.

Jonathan plays her on his show High Standards: "Maude's audience fall to silence when she

starts to sing from the Great American Songbook," he says.

Jane Monheit - A New Class of Singer

Madeline and I went to see and hear Jane Monheit, who hails from our neck of the woods. She travels world-wide with her husband's troup and takes her two little ones in tow. Someday those kids will say, "We were born in a trunk." Jane Monheit is one of the new

top draw winners in the singing sweepstakes. Besides being beautiful, she sings beautifully, and that includes all the songs from the American Songbook and lots of Sinatra favorites.

Watching Jane Monheit close-up singing her wonderfully different arrangements of familiar songs is an exhilarating experience. She flips her hair and delves deep into "Over the Rainbow," and you know you are listening to someone special singing something special.

A product of the south shore of

Long Island, Jane Monheit is a jazz singer with a voice that burst forth from her fledgling beginning in 2001. She has since performed in London and Tokyo as well as everywhere else. Her husband, Rick Montalbano, is the trio's drummer who backs her so well. "Moon River" is a favorite of her fans and she can move along with a bossa nova beat as well as anyone.

Dana Marcine

Dana Marcine dropped in my office today, April 16, 2010. In front of our office is a larger than life replica of the Statue of Liberty,

where Dana took photos for her next album. She came in and asked permission and I discovered a new, up-and-coming singer, who is in love with the great songs of the American Songbook. She sang a few bars and told me her story and I invited her into this book because Frank Sinatra was her main influence.

"Jazz is where my heart is," said Dana. My musical influences are, of course, Frank Sinatra, and Ella Fitzgerald, Diana Krall, the great Tony Bennett and many of the fine musicians and singers I've worked with and have watched."

Dana: "Richard: I grew up in a musical family where mom and dad had wonderful singing voices and on any given day I might hear my dad singing along with his favorite opera albums. I was always singing too, either in the car or making shows for family members in the living room. My first real performance was singing a solo at kindergarten graduation. I loved it all.

"In our Long Island home we also played the music of the great popular singers of the time. I remember being surrounded by the sounds of Frank Sinatra, Ella Fitzgerald, Peggy Lee, Dean Martin, Bing Crosby, Perry Como, and Tony Bennett. I admired and was influenced by each of them. To this day I am amazed and awed by the artistry of Tony Bennett. His talents in the visual arts and musical arts are an inspiration. His decision to name his school of the arts in Queens, New York, after Sinatra, is a legacy to the man who inspired him.

"Sinatra had a way with a song. When I select a song to add to my repertoire, I first ask myself if there is a story to tell. I want to know if there is an emotion that I can connect with and relate to an audience. Sinatra was a master storyteller and could get to the heart of a song. This is also what I want to do. I concentrate on my phrasing and try to interpret a song in a personal way. If the tune is a ballad, jazz, or swing, I always remember the greats and learn from them. I study their jazz timing and soulful ballads. I hear their whispers and crescendos.

"Sinatra had an incredible vocal range. I keep my own voice in good shape by vocalizing daily and taking good care of myself in general. I have never smoked and I get plenty of rest. I try not to abuse myself in any way. If you treat your voice well, it will serve you throughout your lifetime. As a singer/songwriter I also understand the partnership between lyrics and music. It is all about evoking a feeling in the listener. Besides Bennett, some of my current favorites are

Diana Krall, K. D. Lang, Holly Kole, the late Nancy LaMott, Michael Bublé, Claire Martin, and Peter Cincotti. Each of them is wonderful to listen to. Each has a story to tell.

"Sinatra told his story well. In his unique suave style he could be soulful, sassy, swingin', or hip. His phrasing and ability to find the nuances in a song showed that he was an artist at the top of his craft. I remember Sinatra when I am singing a tune like "New York, New York," which I sang for former New York City mayor Rudy Giuliani. I hope somewhere Sinatra is smiling."

Dana Marcine is a New York based singer/ songwriter. Her latest CD *It's Just So* is due out in summer 2010. It features "Long Island Serenade", a tribute to life on Long Island. She is one of the new citizens of Jazz singing that includes the American Songbook.

Tony DeSare
What is Frank Sinatra to me?

"I honestly don't remember the first time the voice of Frank Sinatra vibrated through my formative ears. I'm sure that it played through the tinny speakers of my parents' cabinet-implanted television set before I could even walk or talk. I also remember seeing the stately looking *Trilogy* vinyl album set rounding out my dad's album collection, though I think the music contained on its vinyl grooves was as much a mystery as the platinum outline of the man on the cover.

"I do, however, remember the first time I really heard Frank Sinatra. I was about fifteen years old and I had grown up with an insatiable love of music. At this time I was playing violin in the school orchestra, playing Scott Joplin rags on the piano and also moonlighting as the jazz piano player in my school jazz band. I also played percussion in the concert band. My mom, Louise, brought home a cassette tape called Frank Sinatra Gold and set it on the dining room table without any fanfare. That night before bed I decided to snatch it off the table and give it a try out of curiosity. I was mostly wondering what else that "New York, New York guy" could sing. The next hour of music shaped my destiny in a way I could never have expected.

"For me, Frank Sinatra has always been about his artistic output as a singer. Though an undeniable force in 20th Century pop culture, a fine actor and quite a controversial personality, it was never

those things that made such an indelible mark on me. It was the seemingly effortless, yet perfect, phrasing matched with a voice that was warm and comforting and brash and defiant at the same time. It was that voice that helped me congeal my musical loves into a direction that has propelled me into a daily life and life's work that I'm constantly challenged by and eternally grateful for.

"So much has been written about Sinatra's music and life, that it presents a challenge for one to contribute something that hasn't been already reiterated so many times before. It is redundant and even a bit cliché, I think, to cite Sinatra as an influence or to argue his relevance in American music and culture. Personally, I think that the legend and impact of Frank Sinatra will gather momentum as we move further and further from the century that he owned. For me, as a member of the generation that has come of age in a new century, the specter of Sinatra is a fascinating and mysterious thing. I think others my age and younger who love the genre and style that Sinatra built and lived in will always have a bit of the feeling that we arrived right after the party ended. Sure, there are a few people left still singing around the piano and some good looking dames in the corner, but "you should have seen it a few hours ago!" The question then pops into my mind, what next?

"I feel very fortunate to be on the relatively short list of people who are considered the "carriers of the flame" to the wonderful style of singing that Frank Sinatra, with the aid of a microphone, invented. There is an undying magic contained in so many of those songs and recordings that they are sure to survive as master works of art, just like a Da Vinci or a Picasso. I have made it one of my hopes that something I do could live on and be part of the lexicon of a language that I have adored and will adore the rest of my life. No one knows for sure if the best is yet to come or not, but I plan on doing my part.

Thank you, Frank Sinatra, you're marvelous!"

ONLY THE LONELY
The Iconic Album Of Sinatra's Career

Among the masterpieces that Sinatra's vocalizing has created with one of America's very best arrangers, *Only The Lonely*, this album stands alone as Sinatra's very best album.

Sinatra's ballads performed in this album are nothing short of perfection of interpretation. The songs are essentially unmatchable, emotional, and unparalleled. Ironically Gordon Jenkins was slated to do the album with Frank, but could not break an earlier contract to appear in Las Vegas, so Nelson Riddle was signed to arrange. There were three sessions at the Capitol studios that began on May 29, 1958. Riddle was to conduct the second and third and Felix Slatkin directed the first, which covered seven tracks, but never got any written credit, all the credit going to Riddle.

The selections were Johnny Mercer's "Blues in the Night," and "One for My Baby," Ann Ronell's "Willow Weep for Me," Matt Dennis and Earl Brent's haunting "Angel Eyes," and Gordon Jenkins masterpiece "Goodbye." You can add in "It's a Lonesome Old Town," a Harry Tobias evergreen, a tune that has been rarely recorded. The title song "Only the Lonely" is a perfectly crafted Sinatra vocal that keeps most eyes moist upon listening to this Sammy Cahn and Jimmy Van Heusen piece of musical perfection.

Riddle acknowledges *Only the Lonely* as his best vocal album. There were more than many musicians involved in the making of *Only the Lonely*. It is said that Riddle wrote the arrangements while his mother was in the hospital suffering from cancer. Three months earlier Nelson had lost his daughter of six months to a respiratory illness. Did these events contribute to the somber tone of the arrangements? Who knows!

The technical qualification of Sammy Cahn and Jule Styne, "I Guess I'll Hang My Tears Out to Dry" is clearly a Sinatra specification. Al Viola even had to retune his guitar for one special note at the short verses (voice and guitar only), and at one point, in the key of F sharp, the song and voice rang out clear as a bell, which heightened the performance.

In this album Sinatra was the consummate actor/singer along with his rendition of "Here's That Rainy Day" another terrific offering, and a well complimented "Gone with the Wind," Ally Wrubel and Herb Magidson's big success and a standard set for all time by Sinatra and others, like Julie London's classic recording of some years ago. Add in "Ebb Tide," "What's New,?" and "Spring is Here." As Frank punctuated, "Spring is here, I hear!"

Comments by the author: "Angel Eyes," the finest rendition of this song ever recorded and you can add "Only the Lonely," and "Willow Weep for Me" to be placed in the same category.

Sinatra Impressions

In 1992, while attending a creative writing class, a young man named Matthew Pacciano was handed an assignment to write a snippet about a popular figure and not mention the name, yet compose it so a reader can readily identify the subject. He chose to write about Frank Sinatra whom he witnessed performing at a Sloan-Kettering Benefit in New York City.

Ol' Blue Eyes

The smoke in the room, a bluish veil clinging to the ceiling, was as much a part of the setting and the staging as was the microphone and stool he would sit upon. The clinking of a sea of glasses and subdued chatter of voices, coupled with the movement of the waiters, placed a final touch to the mood.

Soon he would appear to make his usual entrance: sauntering across the stage, cigarette in hand, so sure, almost cocky, as he reached for the stool and microphone. The orchestra was waiting: tuned, poised, ready.

The house was full. People were dressed to the hilt, some with diamonds reflecting their flickers of light as women moved about. The waiters carefully moved to the rear. There was a hush, followed by the eerie silence, and then darkness. The spotlight cut a path throughout the smoke, and a hidden voice, quietly at first, then suddenly booming, announced his name. The crowd quickly came to life.

The orchestra played his familiar theme and there he was moving ahead gracefully to the center of a gigantic ball of light. He bowed and thanked his audience for the thunderous applause and began. He belted out song after song, holding his head at a provocative tilt as he reached certain notes. Then, looking up, then down, arms close to the body, then outstretched, his intense blue eyes always reached out to someone.

**Sinatra with Wife Barbara at the
Waldorf-Astoria, April 1977**

His voice never over-powering, although sometimes strained when demands required. It was a voice of character and experience. His diction was flawless, his phrasing and timing masterful. He was a craftsman, putting together a powerful performance with a believable voice with a host of meticulous details.

The applause, the smiles, the tears, told why they were there. Each song touched someone. Some bought back memories of youth, or carefree days gone by. Others reminisced-perhaps broken hearts, shattered romances, and the 'why didn't this ever happen to me look' appeared on many faces. For the few young people present, he created a temporary mystique.

Matthew Pacciano

The man, middle aged. The songs, dug up from archives. The voice, legendary perfect. A dynamic personality with unbound charm and charisma held them all in awe for almost two hours. When he made his final bow, he seemed humble. And when he looked up and smiled broadly-his blue eyes actually twinkled. You knew who he was. And so did he.

THE BEST POPULAR MUSIC SINGERS OF 1940 - 1985

AL JOLSON	BILLIE HOLIDAY
BING CROSBY	ELLA FITZGERALD
PERRY COMO	HELEN FORREST
FRANK SINATRA	JUDY GARLAND
TONY BENNETT	MARGARET WHITING
DICK HAYMES	DORIS DAY
FRANKIE LAINE	ROSEMARY CLOONEY
NAT "KING" COLE	CONNIE HAINES
JERRY VALE	SARAH VAUGHAN
VIC DAMONE	PEGGY LEE
	DEAN MARTIN
	BOBBY DARIN

Sarah Vaughan
with Frank Sinatra

Harry James with Helen Forrest

The Greatest Disc Jockey - Martin Block
of WNEW Radio - New York

The Great Singer - Frankie Laine

WAS SINATRA ALL WASHED UP?

In 1948 FRANK SINATRA was pouring out a lot of below par recordings while his competition, the stalwart voice of Bing Crosby was riding high.

"Bing is the guy who ran a nodule in his throat into a million dollars, served as my chief and only source of inspiration to become a professional singer." said Frank.

Fans had become disappointed because Frank's voice was not in top condition. He was losing work to another competitor in the voice of Buddy Clark, a fine singer who had to sub for Sinatra in recording an album of songs from the Broadway play *Inside U.S.A.*

Well, perhaps Sinatra was overdoing his tonsils. A guy named James Petrillo, union boss of musicians, prevented these musicians from recording, so Sinatra went into the recording studio to record a ton of records to fill the bank before the deadline; add work on his radio show, five or six shows a day in theaters, making movies in between, keeping late hours, playing baseball and attended horse races- shouting for his horse to come in first.

So, guess what? The Voice began to strain badly. Was he all washed up? Of course not! Reason and logic would eventually prevail, as we all subsequently learned.

He now understood about exhaustion and the need for sleep. He would no longer miss notes, cracked phrasing, or sing mediocre songs arranged by mediocre arrangers. He restored grace and eliminated fatigue.

Coast-to-coast, he was and remained Frank Sinatra, now America's newest Best Singer.

JOLSON AND BING, step aside, dim the lights, turn up the mike, for Frank Sinatra has come back.

OCTOBER 13, 1974
THE MAIN EVENT
MADISON SQUARE GARDEN

Twenty thousand fans. The great Woody Herman with his Herd conducted the orchestra.

Songs: "The Lady is a Tramp," "I Get a Kick Out of You," "Let Me Try Again," "Autumn in New York," "I've Got You Under My Skin," "Leroy Brown," "Angel Eyes," "You Are the Sunshine of My Life," "The House I Live In," "My Kind of Town," and "My Way."

Many say Sinatra's interpretation of "The House I Live In" was one of his best live performances of a song ever, his voice powerful and stunning in this version, still effective.

According to Frank: "I don't care how long you've been in this business, there's nothing like singing to live people."

That's what stellar trombonist Milt Bernhart once opined dramatically and emotionally when I interviewed him while he was President of the Big Band Academy of America.

"Richard, you had to be there. I felt for as long as I can remember that records have an important role to play in the scheme of things---pleasure, education, promotion---all of that and more.

"But they can't come close to the real live thing. If you are too young to have heard Duke Ellington and His Famous Orchestra live, then... you never will. But you say you've heard recent re-releases, and what do I mean, well, it means it's not the same?

"That's just what I mean...it's not the same! The playing on the record may be fabulous, but the player was playing to a microphone, not an audience. And that makes the big difference, in my humble opinion. The microphone hears all, but couldn't care less. It's more than a rumor that the best music ever was not recorded. Is that bad? No! It's wonderful. You had to be there. Am I reaching you?

"And if you were there, you may have even tried to describe what you heard to someone who wasn't there. But, it didn't work, did it? You just had to be there!

"In life itself, you go with the bumps. It's worth it! And besides...for all of us, both performers and listeners, there's more good music up ahead. Don't you hear the orchestra warming up, and the excited buzz of the audience as they find their seats? Anticipation is in the air. Music is about to claim us.

Thank you, God!"

Sinatra's *Main Event* may have been his best ever. His 70s voice was built of a towering strength of voice that tattooed his audiences memory bank deeply and significantly. They would talk about it for years to come as I talk about it now. Don't forget, this Sinatra singing event attracted over 20,000 ticket holders. Besides, the second audience was listening around the world.

The song quality exceeded the recordings of many of the same songs recorded earlier. This was 1974 with Frank Sinatra in top form. The concert was held in the middle of a boxing ring. And, famed sportscaster Howard Cosell was the host. They say 350 technicians worked on that performance. The show was nothing short of perfection and the critics certified it calling the show "superb" and claimed the audience was in rapture. Sinatra was called "the master of his generation.."

The producer of the show was George Schlatter, a veteran television producer and said this: "Frank himself is the event. He's more than a singer. He exudes powerful energy. Everyone knows this about America: Coca-Cola, the Statue of Liberty, and Frank Sinatra."

Sinatra loves Christmas, he loves birthdays, he's patriotic and he loves to laugh.

He could have sung children's nursery rhymes and they would have loved him without "My Way" or even "Chicago."

Richard Grudens with Woody Herman at LeMans - Southampton, NY

FRANK'S COLOSSAL CONCERTS

Over his prolific career Frank Sinatra has performed at hundreds of concerts all over the world and over many years. We spotlight the greatest concerts:

OCTOBER 13, 1974, MADISON SQUARE GARDEN-THE MAIN EVENT

The Garden held 20,000 seats. Sinatra was at his best with "The House I Live In." Jonathan Schwartz pronounced this concert as Sinatra's very best.

NOVEMBER 13 THROUGH 20, 1975, THE LONDON PALLADIUM

The Palladium held 2286 seats. The requests for tickets was 350,000. The concert featured Frank Sinatra and Sarah Vaughan with the Count Basie Orchestra.

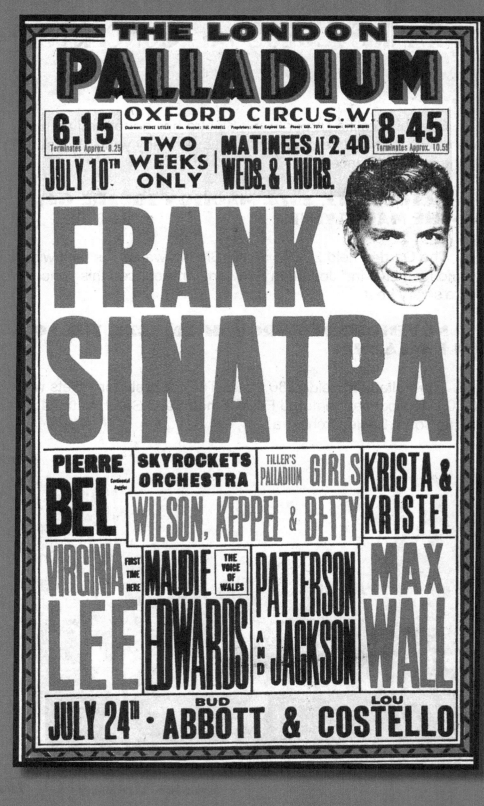

SEPTEMBER 27, 1979, EGYPT - AT THE BASE OF THE GREAT PYRAMIDS.

Frank Sinatra performed a benefit for THE FAITH AND HOPE REHABILITATION and HANDICAPPED. His generosity became legendary world wide.

JANUARY 26, 1980, RIO DE JANEIRO, BRAZIL, Maracana Soccer Stadium.

The 175,000 people who attended the event witnessed one of Frank Sinatra's best career performances singing on a center stage with six runway wings so he could get closer to his fans.

SEPTEMBER 27, 1986, MADRID, SPAIN - THE ULTIMATE EVENT

Frank Sinatra was now 70 years old and sang to an excited crowd of 40,000 fans in front of Chris Smith's 45 piece orchestra. When he sang "New York, New York" he received a 10 minute standing ovation.

Fabulous Frank wows at 70

FRANK SINATRA stepped out in front of his 45 piece orchestra to sing all his classic hits. From 'Come fly with me' to 'I've got you under my skin', Sinatra, 70, had the 40,000 audience eating out the palm of his hand.

Promoter Julio Mario said: "I've never seen a crowd so excited."

When he finally sang his classic signature New York, New York, he received a 10 minute standing ovation.

... and soloing on
"I've Got You Under My Skin'
whilst leading the
Trombone Section on
FRANK SINATRA's
world tour
"The Ultimate Event".

Chris Smith, soloing on Trombone, with His Orchestra

THE GREAT 1980 CONCERT IN RIO

175,000 people share the joy of a great concert. Over his career Frank Sinatra had established tens of thousands of fans all over the world, especially in the teeming city of Rio de Janeiro, Brazil. There was a legend in Brazil that said: "When a young man was courting his girl and she began pressing for a proposal of marriage from her amorous suitor, the man would stall her with the legendary exclamation, "Sure, when Frank Sinatra comes to Brazil." Well, it is presumed that Brazil's population expanded over the ensuing year.

On January 26, 1980, Frank Sinatra came to the Maracana Stadium in Rio, a place that could hold 175,000 people. It is a soccer stadium. The fans began arriving at eight o'clock in the morning. It was raining. The early birds sat through a full day of mostly heavy rain. The stadium was soon sold out.

The stadium was set up with a huge center stage with six wings extending in all directions with microphones everywhere, for Frank Sinatra repeating what Al Jolson did before him, being among the first entertainers to use the runway in performing his act. When Sinatra picked up the mike to begin his concert the rain abruptly stopped. "I looked up at the sky, toward Heaven, and thanked the Lord for this amazing favor. And when the concert was over, as I completed the encore, it began to rain again."

At one point in the concert, Sinatra lost the lyric during "Strangers in the Night," and the audience picked it up and the stadium full of fans began singing the song for him.

Then, a fan rushed up on the stage and grabbed Sinatra and kissed him as he tried to fight him off. It was the famous "Kissing Bandit" known to all of Brazil who has even kissed the shoe of the Pope. The audience enjoyed the incident overwhelmingly.

FRANK SINATRA had performed dozens of concerts in and outside of the United States over the length of his career. This along with his two weeks at New York's Carnegie Hall, always selling out completely, and usually on the first day of issue.

Maracana Stadium Today

Frank Sinatra and Beryl Davis

YOUR LUCKY STRIKE HIT PARADE
Starring Frank Sinatra

Tag Line "Lucky Strike means fine tobacco."

Be Happy, go Lucky,
Be Happy, go Lucky Strike
Be Happy, go Lucky
Go Lucky Strike today!

Mark Warnow 1943 Rehearsal of *Your Hit Parade*

A VERY POPULAR RADIO, AND THEN TV SHOW, *YOUR HIT PARADE* PARADED THROUGH 19 DIFFERENT ORCHESTRAS AND 52 DIFFERENT SINGERS FROM ITS 1935 RUN THROUGH 1959.

Some of the singers were Bea Wain, Buddy Clark, Dinah

Shore, Georgia Gibbs, Martha Tilton, Ginny Simms, Dick Haymes, Johnny Mercer, Doris Day, Andy Russell, Eileen Wilson, Lanny Ross, Joan Edwards. Lawrence Tibbett, Barry Wood and Wee Bonnie Baker, Beryl Davis, and, of course, the most famous of all - Frank Sinatra. When television came in it was Dorothy Collins, Gisele Mackenzie, Russell Arms and Snooky Lanson.

Some of the bandleaders were: Lennie Hayton, Al Goodman, Harry Sosnik, Harry Salter, Leo Reisman, Ray Sinatra, Mark Warnow, Peter Van Steeden. Lyn Murray conducted the chorus and served as musical director.

The program showcased mostly standard arrangements of the week' s most popular recordings with an added "Lucky Strike Extra," an up and coming tune not yet in the top ten. Sinatra would sing it even if he didn't like the tune. It was in the contract.

Gerald Nachman from Raised on Radio: "Long before the onslaught of Top 40 formats, *Your Hit Parade* was the sole oracle of pop music trends - a kind of weekly Grammy Awards. At first, the song s were the stars:. The singers, who earned a hundred dollars a show, weren't even credited. How songs were surveyed and selected was a secret highly guarded by the agency that ran the show, which insisted that its system was beyond reproach and, as announcer Andre' Baruch stated smartly each week, was the result of a tally of sheet music sales, listener requests, and jukebox selections 'coast-to-coast.' In fact, it was fairly random, and allegedly 'scientific' sam-

pling put together by hundreds of 'song scouts' across the country who talked to DJs, bandleaders, and record and sheet-music sales clerks and then reported the week's best-selling tunes. The show in turn, boosted record and jukebox sales, so the show's hits became self-perpetuating."

The show started a few years earlier when Lucky Strike aired the *Lucky Strike Dance Orchestra Show* that featured popular songs on Saturday night at ten and urged their listeners to" reach for a Lucky instead of a Sweet."

Frank Sinatra joined the show and remained for two years, then returned to appear with Doris Day from 1947 through 1949. Beryl Davis, the singer from England, was chosen by Frank Sinatra to replace Doris Day, who was off to Hollywood for her first movie, *Romance on the High Seas* in which she sang her signature song, "It's Magic."

Beryl Davis: "Richard, Frank was always kind to me and very supportive. He always included me, as after each show we would go out to dinner."

During the war years the show's theme was "This is Your Lucky Day," written by Ray Henderson, Buddy DeSylva and Lew Brown.

RECORDING SONGS AT THE FILM STUDIO VS THE REGULAR COMMERCIAL STUDIO

HOW IT WAS DONE

    1. It was called the prerecording process, a more superior method when producing film musicals.

    2. In the commercial recording studio a singer (Sinatra in this case) enters the studio, sings his song with the orchestra present,

listens to a playback of each take on an album, then selects the best performance, and heads for home. He takes home a disc and listens in case he want to change and re-record again.

3. Recording for films needs overdubbing songs to the vision afterwards.

4. Only dialogue is recorded on a movie set. Prerecording the musical numbers is the first step in a movie's production. To begin, the orchestra and vocalists record their parts on the soundstage (a film studio version of a recording studio).

5. When it comes time to film a scene, the performers act out the scenes containing musical numbers, while lip-synching along to the recording of the song made earlier.

6. Before the recording, however, the singers were handed a set of 78RPM playback discs, intended for rehearsal and reference only. There was a signal on the disc that allowed you come in on cue. It was like an alarm clock, but it was a popping sound. It worked well.

7. Lip-synching was at best difficult because, as Sinatra pointed out, "I never sing a song exactly the same way twice, so when I come to mime, I find it very hard. Sometimes miming seems to take away a lot of the spontaneity, and I find myself unconsciously thinking of different ways I might sing the song."

8. With films made at the studio, lighting and sound can be expertly controlled to remain consistant from shot to shot on a daily basis. The problems encountered in singing to playback when a production shoots on location are multiplied ten times, as many uncontrollable factors enter the equation. But every so often, a location shoot provided an opportunity for art to imitate life.

FROM THE LINER NOTES OF THE BOXED SET' FRANK SINATRA IN HOLLYWOOD (1940-1964)

PITCH, NOTE & TONE IN SINGING

You may be an amateur, perhaps one who sings karaoke at the local bar, or you may be a budding, serious singer looking to become professional. In any case there are three important terms you will have to know about to accomplish either cause.:

1. Pitch: which is the high or low frequency of a sound. When you sing you create pitch because your vocal cords vibrate at a specific speed. While you are singing and your vocal cords are vibrating at that specific speed, you sing a higher pitch than when they vibrate more slowly. For example, an A just above Middle C vibrates at 440 cycles per second which means your vocal cords open and close 440 times per second.

2. Notes are musical symbols that designate the pitch location.

3. Lastly, Tone: is the what they call color or timbre of pitch and may be described as an infinite term like warm, brilliant, dark, rich, lush, shrill, or rasping, harsh or scratching, and even jarring, squawky, or loudmouthed.

Young singer Julia Keefe sings with a warm tone, and Judy Garland can be warm, especially when she was young and under management of a singing coach and director, but became strident in her later singing tone.

THE SONGWRITERS

The Songwriters of Tin Pan Alley Who made the Big Band Era Come True for Singers like Frank Sinatra.

*I Like New York In June,
How About You?
I Like a Gershwin tune
How about you?*

Once during an interview, composer Harold Arlen said, "A good lyric is the composer's best friend." According to Arlen, a close bond between composer and lyricist is essential to the success of a song. Normally, a song is created when the usual thirty-two bar melody is written, and lyrics (words), are added and then arranged for interpretation by a musician, a group of musicians (band or orchestra), or a vocalist or group of vocalists. To become a song, a composition must include words. Reversing that role, a song may be defined as poetry set to music. A question may be: What came first, the chicken or the egg? The lyric or the melody? To which George Gershwin once glibly replied, "it's the contract."

Jule Styne with Sammy Cahn (Bottom)

A notable composer is distinctive in melodic line and construction. A distinguished lyricist is able to formulate words for already written music, which is extremely difficult to accomplish, by any stretch of the imagination. Is it easier to write music to words, or words to music?

During the course of my career, I've known a few notable songwriters. When I co-managed the NBC radio and television Ticket Division in New York back in the 1950's, I became a friend to songwriter J. Fred Coots who had written the legendary, perennial Christmas song "Santa Claus is Coming to Town" and the standards "You Go to My Head," said to be Glenn Miller's favorite song, and another now-standard "For All We Know." We always wound up talking about music and how his life consisted of an unending effort to plug his songs and help maintain them in public use in order to earn royalties, by which he lived.

Sammy Cahn

A songwriter named Joe Howard, who also wrote tunes for entertainer Beatrice Kay (mostly about the Gay Nineties), would keep me company on some days. He was down and out, and aging, so what available broadcast tickets I could spare he would give to friends in an effort to restore his validity in a world that seemed to have forgotten him. Late in 1952, comedian Milton Berle, known then as Mr. Television, honored Joe Howard on his *Texaco Star Theater* television show.

During the same period I spent many a lunch hour with a young piano-player who fronted an instrumental trio who performed gigs at local New York Hotels, as well as on Steve Allen's daytime, pre-*Tonight Show* television program *Date in Manhattan*. His now familiar name is Cy Coleman. In one of the unused third floor radio studios, I would sit alongside Cy on his piano bench while he practiced with his trio. I would woefully sing along. Stan Kenton sideman, and then NBC studio musician, Eddie Safranski played bass. We became lunch-time buddies. I often attended those Cy Coleman gigs at the Park Lane Hotel on weekend evenings with my friends. Cy was experimenting writing songs even then. "Witchcraft, "The Best is Yet to Come," and "The Colors of My Life" remain some of his best.

In my last three books, The Best Damn Trumpet Player, The Song Stars, and The Music Men, I wrote about many of the musicians, vocalists, and arrangers of the Big

Jule Styne

Band Era and beyond. None of these books could have been written unless somebody first wrote the songs these musicians were to play, the vocalists sang, and the arrangers arranged, and orchestrated.

Tin Pan Alley

Although not known as songwriters, some of the subjects of those books also composed music or wrote lyrics at one point or another in their career : Mel Torme' ("The Christmas Song"), Peggy Lee ("Manana"), Paul Weston ("I Should Care"), Ella Fitzgerald (with Van Alexander - "A Tisket, A Tasket"), Lee Hale ("The Ladies Who Sang with the Bands"), Frankie Laine ("We'll Be Together Again"), Al Jolson ("My Mammy"), Bing Crosby ("Where The Blue of the Night"), Duke Ellington ("Sophisticated Lady"), Larry Elgart (The theme of "American Bandstand," "Bandstand Boogie".

Today, Tin Pan Alley is essentially The Brill Building and immediate vicinity in New York City, the singular place where music publishing offices were located and where songwriters and song plugger's congregated. The fourteen story Brill is located on the Northwest corner of Forty-ninth Street and Broadway, once having housed the Zanzibar nightclub and Dempsey's Restaurant. Jack, the great heavyweight champion, used to sit at a table next to the window so passerby's could see him and be lured to enter the place. Two blocks north, at 51st Street was 1650 Broadway, home of Irving Berlin Music Publishing and the second "Tin Pan Alley." I understand that Ervin Drake wrote the Frank Sinatra standard "It Was a Very Good Year" in the office of publisher Artie Mogul at 1650 Broadway.

Ervin tells the fabled story of two music publishers. "Way back, two such firms were Mills Music, headed by Irving and Jack Mills, brothers. Their reputation was not the best. Across town in Radio City, was the home of Edward B. Marks Music and they had a like reputation.

The joke among old-time songwriters was that when it came to pay royalties to writers, Marks paid off in mills (1/10th of a cent) and Mills paid off in marks. (In Germany the mark had fallen to an all time low.)

The original Tin Pan Alley first centered around West 28th Street in New York City at the turn-of-the century and up to World War I, where many of the music hall singers and vaudevillian actors once lived. Their many song-publishing offices, like the

George Gershwin

old Jerome Remick Company, employed piano players to demonstrate newly published songs for vaudeville performers who may have been searching for new musical material and for the general public at large. One of these pianists who worked as songpluggers for the Max Dreyfus firm, Chappell Music was young George Gershwin. But Dreyfus soon learned he had a young genius on his hands and signed him up as a composer, like Jerome Kern and Richard Rodgers. They all started with Dreyfus.

The location later moved uptown to Forty-Sixth Street, between Broadway and Sixth Avenue, and when sound of radio dominated the music business, Tin Pan Alley re-located into lush office suites beneath the shadow of NBC's Rockefeller Center, extending up to Fifty-second Street where CBS radio was located.
The designation Tin Pan Alley , actually a sobriquet for the sheet-music publishing industry, was adopted from the tinkling, sometimes out-of-tune pianos being intensely exercised, sounding to a passerby like tin pans being drummed upon as groups of songwriters simultaneously demonstrated their craft at the offices of various publishers through sometimes open windows. Tin Pan Alley was the place where sheet music was written, demonstrated, packaged, and vigor-

Harold Arlen

ously peddled. Remember, with no radio or television, sheet music had to thrive and survive on the strength of song sheet demonstrators playing a new tune in those store-front offices of publishers who also relied upon the illustrated sheet music covers that artfully portrayed the allegory of a tune, sometimes featuring photos of a popular musician or vocalist who had successfully performed it on stage or on recordings. To create a hit song, the axiom of the time was, You got to say "I Love You" in thirty-two bars," and "keep the title short and memorable."

The participants called themselves *Alleymen*. The Alleymen, faced with radio companies refusal to pay songwriters for airing songs, and restaurants blatantly playing songs without compensating their authors, organized ASCAP , the American Society of Composers Authors and Publishers, which still solidly and securely represent the song writing community in all aspects.

Some composers collaborated with a single lyricist or maybe just a few, and some with many. Irving Berlin and Cole Porter were noted to write both the music and lyrics to almost all their compositions. Richard Rodgers collaborated first with Lorenz (Larry) Hart and later with Oscar Hammerstein II. Composer Harry Warren, noted mostly for songs composed for Hollywood musicals, collaborated with lyricists Al Dubin, Mack Gordon, Ralph Blane, Arthur Freed, Ira Gershwin, Leo Robin, Billy Rose, and others. Like Warren, Harold Arlen acquired many additional lyricists when he first split with Tin Pan Alley and Broadway and went to California to work for the movies. After all, being work for hire, composers were not always able to select their lyricists. Lyricist Ted Koehler was Harold Arlen's early, principal collaborator especially during their two shows-a-year job at Harlem, New York's famous Cotton Club. Along the way Arlen linked up with E.Y. "Yip" Harburg (who wrote the lyrics for Arlen's *Wizard of Oz* music); Johnny Mercer, Leo Robin, Ralph Blane, Dorothy Fields, Ira Gershwin, and even author Truman Capote, back on Broadway for their show *House of Flowers*.

Although most of us are more familiar with the names of Irving Berlin, Richard Rodgers, Cole Porter, or George Gershwin, it must be realized that the names of Harold Arlen and some others surely belong among this unique group of musical geniuses. No one can say why the name of Harold Arlen, who composed the great standards "Come Rain or Come Shine," "Over the Rainbow," "That Old Black Magic," "Stormy Weather," and my favorite Arlen piece "My Shining Hour," all songs perfected in recordings by Frank Sinatra. It may be argued that Arlen had perhaps too many collaborators, thus his name became somewhat diluted. This was due partially to the lyricist selection process when he composed for the Hollywood studios, known then as the "composer's haven."

THE FRANK SINATRA I KNEW

By ERVIN DRAKE

A man whose talents are as diverse as they are successful, Ervin Drake's impressive life in music includes contributions as
a composer, lyricist, impresario and copyright champion. He wrote
he words and music to the Sinatra blockbuster "It Was a Very Good
Year," and "Frankie Laine's favorite, "I Believe," just to name two.

Ervin produced hundreds
of music programs on
television. As president of
the Songwriter's Guild, his
tireless efforts to cham-
pion the rights of songwriters helped establish the
monumental copyright
act of 1976. I'm proud to
say that Ervin Drake has
been my friend of over 20
years.

The first time I
heard Frank Sinatra's
recording of my song, "It
Was a Very Good Year,"
it was definitely not under
the best set of circum-
stances. I had checked
into a London hotel suite
in the late summer of 1965
with my wife and two young

Ervin Drake and Richard Grudens
Five Town Music College - 2007

daughters. Having been out of the states and out of touch for two
months, I phoned a music publisher David Platz, who handled work
of mine in the UK. He asked with some excitement: "How do you like
your new Sinatra record?" I confessed to total ignorance. "Hold on, I'll
play it for you."

And so, through the very Lo-Fi earpiece of a wall phone, with one teenager and one sub-teen racketing in the background, I heard my song performed incomparably. The genius of the singer and the orchestra were both evident, even though the boiler factory din of my

darling family. "How do you like that?" asked David.

"Play it again!" was my answer. And after issuing heavy threats to my kids I listened again to the 4-minute, 12-second recording - (very long for 1965) and I was ecstatic. When we returned home, the first thing I did was to buy the LP and play it at least thirty times the first day. To this day I get a real charge whenever that recording is played.

In 1979 Frank Sinatra was preparing a celebration of forty years in show business. It was to include a taping for NBC at a show-room in Caesar's Palace. He invited people in his life. I was one of those. Edith, my wife and I flew to Las Vegas. I was determined to make this a big event because Edith had never been to Vegas. We dined high on the hog. Excellent wines. Three days later at check out there was no bill. How come? "Mr. Sinatra has taken care of it."

As they say, that was not in the contract, but that's how he was. And always, always, never to the contrary-Francis Albert was

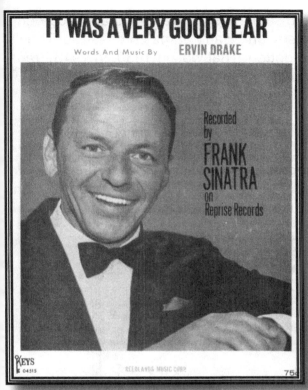

IT WAS A VERY GOOD YEAR

Words And Music By **ERVIN DRAKE**

Recorded by **FRANK SINATRA** on Reprise Records

KEYS
04515   REDLANDS MUSIC CORP   75¢

gracious. I have heard and read all the other stories you have, but the man I knew was beautiful.

When the Voice and I became friends, he would phone me at the house two or three times a year. "Hello, Ervin, it's Frank!
"Hi Frank."
"How are you, Ervin?"
"I'm fine."
"You need anything?"
"No, Frank, but thanks for asking."
"All right, but if you ever need anything, don't forget to give me a holler!"

That was the Sinatra I knew. I gave more songs to Perry Como and Barbra Streisand, but they never called me. Sometimes I doubt they even knew I existed, but Francis Albert Sinatra was the warmest public figure I've ever had the joy of knowing." "It Was a Very Good Year" was arranged by Gordon Jenkins and it won not one, but two Grammy's.

JACK LAWRENCE

Songwriter Jack Lawrence, whom we lost during the Spring of 2009, the composer of an early Sinatra success "All or Noth-

ing at All," (with Arthur Altman) said the song was originally recorded by Freddy Martin, Jimmy Dorsey and Harry James orchestras. They were released and quickly forgotten. That was in 1939. In 1943 Frank Sinatra, now on his own, recorded the song and broke box office records

In his first appearance at the New York Paramount. Columbia had signed Sinatra, whose popularity was great. Before they could get him into the recording studio, the American Federation of Musicians called a strike causing the companies to experiment with a cappella recordings, but the public would not buy them.

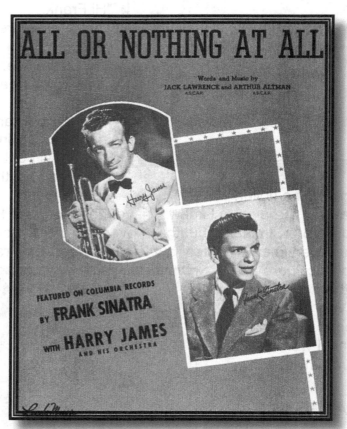

Jack Lawrence: "Then clever Lou Levy, the songs publisher, reminded Columbia that it had a perfect Sinatra recording to re-release: "All or Nothing at All." The original had carried the label crediting 'Harry James and His Orchestra" in large print and in smaller letters, 'Vocal by Frank Sinatra.' Lou pointed out that the entire record sounded llike a solo by Frank because of the length of the song." Columbia gleefully rushed out this recording, but with a new label which read in bold print: 'Frank Sinatra accompanied by the Harry James Orchestra.'"

Talking with Louella Parsons in 1944 Sinatra said: "'All or Nothing at All' was the song that gave Harry James and me our walking papers out of the old Victor Hugo café - and incidentally, out of Hollywood. The manager came up and waved his hands for us to stop. He said Harry's trumpet was too loud for the joint and my singing was just plain lousy. He said the two of us couldn't draw flies as an attraction - and I guess he was right. The room was empty as a barn. It's a funny thing about that song; the recording we made four years ago is now one of the top spots among the best sellers, but it's the same old recording. It's the song I used to audition for Tommy Dorsey, who signed me on the strength of it. And now it's my first big record hit."

Frank Sinatra has recorded this song in many new versions over the years and Jack Lawrence was always grateful to him for having included it in practically all of his retrospective albums.

MATT DENNIS AND TOM ADAIR
FRANK SINATRA'S FAVORITE DORSEY ERA RECORDINGS WERE BY MATT DENNIS AND TOM ADAIR

- "Angel Eyes"
- "Violets for Your Furs."
- "Everything Happens to Me."
- "Let's Get Away from It All."
- "The Night We Called It a Day."

All which he re-recorded once again before his joining Capitol Records. It has been said that the team wrote "Will You Still Be Mine," Everything, and Let's Get Away, in one week. Later, Matt and Tom were introduced to Tommy Dorsey by Jo Stafford.

Matt Dennis:

I have very special memories of Frank Sinatra, and it is with good reason that I will be ever grateful to him. In the fall of 1941, when I joined the Tommy Dorsey band as a song writer-composer along with my lyric-writing pal from California, Tom Adair. Frank was singing with the band in New York and, because of his special way with a song, was causing quite a stir. It was during this time that he became most known by the most famous of his many nick names: "The Voice." It wasn't to long before he recorded three of our new songs: "Everything Happens to Me," "Lets Get Away from it All" and "Violets for Your Furs," all of which to my benefit as a young song- writer became hits. Frank's vocals were wonderful, and he did me a great favor by continuing to perform and record these songs for the rest of his life and career. I am proud to have written a song especially for him "The Night We

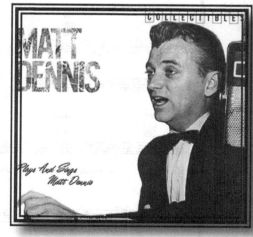

Tom Adair Later in Life

Called It A Day." It appeared on his first solo recording date after leaving the Dorsey band. His increased following, bolstered by outstanding performances around the world and his emergence as an actor, soon made his career one of epic proportions. In 1953 I wrote "Angel Eyes" with Earl Brent, who penned a remarkably potent lyric. Frank recorded this on his memorable album *Only The Lonely* on capital records, and it has never sounded better. Our song caught on, and I am proud of the fact that because Frank loved it so much he included it in many of his dramatic performances. I am reminded of an important moment in Frank's fine career. In 1971, after so many years of outstanding shows, he shocked the world by announcing that he would retire. At the Shrine Auditorium in Los Angeles, Frank closed his final concert by dramatically performing "Angel Eyes." With a sadness in his voice, under a spotlight which would gradually fade to black he sang the final lines of the lyric "'scuse me while I disappear" - a true climax to what had been such a fantastic career.

The worldwide reaction to his retirement announcement was one of devastation, a really stark surprise to the Sinatra following. The media made most of this, and while I was so flattered by the importance Frank had made of my song, it was a sad time for us. But happily, Frank could not stay idle for long. Ol' Blue Eyes is back! became a popular expression, and for the next 27 years, Frank would continue his extraordinary career to even greater success. I am pleased to say that Frank recorded yet another song of mine- "It's Over, It's Over, It's Over" with a fine Nelson Riddle arrangement. That year, fate stepped in, and after an outstanding life as a superstar and a wonderfully talented performer who championed the songs that he loved, Frank Sinatra passed away. He has been so active through the years and it is sad that he will no longer be with us. A documentary was repeated on television the first few weeks after his passing, including scenes from his very last concert. Again, he performed his familiar closer "Angel Eyes," and as the spotlight faded to darkness, he sang that last poignant line: "'Scuse me me while I disappear." This time it was for real! Thanks, Frank... I am forever grateful for a lifetime of your support, your belief in my songs, and for including them alongside those of the songwriter masters. I will never forget that you made my life as a songwriter a successful one, and nobody sang my songs better than you did!... God Bless You!"

JOE BUSHKIN

Sinatra: "One of the things I hated to leave when I quit the Dorsey Band was the piano playing of Joe Bushkin."

Joe Bushkin wrote a few great Sinatra songs when they were both with Dorsey. One was "Oh, Look At Me Now." My lovely friend and Dorsey vocalist Connie Haines was the other voice on the landmark recording of that tune. Connie always said that "Joe Bushkin was the best piano player she ever knew."

Buskin said: "I'll never forget opening night at the Astor Roof in New York with the Dorsey band back in June of 1940. The joint was loaded with celebs---Oscar Levant, Benny Goodman and Ira Gershwin and a few others I recall. Frank usually sang just a chorus of each song in the middle of the arrangement. The only song he actually ended on was 'Begin the Beguine.'

"That night, the end of 'Beguine' a big shout went up, and the crowd was yelling for more Frank. He'd been used to singing with the Pied Pipers, and was really taken with the response. Next came 'Polka Dots and Moonbeams'---and right after the vocal chorus, the crowd again wanted more from him; so Tommy just cut the band off and told Frank to start calling tunes and for me to back him up, just the two of us."

Frank Sinatra called out songs to Joe Bushkin. Back then Frank's range only went up to a D, although later he was able to reach F natural. Bushkin was being careful not to go beyond the range and in the song "Smoke Gets in Your Eyes" at the bridge Bushkin drew a blank and walked off the bandstand. Frank carried on *a cappella* and then Bushkin returned to finish the tune. The crowd reacted well and laughed, and when Joe saw Tommy Dorsey coming off the stand he thought he would be fired for walking off.

"Thank God, Tommy got a kick out of the situation," Joe said.

That night was an important turning point for Joe Bushkin and the history of popular music. The entire focus of the music shifted from the band to the band singer. It was a meaningful change and it all started with Joe Bushkin and Frank Sinatra.

THE CHRONOLOGICAL

JOE BUSHKIN
1940-1946

piano solos
and with Hot Lips Page, Zoot Sims, Cozy Cole,
Specs Powell, Barney Kessel, Al Morgan...

CLASSICS

LONDON BY NIGHT
Songwriter Carroll Coates

'Yes, for me, 1950 was a "a very good year." 'I was playing my first steady piano gig at a little private club just off Piccadilly Circus in London. One of the members was an American screenwriter who eventually asked me the name of the tune I was playing so often. It was my melody of "London by Night" and, after I'd talked the lyric, he asked if I had a copy he could give to his friend Julie Wilson, who was about to open a cabaret engagement at London's Embassy Room. A copy? All I could offer at the time was a rough penciled effort, but Julie figured it out and decided to include it in her act as a gesture to her London audiences.

"Frank Sinatra was concurrently appearing at the London Palladium. One night, after his own show, he stopped in to hear Julie and partake of a late supper. When she finished her act, closing with my song, I saw her stop by his table for a chat, punctuated with a few glances in my direction. Gliding over to me she said, 'You'd best go and introduce yourself. He asked me who wrote the song I closed with.'

"Somehow my legs covered the distance to his table." 'Great song, kid!' said the Voice. 'I'd like to take it back to the States and record it, OK?'

"I can't recall my exact reaction beyond a gulp, but I do remember clearly our second meeting. One on one at his room in the Hyde Park Hotel, the then number one singer encouraged me to come to America and pursue a song writing career.'

That was in 1950 and young Coates went to America and did what the young Sinatra advised. He moved on to Hollywood where Sinatra arranged for him to play at his Villa Capri restaurant. Sinatra re-recorded the song "London by Night" and included it in his album *Come Fly with Me* and *Great Songs of Great Britain*. In 1957 Sinatra included his other song "No One Ever Tells You" in the Capitol album *A Swingin'Affair*.

Sinatra had opened the door for Carroll Coates as he had for many others and he has always been grateful to the guy with the smiling blue eyes.

SAMMY CAHN

Talk about Sinatra's songwriters and you instantly come up with Sammy Cahn, an absolute romantic writer of some of the best popular music of all time. Consider "Love and Marriage," "I've Heard That Song Before," "It's Magic," the song that catapulted Doris Day into a movie singing queen, "Sinatra favorites "I Fall in Love Too Easily," "All the Way," a Sinatra anthem almost always performed at his concerts, "I'll Walk Alone," "The Tender Trap," "Be My Love, "and "Because You're Mine," both songs introduced by, and almost always associated with, the great Mario Lanza.

Sammy, supreme lyricist, was born Samuel Cohen on the lower East side of New York City in 1913. He walked off with four Academy Awards for his life's work of attaching suitable, loving, and clever words to songs of many composers. Among them Saul Chaplin, Jule Styne, Jimmy Van Heusen, Nicholas Brodszky, Victor Young, and Alfred Newman. The Oscar-winning songs were "Three Coins in the Fountain" -1954: "All the Way," -1957; "High Hopes,"-1959: "Call Me Irresponsible" in 1963 - Sinatra hits all. Besides winning four Oscars, he was actually nominated for twenty-three. "Lyric writing has always been a thrilling adventure for me, and something I've done with the kind of ease that only comes from joy. And, through my association with Tommy Dorsey way back when, came the enduring and perhaps the most satisfying relationship in my lyric-writing career. Frank Sinatra, of course.

Cahn was first a member of the "Songwriters Hall of Fame" in 1972, and later its President, succeeding another great songwriter,

Johnny Mercer.

It was generally considered that the team of Sammy Cahn and Jimmy Van Heusen were the personal song-writing team for Frank Sinatra.

SOME OTHER SINATRA DRIVEN SONGS BY SAMMY CAHN

- "COME DANCE WITH ME."
- "FIVE MINUTES MORE"
- "SATURDAY NIGHT."
- "COME FLY WITH ME."
- "I GUESS I'LL HANG MY TEARS OUT TO DRY."
- "TIME AFTER TIME."
- "I SHOULD CARE."

I should not neglect to mention that it was Sammy Cahn who wrote the English lyrics for the song that elevated the Andrews Sisters to fame: "Bei Mir Bist Du Schoen" a Yiddish folk tune written for the theater in 1933. The song became the first million-selling recording by a female vocal group.

Jimmy Van Heusen

JIMMY: "I'd say Frank Sinatra is my favorite singer because he's the best there is!"

Jimmy Van Heusen is a prolific songwriter who made his fame writing songs that Bing Crosby made famous. Jimmy's early success, besides the Billy Rose Aquacade in New York, was his work with the great Harold Arlen, writing songs for the original uptown Cotton Club in collaboration with Arlen back in 1932.

"At that time Lena Horne was fifteen years old and in the front line of dancers. I was eighteen and my real name was Edward Chester Babcock." Jimmy had his name changed when his boss at WSYR where he was a

disc jockey and didn't like the name Babcock, so I looked out the window and saw a Van Heusen collars ad, before they made shirts, and figured it would be a pretty good name for me to use. So, that how it happened.

Jimmy's first big song was "Imagination" and it became a big hit. Mark Sandrich, the producer of the Astaire-Rogers movies heard the song and said to an underling "Get me the guy who wrote that song."

"They found me at the Oyster Bar on Long Island and they hired me for two pictures. Johnny Burke wrote the songs for the picture even though he was working for Crosby and already making big money."

The movie was *Love Thy Neighbor* with comedians Jack Benny and Fred Allen. There Jimmy met Bing Crosby. He invited Jimmy to write the songs for his next picture....*The Road to Zanzibar* with Bob Hope. Not bad. Writing for Bing and Bob.

Jimmy wrote songs for Crosby for forty years and for Sinatra for forty-four years.

"They were both beautiful people," Jimmy told Fred Hall, the famed disc jockey in his book Dialogues in Swing, "But Bing was the granddaddy of them all. He taught them all how to sing. And Sinatra was first to admit it. Crosby liked Sinatra and they always worked well together. "

Jimmy with Johnny Burke

Jimmy wrote "Swinging on a Star," "Polka Dots and Moonbeams," "All the Way," "Come Fly with Me," "Here's That Rainy Day," "Darn That Dream," "Going My Way," and for Frank Sinatra's first daughter, "Nancy with the Laughing Face," with lyrics by actor/comedian Phil silvers, "Call Me Irresponsible," "Moonlight Becomes You," and all the songs for the Bing Crosby, Bob Hope Road pictures and a whole lot more. His collaborators were Eddie DeLange, Johnny Mercer, Jules Styne and Sammy Cahn.

JImmy Van Heusen and Margaret Whiting

Jimmy never left Frank Sinatra's side when he was down and out in the early fifties. "I had it out with Frank in Toot's Shorr's and after that we were close forever." Jimmy went on to write songs for Sinatra like "Tender Trap" that won an Academy Award, and the songs for *The Joker is Wild.*

"'All the Way" was a great song for both of us. And Frank recorded 'Second Time Around' and it was a hit for Sinatra, although I wrote it for Bing. The best song I wrote for Sinatra was 'That Rainy Day.'"

Jimmy was the pianist for Frank Sinatra in London at the Command Performance in 1951.

"Rainy Day" is a great song because of all the changes and it is haunting and is also a wonderful instrumental on its own. For me "Rainy Day" is my most played song. Let me add, Richard, I loved writing for Frank Sinatra. He did justice to every song he ever sang."

Jimmy Van Huesen won four Academy Awards for his songs,"Swinging on a Star," "All the Way," High Hopes," and "Call Me Irresponsible," with the exception of "Swinging on a Star," the last three were Sinatra singing masterpieces.

JOHNNY BURKE

Well, I guess Johnny Burke has put enough lyrics to songs that Frank Sinatra sang over his career that qualify him for an appearance in this book. Let's see, there's "Pennies from Heaven," although it really is a Crosby song, and Burke was essentially a staunch Crosby songwriter first, but that didn't stop Frank Sinatra from singing some pretty good Burke songs.

Here are some Sinatra-Burke beauties that will be played for the next one-hundred years. "Polka Dots and Moonbeams," with Jimmy Van Heusen, "It Could Happen to You," "But Beautiful," "Like Someone in Love," "Here's That Rainy Day," " Imagination," "What's New?" (the previous one not with Van Heusen), among others.

Johnny Burke passed from us at a very young fifty-five. His longest and most productive works are, of course, those produced

with Jimmy Van Heusen. He once worked as a pianist and song salesman in Chicago in the firm of Irving Berlin Publishing. Berlin transferred him to the New York office where he collaborated with a composer named Harold Spina. They wrote songs that were played by Paul Whiteman and Guy Lombardo. Their big hit was a tune called "Annie Doesn't Live Here Anymore,"

Burke emigrated to Hollywood, where he soon met Jimmy Van Heusen with whom he wrote most of his successful songs, after some minor works with Arthur Johnston and Jimmy Monaco. Burke worked his craft with Paramount exclusively. The song team won an Academy Award with the Crosby tune from the film *Going My Way*, "Swinging on a Star."

RECORDING STATISTICS
THE BEST OF SINATRA

Frank Sinatra recorded over 150 singles and enough albums to reach over 2000 total songs recorded. This was accomplished over more than 50 years.

Before the new and revised Sinatra evolved into a major star, he released the album *Swing and Dance* with Frank Sinatra, which may well be his best album before those lush performances in Las Vegas and beyond. The album had it all. "It's Only a Paper Moon," "My Blue Heaven, "You Do Something to Me," "When You're Smiling," and (shades of Fred and Ginger), "The Continental."

Yes, these were all established standards and swing with them he did. The old folks and young new fans were enamored of this wonderful album. The album, *Songs for Swingin' Lovers*, one of the seventeen concept albums, was released in 1956, and is considered by many critics and fans as the best of the collection.

Songs are "It Happened in Monterey," "Old Devil Moon," and my favorite (also done recently by Michael Feinstein) "How About You," "You're Getting to be a Habit with Me," "Anything Goes," and ten more fun-filled evergreens arranged and orchestrated by you know who, the master himself: Nelson Riddle.

Nelson continued with Frank's next

blockbuster, *A Swinging Affair* in 1957 that firmly established Frank as the then current King of popular music, despite the proliferation of rock and roll material filling the airwaves. The track with Frank singing "Night and Day," with Duke Ellington's own Juan Tizol swinging his legendary trombone, and Nelson's rich genius. This has to be one of Frank's perfect albums.

Sinatra and Friends featured Frank with a handful of artists that included Nat "King" Cole, ("Exactly Like You") Dinah Shore and Frank doing "Tea for Two," and Louis Armstrong dueting with Frank on "Birth of the Blues." Added in were a couple of Bing Crosby joint ventures. All of this, of course, before the famed *Duet* Albums appeared much later.

In the remarkable, emotionally charged album of music, 1958's *Only the Lonely*, Sinatra, complex and sad and dark, was working with arranger Nelson Riddle once again. The song "Only the Lonely" proved to me that Sinatra understood his craft and knew how to reach deep into his own heart and soul. The twelve tracks project despair and sadness, and you feel the pain if you happen to be in the same condition. Here, too, Sinatra's longtime pianist Bill Miller assists beautifully on the great saloon song, Harold Arlen and Johnny Mercer's "One for My Baby," a Sinatra benchmark classic. Sinatra is the singing genius at this point in his career. His best overall is still yet to come, but this rivals all his other works.

And finally, Sinatra's 80th-Live in Concert is a brighter affair, an album he dedicated to his wife Barbara and rides high in energy with a handful of great tunes: "You are the Sunshine of My Life," "New York, New York," "Soliloquy" from Rodgers and Hammerstein's earlier Broadway smash, *Carousel*; "Strangers in the Night," all these cuts longtime favorites, topped by the thrilling classic, Paul Anka's "My Way." No one sings it like Sinatra. Who could ask for anything more, as Ira Gershwin once inquired of life in a song. Frank was a happy man at this late stage of his life thanks to his hitching up to Barbara Marx, who helped him settle down to a more stabile life.

Trilogy carried much success, and the hit single "New York, New York."
By now, Sinatra had become he most enduring entertainer in the history of pop
music, except Al Jolson, who, decades earlier had earned that sobriquet in spades-
Americas' Greatest Entertainer. In the modern version of such success, Sinatra
had placed songs on the charts for fifty years. Thirteen years afterwards, he had
the number two album on the popular charts. (*Duets*, selling more than six million
copies), increasing his amazing record to over 60 years. On Frank's seventy-ninth
birthday, *Duets II* was on the *Billboard* Top 10, the thirty-sixth album to reach that
plateau.

SINATRA SINGLES

1939-Harry James (Uncredited) - Columbia - Re-Released In 1943 With Sinatra's Name On The Label.
- *ALL OR NOTHING AT ALL*

1940-DORSEY ON VICTOR
- *I'LL NEVER SMILE AGAIN*
- *IMAGINATION*
- *OUR LOVE AFFAIR*
- *STARDUST*
- *TRADE WINDS*
- *WE THREE*

1941-DORSEY ON VICTOR
- *DO I WORRY?*
- *DOLORES*
- *EVERYTHING HAPPENS TO ME*
- *LET'S GET AWAY FROM IT ALL*
- *OH, LOOK AT ME NOW* (with Connie Haines)
- *THIS LOVE OF MINE*
- *TWO IN LOVE*

1942-DORSEY ON VICTOR
- *DAYBREAK*
- *JUST AS THOUGH YOU WERE HERE*
- *TAKE ME*
- *THERE ARE SUCH THINGS*

1943-DORSEY ON VICTOR

- *IN THE BLUE OF EVENING*
- *IT'S ALWAYS YOU*
- *IT STARTED ALL OVER AGAIN*

1943   ON COLUMBIA with James

- *ALL OR NOTHING AT ALL*

ON COLUMBIA with Dorsey

- *CLOSE TO YOU*
- *PEOPLE WILL SAY WE'RE IN LOVE*
- *SUNDAY, MONDAY OR ALWAYS*
- *YOU'LL NEVER KNOW*

1944 ON COLUMBIA

- *I COULDN'T SLEEP A WINK LAST NIGHT*

1945
- *DREAM*
- *I DREAM OF YOU*
- *NANCY*
- *SATURDAY NIGHT*

1946
- *DAY BY DAY*
- *FIVE MINUTES MORE*
- *OH! WHAT IT SEEMED TO BE*
- *THE COFFEE SONG*
- *THEY SAY IT'S WONDERFUL*
- *WHITE CHRISTMAS*

1947
- *MAM'SELLE*

1948
- No Sinatra singles made Billboards Top Ten

1949
- *THE HUCKLEBUCK*

1954
- *THREE COINS IN THE FOUNTAIN*
- *YOUNG AT HEART*

1955
- *LEARNIN' THE BLUES*
- *LOVE AND MARRIAGE*

1956
- *HEY, JEALOUS LOVER*

1966 ON REPRISE
- *STRANGERS IN THE NIGHT*
- *THAT'S LIFE*

1967
- *SOMETHIN' STUPID* **with Nancy Sinatra**

SINATRA'S ALBUMS

CHRONOLOGICALLY- CAPITOL & REPRISE ALBUMS

CAPITOL

1954
- SONGS FOR YOUNG LOVERS
- SWING EASY

1955
- IN THE WEE SMALL HOURS

1956
- SONGS FOR SWINGIN' LOVERS

1957
- CLOSE TO YOU
- A SWINGIN' AFFAIR
- WHERE ARE YOU?
- A JOLLY CHRISTMAS

1958
- COME FLY WITH ME
- ONLY THE LONELY

1959
- COME DANCE WITH ME
- LOOK TO YOUR HEART
- NO ONE CARES

1960
- NICE 'n' EASY

1961
- SINATRA'S SWINGIN' SESSION
- ALL THE WAY

- COME SWING WITH ME

1961
- RING-A-DING-DING (REPRISE)
- COME SWING WITH ME (Capitol)
- SINATRA SWINGS
- I REMEMBER TOMMY (REPRISE)

1962
- SINATRA AND SWINGS (REPRISE)
- POINT OF NO RETURN
- SINATRA SINGS OF LOVE AND THINGS
- SINATRA AND SWINGIN' BRASS (REPRISE)
- ALL ALONE (REPRISE)
- ALL THE FOLLOWING ALBUMS ARE REPRISE RELEASES

1963
- SINATRA-BASIE
- THE CONCERT SINATRA
- SINATRA'S SINATRA

1964
- DAYS OF WINE AND ROSES
- SINATRA-BASIE: IT MIGHT AS WELL BE SPRING
- SOFTLY,AS I LEAVE YOU

1965
- SINATRA '65
- SEPTEMBER OF MY YEARS
- A MAN AND HIS MUSIC
- MY KIND OF BROADWAY

1966
- MOONLIGHT SINATRA
- STRANGERS IN THE NIGHT
- SINATRA-BASIE: SINATRA AT THE SANDS
- THAT'S LIFE

1967
- FRANCIS ALBERT SINATRA & ANTONIO CARLOS JO-BIM
- FRANK & NANCY

1968
- FRANCIS A. & EDWARD K.
- CYCLES

1969
- MY WAY
- A MAN ALONE

1970
- WATERTOWN

1971
- SINATRA & COMPANY

1973
- OL' BLUE EYES IS BACK

1974
- SOME NICE THINGS I MISSED
- THE MAIN EVENT-Live from Madison Square Garden

1980
- TRILOGY

1981
- SHE SHOT ME DOWN

1984
- L.A. IS MY LADY (Q.WEST)

1990
- Released on Capitol:
- Frank Sinatra-The Capitol Years
- Released on Reprise:

1991
- Sinatra-The Reprise Collection

1990
- Sinatra-The Main Event (Live from Madison Square Garden)

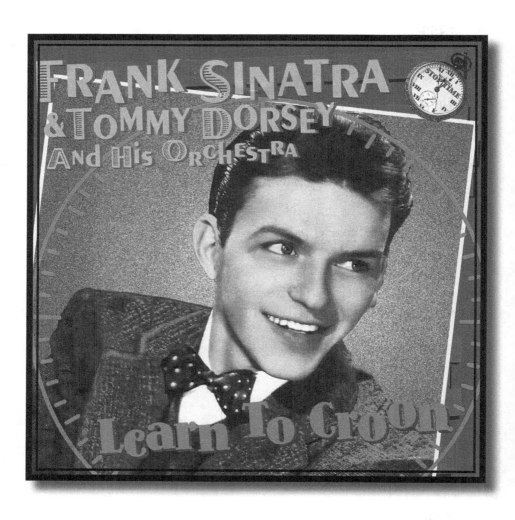

BEST RECORDINGS

FRANK SINATRA'S 25 Best Recordings

1. "SWEET LORRAINE" with Sinatra on vocal, and an amazing group of jazz all-stars Nat "King" Cole on piano, Johnny Hodges on alto sax, Charlie Shavers on trumpet, Coleman Hawkins on tenor sax, Eddie Safranski on bass. w. Mitchell Parish, m. Clifford Burwell.

2. "THE HOUSE I LIVE IN" w.Allen Lewis m. Earl Robinson.

3, "OH, WHAT IT SEEMED TO BE" w.m. Bennie Benjamin, George Weiss, Frankie Carle.

4. "LAURA" w.Johnny Mercer m. David Raksin.

5. "ALL OR NOTHING AT ALL" w.m. Jack Lawrence, Arthur Altman.

6. "PUT YOUR DREAMS AWAY FOR ANOTHER DAY: w. Ruth Lowe m. Paul Mann, Stephan Weiss.

7. "TIME AFTER TIME" w.Sammy Cahn m. Jule Styne arr. Axel Stordahl.

8. "I'M A FOOL TO WANT YOU" w.Jack Wolf/Frank Sinatra m. Joel. Herron arr. Axel Stordahl.

9. "A LOVELY WAY TO SPEND AN EVENING." w. m. Jack Lawrence, Arthur Altman.

10. "IN THE WEE SMALL HOURS OF THE MORNING" w. Bob Hilliard m. David Mann Arr. Nelson Riddle.

11. "I'VE GOT YOU UNDER MY SKIN" w.m. Cole Porter arr. Nelson Riddle.

12. "NIGHT AND DAY." w.m. Cole Porter Arr. Axel Stordahl.

13. "ONLY THE LONELY" w. Sammy Cahn m. James Van Heusen Arr. Nelson Riddle.

14. "LETS GET AWAY FROM IT ALL" with Connie Haines original.

15. "FIVE MINUTES MORE" w. Sammy Cahn m. Jule Styne.

16. "A COTTAGE FOR SALE" w. Larry Conley m. Willard Robison.

17. I'LL NEVER SMILE AGAIN" w.m. Ruth Lowe. Arr Fred Stulce.

18. "TRY A LITTLE TENDERNESS" w. m. Harry Woods, Jimmy Campbell, Reginald Connelly.

19. "ALL THE WAY" w. Sammy Cahn m. James Van Heusen Arr. Nelson Riddle.

20. "STARDUST" w. m.Hoagy Carmichael.

21. "ONE FOR MY BABY" w. Johnny Mercer m. Harold Arlen, Arr. Nelson Riddle.

22. "IT WAS A VERY GOOD YEAR" w. m. Ervin Drake, Arr. Gordon Jenkins.

23. "SUMMER WIND" w. Johnny Mercer, w. Henry Mayer.

24 "ANGEL EYES" w. Earl Brent m. Matt Dennis Arr. Nelson Riddle.

25. "GOODBYE" w.m. Gordon Jenkins, Arr. Gordon Jenkins.

Bonus-One of America's best written songs, from Oklahoma, "If I Loved You."

(w. = words , m. = music)

SONG POLLS AND CONTESTS
Involving Frank Sinatra

Radio Station WQEW-AM 1560 on the dial, New York City Station had once held a contest to determine the most popular songs among their listeners back in 1983.

Here are the winners: Frank Sinatra held the # 9 Spot with "My Way," and # 11 "I've Got You Under My Skin," with that Milt Bernhart trombone solo of note; # 15 Theme from New York, New York," # 20 " Night & Day," # 22 Summer Wind," # 64 "Fly Me to the Moon," # 87 "I'll Be Seeing You," # 88 " I Have Dreamed," : # 93 Strangers in the Night," # 97 "Young at Heart," # 99 " All the Way," : # 102 " Come Fly with Me," for a total of 12 winners, more than any other artist.

A few years earlier WNEW radio in New York held the Greatest 50 Recordings the results of a poll with DJ Bob Jones. Frank held with " I'll Never Smile Again," "New York, New York," Night & Day," My Way," for a total of four winners.

In 2004 the Recording Industry Association of America and the National Endowment for the Arts compiled the 365 Top Selling Songs of the 20th Century. The list began in 1894 and ended in 2000.

Sinatra fared: 1965 "Strangers in the Night," and "1969 "My Way," In November, 1943 Downbeat ran a Seventh Annual Big Band and Vocalist Poll.

In the singing category Frank Sinatra was # 1, Bing Crosby # 2, Dick Haymes # 3, Bob Eberly # 4, Harry Cool #5, and Ray Eberle #6. With the songbirds it was Peggy Lee # 1, Helen Forrest #2, Jo Stafford #3, Anita O'Day # 4, Kitty Kallen # 5, Nan Wynn # 6.

The great Jazz writer Leonard Feather polled the top one hundred jazz musicians in the world for their all-time favorite vocalists and fellow musicians. Sinatra won by a three-to- one margin over closest singer Nat King Cole, as the best male vocalist.

Frank Sinatra spent nine years at Capitol. In that time he recorded 330 tracks.

In his early years at Reprise, Sinatra's first seven albums were each with a different arranger. They were: Johnny Mandel, Billy May, Sy Oliver, Don Costa, Neal Hefti, Robert Farnon, and Gordon Jenkins.

SINATRA SINGLES TO MAKE NO.1 ON *BILLBOARD'S* SINGLES CHART

- 7/20/40 - I'LL NEVER SMILE AGAIN - 15 WKS ON THE LIST
  11/5/42 - THERE ARE SUCH THINGS - 24 WKS ON THE LIST

- 7/1/43 - IN THE BLUE OF EVENING - 17 WKS ON THE LIST

- 8/1/46 - FIVE MINUTES MORE - 18 WKS ON THE LIST

- 5/7/66 - STRANGERS IN THE NIGHT - 15 WKS ON THE LIST

SINATRA SINGLES MAKE NO. 1 TO MAKE *CASH BOX* SINGLES CHART

- 5/7/66 - STRANGERS IN THE NIGHT 15 WKS ON THE LIST

- 3/18/67 - SOMETHING STUPID 14 WKS ON THE LIST

American Bands Database

156 WINNERS - 2004

Radio station WQEW, 1560 on the AM dial, which was the heir to the original WNEW after it went off the air, held a call-in contest in determine the most popular songs among their listeners. Here's how Frank Sinatra fared:

No. 9 - My Way w. Paul Anka, M. Claude Francois, Jacques Revaux, Giles Thibaut.

No. 11 - I've Got You Under My Skin w.m.Cole Porter

No. 15 - Theme from: New York, New York with Fred Ebb and John Kander

No. 20 - Night and Day w.m. Cole Porter

No. 23 - The Summer Wind w. Johnny Mercer, m. Henry Mayer

No. 64 - Fly Me to the Moon w.m.Bart Howard

No. 66 - I'm a Fool to Want You w.m. Frank Sinatra, Joel Herron, Jack Wolf

No, 87 - I'll Be Seeing You w. Irving Kahal, m. Sammy Fain

No. 88 - I Have Dreamed w. Oscar Hammerstein, m. Richard Rodgers

No. 93 - Strangers In the Night w.m. Bert Kaempfert, Eddie Snyder, Charles Singleton

No. 97 - Young at Heart w. Carolyn Leigh, m. Johnny Richards

No. 99 - All the Way w. Sammy Cahn, m. Jimmy Van Heusen

No. 102 - Come Fly with Me w. Sammy Cahn m. Jimmy Van Heusen

No. 119 - All or Nothing at All w.m. Jack Lawrence, Arthur Altman

Fourteen winners, more than any other artist. Earlier a WNEW 1130 AM ran a poll on the Make Believe Ballroom program on Sunday, September 25th with Bob Jones, called:

The 50 Greatest Recordings

No. 8 - I'll Never Smile Again w.m. Ruth Lowe

No. 19 - New York, New York w. Betty Comden, Adolf Green, m. Leonard Bernstein

No. 38 - My Way w. Paul Anka, m. Claude Francois, Jacques Revaux, Giles, Thibaut

No. 40 - Night and Day w.m. Cole Porter

SINATRA'S DRESSING ROOM REQUIREMENTS

Frank Sinatra was a legend and a music icon, but he didn't have nearly the requirements that some of today's big-name rock groups do. His needs were not exactly simple, but if something was missing, it was no big deal to him-he worked around it. No chairs were thrown: there was no refusal to go on stage. There were no drugs, no hookers, and no tantrums. Frank Sinatra's requirements were simply as follows, and according to his contract:

DRESSING ROOMS:

(1) Star Dressing Room- Frank Sinatra
This dressing room is for the exclusive use of Frank Sinatra. This room must contain a carpet, perfect and adjustable climate control, running water, sanitary toilet facilities, a shower, a full-length mirror, a dressing area, and at least four cushioned armchairs or a large couch

with two armchairs. A selection of plants and flower arrangements would be appreciated.

(1) Support Act Room- (Confirm number of rooms with production manager). This dressing room is for the exclusive use of the opening act. This room must contain a carpet, perfect and adjustable climate control, running water, sanitary toilet facilities, a shower, a full-length mirror, a dressing area, and at least several cushioned armchairs.

(1) Production office - This room is for the exclusive use of artist's production personnel. It should contain two eight-foot tables and eight chairs

(1) Artist's Personal Musicians and Conductor - This room is for the exclusive use of artist's musical personnel. It should be large enough to accommodate eight people.

(2) Band Rooms

Male Orchestra Dressing Room:
It should be large enough to accommodate thirty people.

Female Dressing Room:
It should be large enough to accommodate eight people.

Telephones
Four single, private dedicated lines: two in the production office and one in each star dressing room.

Medical Doctor
Local Promoter is to make available on call, if required on the day of the show, an ear,nose, and throat specialist with appropriate medication and sprays, including Decadron

Frank Sinatra's Dressing Room Contents
- Color TV (with a second imput for in-house video feed)
- Upright piano
- Private telephone with a dedicated line, direct dial out
- One bottle each:
- Mouton Cadet red wine

- Absolute or Stolichnaya vodk
- Jack Daniels
- Chivas Regal
- Courvoisier
- Beefeater Gin
- Premium white wine
- Premium red wine
- Bottled spring water
- Large bottle of Perrier
- 24 Diet Coke

- 12 Regular Coke
- Club soda
- Assorted mixers
- One platter of sliced fruit (to include watermelon when available)
- One cheese tray (included brie) with assorted crackers
- Dijon mustard
- Sandwiches (two of each): egg salad, chicken salad, sliced turkey
- 24 chilled jumbo shrimp
- One platter of Nova Scotia salmon and hors d' oeuvres
- 3 cans of Campbell's chicken and rice soup
- 12 rolls of cherry Lifesavers
- 12 rolls of assorted Lifesavers
- 12 boxes of Ludens cough drops (cherry, honey, etc..)
- One bag of miniature Tootsie rolls
- One bowl of pretzels and chips
- Salt and Pepper
- Tea bags (Lipton or Tetley)
- Honey, lemons, limes
- Sugar and Sweet n' Low
- 6 bottles of Evian spring water
- 12 water glasses
- 12 wine glasses
- 12 rocks glasses (eight to ten-ounce size)
- 4 porcelain soup bowls with knives, forks, spoons
- One double burner hot plate
- One teakettle with spring water
- One crockpot for soup with ladle
- One coffee pot, set-up with milk, cups, saucers
- 6 linen napkins
- 6 white towels
- 2 bars of Ivory soup
- 6 boxes of Kleenex tissues
- One carton of Camel cigarettes (no filter)
- One bucket of ice cubes

Thanks to Vincent Falcone & Bob Popyk, the above taken from their entertaining book, Frankly Just Between Us, My Life Conducting Frank Sinatra's Music.

FRANKLY
JUST BETWEEN US

My Life Conducting Frank Sinatra's Music

VINCENT FALCONE & BOB POPYK

THE CONTRIBUTORS
JULIANO FOURNIER

Frankie Laine with Juliano Fournier

It's my idea that a good percentage of Sinatra fans deep inside wanted themselves to be a singer. What a better choice in the best way..

It's different for a woman, they saw him as the lover, the son to cuddle and love, but that's another story.

Today there are many imitators around, but that's easy to be qualified just an imitator,for the fact that you give importance to the words you are singing, you are just another imitator.

It's quite easy to be involved and imitate someone you like, even Sinatra wanted to be a singer by listening to Bing Crosby. What is different between Sinatra and Bing Crosby? Probably the way Sinatra conducted his life style, his attitude and a broad of arrogance that was part of his success. But most of the way he delivered a story. You lived the story.

I met Sinatra three times. I gave him records released in Italy, of Nancy and Frank, Jr. singing in Italian. He was surprised!

The last time I met him, I remember very well, it was at the Desert Inn pool when I heard them paging my name. It was Dorothy

Uhlemann saying Mr. Sinatra was so happy to meet you and to take you back stage after the show at the Golden Nugget.

What a beautiful chance. Naturally I dressed up in a fancy tuxedo for the occasion. I could hardly watch the show and for the first time in my life I could hardly wait until it was over so I could meet the man.

I went to his dressing room and I was happy to meet Dorothy, who introduced me to Mr.Sinatra I spent half an hour and, with a photographer took some pictures.

The funny part was that he asked my wife if she could prepare "The pesto"and he was satisfied by the Italian recipe and ingredients, in fact my wife cooks great.

Speaking of imitators, the best and undoubtedly the only real imitator was Sammy Davis Jr. That reminds me of a story I think I should tell:

Nat "King" Cole was listening to a song over Muzak, his wife, Maria, said "Honey, they are playing your song: Nat said, "Gee, I don't remember when I recorded that. He didn't: it was Sammy Davis Jr.

Sammy was able to imitate many singers, but not Frank Sinatra. Even Michael Buble, doesn't come close to FS, he lacks the vocal cords that gives you a certain intonation or sound that reflects the correct delivery of interpretation and touch of swing that Mr. Sinatra perfected.

In Las Vegas you find a lot of sound-a-likes but it is just like going to a 10 cents store, which doesn't exist anymore, where everything starts at a dollar. You enjoy the music, the arrangements and the mannerism, but that's all. Anyway they are much better than what is available nowadays.

One of my favorite Sinatra songs, and I think that no one can sing that song with the same feeling,is watching him performing "Lonely Town." That's why Sinatra is so unique.

I listen to many songs and many singers and most of the time I just listen to the song and don't pay much attention to the words. With Sinatra, it's different. He tells you a story and is very difficult not to listen very carefully to what he's saying. That's why Sinatra is unique.

Even when he talks he is always singing. He is just the best in the trade and business.

Much of the craft Sinatra had was holding his breath that he learned from Tommy Dorsey and he acquired that in his lungs swimming under water.

What I wrote is well-known because so many books have been written about Frank Sinatra, and many things have been said by the man himself. You have to hear the story directly from the man.

The artist is incomparable.

In the world of song we had the great Caruso, then Mario Lanza in opera, then Frank Sinatra the swing and saloon singer. I could tell it to the man myself: "Frank, you stand alone and that is what you can call fame.

There will never be another you.

JOE FRANKLIN
KING OF NOSTALGIA

When Joe Franklin was seventeen, he worked as the music librarian and record picker for New York's legendary "Make Believe Ballroom" disc jockey Martin Block on radio station WNEW. He would send Block his favorite Sinatra recordings to play for the listening faithful which helped Sinatra's career. That was back in the 1940s. Since then, Joe has become an icon of his own. Joe had interviewed his old friend Frank Sinatra four times, perhaps more than any other interviewer was able to accomplish.

Joe started in television in 1950 and is credited with pioneering the talk show format spawning shows like the *Tonight* Show, *David Letterman, Conan O'Brien,* and the *Today Show*. His show, simply called the *Joe Franklin Show*, was the longest running show in television when it dropped the curtain in 1990. It ran for 43 consecutive years. But, by now, the *Tonight Show* has broken his record, but there were many more hosts. Joe was always alone as host. The Guinness Book of Records claims that Franklin holds the record for hosting 31,015 shows, and has been credited with helping to establish the careers of a number of popular show business personalities along the way. "I did more than 28,000 episodes, interviewing everybody and anybody, which someone told me works out to about two episodes a day for over forty years."

"Anyone in show business was welcome to appear on my show. Sammy Davis, Jr., Bill Cosby, Barry Manilow, Barbra Streisand, and even Woody Allen got their jump-start on my show. My Bing Crosby's interview, with his wife, Kathryn, is still the interview to beat. And, Frank Sinatra revealed many of his inner thoughts and secrets of and about the singing business on my show. In Richard Grudens book *Bing Crosby-Crooner of the Century* the entire Crosby interview is printed exactly as we aired it. I always preferred the early voices of Jolson, Crosby and Sinatra. Crosby's voice was different over six different decades, and you can say Sinatra had six different voices, too. "I watched Frank Sinatra grow into a mature singer as on each interview you could look back at a different Frank Sinatra as he climbed the long ladder of success through his excellent singing and acting."

Joe Franklin in his New York Office, surrounded by a lifetime of memorabilia

THE ART OF VOCAL AUDACITY

by John Primerano
Songwriter, Pianist/Vocalist

Everyone knows about Sinatra's exceptional breath control where he is able to carry a seamless melodic line longer than most wind instrumentalists. Why couldn't a vocalist accomplish that, Sinatra must have wondered!

Phrasing is not the lyrical or melodic liberties a vocalist takes

in performing a song. Rather, it is the grouping of notes to make musical sense --a musical sentence, if you will --without a break in sound. However, lyrics do not always comply with the melody and sometimes may be sustained in mid-sentence, ending the phrasing -- but not the thought.

Sinatra's developed breath control also allowed him to carry the lyrical message to its logical conclusion where other singers with less power might interrupt the thought with a breath.

That being the case, I believe what really made Sinatra different was audacity. Certainly it had its roots in his personality--the swagger, the self-assured "Il Padrone" persona-- that played into his vocal delivery. But it really transcends his nonmusical identity. The art of audacity is the Sinatra of "I've Got the World on a String," "I Get a Kick Out of You," and "I've Got You Under My Skin." It is the Sinatra that played with the music, bending the notes and ad-libbing lyrics to enhance their meaning. No so-called phrasing here, just total command; proof positive that a performer becomes an artist when he is secure enough to take such chances.

Frank Sinatra was not relaxed as a singer compared to his predecessor Bing Crosby, or contemporaries Dean Martin and Perry Como. Crosby, Martin and Como, to be certain, could have fun with a novelty song or touch your heart with a ballad. Martin, like Crosby, had a richness to his voice which was perfect for the laid-back, romantic approach. While Como had a lighter quality as he eased his way into a song. However, Sinatra planted his two feet on the ground and confronted a song head -on. Just listen to "Luck Be a Lady" or his swinging version of Cole Porter's "Night and Day."

Frank Sinatra also had the audacity t o musically wear his heart on this sleeve. He torched for an unrequited or lost love openly and unashamedly and like no other male vocalist had ever done before, yet resisted sounding dependingly weak. Where other singers might elicit listeners to exclaim, "Get over it , Buddy!"

Sinatra had the effect to make the hardiest of men nod with experienced empathy. The self-pity in which he wallowed had a resignation to it that made others feel they had found a confidant in him, and in truth, was how his listeners envisioned his private life and how it influenced his selection of those songs of heartbreak.

Frank Sinatra did not sing like a singer who is only concerned with tonal quality while interpretation, as well as technique, takes a back seat to a song's delivery. Sinatra sang like a musician, learning from the skilled instrumentalists around him. His technique, including articulation, dynamics and perfect diction, made him stand out and he remains forever the gold standard in popular singing and lyrical interpretation. But what truly made Frank Sinatra different was his audacity with a song. It is the quality of making even the songs "Old Mc Donald" or "Mrs. Robinson" his own, personal statement.

Many performers have unique styles, but Sinatra was one-of-kind singer whose art of vocal audacity was his unmistakable signature.

KAREN LAKE

Frank Sinatra was gifted with voice and charm. His string of great songs were played on the airwaves in all the great cities like a gift with an aura of romantic charm.

As a kind of new songwriter and composer, it was many a tune that Sinatra sang that influenced me. The great love tunes from the

golden years of great songs from the mid 50s forward inspired me to begin writing songs of my own.

He inspired me with his strong sense of trying to get to the top. It was a great wonder to me in those years, in how he and his songs managed to become so successful.

At that young age I didn't know about 'clout' and how the money wheels turned. I simply thought that if you loved to sing or write and you were good you could go anywhere. You just had to climb that ladder.

For many it has been a lot harder to achieve the strides Frank Sinatra achieved.

Being in the right place, meaning the big cities on either the East or West coast where the action is also was a factor. When I heard Frank sing, I didn't listen with my ears, I listened with my heart. His voice would touch my heart, and sometimes my soul, the process being almost automatic. It would ignite something deep inside and fed my fire to create a new song or poem. I could actually feel the melody or the lyrics created in the depth of wherever it came from - I am still not certain. It's just there, perhaps like it was with Frank, just waiting to be released.

The way Frank Sinatra dressed was important; his suits and his hats. He always appeared to be all-together and I admired that. He, like Frankie Laine, always wore a smile and you could tell they loved what they did -sing their hearts out and fully entertain.

Earlier, when Frank Sinatra performed his songs with the Big Bands, it was music made in Heaven. And when the saxophone played within the band it added excitement for me. If the song arrangement employs a sax, it reaches the depth of my soul like no other. And, a piano and guitar in a Frank Sinatra recording always reaches me.

They say the music circles round and I feel that his great music, and the great American songbook will be back in full swing once again. My granddaughter Anna is beginning to enjoy the songs of Frank Sinatra, as do I. His recording of "That's Life" is a true example of how he lived his own life. He experienced so much and so he truly believed what he sang about. Torch song or uplifting song, he sang them all.

There will never be another Frank Sinatra, Bing Crosby, or Mildred Bailey, but there will be other performers who have been influenced by them so they too, may experience the greatness one day as Frank Sinatra, the Voice of the Century did before them.

LEE HALE

In 1943 I was in the Navy's V-12 program in Salem, Oregon, and one of the civilian pleasures we were able to enjoy was listening to the hit records of the day. I was a big Bing Crosby fan, and I was outraged that a young Italian singer called Sinatra could be threatening to take his place as America's top crooner.

Lee Hale, Orson Wells and Dean Martin

Yet, as time went on, I concluded that there was room for both Der Bingle and The Voice.

Some months later, in Midshipmen's School in Plattsburg, New

York, two other midshipmen and I took the train down to Manhattan for a very short weekend. We had no money in our pockets, but when I saw that Harry James was playing in the Astor Roof, the three of us ventured up the elevator to see if I could see my high school chum, Corky Corcoran, the extremely talented sax player who had just been adopted by Harry and Betty Grable and added to the James band. The perky hatcheck girl, saying that "anything sailors want to do is okay with me," dashed back to the dressing room and brought Corky out to us. He gave me a hug and insisted on putting us in a stage-front table for the show, picked up the tab on drinks and dinner, and gave us tickets to the West Coast radio broadcast of *Your Hit Parade*,

Starring his friend Frank Sinatra and, singer Bea Wain.

I was so impressed hearing that smooth-as-silk Sinatra voice, that I immediately put him ahead of Bing.

In the '60s, when I was musical director of *The Dean Martin Show*, Frank made several appearances. He and Dean were close as scotch and soda in those days, and although I was fearful that what I had put together for the two of them to sing might not get Frank's approval, I didn't have to worry.

Like Dean, he accepted everything I put before him. He told me he liked the fact that he knew all the songs, the keys were fine and that he didn't have to rehearse. I wrote a 10-minute medley for them, which they performed only once. Their only dependence was on the cue cards to lead them from one song to another. Frank assured me that although Dean wasn't as fast as he was in going from one song to another, he would throw Dean into it, no matter what. It turned out to be an exceptionally fun-filled 10 minutes that only these two superb performers could pull off.

In another show, I had put "Auld Lang Syne" into a 3/4 waltz tempo. "That sounds interesting," Frank said as we were ready to roll cameras. Our arranger, Van Alexander, had made the waltz beat so strong that Frank had no problems with it and said he would always sing "Lang Syne" in that tempo from then on.

In a show biz world where almost everything is rehearsed and over rehearsed, I felt privileged to be in the company of two top stars who didn't want to rehearse, and, didn't have to rehearse. They simply knew what they were doing at all times. They were both rarities. When Frank was leaving the studio at one of the tapings, he grabbed me by the arm and said, "You're doing great work for Dean...he needs you, you know." I carried that in my pocket for years.

When we were putting together a Special for Dean, our producer called Frank to ask if he would like to say a few words about his pal. We would tape Frank in Palm Desert at his home at his convenience. Frank agreed, and I set out on Highway 10 with a camera crew. Frank couldn't have been more hospitable. After we taped his spot in his garden, we were invited in for drinks and supper.

Easy to work with? No question about it! I'm not sure whether he was kind to me because of his relationship with Dean or that he was simply a nice guy who appreciated what those around him were doing for him. Whatever, I have nothing but fond memories of Frankie.

And who's this fellow Bing, anyway?

ALAN BROWN

SETTING THE STANDARD ON GMMY RADIO

"Frank Sinatra was the man who set the standards by which we judge all great singers. These singers came along after the period which was dominated by the crooners Bing Crosby, Rudy Vallee, Al Bowlly and Russ Columbo.

"Mr. Sinatra is judged by the years he spent with various recording companies, with that being the case, I regard his years with Columbia his best. The reason is that behind the great man was another great musician, arranger Axel Stordahl. Between them they cast the die.

"The connection between Frank Sinatra and Axel Stordahl was their mutual membership in the Tommy Dorsey Orchestra. Stordahl, originally a trumpet player and singer, was also an arranger for Dorsey, and he knew just how to bring out the best of the Sinatra voice. That was the reason Sinatra took Mr. Stordahl with him when he left to go solo.

"Sinatra held the crown that was always his, and although there were other good singers, who some people thought were better, Frank Sinatra never deviated from his style of singing which he coined the standard. Some singers came along and tried to keep up with "The Flavor of the Month" but found it just didn't work and they had to find their own voice or quit.

"Listen to Frank Sinatra's tracks on *The Essential Years* on the Columbia label, then listen to the last album he made for Capitol *Point Of No Return* where he turned to Stordahl to back him, even though the presence of Nelson Riddle existed at Capitol. Nothing between those albums were better. Tracks from *The Essential Years* showcased the talent that was maintained over Sinatra's reign (Poinciana," " One Love," " I'm a Fool to Want You") Then listen to, "I Remember April," " I'll See You Again," " I'll Be Seeing You" from *The Point Of No Return* album and you will hear Sinatra and Stordahl together proving that the die they had cast produced music that has never been improved upon.

"All the great singers that came along after Frank Sinatra (there were probably less than twenty-five, they will all say the same thing in that he was the best of them all. HE SET THE STANDARD.

"My two all-time favorite tracks by Frank Sinatra are, "You'll Know When It Happens" and "Was the Last Time I Saw You, the Last Time."

AL PETRONE ON FRANK

Mr. Sinatra. Frank Sinatra
Gannett Newspaper. May 30, 1998

by Al Petrone

Mr. Sinatra was you and me. He lived and enjoyed his triumphs, suffered his failures and endured his frustrations. Sometimes, like you and me, he became irascible and lost out to his frustrations.

We've lived all these things, too. Of course, we had to. However, the outlets for expressing ourselves were limited.

Enter Frank Sinatra: The singer, the actor, the entertainer. He was the you and me we wanted so much to be. We wanted to be as good at our job as he was at his job ---singing. We wanted to be as capable in our life's role as he was at acting. We wanted to be accepted in our lives as he was accepted in his --- a great entertainer. We'd like to be as good at just being us as he was at being himself. We wanted to be all of these things and couldn't.

So we gravitated to Frank Sinatra.

He took us on a marvelous journey beyond our belief. A journey deep into the history and the magic of love. He enjoyed love's creative pleasures and its debilitating loss. And, yes, accepted its lack.

Lack -- that's the word for you and me. We lacked that courage of his ability to accept or reject the many faces of love. Love was an enigma to us, a profound, complex part of our being.

Frank Sinatra welcomed love ----it's joy, it's despair, it's strength, it's weakness, it's vulnerability. He grasped love with all of its ramifications, exposed his vulnerability and turned that vulnerability into an asset.

He knew the vision of love and embraced it. He stood alone with this vision on a stage with no flashing lights, no huge, deafening sound systems. There was no acrobatics, running back and forth from one end of the stage to the other, no outrageous costumes--nothing to distract us from his message drawn from words of the great poets--- the songwriters.

He stood alone---sometimes using subtle body movements to emphasize a melody line, a phrase, a chosen lyric. He did this as we stood by in absolute admiration and awe. Then we---hesitating slightly---responded with a thunderous ovation.

Thank you, Frank Sinatra.

(Al Petrone is the composer of "A Christmas Gift.")

SINGING NOTATIONS OF INTEREST TO SINGERS

Explaining Intro, Interlude, And Postlude:

The introduction is the beginning of a song. the accompanist plays it on the piano before the vocalist starts to sing. An introduction is important because the first word and note grows out of the introduction.

The interlude is a segment of music in between sections of a composition. In songs, the interlude usually occurs between segments of the song, and the pianist plays alone (or an orchestra plays without the vocalist)

The postlude is the song's ending that concludes the musical and dramatic thoughts. the song isn't over until the pianist or orchestra releases the last note(s) of the postlude

Breathing - As In Breathing While A Singer Is Singing:

Attached to the ribs, the lungs are made of pliable tissue--not muscle. when you inhale, the muscles in between the ribs (intercostals) move the singer's ribs up and out as the lungs expand downward. When the intercostal muscle relax back inward, the lungs move back to their normal resting position. another muscle that helps a singer breathe is his diaphragm -- a dome-shaped muscle located underneath the lungs and attached to the ribs and the spine. when a singer inhales, the diaphragm flexes downward and move back downward as the singer inhales, the organs below s singer's diaphragm have to move out of the way. The organs move down and out, which is why the abdomen moves out as he or she inhales. As you exhale, the organs gradually move back to their normal resting position. This is where the importance of good posture and breathing for singing connect. If you stand in a slouch or a rigid military-like position, the diaphragm locks, and it can't descend when you need to inhale. This prevents the lungs from getting the full breath that they need for a singer to sing.

Vocal Cord Problems and Polyps

BY CLARENCE T. SASAKI, MD

Vocal cord nodules and polyps are noncancerous (benign) growths that cause hoarseness and a breathy voice.

When relaxed, the vocal cords normally form a V-shaped opening that allows air to pass freely through to the trachea. The cords open when air is drawn into the lungs (inspiration) and close during swallowing or speech.

Holding a mirror in the back of a person's mouth, a specially trained doctor can often see the vocal cords and check for problems, such as contact ulcers, polyps, nodules, paralysis, and cancer. All of these problems affect the voice. Paralysis may affect one (one-sided) or both vocal cords (two-sided—not shown).

Vocal cord polyps are often the result of an acute injury (such as from shouting at a football game) and typically occur on only one vocal cord. Vocal cord nodules occur on both vocal cords and result mainly from abuse of the voice (habitual yelling, singing, or shouting or using an unnaturally low frequency).

Symptoms include chronic hoarseness and a breathy voice, which tend to develop over days to weeks. A doctor makes the diagnosis by examining the vocal cords with a thin, flexible viewing tube. Sometimes the doctor removes a small piece of tissue for examination under a microscope (biopsy) to make sure the growth is not cancerous (malignant).

Treatment is to avoid whatever is irritating the larynx and rest the voice. If abuse of the voice is the cause, voice therapy conducted by a speech therapist may be needed to teach the person how to speak or sing without straining the vocal cords. Most nodules go away with this treatment, but most polyps must be surgically removed to restore the person's normal voice.

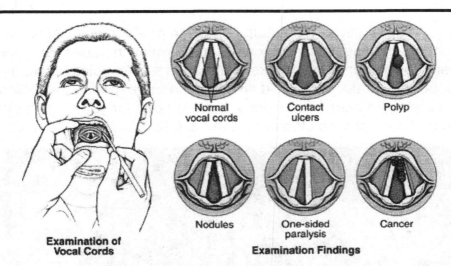

Examination of Vocal Cords

Normal vocal cords

Contact ulcers

Polyp

Nodules

One-sided paralysis

Cancer

Examination Findings

When relaxed, the vocal cords normally form a V-shaped opening that allows air to pass freely through to the trachea. The cords open when air is drawn into the lungs (inspiration) and close during swallowing or speech.

Holding a mirror in the back of a person's mouth, a specially trained doctor can often see the vocal cords and check for problems, such as contact ulcers, polyps, nodules, paralysis, and cancer. All of these problems affect the voice. Paralysis may affect one (one-sided) or both vocal cords (two-sided—not shown).

Vocal cord polyps are often the result of an acute injury (such as from shouting at a football game) and typically occur on only one vocal cord. Vocal cord nodules occur on both vocal cords and result mainly from abuse of the voice (habitual yelling, singing, or shouting or using an unnaturally low frequency).

Symptoms include chronic hoarseness and a breathy voice, which tend to develop over days to weeks. A doctor makes the diagnosis by examining the vocal cords with a thin, flexible viewing tube. Sometimes the doctor removes a small piece of tissue for examination under a microscope (biopsy) to make sure the growth is not cancerous (malignant).

Treatment is to avoid whatever is irritating the larynx and rest the voice. If abuse of the voice is the cause, voice therapy conducted by a speech therapist may be needed to teach the person how to speak or sing without straining the vocal cords. Most nodules go away with this treatment, but most polyps must be surgically removed to restore the person's normal voice.

STAGE FRIGHT GOODBYE

Whether you're a standup comedian or a pop vocalist singing in front of an audience large or small, performing in public can send shivers down your spine - make your hands shake, voice crack, heart race, or body break into a cold sweat. If the mere thought of getting up on a stage makes you anxious, there is hope for you singers out there and here are the steps you need to follow:

1. If you constantly sweat it out, then dress in loose-fitting garments or a sleeveless shirt to prevent this symptom from taking control of you. Practice deep breathing before you begin to sing. Inhale slowly through the nose, and exhale through your mouth. And, in any case, prepare yourself for a successful performance and don't worry about experiencing a quivering voice or butterflies in your stomach. Al

Jolson, the worlds greatest entertainer, had this negative experience almost every time he faced an audience.

You have to enjoy the experience no matter what because the show must go on. Wait for a moment, the sweat will dissipate and the negative feelings will pass, rest assured. Any psychologist will tell you that in your first visit to his office. The symptoms lessen as you wait it out and let yourself relax, something difficult to do while you are on stage. But, believe me, the audience will never know.

2. On stage dry mouth is another common symptom you may experience. Try to bring a glass of water with you or arrange for someone to keep one handy. Also, volume makes a difference in how your audience reacts to you. Breathe deeply frequently, you will relax much sooner.

3. If your hands are still shaking , remember that only a few in the audience may notice. Hold the microphone loosely and hide your other hand behind you or clutch the mike with both hands and alternate them.

4. After the performance , and especially if your audience praises you,you know you got the job done. You now realize your fears were irrational. Now you will be prepared for the next time you have to get up there and sing "Stardust" or some other great song.

LADIES SINGERS HAVE THEIR THROAT TROUBLES TOO!

Beginning with the incomparable Helen Forrest, I recall Helen telling me about her throat problems acquired when she was the girl singer with Artie Shaw and in the midst of a tour with the band. One morning when she woke up and no sound came out of her at all. This was before her vocal chords developed strength.

Helen flew down to New York from Boston and met with an osteopath. "I couldn't even whisper. He treated me with massage and heat-- infrared and diathermy. Ninety minutes later I walked out and I could talk." Helen flew back to Boston and performed her shows without a further hitch.

Helen's voice was a "natural." She really never studied voice,but once went to a voice teacher because she wanted to raise her range. The teacher told her that the range was there, that she just had to learn how to use it by just raising her key, something the orchestra leader had to do for and with her.

Helen started her singing career by trying to emulate Mildred Bailey, but gradually found her own way. When she did, no other singer could emulate her because her voice was different, being one of a kind, so to speak.

"Frank Sinatra has been tops at communicating the subtle meaning into a lyric and does equally well with slow ballads and up-tempo tunes. I also believe that Dick Haymes was the balladeer supreme and Mel Torme was always exciting to hear and sing with as well."

"Johnny Carson was always saying to his singing guests that he wished he could be a great singer. A great singer can cast a spell on an audience. But it takes a lot of work, a lot of experience, and a lot of practice to get to the point where you can cast that spell."

Patty Andrews told me, when she was ninety years old just last year, that she had to have voice retraining, which she said helped her career because she learned to breathe better and was able to avoid the problems of strain which plagued Kay Starr and many other singers.

Patty Andrews

BEL CANTO

An Appreciation

Musicologist, Professor Richard Grudzinski of Berklee Music College explains Bel Canto

"An Italian phrase meaning 'Beautiful' is an expression that evolved from the 18th and 19th century Italian opera aria. The spectacular growth of the vocal virtuosity in Italy coupled with the tremendous range of emotional expression from the first operas of Monteverdi up to and beyond Donizetti, Bellini and Puccini produced an art form unrivaled in vocal agility, and packed with dramatic and emotional sensuality. *Bel Canto* became a powerful and popular musical style. "Over the years the concept of *bel canto* spilled over into the provenance of popular song. The composers and the singers of popular music gradually evolved a crossover - a blend of what previously were two mutually exclusive styles of music. This was most evident in the recordings of ballads, sung and recorded by crooners such as Frank Sinatra, Perry Como and Bing Crosby. Many of these songs in <u>bel canto</u> style came out of the Broadway musi-

cal. ' Ol' Man River,' 'September Song,' ' Begin the Beguine,' 'You'll Never Walk Alone,' and 'Night and Day,' all sung and recorded by Sinatra. Of course, many other songs share the aesthetic of *bel canto*.

A teacher by the name of Mathilde Marchesi was a famous teacher of 'bel canto' singing, in the mid 1850s. Today, singers Joan Sutherland, and Beverly Sills, and a bit earlier, Maria Callas, among modern singers sang in the 'bel canto' style. Bel canto is considered a style rather than a vocal technique.

Another View of Berklee

SONG ASSOCIATIONS

The list of singers and the song they "own" and have been associated with for many, many years.

1. FRANK SINATRA - **MY WAY**

2. BING CROSBY - **WHITE CHRISTMAS**

3. TONY BENNETT - **I LEFT MY HEART IN SAN FRANCISCO**

4. JUDY GARLAND - **OVER THE RAINBOW**

Richard with Don Cornell

5. FRANKIE LAINE - **THAT'S MY DESIRE**

Tex Beneke

6. VIC DAMONE - **YOU'RE BREAKING MY HEART**

7. JERRY VALE - **TWO PURPLE SHADOWS**

8. JULIUS LA ROSA - **EH! COMPARI**

9. DEAN MARTIN - **THAT'S AMORE**

10. DON CORNELL - **IT ISN'T FAIR**

11. TEX BENEKE - **CHATTANOOGA CHOO CHOO**

12. HERB JEFFRIES - **FLAMINGO**

Judy Garland

13. JOE WIL-LIAMS - EVERY-DAY I SING THE BLUES

14. AL MAR-TINO - SPANISH EYES

15. EDDIE FISHER - OH, MY PAPA

Al Martino

16. GUY MITCHELL - MY HEART CRIES FOR YOU

17. DICK HAYMES - **LITTLE WHITE LIES**

18. NAT "KING" COLE - **NATURE BOY**

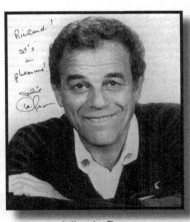

Julius LaRosa

19. BOB HOPE - THANKS FOR THE MEMORY

20. JIMMY ROSELLI - WHEN YOUR OLD WEDDING RING WAS NEW

21. MILLS BROTHERS - PAPER DOLL

22. PEGGY LEE - GOLDEN EARRINGS

23. LENA HORNE - STORMY WEATHER

24. CONNIE HAINES - LET'S GET AWAY FROM IT ALL (WITH SINATRA)

25. DORIS DAY - **SENTIMENTAL JOURNEY**

26. HELEN FORREST - **I HAD THE CRAZIEST DREAM**

27. BOBBY DARIN - **MACK THE KNIFE**

TIPS ON POPULAR SINGING
By Frank Sinatra And John Quinlan.

Author note - This book was probably written by the teacher, John Quinlan, without help from Sinatra. Quinlan was an opera singer who came from Australia. The book teaches the student to avoid strain and to annunciate words (lyrics) clearly and well-explained by Quinlan. Sinatra said he also worked with famed opera singer Dorothy Kirsten' voice teacher, sought voice/singing advice from opera singer Robert Merrill whenever possible, and always followed a special routine of vocal practice before concerts or when recording.

Tips On Popular Singing

by

FRANK SINATRA

in collaboration with his vocal teacher

JOHN QUINLAN

Price 2/6

A WORD OF COMMENDATION

by

TOMMY DORSEY

From the standpoint of convention, it would seem rather bizarre for me to step out of my role as an orchestra leader and master of ceremonies in the field of entertainment and enter the realm of belle-lettres, even in a minor capacity, but the subject matter of "Tips On Popular Singing" appealed to me so forcibly that, when I was requested to write an opinion on it, I immediately followed up the idea.

In my travels, throughout the country, I have always made it a point to assist the aspiring song writer, the singer and the musician, in their respective careers. Now that Frank Sinatra and John Quinlan have given the public "Tips On Popular Singing," I wish to further voice my co-operation by highly recommending this book.

Frank Sinatra, who is a member of my organization, is an unusually talented, conscientious artist. Through his interpretive qualities, he has not only brought success to himself, but he has made many hits for the various music publishers and, of course, has brought pleasure to thousands of listeners.

In writing this book, Mr. Sinatra was extremely fortunate in securing the collaboration of his well-known coach and voice teacher, John Quinlan. They have written a work which, I hope, is the beginning of a subsequent series of books of this type.

"Tips On Popular Singing" is the answer to many a query I have received as to whether or not such a book might be procured — and where.

It goes without saying that "Tips On Popular Singing" has my very best wishes for success, and I trust that the untiring effort put into it by the above mentioned authors will prove to be of great help to those who are at the beginning of a road which may ultimately lead to fame and fortune.

PREFACE

In the music world of today, the popular song seems to play a more important part than at any time in previous history; in camp, at community sings, at parties and wherever entertainment of any sort holds sway, the popular song has proven to be the best means of establishing joviality, hilarity and good fellowship and maintaining a general spirit of fun in a crowd.

Whether it is a ballad, a hill-billy, a swing number, a novelty song, a marching song or a comedy number, the popular song has that "something" which makes people forget their troubles and cares, when together, better than any other medium.

Everyone can sing a little; some have better voices than others. Those with trained voices are, as we all know, not nearly as numerous as those with non-trained voices. However, the fact remains that a great many of the latter have an earnest desire to become popular singers.

This book, "Tips On Popular Singing," was written for anyone with the ambition to become a popular song stylist of the type now appearing with the various bands on the radio, in night clubs and other places of amusement.

"Tips On Popular Singing" contains all that is necessary, in the way of vocal instruction. All instructive matter in this book is written in a clear, understandable manner and, if strictly followed, it will be of great help to the aspiring student in the popular field.

"Tips On Popular Singing" was written by Frank Sinatra, in collaboration with John Quinlan, only after numerous requests for a work of this kind had been made.

It is needless to say that Mr. Sinatra, at present connected with Tommy Dorsey's famous orchestra, is one of the country's outstanding popular vocalists. Not only have his records enjoyed a tremendous sale, but he is also given credit for popularizing many songs in the hit class.

Mr. Sinatra's marvelous success is due, to a great extent, to the careful and systematic coaching given him by Mr. Quinlan, one of America's leading voice teachers. Mr. Quinlan's success is backed up with many years of experience as a professional singer and teacher.

It is our opinion that the authors, Mr. Sinatra and Mr. Quinlan, have done excellent work in writing a book which will prove invaluable to the ambitious singer of popular songs.

We sincerely hope that the student will enjoy the study of "Tips On Popular Singing."

The Publisher

INTRODUCTION

Many young people are under the erroneous impression that, in order to become a successful singer, it is necessary for them to have had years of intensive voice training. The truth of the matter is that the popular vocalist, who has had voice training, beyond a few simple exercises, is the exception rather than the rule.

The comparatively simple procedure of analyzing a melody often results in the birth of a certain style which, as a matter of fact, is nothing more than an individual's own interpretation of phrasing, breathing and diction.

It is suggested that the student listen to the records of as many different vocalists as possible, take, for instance, the Vallees, the Columbos and the Crosbys, down to the present era of the Eberleys and the Leonards. Then select some of their little mannerisms of phrasing and diction, from which it may be possible to invent an individual style of interpretation and expression, being careful to always employ intelligence and good taste.

If the student desires to attain success in the popular field, good health, hard work, and plenty of patience are obligatory.

At the very beginning of one's career it is absolutely necessary to take up the correct method of voice culture.

The examples in this book have been selected with great care. They are simple and effective, and have been written for the sole purpose of developing and broadening the voice range.

THE CARE OF THE THROAT

It is only natural that a singer should take excellent care of his throat which, it seems, is the most susceptible part of his anatomy. Great caution must be taken, at all times, to avoid a cold or sore throat, in any form. One may ask the question, "How do I go about avoiding a cold?" In answer to this, using a little common sense is a great help, but the best advice on this subject is: "Keep the feet dry and avoid sitting in a draft."

The throat, as a rule, is always in a healthy condition; otherwise you wouldn't possess a voice. It is advisable not to pay too much attention to the throat but, at the same time, it would be foolhardy, in the event of symptoms appearing, such as a slight burning feeling in the throat, stuffiness in the head, a catarrhal condition in the nose, etc., not to act at once. A singer cannot afford to procrastinate, hoping against hope that a slight cold will disappear over-night. It is extremely dangerous to allow a cold to become chronic, as that would not only prove harmful to the voice, but it would also interfere with one's health in general.

When the symptoms of an approaching cold appear, it is beneficial to drink hot water with a little lemon juice added. The latter not only tends to make the hot water more palatable, but it also helps to counteract any acid conditions in the system. Should the hot water remedy, after a fair trial, prove insufficient in restoring the voice, it is suggested that the singer consult a throat specialist of the highest reputation.

THE ART OF BREATHING

It is wise to stress the importance of breathing, as it is the most essential part of singing, yet is far from being the complicated procedure which some teachers claim. There is but one way to breathe, and that is in the natural way. Stand erect, relax the chest and inhale deeply through the nostrils. Avoid making the mistake of pushing the chest out as you inhale — let the breath do that. You'll be surprised at the amount of breath you can inhale.

When exhaling, do not let the chest collapse. Hold the position you had when you finished inhaling, and then slowly exhale through the mouth. You will notice that the stomach takes an inward direction toward the spine. This is also what eventually happens when the singer sustains high notes; it gives the appearance of the voice *floating* out, instead of being *pushed* out. Practice the above exercise twice a day for ten-minute periods.

A splendid breathing exercise is to lie flat on your back, hands extended at your sides with the back of the hands on the floor. Relax completely and take a slow deep breath through the nostrils; then exhale slowly through the mouth. While doing this, do not push the chest out but let it gradually rise of its own accord. This is extremely important.

Shallow breathers are so called, because they do not relax the chest while inhaling. In order to get the real significance of this, try extending your chest as far as you can, before inhaling. See how much breath you can inhale. Practically none. While exhaling, do not let the breath *rush* out, but try to control it. This also applies to singing. It is not advisable to allow a great amount of air to escape on the first word you sing. Observe all words commencing with the letter H, such as the words HERE, HE, HER, etc., as some singers, for want of knowledge, are inclined to let a lot of air escape on these words.

As you exhale, you will discover that, by holding the chest in the position it was in at the end of the intake, the stomach will recede. Do not think too much about this! The chest, diaphragm and stomach will all co-ordinate in the natural manner.

Walking is one of the best physical exercises for a singer. However, this does not mean just strolling along, neither does it mean rushing, as though you had to catch a train. Set a good medium pace, and, while walking, remember the instructions given in the aforementioned exercises on breathing.

Golfing, when done in moderation, is also good exercise for a singer. It is advisable, however, not to overdo golfing by playing an extra round, especially when you have a singing engagement that same evening. A good rule to follow is: "Be moderate in all physical exercise."

GENERAL INSTRUCTIONS

When singing a descending passage in an exercise, try to keep each succeeding lower tone in the same position as the one that precedes it. In this way, you will learn to place the voice correctly and, at the same time, eliminate all throat strain.

Whenever you feel a little pressure on the throat, you'll know that you are singing incorrectly. Concentrate on the tone and on the throat. You can only overcome that harmful throat pressure through the mind. After a while, when your voice is properly placed, you will be able to relax somewhat against the incorrect habits you may have had.

Never practice too long at a time! It is better to practice four fifteen-minute periods a day than one hour steady, or two half-hour periods. The throat and vocal chords are quite sensitive and need an occasional rest. Whenever the throat begins to feel tired, take a rest and continue to practice later. Never force the voice, for harsh tones eventually wear out the vocal chords.

All of the exercises in this book are suitable to any voice, regardless of range. For instance, if the lowest clear tone in your voice range is low F, start the exercise one tone higher, on G, and continue, ascending to your most comfortable high tone, without straining. When this is done, complete the exercise by descending, phrase by phrase, until you arrive at your starting point. This rule applies to all exercises, except when otherwise mentioned.

EXERCISE 1

This exercise is based on a series of five notes, the first three of which form a major triad (chord). Each group of five notes is a separate phrase which is slurred by a curved line. This means that the entire phrase, or group, should be sung in a legato, or smooth manner, using the syllable UH, as in UP. Do not use an UH for each note!

On the first and second notes in each group, the mouth should be opened just a little (see FIG. 1, p. 31); on the third, or top note, it should be opened a little more (see FIG. 2, p. 31), and this mouth position should be retained for the two remaining notes.

Breathe before each phrase. (See chapter on "The Art of Breathing." p. 7.)

EXERCISE 2

The same instructions for the mouth position, given in exercise 1, p. 9, also apply to the singing of MUH in exercise 2. Bear in mind the difference between the mouth opening at the beginning and that on the top note.

Breathe before each phrase.

For the words CARRY and HOME refer to the mouth positions on p. 31. CAR (FIG. 1), RY (FIG. 3) and HOME (FIG. 4).

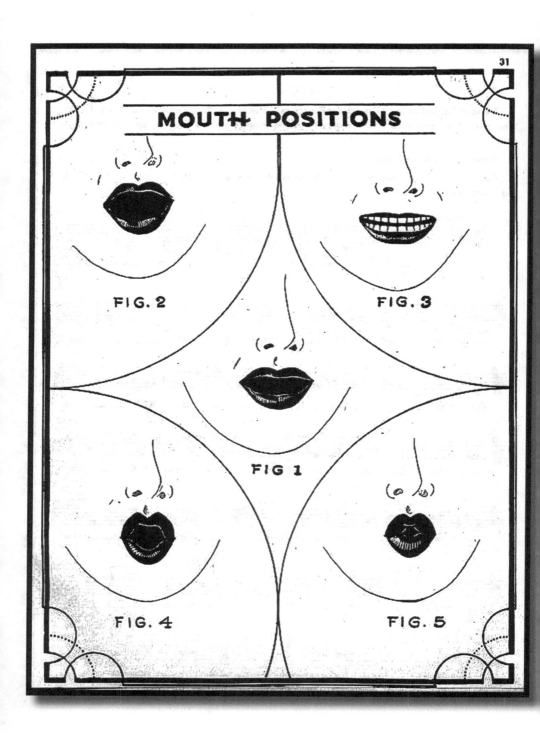

MOUTH POSITIONS

FIG. 2

FIG. 3

FIG 1

FIG. 4

FIG. 5

CONCLUDING REMARKS

Now that you have concluded the foregoing exercises you will, undoubtedly, notice the marked improvement in your voice; that is, if you have followed all the instructions carefully.

You may now select a song of medium range and try to sing it according to the various ideas you have learned from this book. Just sing the song in a natural way, without straining, and you will find that the voice will do what is expected of it. You'll be surprised at your progress.

Never be careless when learning new songs. If a certain phrase does not sound as it should to you, go over it again and again, until you are perfectly satisfied.

Remember that a good voice cannot be developed overnight, and that only through ambition, intelligent study, hard work and patience will you be able to gain perfect voice control.

The instructions and exercises in this book have been written for the purpose of giving the student all that is necessary for him to become a successful singer of popular songs. If, however, he should feel the need of individual instruction, it is suggested that he engage a reliable competent voice teacher.

SINATRA BIBLIOGRAPHY

Alexander, Van & Stephen Fratallone. *From Harlem to Hollywood-My Life in Music*. Albany, Georgia: Bear Manor Media. 2009

Balliett, Whitney. *American Musicians - 56 Portraits in Jazz*. New York, New York: Oxford University Press. 1986.

Damone, Vic and David Chanoff - *Singing Was The Easy Part*. New York, New York. Saint Martins Press. 2009

Falcone, Vincent * Bob Popyk. *Frankly Just Between Us*. Milwaukee, WI: Hal-Leonard Corporatiion. 2005

Feinstein, Michael. *Nice Work if You Can Get It*. My Life in Rhythm and Rhyme. New York, New York: Hyperion Publishing 1995

Forrest, Helen w/Bill Libby. *I had the Craziest Dream*. New York: Coward, McCann & Geoghegan, Inc. 1982

Friedwald, Will. *Sinatra-The Song is You*. New York, New York: Da Capo Press. 1997

Grudens, Richard. *The Song Stars*. Stonybrook, New York: Celebrity Profiles Publishing. 1998

Grudens, Richard, *Stardust-The Bible of the Big Bands*. Stonybrook, New York: Celebrty Profiles Publishing. 2008

Hall, Fred. *Dialogues in Swing*. Ventura,California. Pathfinder Publishing. 1989

Harris, Jay S. *TV Guide-The First 25 Years*. New York, New York. Simon and Schuster. 1978

Jenkins, Bruce. *Goodbye-In Search of Gordon Jenkins*. Berkeley, California: Frog, Ltd. 2005

Lahr, John. *Sinatra's Song-Profile*. New Yorker Magazine, New York, New York 1997 (November 3rd issue)

Levinson, Peter, J. *September in the Rain -The Life of Nelson Riddle*. New York, New York. Billboard Books 2001

O'Brien, Ed. With Robert Wilson. *Sinatra 101-The 101 Best Recordings*. New York, New York. Berkley Publishing Group. 1996

O'Brien, Ed with Scott Sayers, Jr. *The Sinatra Sessions 1939-1980*. Dallas, Texas. The Sinatra Society of America. 1980.

Phillips, Pamelia, *Singing for Dummies*. New York, New York. Wiley Publishing. 2003

Pleasants, Henry. *The Great American Popular Singers*. New York, New York: Simon & Schuster. 1974

Shanaphy, Edward, Editor. *Sheet Music Magazine*. New York, New York: Oct. 1998

Sinatra, Frank. John Quinlan. *Tips on Popular Singing*. New York, New York: Embassy Music Corp. 1941

Sinatra, Nancy. *Frank Sinatra-An American Legend*. Santa Monica, California: General Publishing Group, Inc. 1998

Torme, Mel. *It Wasn't All Velvet*. New York, New York: Viking Penquin Group: 1988

Torme,Mel. *My Singing Teachers*. New York, New York. Oxford University Press. 1994

Ulanov, Barry. *Down Beat Magazine.* Various Commentary. 1955-on.

WEB MD Magazine Scare Tactics July/August 2009

Zehme, Bill. *The Way You Wear Your Hat*. New York, New York: Harper Collins Publishers, Inc. 1997

Zinsser, William. *Easy to Remember*. Jaffrey, New Hampshire. David R. Godine. 2000

AUTHOR'S ACKNOWLEDGEMENT

This Frank Sinatra book is filled with lots of information gathered from myriad sources and information accumulated by myself and others. A book can not be accomplished by any one person, no matter whose name appears as author.

First, my appreciation goes to the most gracious and talented Kathryn Crosby, the late Frankie Laine, legendary Jerry Vale and his wife Rita, Vic Damone, and Barbara Sinatra, for her gracious approval and encouragement.

Kathryn passionately circumvents the earth to tell the story of her wonderful husband, Bing Crosby, so the world will continue to remember his great career and contributions to the formation of almost all future vocalists. Bing led the way. As we know, Sinatra validates and acknowledges it between these pages. Everyone else followed Bing.

Frankie Laine, however, was one of a kind. An accomplished performer, recording artist and mentor, I will always be grateful to him and will never forget his unselfish contributions to my works and the wonderful recordings he gave the world. God bless him. My personal appreciation and thanks go to legendary Patty Andrews, Margaret Whiting, Ann Jillian, Joe Franklin, Tony B. Babino, and Max Wirz, whose consistent and direct assistance helped this and all my other books come to fruition.

Professionally, I acknowledge the help of counterparts Anthony DiFlorio III, Jack Ellsworth, Al Monroe, John Tumpak, and Jack Lebo. Appreciation also goes to the great Ervin Drake, songwriter and producer, for his contributions and friendship. And to two new friends, Al Petrone, former producer, songwriter and author, who has extended his hand, and Sinatra collector Seymour Silverberg.

With recognition to those who have passed - the late Jerry Fletcher, Camille Smith, Joe Pardee, and Gus Young.

Personally, I thank Ben Grisafi, my son Robert Grudens, long time friends Bob Incagliato and Jerry Castleman (both who doubled as Jerry Vale's chauffeur when it was needed), and who assisted during Jerry Vale's, Connie Haines's and Kathryn Crosby's engagements.

And, to Madeline Grudens, my wonderful wife and companion. It is she who designs, formats, edits, provides photo magic, and shares in every aspect of the production of this project.

Thank you all.

ABOUT THE AUTHOR

Richard Grudens of St. James, New York, was initially influenced by Pulitzer Prize dramatist Robert Anderson; New York Herald Tribune columnist Will Cuppy; and detective/mystery novelist Dashiell Hammett, all whom he knew in his early years. Grudens worked his way up from studio page in NBC's studios in New York to news writer for radio news programs, the Bob and Ray Show and the Today Show.

Feature writing for Long Island PM Magazine (1980-86) led to his first book, The Best Damn Trumpet Player - Memories of the Big Band Era. He has written over 100 magazine articles on diverse subjects from interviews with legendary cowboy Gene Autry in Wild West Magazine in 1995 to a treatise on the Beach Boys in the California Highway Patrol Magazine, and countless articles on Bing Crosby, Bob Hope, including a major Hope cover article covering Hope's famous wartime USO tours published in World War II Magazine. He has written extensively about Henry Ford, VE Day, Motorcycle Helmet Safety, DNA History, among other subjects.

His other books include The Song Stars, The Music Men, Jukebox Saturday Night, Snootie Little Cutie - The Connie Haines Story, Jerry Vale - A Singer's Life, The Spirit of Bob Hope, Bing Crosby-Crooner of the Century (winner of the Benjamin Franklin Award for Biography-Publishers Marketing Association), and Chattanooga Choo Choo - The Life and Times of the World Famous Glenn Miller Orchestra, The Italian Crooners Bedside Companion, When Jolson was King, Mr. Rhythm - A Tribute to Frankie Laine and Star*Dust - The Bible of the Big Bands.

Commenting about his books, Kathryn (Mrs. Bing) Crosby wrote: "Richard Grudens is the musical historian of our time. Without him, the magic would be lost forever. We all owe him a debt that we can never repay."

Richard Grudens, and his wife Madeline, reside in St. James, New York.

ACKNOWLEDGEMENTS

We are grateful to:

Kathryn Crosby

Frank E. Dee

Al Petrone

Ben Grisafi

Jack Ellsworth

Max Wirz

Bob Incagliato

Al Monroe

Jack Lebo

Jerry Castleman

Robert Grudens

Madeline Grudens

DEDICATION

This book is dedicated, in fond memory, of my photographer, interview partner and friend, C. Camille Smith.

Additional Titles by Richard Grudens
www.RichardGrudens.com
Explore the Golden Age of Music when the Big Bands and their vocalists reigned on the radio and all the great stages of America.

Sinatra Singing

This is a book about SINATRA SINGING. Inside you will meet his arrangers, conductors, musicians, songwriters, the songs, and all of the singers who were influenced by him, over many years, from Bennett to Damone and many others, technical notes on bel canto, breathing, vocal cord problems, conquering stage fright, song polls taken over the years, singing instructions, the albums, and more.

Mr. Rhythm - A Tribute to Frankie Laine

This book celebrates the life and times of Frankie Laine: the trials, the rejections, the heartbreak, the hard work, and eventual victory punctuated by all the complexities that make up the ubiquitous profession called show business. The foreword is written by one of America's greatest films stars, five time Academy Award actor and director, Clint Eastwood, an admirer and true friend of Frankie Laine.

Star*Dust - The Bible of the Big Bands

Star*Dust is America's best and biggest book of the Big Bands with 700 pages and 650 photos that cover the glorious years of the best music ever played and featuring the musical giants of the twentieth century: Glenn Miller, Artie Shaw, Les Brown, Stan Kenton, the Dorsey's, Woody Herman, Duke Ellington, Count Basie, Harry James, and every band, musician, vocalist that ever played or recorded.

The Italian Crooners Bedside Companion

The Italian Crooners is a compendium of your favorite Italian male singers, presented in a shower of photos, stories, favorite recipes and selected discographies, with a foreword by Jerry Vale.

Chattanooga Choo Choo - The Life and Times of the World Famous Glenn Miller Orchestra

Commemorating the 100th Anniversary of Glenn Miller's life and the 60th Anniversary of his disappearance over the English Channel in late 1944, we present the tribute book Glenn Miller fans all over the world have been waiting for.

Bing Crosby - Crooner of the Century

Here is the quintessential Bing Crosby tribute, documenting the story of Crosby's colorful life, family, recordings, radio and television shows, and films; the amazing success story of a wondrous career that pioneered popular music spanning generations and inspiring countless followers.

The Spirit of Bob Hope:

Tracing Bob's charmed life from his early days in Cleveland to his worldwide fame earned in vaudeville, radio, television and films and his famous wartime travels for the USO unselfishly entertaining our troops. The best Bob Hope book with testimonials from his friends and a foreword by Jane Russell.

Jerry Vale - A Singer's Life

The wondrous story of Jerry's life as a kid from teeming Bronx streets of the 1940s to his legendary appearances in the great theatrical venues of America and his three triumphant Carnegie Hall concerts, with appearances at New York's Copacabana, whose magnificent voice has beautifully interpreted the 20th Century's most beautiful love songs

Snootie Little Cutie - The Connie Haines Story

The story of big band singer, Connie Haines, who sang shoulder to shoulder with Frank Sinatra in the bands of Harry James and Tommy Dorsey, and for years on the Abbott & Costello radio show, and who is still singing today.

Jukebox Saturday Night

The final book in the series; interviews with Artie Shaw, Les Brown and Doris Day, Red Norvo, Les Paul, Carmel Quinn, stories about Glenn Miller and the Dorsey Brothers, songwriters Ervin Drake ("I Believe," "It was a Very Good Year,") and Jack Lawrence ("Linda," "Tenderly,") and a special about all the European bands past and present.

Sally Bennett's Magic Moments

This book is filled with extraordinary events in the life of Sally Bennett who established the Big Band Hall of Fame and Museum in West Palm Beach, Florida. Sally is a composer, musician, playwright, model, actress, poet, radio and TV personality and the author of the book *Sugar and Spice.*

The Music Men

A Companion to "The Song Stars," about the great men singers with foreword by Bob Hope; interviews with Tony Martin, Don Cornell, Julius LaRosa, Jerry Vale, Joe Williams, Johnny Mathis, Al Martino, Guy Mitchell, Tex Beneke and others.

The Song Stars

A neat book about all the girl singers of the Big Band Era and beyond: Doris Day, Helen Forrest, Kitty Kallen, Rosemary Clooney, Jo Stafford, Connie Haines, Teresa Brewer, Patti Page and Helen O'Connell and many more.

The Best Damn Trumpet Player

Memories of the Big Band Era, interviews with Benny Goodman, Harry James, Woody Herman, Tony Bennett, Buddy Rich, Sarah Vaughan, Lionel Hampton, Frankie Laine, Patty Andrews and others.

Order Books On-line at:
www.RichardGrudens.com
Or Fax or Call Your Order in:
Celebrity Profiles Publishing
Div. Edison & Kellogg
Box 344, Stonybrook, New York 11790
Phone: (631) 862-8555 — Fax: (631) 862-0139
Email: celebpro4@aol.com

Title	Price	Qty:
The Best Damn Trumpet Player	$15.95	
The Song Stars	$17.95	
The Music Men	$17.95	
Jukebox Saturday Night	$17.95	
Magic Moments - The Sally Bennett Story	$17.95	
Snootie Little Cutie - Connie Haines Story	$17.95	
Jerry Vale - A Singer's Life - *SOLD OUT*	$19.95	
The Spirit of Bob Hope - One Hundred Years - One Million Laughs	$19.95	
Bing Crosby - Crooner of the Century	$19.95	
Chattanooga Choo Choo The Life and Times of the World Famous Glenn Miller Orchestra	$21.95	
The Italian Crooners Bedside Companion	$21.95	
Star*Dust - The Bible of the Big Bands	$39.95	
Mr. Rhythm - A Tribute to Frankie Laine	$29.95	
Sinatra Singing	$29.95	
TOTALS		

Name:		
Address:		
City:	State:	Zip:

Include $4.00 for Priority Mail (2 days arrival time) for up to 2 books. Enclose check or money order.

FOR CREDIT CARDS, Please fill out below form completely:

Card No.:

Name on Card:

Exp. Date:

Signature:

Card Type (Please Circle): Visa — Amex — Discover — Master Card